Shadow of the Moon

SHADOW
OF THE
MOON

by M. M. Kaye

JULIAN MESSNER, Inc.   New York

FIRST PUBLISHED IN THE UNITED STATES OF AMERICA
BY JULIAN MESSNER, INC., 1957
8 WEST 40 STREET, NEW YORK 18
PUBLISHED SIMULTANEOUSLY IN CANADA
BY THE COPP CLARK PUBLISHING CO. LIMITED
© COPYRIGHT M. M. KAYE, 1956

PRINTED IN THE UNITED STATES OF AMERICA

To

Sir John William Kaye
who wrote a history of the Indian Mutiny,
Major Edward Kaye
who commanded a battery at the Siege of Delhi,
my grandfather, William Kaye of the Indian Civil Service,
my father, Sir Cecil Kaye,
my brother, Colonel William Kaye,
and to all other men and women of my family and
of so many other British families who
served, lived in and loved India.
And to
The Lovely Land
and all her peoples,
with admiration, affection and gratitude.

'. . . . . ; and there you can see'
'Our English sun, convalescent after passing'
'Through the valley of the shadow of the moon.'

Christopher Fry (*Venus Observed*)

Shadow of the Moon

Ware

1

THE chill wind that was driving tattered regiments of cloud across a watery moon brought with it a sudden and vicious spatter of raindrops and a hint of snow. It jerked unexpectedly at the folds of a long military cloak that wrapped the solitary rider on the moor road, and sent it flapping out behind him like the wings of some monstrous bat.

Captain Alex Randall swore into the cold night and reining in his horse gathered the heavy folds about him again, gripping the slack beneath his arm. He rose in his stirrups and peered ahead into the wind-torn darkness, but could see no sign of light or human habitation. The moon, momentarily shaking itself free from the millrace of the clouds, showed nothing but a desolation of moorland, across which the lonely road cut a pale track like the wake of a ship running before the wind.

A fresh gust of rain whipped out of the darkness and Medusa jerked at her bit and sidled on the rough roadway, impatient to be off.

It was on Medusa's account that Captain Randall was on the road at this late hour. He had hoped to reach Ware before dark, but just beyond Highelm the mare had cast a shoe. There had been a considerable delay before a new shoe could be fitted and Medusa ready for the road again, and the smith in Highelm, inquiring as to Captain Randall's destination, had advised against a resumption of his journey that day. Only last week, said the smith, a London doctor, hastening to his lordship, had been overtaken by darkness on the moorland road and had perforce to spend the night in his stationary coach owing to the loss of a wheel. "An' 'e might 'av saved hisself the journey. It's for Thursday, we hears. There's bin many goin' past this day."

The smith, a well-meaning man, had urged Captain Randall to spend the night at The George and resume his journey on the morrow, but Randall was not to be persuaded. He thanked the smith for his well-meant advice but persisted in his intention of continuing on his way, and night

had overtaken him while some eight to ten miles still lay between him
and the tall towers and florid battlements of Ware.

The rain drove under Captain Randall's hat brim and trickled icily
down his neck despite the close-wrapped folds of his cloak. His hands,
incased in heavy gauntlets, were so frozen that he could barely feel the
reins, and his booted feet ached with cold. He flexed his numbed fingers
and smiled wryly into the darkness.

How many times during the last ten or eleven years, in the merciless,
grinding heat of an Indian summer, lying panting under a flapping punkah
that merely disturbed but could not cool the molten air, had he yearned
in imagination for the ice and frost and snow of an English winter? Well
he had them now, and he should be satisfied. But perhaps the blazing
suns of the last twelve years had thinned his blood, for the icy wind that
disputed his passage chilled him to the bone and his whole body ached
with cold and fatigue.

To distract his thoughts from his physical discomforts, he reviewed for
perhaps the hundredth time, and with a deepening sense of exasperation
and distaste, the events that had led to his riding along this moorland
road by night and in the teeth of a rising gale toward the great house
of Ware.

Almost twelve years ago, in the autumn of 1843, Alex Mallory Randall,
having completed his training at the Honorable the East India Company's
Military College at Addiscombe and celebrated his eighteenth birthday,
had embarked for the shores of India. He had served with distinction in
that vast and turbulent land, and had been rewarded by a brevet to the
rank of lieutenant. As a result he had been removed from regimental duty
and set to work in an administrative capacity under the eye of that great
administrator Henry Lawrence. Under Sir Henry's tutelage Alex had been
in turn surveyor, road builder and magistrate, and had helped to govern
and control vast expanses of lawless territory at an age when many a man
is licking stamps or running errands. His handling of a swift and ugly
crisis on the North-West Frontier had led to a second brevet, but he had
not been permitted to return to his regiment, and had once more found
himself employed in a capacity that was more political than military.

His immediate superior in his present appointment was one Mr. Conway Barton, Commissioner of Lunjore. Alex Randall had not taken to his
chief. There were too many aspects of Mr. Barton's character and habits
that failed to commend themselves to him, but as that gentleman was
only too willing to transfer the bulk of the work to his junior's shoulders,
Alex went his own way to a large extent, unhampered by much interference.

It was on the eve of his departure on a year's furlough that Mr. Barton
had thrust an unwelcome commission upon him, and looking back on it
Alex was surprised to find how clearly he remembered that evening . . .

The monsoon was late that year and the scorching earth seemed to pant

for breath under the weight of a brazen sky. Alex had seen that the last
of his packing was completed, and in response to an unexpected summons
from Mr. Barton he had walked over in the hot, harsh moonlight to the
Residency.

He was to leave next day for Calcutta, and from there, via the overland
route, for England. What would England look like?—feel like?—smell
like? Could it really be as cool and green and fragrant as his memory had
painted it for him during the last hot and crowded and eventful years?

The night was very still, and no breath of wind stirred the shriveled
leaves or the dried, parched grasses. But the air under the arch of the
great Residency gateway was cooler than that of the hot night outside,
and lingering there, grateful for the small relief of that coolness, Alex became aware of an interruption of the silence: a whispering voice that despite its inaudibility conveyed an indefinable impression of authority, and
that appeared to come from somewhere deep in the tangled shadows of
a banyan tree that grew to the left of the gateway and just inside the
Residency walls.

There was a stone idol among the roots of the great tree; a crude, obscene figure roughly carved on an upright slab of stone, hideously
bedaubed with orange paint, and, on feast days, wreathed with garlands of
fading marigold flowers. From an angle of the archway, where the black
shadow of the gate cut across the moonlit drive, Alex could see the dark
mass of the banyan, and as his eyes became accustomed to the shadows
he could make out figures crouched about the main trunk where the idol
stood. One of these, surely, was Akbar Khan, the gatekeeper, while another was the oily down-country khansamah, cook to the Commissioner,
and a third the havildar of one of the native infantry regiments stationed
in Lunjore. There were at least a dozen men in the shadow of the banyan,
and Alex came to the conclusion that they were for the most part Residency servants—Mohammedans, with a sprinkling of low-caste Hindus.
But the havildar was a Brahmin. What, then, were they all doing, meeting
at this hour at the feet of a Hindu idol?

As he listened the speaker ceased, and a low-toned murmur of general
conversation broke out, and presently a lone figure detached itself from
the group among the tree roots and moved out into the moonlight. Alex
saw with surprise that it was a sadhu, a Hindu holy man. The tall, spare
figure was naked except for an intricately tied loincloth, and in the clear
moonlight the man's ash-smeared body and long ropelike locks of ash-
covered, uncombed hair appeared gray and ghostlike.

The sadhu reached the path before the gateway and without pausing
walked directly toward Alex, his naked feet making no sound on the baked
earth. Alex had a momentary glimpse of a gray, skull-like face blotted with
a dark caste mark, in which a pair of glittering eyes showed astonishingly
alive, and then, before he had quite realized it, the man had walked
swiftly past him and through the dark arch of the gateway.

Alex swung round and ran after him, but the road beyond the gateway was empty. The sadhu had vanished as completely as though he had indeed been a ghost, for the road was lined with shade trees, gray with the dust of breathless days, and the sharp-edged shadows of any one of them might have swallowed up the ash-smeared figure.

He heard a slight sound behind him and turned quickly to find Akbar Khan, the gatekeeper, a shadow among the shadows, salaaming under the archway.

"Where hast thou been?" demanded Alex harshly in the vernacular, "and what hast thou and the others to do with a sadhu? What evil is toward?"

"No evil, Huzoor," said Akbar Khan tranquilly. "We do but make prayer for rain."

"What child's talk! Thou art a follower of the Prophet. Imam Din also, and Ustad Ali. Since when have Mussulmans made prayer to the gods of the Hindus, or consorted with their holy men? And what has Havildar Jodha Ram to do with such as Bulaki of the sweeper-*log*?"

"Huzoor," said Akbar Khan, "in evil times, when the rains fail, we suffer as one. The monsoon tarries and the crops die. Soon, if the rains delay overlong, there will come a great famine and many will die—Mussulman and Hindu, Sikh and Bengali together. Yonder fakir makes petition to his gods for rain. While we Moslems call upon Allah for rain the Hindus of the city call also upon their gods. That is all."

"Hmm," said Alex. "In the circumstances it is almost conceivable that you might be speaking the truth. But I don't believe it and I don't like it. And don't leave the gate unattended again, you old reprobate."

Akbar Khan, to whom these last remarks, spoken in English, were unintelligible, salaamed deeply and drew back against the wall as Alex walked past him and up the long curving drive toward the big white single-storied house among the flame trees.

From a courtyard behind the house a woman's voice could be heard singing a shrill, quavering Indian song to the accompaniment of a sitar. It stopped suddenly, as though checked by an order, as Captain Randall mounted the veranda steps, his boots ringing loud on the stone.

A white-clad figure rose with a rustle from the matting and salaaming low, pattered away to a lighted doorway screened by a curtain of split cane that led into the Commissioner's drawing room. Alex could see the crouching figure of a punkah coolie seated cross legged in the shadows, his body bowing to the rhythmic tug and release of the rope, and from inside the room came the familiar flap and fall of the punkah cloth, a clink of bottles and glasses and the murmured Urdu of the native servant.

"Wha's that? Wha's that?"

The Commissioner's bulky figure appeared in the doorway, outlined blackly against the yellow lamplight.

"Tha' you, Alex? Come in! Come in! Jus' the man I wanted t'see. Siddown. Have a drink. Know why I sent f'yer?"

"No, sir. Nothing gone wrong with my furlough, I hope!"

"No, no. Tha's all right. It's about that I wan't' talk. Wan' you t' do something for me. Favor. Long story. It's m' future wife . . ."

He took a deep pull at the glass in his hand while the sweat trickled down his pale, puffy features and soaked into the thin, short-sleeved, Indian-style garment he wore in lieu of more formal attire.

Alex sat down and resigned himself to listen. He knew—as who did not?—that Mr. Barton was affianced to a distant cousin: a great-granddaughter of the Earl of Ware.

Conway Barton was proud of his connection with Lord Ware and lost no opportunity of mentioning the relationship, though in actual fact the connection was of the slightest. The Lady Emily Grantham, only daughter of the fifth Earl, had married an elderly nabob Sir Ebenezer Barton. This Sir Ebenezer's youngest brother was Conway Barton's father. Lady Emily's niece Sabrina Grantham had apparently married a Spanish nobleman while on a visit to India, and it was to her daughter that Mr. Conway Barton was affianced. The match had been arranged some five or six years previously during the Commissioner's last furlough in England, and it had been intended, explained Mr. Barton, that there should be a long engagement—no unusual thing under the circumstances—and that the marriage should take place during his next Home leave. But this would not fall due for several years, and meanwhile the Earl of Ware, the lady's aged guardian, was failing in health and had written to urge the return of Mr. Barton and his immediate marriage to his betrothed. This being impossible, the Commissioner had decided upon an alternative arrangement.

"The mountain must come to Mahomet!" said Mr. Conway Barton, and laughed heartily at his own wit. "An' this, Alex, is where you come in."

"I, sir?" Alex sat up with a jerk.

"Yes, you, m'dear fellow. Wouldn't trust anyone else. An' though yer a sight too good looking fer a man—or would be if yer'd only grow some hair on yer lip—was'er marrer with yer anyway? It ain't decent at your age, shavin' yer face like a demmed nigger—yer don't go much with women. 'Tisn't normal, but there it is. Sho when I had to decide, I said, 'Randall! Just the f'llow. He'll do!'"

The Commissioner stopped as though he had fully explained himself, and lay back in his long cane chair and drank deeply.

"Do what, sir?"

"What? Wh's that? Oh! fetch her of course, m'boy. Bring her out here. Mountain t' Mahomet. Hope she ain't a mountain. Skin and bone fi'—five years ago. But never can tell. Half Spanish, y' know. They can run to fat. Mountain t' Mahomet!"

For a few moments Alex had thought that the Commissioner could not possibly be serious, but he was speedily disabused. The Commissioner was perfectly serious. His plans were all made. Captain Randall was to explain the whole matter in person to the Earl, and add his entreaties to those of the Commissioner that the Condesa de los Aguilares should set sail for India in the following year under the charge of Captain Alex

Randall, and any suitable chaperone that could be provided, when Captain Randall returned from furlough.

Alex had argued and protested, but to no purpose, and as he could not afford to quarrel with Mr. Barton, it had ended with his accepting the distasteful commission. But with certain inward reservations.

Alex had considered those reservations often since that hot night at the Lunjore Residency, but had been unable to come to any definite decision. There were two alternatives before him, and both were distasteful. On the one hand he was to make himself responsible for conveying a gently nurtured woman to an unknown land seething with sedition and unrest—to say nothing of the dangers and discomforts of such things as disease, intolerable heat and an almost total lack of sanitation—and eventually hand this fellow creature into the care of a man whom he knew to be both a drunkard and a libertine. On the other hand, should he warn Lord Ware of these aspects of the affair, he would be betraying the trust of his superior officer.

It was always possible, of course, that the Commissioner's betrothed was well aware of the disadvantages of the match. The marriage had been arranged some five years previously, and as the earliest that a young lady of rank would be likely to be affianced was seventeen, that would make her at least of age. But possibly she was a good deal older than that, and plain in the bargain, which would account for the aged Earl's anxiety to get her suitably bestowed. If so, it was likely that the lady herself was fully prepared to accept the prospect of life in the East, and a drunken husband of loose morals, as an escape from spinsterhood. Women were unpredictable in such matters.

Alex had attempted to dismiss the whole problem from his mind, but for some reason it refused to be banished and lurked uncomfortably in a corner of his brain, weighing heavily on his conscience and troubling his waking hours.

Captain Randall roused himself from his stupor of cold and fatigue and peered ahead. There were trees near by. And surely that was a glimmer of light? They were leaving the moors behind and entering a more hospitable country of fields and hedges and woodland, and Medusa shook her head and snorted as though she knew that a warm stable and a feed of oats lay not far ahead.

A high wall loomed up out of the darkness; sensed rather than seen, for the wind was cut off abruptly and the sound of Medusa's hoofs rang hollowly on the roadway. The wall followed the line of the road for a mile or so and then turned away almost at right angles in front of a vast stone gateway topped by the heraldic wolves of Ware.

Lights glowed behind the windows of the lodgekeeper's cottage and it seemed that Captain Randall was expected, for the heavy wrought-iron gates stood open. Beyond them lay a long avenue of oak trees rising out of a sea of dead bracken, and on either side stretched the open spaces of a park across which the wind blew in savage gusts between the tree trunks.

Medusa broke into a gallop, and ten minutes later the avenue ended in a wide sweep of gravel before the towering bulk of a great house, half castle, half mansion. A faint gleam of light showed from a high window, but except for that the house was in darkness.

Captain Randall dismounted stiffly, and knotting the sodden reins, looped them about the neck of a dimly seen griffon carved in weather-worn stone, and mounted the wide steps that led up to the front door. He tugged at the iron bell chain and waited, stamping his feet on the wet stone to restore the circulation to them. After what seemed an unconscionably long wait he heard a sound of slow footsteps, and the great door creaked open. An aged man, bent and wrinkled, his white hair dressed in the manner of an earlier day, peered out at him, and then setting the door a little wider, drew back to let him pass.

Captain Randall found himself standing in a vast hall that appeared even vaster in the dim light of the single branch of candles that formed the only illumination in all that wide place of shadows. He looked about him in some surprise. In such a hall one might have expected to see family portraits, weapons or trophies adorning the enormous expanse of wall. But here there was nothing. Nothing but a blackness that seemed to move and sway and shiver as the draft blew in through the half-opened door and eddied about the hall.

The candle flames flickered wildly in the rush of cold air, to flare up again as a tall footman in black livery leant his weight against the door, shutting it upon the wild night. Captain Randall stared about him in the grip of an odd sense of unreality. Weariness appeared to be playing tricks with his eyesight. Was it only imagination—or the effects of cold and fatigue that made the shadowy walls about him seem to move and tremble?

The ancient steward who had peered at him through the half-open door tottered across the hall and lifted the branched candlestick, holding it high, and Alex saw with a sense of shock that the walls of the vast hall were hung from ceiling to floor with black curtains. Curtains that still swayed and shifted uneasily from the wind that had blown in from the night.

The old man tapped on the stone floor with the long steward's wand he held in one shriveled hand, and two more somber-liveried flunkeys materialized out of the shadows. "Your horse shall be attended to, sir, and Thomas will see that you have all you require. You will be one of the family? I do not for the moment recall the name. Forgive me, sir—your lordship—we were not expecting—" the old man's voice quavered to a stop and Alex spoke curtly:

"You mistake me. I am Captain Alex Randall. Lord Ware requested me to wait upon him on this date. I was delayed upon the road or I should have reached here before dark. You will find my valise strapped to the saddle."

"His lordship requested you . . . ?"

To Alex' puzzled amazement he saw that tears were standing in the old man's eyes. The feeble tears of old age that brimmed over and trickled down the furrowed, parchmentlike face and flashed in the candlelight. And suddenly several things that had meant nothing to him a moment before took on shape and meaning. The smith at Highelm who had said: "It's for Thursday, we hears. There's bin many goin' past this day." The London doctor who might have saved himself a journey. The open gates at the entrance of the oak avenue, the black liveries of the servants and the funereal hangings that draped the walls of the great hall.

He said suddenly, sharply: "The Earl—?"

"His lordship died five days ago," said the old steward.

2

CAPTAIN ALEX RANDALL awoke with a headache and a sense of acute irritation. He had slept little, and that uneasily, for the problem that he had intended to transfer to the Earl of Ware was once more back upon his own shoulders. Lord Ware, thought Alex crossly, had no right to die before settling his ward's affairs. Now what was to be done? It was one thing to explain the true state of affairs to an elderly man of the world, but quite another to interview Mr. Conway Barton's betrothed herself.

Devil take the Commissioner of Lunjore and perdition seize all women! thought Captain Randall, scowling up at the heavy canopy of the massive four-poster in which he lay. He had a very good mind to abandon the whole business and ride back to London that morning.

He breakfasted alone in a small paneled room warmed by a blazing log fire, where an elderly and sedate secretary waited upon him with a message from the new Earl. Lord Ware, owing to pressure of work, found himself unable to see Captain Randall until late in the day: he trusted that it would be convenient for Captain Randall to spend another night or so at Ware, as the business he had come upon was not one to be dealt with in haste.

"It is most damnably inconvenient," said Captain Randall sourly. "But I suppose there is no help for it."

Left to his own devices he passed a tedious morning, and the company at luncheon proved unenlivening. They were all, with the sole exception of himself, relatives who had assembled for the funeral of the late head of their house, which was to take place on the following day. They were dressed in deep black, and conversed in the hushed undertones apparently deemed suitable to a house of mourning, but bereavement had evidently

not impaired their appetites. The meal was rich, indigestible and interminable, and the conversation, of necessity, lacking in sparkle.

Alex spent the greater part of the afternoon moodily watching a stream
of black-clad tenants who, despite the inclemency of the weather, were
moving slowly up the oak avenue to pass through the guardroom where
the late Earl's coffin lay in state. Eventually, more for lack of other oc-
cupation than from any desire to pay his respects to the unknown dead,
he went down to join them. The somber procession moved forward slowly
and in silence, and passing through a low porch in the oldest part of the
castle, entered a long passage that ended in a flight of stone steps leading
down to the guardroom and the catafalque.

Alex drew to one side and stood looking down on a strangely impressive
scene. The walls were draped in the same unrelieved black, and the catafalque itself and the floor about it was covered with heavy black cloth
and lit by four massive candles in iron sconces. But the rest was color
and glitter and magnificence. A magnificence made even more startling
by very contrast to its funereal setting. A defiance and a boast in the face
of death.

The ornate hatchment suspended above the coffin head gleamed with
all the color and gilding and pride of heraldry, and below it crimson velvet
drapery decorated with gold covered the heavy oak of the coffin. Placed
upon the coffin on a velvet cushion stood the Earl's coronet and the Star
and Garter. The diamonds flashed and blazed as the candle flames wavered in the draft, sending out splinters of brilliant light—violet and green
and blue, scarlet and white. The breastplate, surrounded by various orders
and badges of honor, was surmounted by the Earl's own arms, and below
them, together with the gilt spurs of knighthood, lay two crossed swords;
the dress sword of a Knight of the Garter and one which Alex took to be
the sword of some militia regiment. At the foot of the coffin hung a
Knight's gold collar and beneath it were grouped on either side of the bier
the Earl's mantle and the velvet and ermine of a Knight of the Garter, the
hat of a Colonel of Militia and a military scarf. Servants dressed in black
livery stood guard at each side of the coffin as the silent procession of
mourners passed slowly by the bier and out through the low stone arch at
the far side of the room, and Alex found his lips moving in scraps of remembered poetry: "*The boast of heraldry, the pomp of pow'r, and all that
beauty, all that wealth e'er gave, await alike the inevitable hour: The paths
of glory lead but to the grave.*" Yet there was no meek acceptance of the
latter end here. His aged lordship was moving to the grave with all the
pomp and ceremony that had attended him in life.

The steady stream of mourners thinned gradually to a mere trickle, and
beyond the narrow stone embrasures of the guardroom windows the gray
daylight took on the purple hue of dusk.

A woman, veiled and in heavy mourning, brushed past Captain Randall
and went swiftly down the steps to pause beside the resplendent bier, her
clothing outlined with a faint nimbus of gold from the candlelight beyond.

The thick veil that fell from her bonnet's edge almost to her feet permitted no glimpse of her features and did not even betray the color of her hair. But the vast, hooped crinoline, the heavy crape veil and a deeply fringed pelisse, unwieldy as they were, failed to conceal the wearer's youth. They failed, too, to conceal something else. Despite its rigidity there was about the small figure in its cumbersome mourning a poignant impression of intense and hopeless grief. Alex could not have explained even to himself why this should be so, for the girl stood stiffly, head erect and black-gloved hands pressing back the spreading skirts of her dress. But he was aware of a sudden sense of guilt, as though he were eavesdropping on some intensely private and personal conversation, and turning abruptly he walked quickly away.

Darkness had fallen by the time the secretary appeared to request Captain Randall's presence in his lordship's private apartments, and to lead the way along interminable corridors to a more recently constructed wing. He turned the handle of an ornate white and gold door and ushered Captain Randall into a large, high-ceilinged room. But it was the Countess and not the Earl who waited to receive him.

Lady Ware rose with a rustle of heavy silks. A tall woman, verging on middle age, with a coldly handsome face and smooth loops of light-brown hair already lightly streaked with gray. She held out a thin white hand with a gesture that was almost royal, and Alex Randall bowed over it and straightened up to meet the critical gaze of a pair of slightly prominent blue eyes; cold, pale and calculating. She studied him for a moment in silence and apparently liked what she saw, for her somewhat thin-lipped mouth relaxed in a faint smile.

"My dear Captain Randall," said the Countess of Ware, "you must forgive me for being unable to receive you earlier, but under the present sad circumstances—well, I am sure that you will understand how difficult it has been for us. My husband has asked me to convey to you his regrets that he cannot, after all, find the time to see you today. He hopes that he will be able to do so later."

The Countess seated herself again, and waved Captain Randall to a chair beside her. Alex sat down warily. He had never had much to do with women, and apart from several light and lovely ladies who had provided him with amusement, had met singularly few of them. Alex Randall was no celibate, but two things obsessed him to the exclusion of all others: India and "John Company." The glamour of India—the vast, glittering, cruel, mysterious land teeming with violence and beauty—and the romance of John Company, that prosaic collection of merchant traders from London who had conquered a subcontinent and now maintained their own armies and administered justice and law to sixty million Indians.

Facing the imposing figure of the Countess of Ware, Alex knew himself to be at a disadvantage. He could have dealt with a man. He disliked having to deal with a woman.

"I must apologize for my inopportune arrival," he said stiffly. "I had expected to arrive a good deal earlier, but I visited the Crimea en route and was delayed. I wrote to Mr. Barton and the late Lord Ware to explain matters."

"We quite understood. You were wounded, were you not? Did you see much fighting?"

"A certain amount," said Alex uncommunicatively.

Lady Ware lost interest in the Crimea and returned to Mr. Barton. ". . . and now that we have had the opportunity of meeting you, and of reading the letters you brought with you," she concluded, "the position is of course quite clear." She lifted one of the letters under discussion from an ormolu table at her side. It was still unopened and the seal intact.

"We have not," said Lady Ware, "given Winter her letter as yet. I shall now do so at the earliest opportunity." The shadow of a frown passed over her face and her narrow mouth drew itself into a tighter line. "Naturally she will be allowed to express her views, but I am convinced that she will consent to dear Conway's plan. It is unfortunate that he cannot come home, but under the circumstances I feel that to delay the marriage for a further, and possibly indefinite, period, would be unnecessarily harsh. Both on dear Conway and on Winter herself."

Winter! thought Alex Randall. What an impossible name! Probably the diminutive of some more lengthy Spanish one.

"I understand," said the Countess, "that you yourself have very kindly undertaken to act as escort to my cousin and whatever chaperone we may select to accompany her. That is most kind of you."

"Have you any knowledge of the East?" inquired Alex abruptly.

Lady Ware looked a little taken aback. "If you mean, have I ever been there, I have not. Why do you ask?"

"I only wondered if you have any idea as to what life, and to what conditions of life, you are sending your cousin? It is no country for a young lady who has been brought up in such surroundings as these."

"Nonsense!" said the Countess crisply. "Thousands of Englishwomen—many of them well bred—have managed admirably out there. I myself am acquainted with some of them. You yourself have spent some years in that country—"

"Twelve," interrupted Captain Randall.

"Then surely you have met many of your fellow countrywomen out there? Are you trying to tell me that none of them find life supportable? I cannot believe that you are serious."

"No," said Alex slowly. "Many of them would be nowhere else if given the choice. But as a general rule these fall into two categories. Those who remain, and endure every hardship that heat and disease and exile can bring, for love of husband or father. And those whose social status in this country is such that India gives them a sense of position and importance that they cannot obtain here. The rest hate it. The latter consideration will hardly apply to your cousin. Can you be sure of the first one? I understand that it is five years and more since she last saw Mr. Barton."

"That is a matter that must be left to my cousin," said the Countess frostily. "It is no concern of ours."

She rose with an impressive rustle of silk and held out her hand. Captain Randall stood up and bowed over it.

"I hope," said the Countess with a return to graciousness, "that you will not mind extending your stay for another two days? My husband hopes to be able to see you tomorrow afternoon. Most of our guests will be leaving after the funeral and he will then be able to give you his undivided attention."

Captain Randall murmured his thanks and turned to go, and as he did so he noticed for the first time a large portrait that hung above the clutter of a velvet-draped overmantel. It depicted a young girl in a white crinoline and a blue sash. A pretty creature, barely more than a child, with pale gold ringlets falling onto sloping shoulders and one small hand holding a single rose. The expression, true to the dictates of fashionable female portraiture, was one of conscious sweetness, but there was a suggestion of petulance and obstinacy about the small pouting mouth that belied the limpid mildness of the blue eyes. He had observed the original of the portrait at luncheon that day and had wondered if by any chance it could be the Condesa.

"Who is that?" he inquired, studying the portrait.

"My daughter," said the Countess complacently, and Alex drew a quick breath of relief. At least the future of that fragile-looking child need not be on his conscience. He turned and smiled at the Countess. Few women were proof against Alex Randall's smile, and Lady Ware proved no exception. She thawed visibly.

"She is very lovely," said Captain Randall.

"Do you think so? As her mother perhaps I should not agree with you. But then so many people are of your opinion. Indeed Herr Winterhalter said that of all his subjects Sybella gave him the greatest pleasure to portray."

The Countess appeared to be launched on her favorite subject and would doubtless have enlarged upon it at some length had not the discreet entrance of an elderly lady, evidently a companion, interrupted her. She dismissed Captain Randall graciously, and turned her attention to the elderly companion.

II

There had been no sign of the young lady of the portrait at dinner that night, and Alex concluded that she must be dining with her parents. He had found himself on this occasion seated next to a Lady Wycombe; a talkative and imposing woman who, having demanded and received an explanation as to his presence at Ware, observed: "You were looking for someone, were you not? Whom did you expect to see here this evening?"

"There was a young lady sitting opposite me at luncheon," said Alex. "I noticed that she is not here tonight."

"Ah, you must mean Sybella. She is having a light supper in her room. Do not tell me that you too have fallen a victim to her charms? If so I must hasten to warn you that you stand no chance, no chance at all! When Bella marries it must be to the heir of a great name or a great fortune. And she will do so, of that I have no doubt. That is, if she can rid herself of her cousin. Winter may yet spoil her aim. It is a way she has."

"Winter? Oh—the Condesa. What is she like?"

Lady Wycombe had laughed on rather an odd note.

"No woman can describe her to you without injustice. But I am sorry for Julia—and Sybella! Do you see that young man over there? On the far side of that candelabrum——" Lady Wycombe gestured with a black lace fan. "That is the Honorable Edmund Rathley, and the greatest *parti* in Europe. He is the nephew of the old Duke of Amberley, and will inherit the dukedom when his uncle dies. He is also Sybella's first cousin; but that will not stop them! There is only one thing that may stand in the way of a satisfactory conclusion, but now that Henry is dead I am quite sure that suitable steps will be taken. Yes, they will certainly get rid of Winter."

There had been no gathering of the assembled guests at the conclusion of the meal, for the ladies withdrew to their several rooms immediately upon leaving the table. After an unusually brief interval with the port the gentlemen followed their example, and Captain Randall, making his way back to his room, took a wrong turning in error and so came upon a curious scene.

He found himself at the entrance of a long, unlighted gallery hung with tapestries and family portraits, at the far end of which, blackly silhouetted against a lighted hall beyond, stood two closely embraced figures. He was preparing to retreat hastily when it was borne in upon him that what he was witnessing was not a love scene, for the woman at the far end of the gallery was being held against her will. Her captor held her with her arms closely pinioned to her sides, and so hard against him that she could move nothing but her head as she strove frantically to avoid his avid kisses. She did not cry out, but struggled silently, and in the stillness of the quiet gallery Alex could hear her short, panting breaths. He started forward at a run.

The floor of the gallery was thickly carpeted and the two at the far end of it too engrossed in their struggle to be aware of his approach.

"Just a moment," said Alex crisply. He caught the gentleman's shoulder in an ungentle grip and jerked him round, and the lady, freed, drew back with a gasp of relief and leant panting against the wall, her hands at her throat. The wide black skirts of her crinoline merged with the shadows of the gallery, and only her face and her small hands made white blurs in the dim light.

Alex turned his attention to the gentleman, but before he could speak yet another figure appeared upon the scene; someone who must have started to run across the wide hall toward the struggling figures at almost the same instant that Alex had started toward them from the far end of the gallery, but who, hampered by a trailing cashmere shawl, had arrived there a close second.

"*Edmund!*" The word was a gasp of fury.

Captain Randall released his captive who took a hurried step backward, bringing his face into the subdued light of the hall. It was the young gentleman whom Lady Wycombe had referred to as the most eligible *parti* in Europe.

The new arrival stared up at him for a moment, her breath coming short. Then suddenly, swiftly, she brushed past him, ignoring Captain Randall as though she were unaware of his presence, and confronted the panting figure in the shadows.

"*You!*" The single syllable was scarcely more than a breath of rage in the silence. It was followed by another sound, equally shocking in its unexpectedness. The crisp, sharp sound of a slap delivered with the full force of an open palm.

The woman in the shadows threw up an arm as though to protect herself from further attack, and then picking up her wide skirts, whirled about and ran down the length of the dark gallery, the heavy silk of her dress rustling in the silence like a rush of wind through dead leaves. In the same instant the eligible Edmund turned on his heel and disappeared with startling suddenness through a door that led out of the circular hall a few paces from the entrance to the gallery, and Captain Randall was left alone with the lady in the cashmere shawl.

She turned slowly, and apparently for the first time became aware of the presence of a stranger, for he heard her startled gasp. The warm light from the hall fell full on her white face and tumbled blond curls. It was the girl of the dining room and the Winterhalter portrait; the Lady Sybella Grantham. The next moment she had swept past him and run lightly across the hall to vanish down a dimly lit corridor beyond.

The whole curious incident had occupied less than two minutes of time, and Captain Randall, unexpectedly involved in the brief drama and left in sole possession of the scene, retraced his steps, and coming upon a hurrying flunkey was redirected to his own part of the house.

III

The morning of the funeral dawned cold and windy. Hurrying ranks of clouds streamed endlessly overhead against a lowering background of gray skies that failed to show a glimpse of blue, and patches of discolored snow still lay about unmelted among the roots of the oaks and the beech trees in the park.

The body of the late Earl had been laid to rest in the ancestral mausoleum attached to a chapel in the grounds of the castle, and, the service over, Captain Randall found himself standing next to his neighbor of the previous evening, Lady Wycombe.

"Let us wait in the porch until the crowd thins," said Lady Wycombe. "At least it is out of the wind. It will take some time to get the carriages away, and I do not intend to walk."

The crowd about the mausoleum was thinning rapidly, for the keen wind did not encourage loitering. Those who had come or were returning on foot had already set off at a brisk pace, and the carriages that waited to one side of the yew-lined avenue were being filled and driven away.

A lone woman was standing apart by the nearest yew tree, using the thick trunk as a shelter against the wind and evidently waiting, as were Alex and Lady Wycombe, until the major portion of the crowd had left the avenue. Something about her, something vaguely familiar, attracted Captain Randall's attention. Despite the heavy veil that obscured her features he had the impression that he knew her or had seen her before. Yet it was not the Lady Sybella; of that he was certain. This woman was not so tall and her hair was dark, not fair, for in the cold light of the windy morning even a heavy black mourning veil could not have entirely disguised the pale gold glint of Lady Sybella's curls.

She stood quite still; so still that Captain Randall suddenly realized where it was that he had seen her before. It was the woman who had entered the guardroom yesterday and had stood in that same rigid attitude before the old Earl's coffin.

He watched her idly, wondering how it was that such complete immobility could yet manage to convey such a vivid and unmistakable impression of grief. And as he watched, a freakish gust of wind, sweeping about the trunk of the aged yew tree, snatched at the long black veil and whipped it out and up above her head, revealing a young unguarded face.

It was a small face, the color of warm ivory. Wide at the brow and pointed at the chin, with enormous dark eyes under delicate black brows that curved like swallow's wings. The mouth was too wide and too full to suit the accepted standards of beauty in that age, but it was a mouth, all the same, to set a man's pulses beating, and the thick waves of hair that sprang from a deep widow's peak on her forehead held the blue, burnished gleam of a raven's wing and made the mourning hue of bonnet and gown appear dull and rusty by comparison.

The girl reached up an arm to recapture her veil, and as she did so she turned her head more fully toward the two in the porch. Upon her left cheek, and sharply visible against the ivory skin, was an irregular blotch that might have been a birthmark—or the mark left by a vicious blow given with an open hand.

Alex' eyes narrowed. So this was the girl who had been in the gallery last night and whom he had rescued from the unwelcome attentions of the Honorable Edmund Rathley!

Captain Randall turned to his companion. "Who is that? The young lady by the yew tree?"

Lady Wycombe turned. "That? We were discussing her last night—the Condesa de los Aguilares. That is Winter."

The Shadow Before

3

"*Winter!* Who ever heard of such a name? It is not a name at all! Pray be sensible, my dear Marcos. You cannot call the poor mite anything so absurd!"

"She will be called Winter."

Kindly Mrs. Grantham threw up her hands in a gesture of exasperation. "But my dear boy!—Winter de Ballesteros de los Aguilares—only think how absurd it will sound!"

"Sabrina wished it," said the distraught young husband stubbornly.

Mrs. Grantham knew when she was defeated. There was no arguing with Marcos in his present frame of mind, and the baby was a sickly infant whose chances of survival were so slight that it had been thought necessary to baptize it without delay. Marcos, who was a Spaniard and a Catholic, had agreed to allow the ceremony to be performed by an Anglican parson—cholera having struck down the only available priest, and the child's mother having belonged to the Anglican Church. He had been sufficiently distraught to agree to anything, but he had been adamant over the matter of his daughter's baptismal name.

"*Winter!*" repeated Mrs. Grantham, dabbing ineffectually at her swollen eyes. "Poor 'Rena must have been out of her mind!"

But Sabrina—poor, pretty Sabrina—dying in childbirth in the merciless heat of an Indian May, had not been out of her mind. She had been thinking of Ware . . .

II

Sabrina had never known her parents. Her father, Johnny Grantham, youngest son of the fifth Earl of Ware, had been killed at Waterloo, and her mother, Louisa, had died in giving birth to his only and posthumous child. Sabrina had been brought up in her paternal grandfather's great house, and she was nineteen when her Aunt Emily, who had married an elderly nabob, asked that her niece be allowed to accompany her on a visit to India.

Sabrina had been enchanted with India. She possessed a gay and uncritical nature, and everything that she saw there delighted her. Her Uncle Ebenezer, as a prominent member of the Governor-General's Council, often went on stately tours during the cold season, upon which Lady Emily and Sabrina would accompany him, and it was in the course of a visit to the court of the King of Oudh that Sabrina met Juanita de Ballesteros.

Juanita's father, the Conde de los Aguilares, was a wealthy and eccentric Spanish nobleman who as a young man had traveled much in the East. Arriving in Oudh almost half a century earlier he had been greatly attracted to the country and the people, and in particular to a nephew of the ruling king. The two young men, Spaniard and Mussulman, had become fast friends.

Ramon de Ballesteros, Conde de los Aguilares, never returned to Spain. Oudh became his home, and the rich, barbaric, colorful kingdom his country. The King of Oudh made him a grant of land on the banks of the Goomti, and there, surrounded by groves of orange and lemon trees and green, formal gardens, he built a house: the Casa de los Pavos Reales—the House of the Peacocks—a vast Spanish castello in the heart of India.

In due course the Conde married: not, as might have been predicted, a daughter of the royal house of Oudh, but the only child of a French émigré who had fled with his family to Pondicherry from the bloody massacre of the Revolution, and had subsequently taken service in the Army of the East India Company. Anne Marie de Lazencourt settled into the colorful polyglot life of her husband's great house on the Goomti and never realized its strangeness. Her friends were the slender, olive-skinned, dark-eyed wives of the princes and nobles of Oudh, and her fourth child, Juanita, was born in the house of Aziza Begum, wife of her husband's great friend, Mirza Ali Shah.

Only two of Anne Marie's seven children survived their infancy: her daughter Juanita and her son Marcos. The others fell early victims to cholera and typhus, those two deadly plagues of the East.

When Marcos was fourteen years old his father dispatched him to Spain in order that his son might complete his education in his native land. Marcos did not return for nine years. By then he was a slim young man with the dark hawklike handsomeness that is so frequently seen among the great families of Aragon and Castile, and his sister Juanita had married her childhood playmate, Wali Dad, son of Ali Shah and Aziza Begum.

Sabrina Grantham, visiting Oudh with her aunt and uncle in the spring of 1837, met Juanita de Ballesteros, wife of Wali Dad, at a banquet in the women's quarters of the Chutter Manzil Palace in Lucknow. They were friends from the first moment of their meeting, and Sabrina came to spend more and more of her time at the Gulab Mahal,* the little pink stucco

* Gul (rhymes with "pull") arb Ma-harl

palace in a quiet corner of the city where Juanita lived, for Sir Ebenezer
Barton was making an extended stay in Oudh.

The Honorable the East India Company—"John Company"—was a company of merchants and traders. They had come to India to buy and sell,
and trade and profits were what they desired. They did not want an Empire. Yet slowly and insidiously, or so it seemed, an Empire was being
thrust upon them.

In the days of the Great Moguls a British ship's surgeon had successfully treated the badly burned and beloved daughter of the Emperor
Shahjahan, and when asked what he wished for in reward had requested
permission for the British to trade in Bengal. Those first small trading
posts had flourished and paid rich dividends, but in their very success they
had aroused the envy and resentment of other traders from beyond the
seas. The French, the Arabs, the Dutch and the Portuguese were also
rivals for the golden prizes of Indian trade, and to protect their factories,
together with their own lives, the British merchants had been forced to
arm themselves and to hire mercenaries. They had succeeded in time in
defeating their rivals and in establishing a monopoly of trade, but as their
interests grew and expanded, and more and yet more factories and ware-
houses were built, the need for larger forces for their protection grew also,
for the times were troublous ones, and India a medieval medley of small
and warring states, riddled with corruption, trickery and intrigue. The
Company of Merchants made treaties with many of these petty kings, and
on behalf of their allies fought with others; and their arms of necessity kept
pace with their profits. The Genie of Force had been let out of the bottle
and it became impossible to replace it. Instead of reaping a harvest of
gold as they had in the early years, the Directors of the East India Company found themselves pouring out treasure upon what had become no
less than a vast private Army, and acquiring, in order to protect their
trade, a huge and ever enlarging Empire.

The men of John Company had defeated Tippu Sultan, ruler of Mysore,
and divided and apportioned his territory. They had defeated the Mahrattas and the Gurkhas, and deposed the Peishwa and added his lands to
the Presidency of Bombay. Would the ancient kingdom of Oudh now go
the same way, and its rule pass from the hands of its royal house into
those of the Company? Sir Ebenezer Barton, for one, was resolved to do
all he could to prevent it. He, and many like him, considered that the
whole question of India was getting out of hand. The greater the Company's territorial power and possessions, the less profit in terms of trade.
John Company was not only losing money, but was heavily in debt. It was
out of the question that they should take over the sole government of
Oudh.

The warm November weather gave place to the sharp, sparkling mornings, cool nights and brilliant days of December, and Sabrina, paying a
call at the Casa de los Pavos Reales with her Aunt Emily, met Marcos de
Ballesteros, newly back from Spain.

It was of course inevitable that they should fall in love. Marcos, dark haired and romantically handsome, with his gay laugh and the novelty and charm of one newly come from that most charming of countries, Spain, and Sabrina Grantham who had, surprisingly enough, not been in love for over a year, and who was so small and slim and blondly beautiful. They had stood looking at each other in the cool white hall of the Casa de los Pavos Reales where the orange trees grew in tubs as they do in Spain, and where the sunlight, filtering through the lemon trees planted about the house, filled the hall with a green, aqueous light.

They stood and looked at each other and fell in love.

Juanita's daughter was born, and the old, old lullabies of Spain and France and Hindustan were sung above her cradle.

For Sabrina it was a time of enchantment. A page cut from a fairy story. But Emily was full of anxiety and foreboding. Lady Emily was staunchly and stubbornly British; possessed of all the ingrained insularity of her race. She did not find India beautiful or exciting. She saw it only as an uncivilized and barbaric country with a medieval standard of morality, justice and sanitation that it was the divinely appointed but distasteful task of men like Ebenezer to govern and control and lead into the path of enlightened Western living.

"We will remove to Delhi immediately," decided Lady Emily, "and I think it would be as well if Sabrina returned to England in the spring."

"But I cannot do that," said Sabrina, starry-eyed with happiness. "I am going to marry Marcos."

"Oh dear," sighed Lady Emily, "I can see that it is all going to be very difficult. I hope you may not find that you have made a sad mistake. You think now that this country is beautiful and romantic, but how are you going to like living all your days here? Heat, disease, dirt, wars, famines—"

"I shall have Marcos," said Sabrina.

Emily gave it up and waited with as much resignation as she could muster for the arrival of the mails from England that would bring her father's answer to the request for his blessing upon the marriage of his favorite grandchild to Marcos de Ballesteros.

III

The new year dawned over Oudh in a blaze of saffron yellow light. A new year that was to see the coronation of the young Queen Victoria, the Austrian evacuation of the Papal States, France declare war on Mexico, the abolition of slavery in India and the start of the disastrous Afghan War. But the year that had dawned for Sabrina with so much sunshine and happiness darkened swiftly. Anne Marie died in the first week of February, and old Conde Ramon, stricken with years and grief, took to his bed and did not rise from it again, and three days later his body lay beside that of his wife in the marble mausoleum of the Casa de los Pavos Reales.

March brought with it a steadily rising temperature, dust storms, the monotonous, maddening call of the Köil whom the British had nicknamed the "Brain Fever Bird," and the dispensation that Marcos had written for from Rome. And on a hot evening toward the end of March, while a dry wind rattled the dying leaves of the bamboos and neem trees, and the pariah dogs of the city bayed a sultry yellow moon rising through the hot dusk, the letter they had been awaiting for so long arrived from England.

It was short and to the point. On no account whatsoever would the Earl of Ware consent to the marriage of his granddaughter to this ex-patriate Spaniard who had settled in the East. He had no intention of allowing Sabrina to throw herself away on any man, however wealthy or well born, who was not only a foreigner but had made his home in such a barbarous and uncivilized spot. Sabrina would return home instantly. In the event of her refusing to do so, and of persisting in this outrageous folly, she would be cut out of his will and cut off from all future contact with him or his family. This was his final word upon the subject.

But Sabrina had no intention of being sent home to England. She had promised her aunt and uncle that she would wait until her grandfather's views on her marriage to Marcos de Ballesteros were made known, but she had not promised to abide by those views. Now that her grandfather's letter had arrived offering her the choice of giving up Marcos or being cast off and disinherited, there was no further need for delay. She left a note pinned to her pincushion in the traditional manner, and slipping out of the house had her horse saddled, and rode away to Marcos.

They were married in the little chapel of the Casa de los Pavos Reales in the presence of two young officers of the 41st Bengal Cavalry, friends of Marcos' on their way to rejoin their regiment after a leave spent shooting in the Terai, and of Juanita, who had been hurriedly summoned from her home in the city.

Sabrina wore a dress of Anne Marie's that she and Juanita had found stored away in a camphor-wood chest in Anne Marie's rooms, for she had brought nothing with her except the clothes she stood up in and the pearls that Marcos' mother had given her on the night of her birthday ball.

Someone had put jasmine and white roses in the chapel, and the *cura* had lighted candles on the altar. The ring that had been one of Anne Marie's slipped onto Sabrina's finger; a broad gold band set round with small pearls. Anne Marie's fingers had been plumper than Sabrina's, and the ring was heavy and a little loose. Sabrina looked down at it—this sym-bol of her marriage to Marcos, that had belonged to Marcos' mother—and as she looked at it she was aware of a strange feeling of timelessness and of the continuity of life. One day this great house would crumble into ruin and be no more than the little heaps of time-worn stones that marked where some forgotten city had stood. But she, Sabrina, would go on into time, as through Johnny and Louisa she went back into time.

I shall live forever and ever, thought Sabrina, exalted. But however long I live I shall never again be happier than I am now.

Wali Dad's father, who had been Conde Ramon's friend, died that spring, and Sir Ebenezer and Lady Emily Barton left for the cool air of Simla, where Emily's health improved and Sir Ebenezer attended those endless conferences that were to result in the disaster of the First Afghan War.

Sabrina remained in her husband's house on the banks of the Goomti, and the furnace heat of the Indian summer closed upon Oudh like a steel trap from which there was no escape. But the high white rooms of the Casa de los Pavos Reales, with their thick walls and shuttered windows, and the patios with their fountains and orange trees, had been built for coolness, and Sabrina did not suffer too greatly from the heat that first summer, though she grew pale from the enforced inaction of the long months.

Old Conde Ramon had left vast estates, for he had from time to time acquired land in outlying parts of Oudh, so Marcos spent the greater part of each day in the saddle, and Sabrina would often have been lonely that summer had it not been for Juanita. Juanita and her baby daughter and her husband, Wali Dad, were frequent visitors at the Casa Ballesteros, and often during the long hot evenings, if Marcos were away for the night, Sabrina would visit the Gulab Mahal, and sit upon the rooftop in the twilight, listening to Juanita's mother-in-law, Aziza Begum, telling long, long stories of her youth and of kings and princes and nobles of Oudh these many years in their graves.

Aziza Begum complimented Sabrina upon her progress in Urdu, and as a mark of her favor sent a woman of her household to be her personal servant. Zobeida was the daughter of a zenana slave; brown-skinned and sturdily built, with a quick brain, light deft hands, willing feet and a faithful heart. Sabrina grew to love her and to depend upon her as though she had been some faithful nurse from the days of her childhood, and Zobeida reciprocated with the protective devotion of a mother for her child.

Among the pines and deodars of Simla Lord Auckland, the Governor-General, encouraged by the irresponsible advice of men whose lust for power and conquest had made them deaf to the dictates of prudence, justice or common sense, had decided to declare war on Afghanistan.

It mattered little to Lord Auckland and his favored advisers that Dost Mahomed, the Amir of Afghanistan, was the chosen ruler of a people who infinitely preferred him to that elderly weakling, Shah Suja—the ex-ruler whom they had driven from his kingdom many years before. The Governor-General's advisers distrusted a man of the Amir's ability, who had proved that he could both think and act for himself. They considered it a vital matter of policy that Afghanistan should be an ally of Britain, and suspecting that Dost might intrigue with Russia, decided to force the rejected

Shah Suja back on his unwilling people in the belief that gratitude and self-interest would bind him to the British. With this end in view they concluded a treaty that amounted to nothing less than an offensive alliance with the dying Ranjit Singh, "Lion of the Punjab" and ruler of the Sikhs, and in November, with the onset of the cold weather, the grandiloquently named "Army of the Indus" assembled at Ferozepore before marching on Afghanistan.

Sabrina was pregnant, but after the new year Juanita did not come so often to visit her, for the birth of her own second child was imminent, and she preferred to remain within the seclusion of her house. But when Marcos was absent Sabrina spent much of her time at the Gulab Mahal, talking and laughing with Juanita and Aziza Begum, and playing with her niece, Juanita's black-eyed, dimpled first-born.

She was there on a golden morning in early February when Juanita's pains began, and would have stayed with her but that Aziza Begum and Juanita herself would not permit it.

"Send her away, my mother," whispered Juanita urgently, the sweat already pearling on her brow. "The English are not as we. They tell their maidens nothing of these things, and because it will go hard with her when her time comes it were better she were not now made afraid."

"Arré! and who should know better than I?" nodded the Begum. "Her time will indeed be hard. She is not made for the bearing of children. Hai mai! I will send her away, do not fear."

Aziza Begum stuffed her mouth with pan leaves and waddled out to summon the carriage and reassure the anxious Sabrina: "Do not fear. It is but a time that comes to all women, and what woman amongst us all would forego it had she the choice? Not one, my bird!—not one. For is not this the end for which we were born?"

Sabrina looked at the obese old woman who was Juanita's mother-in-law, and it was as though she were seeing her for the first time. The wrinkled skin that in youth had had the pallor of old ivory had darkened with age to a brown that was blotched with purplish patches on the cheeks and the pendulous chins. Her immense bulk was clothed in pajamas and tunic of pink silk over which she wore a length of yellow gauze, and her small fat hands, whose size had been the pride of her youth, were decked with rings, the wrists encircled by numerous bangles.

Sabrina had always seen her as a grotesque figure, but now, suddenly, she saw her with new eyes. Saw the kindness and the shrewd wisdom in the bright eyes that peered out of that fat wrinkled mask; the firmness and character that lay in those small dark hands; and, all at once, the vanished beauty and charm that had once been possessed by this obese and shapeless old woman who had been Anne Marie's lifelong friend.

Moved by a sudden impulse Sabrina put out her hand and groping for those small beringed fingers, clung to them tightly. The Begum embraced her. It was surprising how comforting that plump sandalwood-scented shoulder was to lay one's head against. "Haste now, little daughter, and return to thy husband's house, and I will send word when my son's son is born."

Juanita's son was born before moonrise. A lusty, dark-haired creature with his mother's fair skin and his father's black eyes. But Juanita, much to her dismay, made a slow recovery from her son's birth, and many weeks went by before she was strong enough to leave her room.

Sabrina at first went often to the Gulab Mahal to visit her, but as the cold weather neared its end and once again the days began to take on an uncomfortable warmth, she moved abroad less and less, for her slight figure was heavy now and distorted by the coming child.

The Bartons had once again left for Simla, and far to the north, as April drew to a close, Shah Suja with the British Envoy, Macnaghten, riding behind him, entered Kandahar. And in the last week of that month Marcos left for the South.

Anne Marie's father, on his retirement from service in the East India Company's army, had acquired land on the Malabar coast and settled down to the life of a planter. His estate had prospered and he had died a rich man. Anne Marie had been his sole heiress and the property had passed on her death to her two children, Marcos and Juanita. But news had been received of the overseer's death from snakebite and of disaffection among the coolies employed on the estate. Marcos, and Wali Dad, Juanita's husband, discussing the matter, decided that their best plan would be to sell the Malabar estates and invest the money in Oudh, as the property was too far away to be administered except at second hand and at long range; an arrangement which the present news had proved to be unsatisfactory.

Marcos and his brother-in-law rode south in the last week of April, promising to return by the end of May.

"It will not be for long, *querida*," said Marcos, comforting Sabrina. "I shall be back before May is out, I promise you."

"You must come to me," said Juanita. "I know you do not wish to leave Pavos Reales, and that it is cooler there. But it is not right that you should be alone just now. Send her to me, Marcos!"

So Sabrina moved from the Casa de los Pavos Reales to the pink stucco palace in Lucknow city, and watched Marcos and Wali Dad ride away under the flaming glory of the gold mohur trees in Juanita's garden, her eyes misted with tears.

Marcos, turning in his saddle for a last look as he rode under the arch of the gateway, saw her standing among the hard, fretted shadows of the garden—an incongruous little figure with her white skin and soft blond curls in that flamboyant Oriental setting—and did not know that he was seeing her for the last time.

With Marcos' departure it was as if the shining world of beauty and contentment in which Sabrina had walked had shattered like some fragile and iridescent soap bubble at the touch of a rough hand. She missed him with an intensity that grew rather than diminished as the days wore on. She missed the cool stately rooms of Pavos Reales and the quiet of the vast parklike grounds that surrounded it.

The Gulab Mahal—the "Rose Palace"—was full of noise, and the rooms with their walls painted and carved or inlaid with varicolored marbles, semi-precious stones or shining pieces of mother-of-pearl, and their windows screened with stone tracery, were stiflingly hot. Below the innumerable carved balconies lay paved courtyards and gardens thick with mango and orange and gold mohur trees, while beyond and all about the high wall that hemmed them in pressed the teeming city, with its crowded bazaars and gilded mosques, green gardens and fantastic palaces.

The noise of the city beat about the pink walls of the Rose Palace night and day, filling the small hot stifling rooms with sound, as the unguents and essences used by Aziza Begum and the zenana women filled them with the heavy scent of sandalwood and attar of roses, and the cooking pots of the kitchen courtyards filled them with the smell of boiling ghee, curry and asafetida.

Even the nights brought only a diminution of the noise; never silence. Tom-toms beat in the crowded mazes of the city, mingling their beat with the piping of flutes and the tinkle of sitars, the barking of pariah dogs, the crying of children, the clatter of armed horsemen riding through the narrow streets, or the drunken shouts of revelers returning from some debauch at the King's palace.

Sabrina found it possible to sleep a little during the day, for a hot dry wind frequently blew during the daytime, and then the doors and windows would be opened and hung with curious thick matted curtains made of woven roots, which were kept soaked with water. The hot winds blowing through the damp roots cooled the rooms and filled them with a not unpleasant odor. But often the wind did not blow, and always it died at sunset.

Sabrina's thin body felt hot and dry and shriveled with heat, and she began to long for the cool pine-scented air of the hills as a man parched with thirst longs for a draft of cold water, and to regret that she had not gone to the hills with Emily in March as Marcos had wished her to do. But she would never again go to the hills with Emily. Marcos had been absent just over three weeks, and May was halfway over, when a brief letter arrived from Sir Ebenezer Barton. Emily was dead. She had contracted malarial fever, wrote Sir Ebenezer, and had died two days later. Sir Ebenezer's handwriting, normally so clear and firm, wavered like that of an old man far gone in years.

There had been no news of Marcos or Wali Dad beyond a brief note dispatched from the village where they had spent the first night of their journey. The lack of news did not worry Juanita or the Begum, who knew only too well the state of the roads and the difficulties of sending word through the dâk from out-of-the-way stations. But it worried Sabrina, and during the long hot hours of the sleepless nights her imagination would conjure up pictures of horror and calamity. The India that had once seemed to her so glamourous and beautiful a country began to wear a different aspect. She knew now that underneath that glamour and beauty lurked undreamed-of depths of cruelty and terror, just as the graceful minarets and gilded domes of the palaces rose above narrow, filthy streets and the squalid hovels of the poor.

On the far side of the high wall that bounded the garden of the Gulab Mahal, and immediately fronting Sabrina's window, stood a mosque. It was an unpretentious little mosque built of whitewashed brick and plaster, its bulblike dome crowned by an iron horned moon that is the symbol of Islam. The sun rose directly behind it, and with every dawn, while the air was still faintly cool from the long hours of darkness, Sabrina would see it framed by the curve of the open window and silhouetted darkly against the saffron sky. And when, too soon, the sun rose, it would cast the curved shadow of that horned moon across the floor of her room.

The shadow would creep slowly across the matting as the sun rose into a brassy sky, and sometimes at night Sabrina would awake to find it lying black in the moonlight. It came to symbolize for her all the fear and loneliness of those long days, and that growing sense of being alone in an alien country and surrounded by people of an alien race. It was a threat and a warning. A token of the inescapable and grinding heat of the coming day. Heat that sapped the strength from Sabrina's body and the power of connected thought from her brain.

She had not visited the Casa de los Pavos Reales since Marcos had left, but one breathless evening she was seized by a sudden desire to see it again and to walk through the gardens and along the river terrace.

Juanita offered to accompany her, but Sabrina preferred to go alone. Marcos had left a carriage for her use at the Gulab Mahal, and attended by Zobeida she was driven through the narrow burning streets, where the heat appeared to be imprisoned between the houses as water between the banks of a river, and out to the open country where the Casa de los Pavos Reales lay surrounded by acres of parkland and groves of trees.

The dim shuttered rooms were close and stuffy and the patio fountains were silent, but after the noise and heat and color of the Gulab Mahal it seemed to Sabrina incredibly cool and peaceful, and she wandered through the quiet, darkening rooms, touching the heavy Spanish furniture and the fragile French ornaments with a caressing hand, as though they were friends whom she was greeting—or bidding farewell.

Below and beyond the stone terrace flowed the river, its wide expanse dull gold in the light of the late evening and its far bank almost invisible in the dusty twilight. The river was low and barred with the faint silver ripples of shoal water, and white, long-legged birds like a species of small heron picked their way along the warm shallows, ghostlike in the dusk. A peacock called harshly from among the bamboo thickets, its cry catching the echo from the curved wall at the far end of the terrace. Pea-oor! . . . *Pea-oor!* . . . Pea-oor! . . . *Pea-oor!* Sabrina had always loved to hear the peacocks cry at dusk and dawn at the Casa de los Pavos Reales, but tonight it seemed to her that the harsh call held a strange aching note of sadness, and of a sudden she was seized by an uncontrollable spasm of fear. A fear of India. Of the savage alien lands that lay all about her, stretching away for thousands of miles and yet hemming her in. Of the dark, secretive, sideways-looking eyes; the tortuous unreadable minds behind those bland expressionless faces. Of the incredible cruelties that were practiced within the kings' palaces, of which the zenana women whispered. Of queens and dancing girls and zenana favorites burnt alive on the funeral pyres of their lords . . .

Daylight does not linger in the East as it does in cooler lands, and the Oriental twilight is barely a breath drawn between day and night. One moment the river ran gold in the last reflected glow of the sunset, and in the next the moon had laid a shining pathway across its dark surface, and Sabrina's shadow lay black on the moonlit terrace.

A jackal howled from somewhere far out across the darkening plain, and although nightfall had brought little or no alleviation of the oppressive heat, Sabrina shivered as though with a sudden chill. She drew the light scarf of Indian gauze closer about her and turned back to the house, and presently she was driving away down the long moonlit avenue toward the city and Gulab Mahal.

There was a riderless horse standing just within the gateway of the Rose Palace. A tired horse, lathered with sweat, its head drooping and the white dust of the roads thick on its heaving flanks. It stood among the dappled shadows of the flame trees, but Sabrina knew it. She knew all the Pavos Reales horses, and this was Suliman who had been ridden by one of the servants who had accompanied Marcos to the south.

Her heart leapt with a sudden wild joy and she stood up, swaying to the movement of the carriage as it jolted over the uneven paving of the court-yard. But it was not Marcos. A messenger only, bearing letters, said the servant who opened the carriage door. Sabrina brushed aside Zobeida's hand and sprang to the ground. A letter from Marcos at last! Perhaps to say that he would be back in a few days. Only a few more days to wait! She ran down a short passage and up the two steep flights of narrow ill-lighted stairs that led to Juanita's rooms, laughing as she ran.

Juanita's room seemed to blaze with light after the dimly lit stair-way, and it was full of people. Aziza Begum was there and two of her daughters, and Wali Dad's younger brother Faiz Ullah, and several serving women. And Juanita herself was holding a letter in her hand and her face was white and frightened.

Sabrina stopped on the threshold and stood quite still. Then her lips closed stiffly and she said: "Marcos—"

Juanita ran to her, putting her arms about her and holding her close. "Do not look like that, *querida!* He will not die. Many recover. Do not look so!"

Sabrina put her aside, pulling herself free of the clinging arms, and spoke across the small, hot, crowded room to Aziza Begum:

"What is it? Tell me."

"It is the cholera, my daughter. One of thy husband's servants brought a letter from my son. He thought it best that we should know, so that—" The Begum checked herself and then said: "But thy husband is a young man and strong. He will recover, never fear. Many recover from the cholera who are not as young and as strong as he."

But Sabrina did not hear her. She had heard only the one word—cholera! The swift, dreaded plague of the East. Marcos had cholera. Even now he might be dying—dead! She must go to him. She must go at once.

The heat of the small room pressed upon her with an almost tangible weight, but it seemed to her that her brain was suddenly very clear and cold. The only clear thing in this queer hot room full of oddly hazy faces and bright spinning colors. The only cold thing in this furnace-like city. She looked at the faces around her, trying to focus them. Dark anxious faces. Dark anxious eyes. Juanita's blanched cheeks. They were kind. She knew that. But they would try and stop her. They would prevent her going to Marcos. But Suliman was tethered by the gate. If she could only reach him she could ride away to Marcos and they could not catch her.

She backed away from them very slowly, and Juanita took a swift step toward her, her hand outstretched. The roomful of faces seemed to surge up and forward, and Sabrina whirled round and ran toward the stairs. The steep dark stairway yawned below her feet and she heard footsteps running behind her and glanced over her shoulder. And then she was falling, falling—falling into a hot spinning darkness that reached up and engulfed her.

Sabrina's daughter was born as the sun rose, after a night of agonizing labor, and Juanita, watching the white lips move, bent close to catch the whispered words.

"Don't . . . let . . . it . . . touch—"

"No, no," comforted Juanita, not knowing of what she spoke.

"The shadow—" persisted Sabrina. She was too exhausted to turn her head, but her eyes turned, and Juanita following their gaze saw them rest on the curious curved shadow of the crescent moon that the early morning sun threw across the wall.

She rose quickly and drew close the heavy wooden shutters that should have been closed an hour earlier to conserve what little coolth the night had brought into the room.

Sabrina closed her eyes and lapsed into a waking dream in which her mind wandered back to Ware in wintertime; to a white expanse of snow and the sharp blackness of yew trees and leafless woods; to frost patterns on a windowpane, and softly falling snow. All that long hot day Zobeida crouched beside her, fanning her tirelessly, and at sundown she opened the shutters and sprinkled water on the balcony outside, and Sabrina, waking, heard the water hiss upon the hot stone. Aziza Begum, seeing that she was awake, brought her the child.

"What shall you call her?" asked Juanita. "She is half a day old and should have a name."

Sabrina looked at the tiny white-skinned creature that lay beside her, and remembered a fairy story that someone—was it Aunt Emily?—had told her one winter's day at Ware. A story about a queen who had sat at her window on a snowy day, spinning with an ebony spinning wheel, and had wished for a daughter with skin as white as snow and hair as black as ebony.

"Winter," whispered Sabrina.

"*Winter?* But that is not a name, *cara mia*. She must have a beautiful name."

"It is a beautiful name . . ." Juanita did not realize how beautiful! She had never seen the snow and the dark December woods. She only knew the harsh, flaming colors of this sun-scorched country, and the heat was not an intolerable burden to her as it was to Sabrina—pressing her out of life. She did not know what it was to long for gray skies and fresh winds and the cold touch of falling snowflakes.

Outside the shuttered window the sun beat down upon the city like a giant hammer, and beyond and around the city walls lay the scorching plains, stretching endlessly away to the burning horizon. Somewhere out there lay Marcos. *Marcos—Marcos!* Was he dead already? Perhaps he would never know that he had a daughter.

A sudden sharp fear—a purely maternal fear—took possession of Sabrina. If Marcos were to die—if she herself were to die—what would become of the child? Juanita? No—*No!* thought Sabrina, agonized. Not this life for my baby!

Grandpapa! The old Earl had loved her and he would take care of her child. Sabrina was aware of a quivering sense of urgency. Of time running out like sand between her fingers. She must send a letter to Ware, at once, before it was too late. She set her teeth and summoning up all her will power, dragged herself up onto her pillow. There was a quick rustle of silk and Juanita was beside her.

"What is it, *cara mia?*"

"I must write a letter," whispered Sabrina. "A letter to Ware. I must write at once."

"I shall write it for you," said Juanita soothingly. "You shall tell me what to say."

So Juanita wrote at Sabrina's dictation, writing down the words that came so slowly and with such difficulty in that soft gasping whisper. She wrote in French, for although she spoke English well and fluently, she could not write it with ease. And looking at Sabrina's face, and the faces of Aziza Begum and Zobeida, she was afraid, and the tears that she would not let Sabrina see, fell and blotted the written words.

"Look after her," begged Sabrina of her grandfather. "If anything happens to me or to Marcos—if we are not here to care for her—I leave her to you. I do not know how to write a will, but this letter is my will. If Marcos dies I leave everything to my daughter, and I leave my daughter to you."

When she had finished, the Begum and Zobeida lifted her, and with Juanita steadying her hand she signed her name to it. Juanita folded the paper and addressed it and put it away, and Sabrina smiled at her. Then she turned her head on the hot pillow and looked out at the moonlight beyond the open window, and as she looked it seemed to her that the dome of the mosque, the white, moonlit walls of India and the black shadows of the orange trees, were the snow-covered fields and winter woods of Ware; and she began to talk in a clear, light voice.

It was winter and the snow was falling, and Sabrina wept because they had locked her into the hot schoolroom and she could only see through the barred windows the white park where she was forbidden to play. She struggled to reach it but hands held her back. And then all at once the hands fell away and the door was open. She ran out of the room and along the familiar passages and down the wide staircase. The wind blew about her, smelling of the winter woods, and now she had reached the snow, and it was cold and shining and wonderful and she was not hot any more, but cold, cold, cold.

Zobeida and the Begum fetched padded quilts and tucked them about her shivering figure as the fever mounted, but Sabrina did not feel them, and toward morning she died.

IV

Marcos did not die of the cholera. He was, as Aziza Begum had said, both young and strong. He returned home, but by that time Sabrina had been two weeks in her grave, and to stay here in the Casa de los Pavos Reales where he had spent his brief year of happiness was suddenly intolerable to him. Through Sir Ebenezer Barton's influence he obtained a commission in the East India Company's Army: there was always work for the Army, and Marcos yearned for change and hard work, and, if possible, hard fighting. He placed his daughter in the care of his sister Juanita, and having installed a reliable caretaker and overseer at the Casa de los Pavos Reales, he put his affairs in order and rode north to join the Army of the Indus, reaching Kabul by way of the Khyber Pass with the advance guard of a motley army under the leadership of Shah Suja's son.

Left behind in the little pink palace in Lucknow City, Sabrina's daughter grew and thrived. Her nickname among the household was *Chota Moti* —Little Pearl—because of her whiteness, and because her given name had no meaning for them and its syllables were harsh to their ears. Zobeida had taken on the duties of nurse, and a strong and healthy hill woman, Hamida, had been engaged as wet nurse.

The child would lie in the room that had been her mother's, her eyes on the colorful walls where formalized trees and flowers in the Persian style were molded in high relief in chunam, a polished cement that had the appearance of colored marble. As soon as she could crawl she would spend hours running her small hands over the flower designs, tracing their stylized curves with a tiny finger. They were her first toys and her first memory, so that in later years her recollection of her earliest days was that they had been spent in a fantastic garden in which she had played and eaten and slept surrounded by wonderful flowers and curious, beautiful birds.

Every animal and every bird in those colorful friezes had had its own name, but there had been one that was her especial favorite—the first within reach of her small clutching hands—a stylized parrot with a wise expression who held one claw upraised as though he were commanding attention. He was called Firishta, after a celebrated Moslem historian who had lived in the days of Akbar and Jehangir. When she was older, and the days were hot, she would stand by the pink plaster wall, pressing her small cheek against Firishta's cool, smooth greenness, and talk to him as though he were a friend and a playmate.

She had many playmates in the Gulab Mahal, chief among them Juanita's two children, Khalig Dad and the little Anne Marie who was a year and a half her senior and had been named for Juanita's mother. Anne Marie the Second, despite her name, had not inherited her looks from her mother's side of the family. She was all Wali Dad. Golden skin and eyes like sloes, a mouth like a curled rose petal and hair as black as jet. "She is her father again—and as I also, when I was but a child," said the Begum complacently. "My son had great beauty, as also had I, his mother, when I was in the bloom of my youth. *Hai mai!* but that was long since, and I grow old."

But while life in the Rose Palace went its peaceful way, the storm clouds gathered over far-off Afghanistan. Early in November the storm broke. Alexander Burns, the British Emissary, and his brother were hacked to pieces by a screaming mob, and soon all Afghanistan was aflame. The distant outposts were attacked and their defenders massacred. Food became short; there was no hope of relief, and the senile and incompetent Elphinstone was totally incapable of the prompt and daring action that alone might have saved the doomed Army. Akbar Khan, son of the Dost, murdered Sir William Macnaghten, the British envoy, and General Elphinstone remained supine and took no action to avenge his death. Instead, a treaty was made with the chiefs by which the British forces were to be allowed to leave the country under a guarantee of safe conduct, Akbar Khan promising to send a strong Afghan escort to see them safely through the passes.

The retreat began early in the new year, and more than four thousand fighting men, with twelve thousand camp followers including many women and children, marched wearily out of the cantonments toward the snow and the bitter cold of the barren hills that lay between them and the fortress of Jalalabad.

But once among the steep defiles of the passes Akbar Khan's escort deserted them, leaving them to the vengeance of the hostile tribes. Hundreds died of exposure in the intense cold, and those who dropped by the way and did not die met a less merciful death from mutilation at the hands of the tribesmen. At some time during that long martyrdom Akbar Khan, with an eye to the future, offered his protection to those few Englishwomen who were still alive, together with their husbands and General Elphinstone. They had no option but to accept and they turned back with him. The remainder fought their way forward against the snowdrifts and the murderous tribes, and on the thirteenth day of January a sentry on the ramparts of Jalalabad saw a solitary rider; emaciated, ragged, bloodstained, drooping with exhaustion on a starved and exhausted horse. It was Dr. Brydon—the sole survivor of the sixteen thousand souls who had set out from Kabul on that tragic retreat.

Somewhere back in those terrible passes, among the butchered thousands who had paid the price of Lord Auckland's folly, Marcos de Ballesteros had died as Sabrina had imagined herself in her last hours—face downward in the cold and glittering snow. And his corpse, and those other thousands of mutilated corpses that rotted in the passes, were the seeds from which sprang the rank growth of rebellion that was in time to deluge all India in blood. For the power and the prestige of the Company had been humbled into the dust. Their troops had been defeated in battle and herded and butchered like sheep, and their bones lay bleaching in the sun and wind to bear witness that the mighty John Company was mortal. All along the Border and through the length and breadth of India the news spread swiftly, and many men sharpened their swords in secret—and waited.

In the little Pink Palace in Lucknow Juanita wept for her brother, clutching his orphaned daughter in her arms until the child too wept aloud in bewilderment and alarm.

When her first grief had spent itself she wrote to the Earl of Ware, enclosing Sabrina's letter and another packet; papers relating to the de Ballesteros estates, together with the will that Marcos had left with her instructing her to send them to Lord Ware in the event of his death. She wrote in March, but summer had gone and the leaves were falling by the time the packet reached Ware.

The Earl was eighty, but he did not look his age. He read Juanita's covering letter, telling of her brother's death in the Afghan passes, and the will that Marcos had made in favor of his only child in which he had concurred, in the tortuous legal phrases required by the law, with his wife's desire that the child should become the ward of her grandfather. He untied the strings of a small brocaded bag that still smelt faintly of sandalwood, his lip curling with distaste. The letter it contained was written in French, and the ink was blotted in places as though the writer had been crying and her tears had fallen upon the paper.

The Earl read it once slowly, and then again. And suddenly there were tears on his own cheeks.

It was not until the autumn of 1844 that Sabrina's daughter, Winter de Ballesteros, Condesa de los Aguilares, arrived at Ware, for mails were slow and travel slower, and the loss at sea of the Earl's first letters, followed by the death from typhus of a lady who had agreed to bring the child home, had delayed matters considerably.

She was six and a half years old. And with her, to the mingled curiosity and consternation of the Viscountess and the Servants Hall, came a dark-skinned attendant—Zobeida.

Save for one notable exception the small Condesa made an unfavorable first impression. She was a tiny creature, small boned and, according to Lady Julia, sickly looking. The white skin that had reminded the dying Sabrina of snow at Ware had ripened with time and the suns of the East to a warm ivory that her newly found relatives described as "yellow." Her enormous eyes, the dark velvet-brown of pansies, were overlarge for her small face, and the rippling blue-black hair that already fell below the child's waist were pronounced "foreign"; and they resented her sonorous Spanish title.

She was a silent child who spoke English haltingly and with a pronounced accent. The complete change of scene and environment, the contrast between the warm, colorful, casual life of the Gulab Mahal and the cold, gloomy rooms, Victorian discipline and stately routine of Ware, coupled with the bitter pangs of homesickness for the only home she had ever known, reduced her to a state of dumb despair. Her silent, dry-eyed misery was taken for sullenness and her slow speech for stupidity, for her relatives were not as yet aware that the child spoke four languages—Urdu, French, Spanish and English—of which English, owing to the fact that it had been taught her by a woman of Franco-Spanish ancestry, was the least fluent.

To Julia the fact that Sabrina's daughter was a plain, sallow and silent child proved a relief, for the Viscountess possessed a jealous nature, and her own small daughter, Sybella, was the apple of her eye. She did not relish the appearance of a rival, and from what she remembered of Sabrina, Sabrina's daughter might well prove to be a formidable one. The subsequent arrival of such a notably unattractive child therefore relieved her of some anxiety. But her relief was of short duration, for the single exception to the disparaging view that her noble relatives had taken of Sabrina's daughter was provided by the Earl himself. Between the old man and the small silent child there sprang up a strong bond of sympathy and understanding. He alone came to realize what the child must be suffering in heartache and homesickness; and young as she was, she sensed the loneliness and need for affection that lay behind the old man's forbidding exterior and irascible manner.

Julia saw her worst fears realized. It seemed to her nothing less than a deliberate affront that her own beautiful child should fail to hold first place in Ware's affections owing to the presence of this pallid, Anglo-Spanish brat. She could not forgive Sabrina's child for stealing what she considered to be her own daughter's birthright, and her resentment made itself felt in numerous small ways.

The child herself did not know what she had done to earn Julia's dislike. She was merely aware of it and did her best to keep out of her way. She was a lonely child, driven in upon herself by the circumstances of this new life; her only companions the silent Indian woman and the old man crippled by years and gout. It was therefore not surprising that her memory painted India as a place of wonder and beauty where the sun always shone and where people did not live in vast chilly rooms full of ugly dark furniture, but in gardens full of strange and beautiful flowers and tame birds. "One day," Aziza Begum had said, taking tender farewell of the weeping child, "you will come back to the Gulab Mahal and we shall all be happy again."

Zobeida too longed for her homeland, and kept it alive in Winter's memory, retelling the tales that Aziza Begum had been wont to tell of an evening seated on the flat rooftop of the zenana quarters and looking out across the beautiful garish city of Lucknow. "Someday," promised Zobeida, comforting the lonely and homesick child, "we will go back to the Gulab Mahal, and then all will be well with us."

V

Winter was eleven years old when Conway Barton, her distant cousin, accompanied her great-uncle Ebenezer on a visit to Ware. Sir Ebenezer was getting old and his contacts with India, together with his interest in it, had shrunk with the years. But his influence had been sufficient to assist the advancement in that country of his nephew Conway, the son of his brother Joseph. Old Lord Ware had wished to make the acquaintance of Sir Ebenezer's nephew, with a view to asking him to see to certain details connected with the de Ballesteros estates in Oudh that could only be dealt with by someone in India.

Conway Barton was at that time in his thirty-seventh year, and still a personable enough figure of a man. Already moving toward stoutness, he was of sufficient height to make it appear that he was powerfully built rather than overweight, and his blond hair and blue eyes appeared lighter in color than they actually were, owing to the sun-tanned skin of one newly arrived from the East. He was an ambitious man, not too scrupulous where his ambitions were concerned, with an easy address and an excellent opinion of his own capabilities.

The Earl of Ware had always considered himself to be a good judge of character, but he was old and tired and in this instance his judgment was at fault. His eyesight too had dimmed, and so he failed to mark the signs of weakness and dissipation that were already written clear on Conway Barton's face. He took a great fancy to his son-in-law's nephew; entrusted him with much of Winter's affairs, and, when Sir Ebenezer left, pressed the younger man to extend his stay.

It was at some time during this visit that the idea occurred to Mr. Barton, who was already familiar with Winter's story and now heard for the first time the full tale of her possessions and estates, that this sallow and unprepossessing child would one day make a most eligible wife for some ambitious man. From this reflection it was but a short step to substituting Conway Barton for this anonymous future husband. The more he thought about it, the better it appeared. He was only thirty-six. He could afford to wait for six years—or ten if need be. But only if he were assured of the outcome.

Fortune favored him, for he had come from the East—from India; the Enchanted Land that was now but a fast-fading memory in Winter's mind. He had talked of that country once, in tones not untinged with distaste, in the presence of the child, and had been aware of her sudden avid attention. Thereafter he changed his tone and spoke of India as he himself had never seen it. His personal opinion of the country and its inhabitants was not a high one. He considered the former unsanitary and barbaric and the latter uncivilized and contemptible, but having realized that there were fortunes to be made in India he had had every intention of making one. Now however Fate appeared to have presented him with a yet easier way of acquiring wealth, and one which, if he were not mistaken, would entail the exercise of considerably less effort.

Mr. Conway Barton began to speak to the eleven-year-old Winter of life in India, describing fantastic beauties of scene which were for the most part purely imaginary. The India he created for her was apparently entirely populated by Oriental kings and queens who rode on white elephants, decked with golden trappings and attended by gorgeously robed slaves waving fans of peacocks' feathers, and who lived in glittering fairy-tale palaces of white marble in a land where the sun always shone and the gardens were full of flowers and fountains and exotic fruits. It was all so much in tune with the shadowy country of Winter's memory and imagination that she listened with rapture. Except for her great-grandfather and 'Beda, no one at Ware had ever troubled to single her out for attention or kindness. But this tall, yellow-haired man was kind to her, noticed her, talked to her, flattered her. She thought him wonderful.

The Earl was pleased that his favorite should show such partiality for a man who had taken his fancy, and put it down to an unconscious endorsement of the soundness of his own judgment.

Conway Barton left Ware with a pressing invitation to return. It was on his last visit, when less than two weeks of his furlough remained, that he spoke of Winter to the Earl. He had given the matter considerable thought and chose his words with care. He had, he said, become greatly attached to the child and would now be returning to India for a further period of some eight to ten years. He suggested, delicately, that the Earl's expectation of life could not be great, and should anything—er—unforeseen occur, Winter would be left to the care of Lady Julia, with whom the child did not appear to be entirely in sympathy. He realized of course that no such thing as a formal engagement could be entered into with a girl in the schoolroom, but he would like to feel that when he returned from the East he might, with the permission and approval of Lord Ware, approach her as a possible suitor for her hand.

The aged Earl was much moved. Lord Ware had always known that Julia disliked Sabrina's daughter, and he placed no reliance upon her being either kind or considerate toward the child once he himself was dead. She could be counted on instead to seize the earliest opportunity of ridding herself of the girl through marriage with the first who offered for her. But now here was a way out of all his difficulties. Married to this admirable young man, Winter would be safe; and with her affection for him, she would also be happy, for it was safe to assume that this childish attachment would grow and not diminish with the years. As for the idea that Conway Barton should wait until he was next in England before the subject was broached, the Earl would have none of it. He himself might well be dead long before then. In his own long-vanished youth, as it was still on the Continent and in the land of Winter's own father, children were frequently promised in matrimony at a very early age.

Winter was summoned to her great-grandfather's room, the situation explained to her, and her future decided. It seemed to her the most delightful thing in the world. Dear Mr. Barton, who was so kind—almost as kind as Great-grandfather himself—would come for her and 'Beda and take them away, back to that golden, enchanted land whose memories he had reawakened for her.

At the Earl's desire a formal contract of betrothal was drawn up in which he, as the girl's legal guardian, gave his consent to the eventual marriage of his ward to Conway Barton. Mr. Barton signed his name to it in a bold, flowing hand beneath Winter's childish signature. This contract the old Earl had insisted upon, as it was his wish that, in the event of his death, Conway Barton should immediately claim his bride, provided she had reached marriageable age.

Later during the week the Earl's solicitors called at Ware and drew up various legal documents with which Winter, a minor, had no concern; her great-grandfather signing on her behalf. And on the day he left Ware Conway presented her with a ring. It was a small thing, made to fit a slim finger, yet still too large for Winter's childish hand. The unpretentious little trinket—for Mr. Barton knew that Lady Julia would take strong exception to any more ostentatious piece of jewelry—consisted of a small pearl set in a plain gold band. "You cannot wear it on the right finger yet," said Conway Barton, slipping it onto the third finger of Winter's small right hand, "but it is only a token. One day, when you are grown up, I shall put another one there—the brightest diamond I can find for you in

India. You must grow up quickly, and you must not forget me while you
are doing it."

The child flung her thin arms about his neck in a strangling hug. "I
will try and grow up as quickly as ever I can, and I will write you a great
many letters so that you will not forget me."

Conway Barton patted her head encouragingly, disengaged himself and
rode away.

Winter wore his ring for exactly two days, during which it fell from
her finger some two dozen times and Sybella remarked crushingly that it
was a trumpery thing and that she herself would never consent to wear
such poor stuff. Their governess refused to allow her to wear it during
school hours, and when worn out riding under a leather gauntlet it cut
into her finger. Winter gave up the attempt, and threading it on a narrow ribbon she wore it thereafter around her neck, hidden beneath her
bodice.

True to her promise, she wrote long and often to Conway, telling him
of her small doings and asking news of him and his work, but Mr. Barton's
letters were disappointing. They were generally full of complaints about
his superiors who were, it appeared, an envious lot who were jealous of
his outstanding talents and judgment and did their best to keep him from
preferment, and Winter would burn with resentment against these stubborn and mean-minded officials who could oppose so good and kind a
man.

She was fourteen when Zobeida died.

The damp cold and the fogs and frosts of the English climate had always been a torment to Zobeida, and of late years her once-sturdy frame
had shrunk to little more than skin and bone. She had no reserves with
which to combat a chill that had turned to pneumonia, and had died
within three days, babbling in her native tongue words that only Winter
understood.

In the years that followed Zobeida's death Winter turned more and
more to her make-believe world of the future. The years might be passing
slowly, but at least they were passing. Only a few more of them, and
Conway would come and claim her, and after that she would live happily
ever after. She grew paler and thinner and more silent than ever.

But the natural health and resilience of youth eventually reasserted itself, and almost overnight, or so it seemed, Sabrina's daughter grew from
a plain child into a young woman of strange and disturbing beauty. It
was a beauty that many—and these were all women—could not appreciate
or understand. England was in the throes of a sentimental age: an era
where the ideal of feminine beauty consisted of a smoothly oval face of a
stereotyped pink and whiteness, a small rosebud mouth, limpid eyes—
preferably blue—and long, sleek curls à la Stuart caressing the cheeks and
dressed so as to accentuate the oval of the face, or at least to give that
effect to those unlucky enough not to possess the fashionable features.

Sybella was the very embodiment of the Victorian ideal of beauty, but Winter possessed none of these attributes. Her wide forehead and small pointed chin gave her face a heart-shaped appearance, and her mouth was considered far too large. It was therefore not altogether surprising that to the majority of feminine beholders she should still appear entirely unremarkable, if not actually plain.

But it was quite otherwise with their men. By the time Winter had reached her sixteenth birthday men's heads began to turn when she passed by, and men's eyes to follow her whenever she entered a room. The scrawny, angular child had grown into a slender girl whose slim seductive shape even the overblown hoops of the newly fashionable crinolines could not entirely disguise. Her thin little face had filled out, setting her features in proportion at last, and the wide mouth was seen to be curved with beauty and of a rich and lovely redness. The sallow skin had warmed to ivory, and the sweet curve of her young breasts owed nothing to the ruffles and padding so often resorted to by Victorian maidens. Winter's expressive dark eyes tilted slightly upward at the outer corners, which women pronounced unbecoming and men found irresistible. But even the sternest of feminine critics were obliged to allow that her long slender neck and the thick sweep of her silky black lashes were both exceptional beauties.

The girl appeared to have acquired too the graceful carriage that is possessed by so many Spanish women. Perhaps, like her coloring, it was a legacy from Marcos, and possibly she had always possessed it, only no one had troubled to notice it until now.

It was not until the summer of 1855, when Winter was sixteen, that Lady Julia awoke to the fact that the ugly Anglo-Spanish duckling had turned into a swan. Julia had given a young people's party for Sybella—a summer dance. It was not to be termed a ball, for Sybella would not make her official debut until the following spring. Julia's party for Sybella might with more truth have been termed a Private View, for she considered it only fair that the more eligible bachelors in Society should at least know that if they were prepared to wait a few more months, a Beauty of Beauties would shortly be making her debut, and thus be spared the possibility of throwing themselves away on some lesser damsel without realizing what was so shortly to dawn on their horizon. Whatever glamour might attend Sybella's future debut, this comparatively small assembly constituted her real introduction to the social world in which her mother intended that she should one day be queen.

Certainly Julia had every reason to feel proud of her child as Sybella stood before the long pier glass in her mother's bedchamber, complacently admiring her enchanting reflection. Sybella's white satin bodice, tiny waist and soft, sloping, flower-wreathed shoulders rose out of a wide crinolined ballgown of white *gros de Naples* whose overskirt of satin-striped gauze, trimmed with blonde, was looped up at intervals with bouquets of white primroses, heath and lilies of the valley. Her golden curls were .

adorned by a wreath of the same flowers, and in deference to her youth she wore only a simple necklace and bracelet of seed pearls.

Winter's dress had received considerably less attention. It had in fact been selected by the housekeeper Mrs. Flecker, who had been told by Lady Julia to see that Miss Winter had a suitable gown. It would have to be white, and as simple as possible, as Miss Winter was younger than Lady Sybella and therefore must consider herself fortunate in being permitted to attend at all.

Mrs. Flecker procured a sufficient quantity of white Indian muslin and the services of an elderly dressmaker from the market town of Wareburn, and the result was a simple gown that met with Lady Julia's approval. But the effect of the garment when worn by Winter was entirely unexpected. Perhaps the French blood of Anne Marie de Lazencourt, Marcos' mother, had something to do with it, but the fact remained that the simple and unadorned muslin gown acquired from its wearer that look of rare distinction that many Frenchwomen and few Englishwomen can give to an otherwise unremarkable dress.

Winter's wealth of blue-black hair was drawn straight back and confined in a net of white silk, so that its shining weight tilted her little pointed chin as though with pride. She wore no jewels—she was as yet unaware that she possessed any—but Mrs. Flecker, tying the wide white taffeta sash about her slender waist and turning the girl about to see that she was ready to be sent downstairs, had reached out of the window to where the climbing roses nodded just below the sill, and breaking off a white rosebud had tucked it into the dark sweep of hair above one small ear.

Winter had had an astonishing success, and Lady Julia was both angry and bewildered. She could not understand why the girl received so much attention from men whom she had confidently expected to have eyes for no one but Sybella. It was not that Winter had outshone her cousin. She could not do that. Sybella had attracted the lion's share of attention, but Julia was not slow to note how the older and more eligible men turned to look again and yet again at Sabrina's daughter.

Lord Carlyon, handsome, wealthy, bored, thirty-five and still a bachelor, had inquired of Sybella who the beautiful creature in white might be? Sybella had not recognized her cousin by this description, and Lord Carlyon had been more specific.

"You mean *Winter?*" demanded Sybella, astounded.

"Winter?"

"My cousin Winter. Such a peculiar name, is it not?"

"*Winter!*" Sybella had heard him repeat the word almost with awe. "But how perfect!"

"What *do* you mean?" Sybella's fluting voice had a sudden sharp edge to it.

"I mean that it suits so admirably. She is like snow and black shadows. Cool and mysterious, and yet—" He laughed on an odd note. "So this is the plain cousin from the East! I have heard of her. The ugly duckling in person. Pray introduce me, Lady Sybella."

Arthur Carlyon was no impressionable youth but a coldly handsome rake with a considerable experience with women. His confident approach and suavely experienced manner had, however, made no impression on Sybella's young cousin. Winter had not been in the least sensible of the honor implied by his interest, and had considered him impertinent. Carlyon, who had imagined that such a youthful creature would be easy game, found himself being put in his place and dismissed with a cool grace that would have done credit to an experienced London hostess. It was an entirely new and salutory experience to Lord Carlyon—and an unpleasant one.

But he had by no means been the only one to comment admiringly on Winter's unusual style of looks, and Sybella was astounded and outraged and Lady Julia coldly angry. There was only one thing to be done. Conway Barton must come home and marry the girl as soon as possible. She would be seventeen in the spring and quite old enough to be married. "I have already written," said the old Earl.

He had not meant to write. He had not wished Winter to marry until she was eighteen or nineteen—or even twenty. He had celebrated his ninetieth birthday the previous year and felt unusually well—better than he had felt for a long time. But the snow had lain late into the year and spring had been tardy and cold and the rain fell steadily. The damp cold to which he had been impervious for so long seemed to seep into the old man's very bones and he could not keep warm. He had felt the tide of his life running out, and he had written to Conway Barton.

In the early autumn a reply arrived from India. Mr. Barton had received Lord Ware's communication and was deeply grieved to hear of his failing health. He could only hope that Lord Ware was by now fully recovered. Naturally it was the dearest wish of his heart to marry the Earl's ward, but various unforeseen difficulties had arisen which necessitated his remaining at his post for the present. However, he had a suggestion to make that he hoped might meet with the Earl's approval. He had written more fully on the matter and was sending that letter by the hand of a trusted subordinate Captain Alex Randall, who should reach England sometime in the autumn.

But Captain Randall, as it happened, was considerably delayed. He had met with friends at Gibraltar, and instead of continuing on his way had turned back with them and gone instead to the Crimea where he had managed, entirely illegally, to get himself attached to General Windham's Staff, had fought at the taking of Sebastopol and been wounded in the bloody battle for the Redan. He had not reached England until late in February, and it was not until the second week of March that he arrived at Ware.

Kishan Prasad

4

THE majority of the guests who had stayed at Ware for the funeral left the same afternoon, and those few who remained kept to their rooms. Toward dusk on that cold and windy day the sixth Earl sent a footman to find Captain Randall, and once again Alex was led through the corridors and galleries of the west wing. But this time he was ushered into a small paneled room where a fire crackled in the hearth and the new Earl sat warming himself at the blaze.

Huntly, Lord Ware, was a stout and undistinguished man who disguised his lack of character behind an impassive and somewhat pompous manner. He touched only briefly on the subject of Captain Randall's errand, and beyond thanking him for his good offices did not appear to think that any further discussion was necessary. Alex' hard gray eyes ran over him in a comprehensive glance and summed him up dispassionately as a nonentity. The last of the Wares! The old man whose funeral he had attended that morning must have had more hot blood in him than this, if all accounts were true!

Alex had been unable to speak plainly to the Countess, but no such scruples need weigh with him now. This fat, pallid man with his air of consequence had presumably inherited the guardianship of the little Condesa and must therefore be appraised of the truth. But there was a faint chance that he might be dissuaded from sending the girl to India without being informed of the facts about Mr. Conway Barton. It was at least worth trying, and Alex tried it.

"Might I suggest, sir, that it would be advisable to postpone the Condesa's departure for—for a few years? Until the country is in a less unsettled condition? You cannot, I think, fully appreciate the present state of unrest that prevails in India. There have been disturbing signs of late, and Sir Henry Lawrence and many others have warned of the possibility of grave troubles arising out of Lord Dalhousie's policy of annexation of sovereign states. In particular if it is pressed over the matter of Oudh. India and the Bengal Army are far from being in the condition of tranquillity that some would have us suppose."

Huntly raised his eyebrows and observed coldly that Captain Randall was mistaken in supposing that he had no knowledge of the situation prevailing in India. He had occasion to attend, only the previous August, the banquet given at the London Tavern by the East India Company in honor of Lord Canning, the Governor-General designate, and he had been assured, through the medium of public speeches and private discussions that our Indian dependency had never before been so peaceful or so prosperous.

Alex said: "Lord Dalhousie's policy of annexation and lapse, though it has added immeasurably to our territories, has aroused the bitterest enmity among those nobles whom we have dispossessed. Oudh has been one of the greatest recruiting grounds for the sepoys of the Bengal Army, and if it is indeed annexed it may well prove to be the straw that breaks the camel's back. The arbitrary acquisition of Oudh will mean, once again, a province almost the size of England awash with disbanded soldiery and embittered nobles to whom annexation will have meant the loss of power and privilege and, in many cases, of even the bare means of existence. In addition to which, Oudh—although its people are largely Hindu —is one of the last remaining Mohammedan states. Its annexation will not only antagonize all Mohammedans, but give rise to the fear that we intend to swallow the rest of India, and that no state is safe from us."

Huntly said pompously: "You forget, I think, that the bulk of the population cannot but look upon us as their deliverers from the long reign of oppression, torture and extortion inflicted upon them by their native rulers. We are not only giving them better government, but bestowing upon them the blessings of progress and civilization, for which they are bound to be grateful."

"That is a view only too commonly held by our race," said Alex dryly. "It is a comforting one with which to justify conquest, but, unhappily, entirely untrue. The blessings of civilization are seldom appreciated by the simple savage—especially when rammed down his gullet with a musket. I would assure you, sir, that I am no alarmist. We shall hold India. But all that I have heard and seen and felt during the past few years has served to convince me that we are moving blindly toward disaster. This is no time to cumber ourselves with women, or to send out a young girl who knows nothing of the East."

Huntly drew himself to his full height and looked haughtily down his somewhat fleshy nose. "My dear Captain Randall," he observed in chilling tones, "had there been any risk attached to sending my cousin to India, you may be assured that Mr. Barton would never have suggested such a course."

Alex said ruefully: "I am afraid that I shall have to speak plainly, sir. I am well aware that in doing so I am open to a charge of disloyalty to my superior officer, but the occasion appears to me serious enough to war-

rant it." And he spoke clearly and dispassionately on the subject of Mr.
Barton. . . .

Lord Ware's prominent eyes bulged palely in the firelight, and he remarked a little nervously that of course he had no idea. . . . What Captain Randall had divulged was most disturbing. Surely he exaggerated? He
could not bring himself to believe—

Captain Randall cut him short: "I must ask you to believe, sir, that
what I have told you of the Commissioner is less than the truth. Now
that I have acquainted you with these unpleasant facts, I have no further
obligation in the matter, as it will be for you to decide whether the Condesa goes or not. Your servant, sir." He bowed curtly and withdrew.

Once again, as on the evening of his arrival, Captain Randall dined
alone, but at the conclusion of the meal the secretary Mr. Harrowby made
his appearance with a message from Lady Ware. The Countess, said Mr.
Harrowby, wished to see Captain Randall at his earliest convenience, in
order to make him known to the Condesa. Captain Randall heaved a resigned sigh, and pausing only to possess himself of a small package that
had been entrusted to him for personal delivery into the hands of the
Commissioner's betrothed, followed Mr. Harrowby to Lady Ware's
apartments.

"So good of you to come, Captain Randall. You have met my husband,
have you not? This is my daughter Sybella. And this is dear Conway's
future wife—Winter de Ballesteros. Winter, this is Captain Randall—"

Alex bowed briefly. Lord Ware did not meet his gaze but Lady Ware
returned it with a coldly smiling blandness that told its own story. So
her husband has told her, thought Alex, and she means to ignore it. She
will tell that child nothing, and neither will she do anything to prevent
the marriage. That Wycombe woman was right! He looked beyond Lady
Julia into the wide, wary eyes of the Commissioner's betrothed. He looked
long and deliberately, studying that young and guarded face, noting the
wariness and schooled immobility with cool interest.

A faint flush of color rose into the pale cheeks and Alex put his hand
into his pocket and drew out a small sealed packet that the Commissioner
had given him. He said briefly and without preamble: "Mr. Barton requested me to give this into your hand."

The girl's fingers closed about it, holding it tightly, and color and life
flamed up into her face so that she was suddenly beautiful. She made a
small, swift gesture with the clenched hand as though she would have
hidden it among her billowing skirts, but Lady Ware spoke with calm
authority: "You may open it, my dear. It will be your betrothal gift."

Winter looked down at the small packet in her hand. She knew without
opening it what it contained. She had never forgotten anything that Conway had said to her, and had he not said that he would one day give her
a diamond—"the brightest diamond I can find for you in India"—to wear
on her finger instead of the little gold and pearl ring that she had worn
for so long on a ribbon about her neck? He had sent for her, and he had

sent the diamond. All her dreams were coming true at last. She did not want to open Conway's gift in the presence of Cousin Julia and this stranger who studied her with such cool and speculative interest. This was not something for critical and unsympathetic eyes to appraise. It was something intensely personal to herself.

"We are waiting," said Cousin Julia.

The lovely color faded from Winter's cheeks and she broke the seal with cold, unsteady fingers.

The firelight gleamed on an enormous carved emerald in a curiously wrought setting of Indian gold, and Alex, recognizing it, was unprepared for the sudden shock of anger and disgust that the sight of it gave him. He had seen that stone before, many times. Three years ago it had adorned the hand of a member of a princely house, Rao Kishan Prasad.* Alex knew a good deal about Kishan Prasad. There had been odd whispers about him, and the subsequent appearance of that ring in the possession of the Commissioner of Lunjore had caused Alex to wonder more than once just what piece of bribery the fabulous stone had represented? It had been flaunted thereafter by the Indian woman, a dancing girl from the city, who was the latest occupant of the *bibigurh* attached to the Lunjore Residency, and she had worn it as she gyrated for the amusement of the guests at one of the Commissioner's more questionable parties which Alex had attended. Alex had also seen Kishan Prasad comparatively recently and in unexpected surroundings, and he scowled down at the great carved jewel with incredulous distaste.

Sybella gave an audible gasp of envy and admiration and even Lady Julia's cold eyes widened in involuntary astonishment, but to Winter it was as though a small chill wind had momentarily breathed upon the shining warmth that Conway's letter had lit in her breast. He had forgotten! The next second she had taken herself to task. Why should he take literally a sentence spoken to a child? He had meant only that he would one day send her a jewel of beauty and price to wear on her finger in place of the modest trinket he had given her at parting. And he had remembered—and sent it.

She slipped the barbaric thing onto the third finger of her left hand where it hung as loosely as that other ring had done five years before, and thought as she did so that soon Conway would put a wedding ring on that same finger and after that she would be safe and protected and loved —and free from loneliness forever. She smiled down at it, a little secret smile, and looked up to meet the anger and disgust in Captain Randall's eyes.

For a moment the intensity of that cold disgust startled her. This man for some unknown reason was hostile to her. No. Not to her—to Conway. This, then, must be one of those men of whom Conway had written. Men who were secretly envious of him and who intrigued against him.

* Pra-shād

Yet that was surely impossible, for Conway himself had sent this man to be his emissary and to escort his future wife to India. She must have mistaken that expression. And indeed it was there no longer. The face that looked back at her was gravely impersonal; the gray eyes remote and expressionless.

The brief moment of silence was broken by Lady Ware. "You will forgive me, I know, if I say good-by to you now," said Lady Ware, dismissing him. "I fear I am not an early riser, and you will, I feel sure, be anxious to be on your way. I shall of course inform you by letter of the arrangements I have made for dear Winter."

It was plain that the matter was considered as settled and that he was to be given no opportunity for private conversation with the Condesa herself. The entire affair had filled Alex with boredom and irritation and, finally, disgust. He had discharged his mission, and his conscience was clear; but now, unaccountably, he found himself angry.

This was no poised and mature woman who was to be tied in matrimony to the obese roué who was Commissioner of Lunjore. This was a girl. A child. And for reasons that the gossiping Lady Wycombe had made abundantly clear, her august relatives, far from pausing before consigning her to the fate that must inevitably overtake any wife of Conway Barton, had every intention of hurrying her toward it without uttering one word of warning.

All the impropriety of bluntly informing her himself of the true state of affairs occurred most forcibly to Captain Randall. The robust outspokenness of the Regency had given place to an age of extreme and mealy-mouthed prudery in which young girls were sedulously guarded from the facts of life and were expected to have no inkling of the coarser aspects of masculine amusements. Twelve years in the East had, however, robbed Alex Randall of any particular respect for the polite conventions, and he was suddenly and stubbornly resolved that the Commissioner's betrothed should not walk blindly upon her fate if he could prevent it. Once back in his room he found letter paper, a quill pen and a standish, and having written a brief note, folded the paper, sealed it and tugged at the bellpull.

It was answered by a maidservant in a neat print dress. The note and a gold coin changed hands and the girl, her eyes round with pleasurable interest, assured him in a conspiratorial whisper that Miss Winter would receive his communication without fail. Alex yawned largely, scowled at his reflection in the vast oval looking glass that adorned one wall of the room, and retired to bed.

The morning dawned cold and gray, and a white layer of mist lay over the park and pressed against the wet windowpanes. In the great hall a covey of servants were busied with removing the funeral trappings from the walls under the eye of the aged majordomo, and on the wide sweep before the main door Medusa sidled and snorted in charge of a groom. Captain Randall swung himself thankfully into the saddle, grateful to see the last of Ware.

The mist lay thicker under the overarching boughs of the oak trees that lined the long avenue, and the trees themselves appeared pale and ghostly. For a mile or more Alex gave the mare her head, exhilarated by the speed, the rush of the cold misty air and the swift, hollow drumbeat of Medusa's flying hoofs; but presently his ear caught what seemed an echo of that sound, and he slowed Medusa's pace to a trot and then to a walk. There was another rider in the long oak avenue, and Alex, listening, made a wry grimace in which distaste and relief were oddly mingled, and reined to a stop. Medusa whinnied softly as a moment later a horse and rider materialized out of the mist and drew level with them.

There were raindrops like a spangle of moonstones on Winter's dark hair, and cold air and exercise had whipped a glow of color into her pale cheeks. Those enormous dark eyes—the eyes of her father Marcos de Ballesteros, who in turn had inherited them from some long-forgotten Moorish ancestress—were wide and young and wary, and looking at her Alex was conscious once again of that unexpected flood of anger and exasperation. It must have shown briefly in his face, for her voice was breathless and a little uncertain:

"You—you have a message for me, Captain Randall?—from Conway—Mr. Barton?"

Alex shook his head.

"But . . . you wrote—"

"You must forgive me for the subterfuge," said Alex curtly, "but I wished to see you privately. I have something to say to you that your relatives would apparently prefer to remain unsaid. I took this method of insuring that you would see me."

He saw the slender figure stiffen and draw itself erect and the dark eyes became guarded. "What is it you wish to tell me?"

Alex studied her for a moment, frowning. "How old are you?"

The unexpectedness of the question appeared to take her by surprise, and she answered in unconscious obedience to the authority in his voice. "Sixteen. But I shall soon—"

"*Sixteen!*" said Alex, exasperated. "It's not decent! Have you any conception as to what you are going to? Of the life you will be expected to lead? Of the country in which you will live?"

Winter looked at him in surprise. "Why—you are kind!" she said. Her voice held a note of wonder and Alex realized with a sudden stirring of pity that kindness had been a rare thing in this young creature's life. She leant forward with a little confiding gesture and said: "You think that I am going to a foreign land and that I might be unhappy there. But you are wrong. I am going home. Did you not know that my father was a Spaniard who lived and was born in Oudh, and that I was born there too? India is more my home than Ware will ever be."

She saw Alex' mouth tighten, and said breathlessly, watching his face: "What is it? Is Conway ill? Is that what you meant to tell me? Is he—"

"No." Alex' voice was hard and completely expressionless. "He is not ill. Not in the way that you mean. But I imagine that he has changed considerably since you last saw him."

"Of course he has changed!" said Winter quickly. "I have changed too. I was only a child then, and now I have grown up. He has had years more of hard work and sickness and heavy responsibility. He will look older, but it will not matter."

"You do not understand," said Alex curtly. "I cannot say what Mr. Barton may have been five or six years ago. But I know what he is now, and I can do no more than to urge you, in your own interests, to abandon your journey to India and postpone your wedding until such time as he can return to this country, so that you may have the opportunity of judging for yourself."

Winter's eyes were suddenly bright with anger and her voice sharpened to scorn: "So I *was* right! You are one of them! One of his enemies who scheme against him behind his back, because you are envious of him! And you dare to speak against him to me—to *me!*" Her chin lifted haughtily: "I must ask you to be plain, sir. You cannot make veiled accusations and not qualify them. Or do you prefer imputation to plain speaking?"

"No," said Alex slowly, "but I do not wish to offend your ears with matters that cannot be within your comprehension. However, if you will have it, your betrothed is no fit husband for any young or decently bred woman, and—"

He saw the small face turn as white as the mist around it and the gloved fingers clench on the riding whip they held, and knew a fraction of a second before she raised her hand what she would do. But for some reason that he could not have explained he made no attempt to avoid the blow. The lash of the whip cut savagely across his face and he felt a thin trickle of blood run warmly down his chin from a corner of his mouth— and suddenly and unexpectedly he laughed.

"The Ware women," said Captain Randall, "would appear to be remarkably quick with their hands. I see I have misjudged you. You may well be a match for him after all."

The bright color flamed up into the girl's face once more, and she brought the whip down again, but this time on her horse who sprang forward and galloped away down the long avenue to disappear into the mist.

Captain Randall lifted his hand to brush the blood from his chin, and laughed again. So much for the popular conception of gently bred young ladies as frail and tender plants given to swooning and the vapors! He wondered if he had seen the last of Winter de Ballesteros? It seemed likely. He could not believe that after what had just occurred she would avail herself of his escort to India. She would now take a passage on some other ship and dispense with his services, and she would undoubtedly warn her betrothed against him. In that event the Commissioner could be counted upon to effect his removal from Lunjore. He had in fact bungled the whole affair; branded himself as disloyal to his chief, incurred the enmity of the young Condesa and her influential relations, and probably brought about his own dismissal—and all for nothing.

Firm in the belief that he would not now receive any further communication from Ware he was surprised, and more than a little annoyed, by the arrival some three months later of a letter from the Countess. A passage had been procured, wrote Lady Ware, for her young cousin on board the steamship *Sirius* sailing from London to Alexandria on the fifth of July. Mr. Barton was to meet his betrothed in Calcutta and the marriage would take place almost immediately following her arrival at that port. She would be traveling in the company of a Mrs. Abuthnot, who with her two daughters was proceeding to India in order to rejoin her husband who commanded a regiment of Bengal Infantry at Delhi. The ladies would be pleased to avail themselves of Captain Randall's protection and assistance on the voyage.

Captain Randall scowled at the single sheet of paper with its thinly elegant handwriting and florid seal, and crumpling it in his hand he tossed it impatiently into the wastepaper basket, mentally consigning all women —with the possible exception of a certain charming and accommodating *première danseuse*—to the same receptacle.

He had other things to think about than the doings of the Granthams. On the thirtieth of March the news had spread slowly that the Great Powers of Europe, together with Turkey and Sardinia, were at last at peace after one of the most futile and wasteful of wars. It was Sunday, and in order not to interrupt the evening services the salute of a hundred and one guns was fired at ten o'clock that night and, listening to the crash of the cannonade in the cold darkness of St. James's Park, Alex thought of the dead who rotted on the heights of Sebastopol—and of the smiling face of Kishan Prasad taking gloating note of the ragged and demoralized British Army as they fell back after their failure to capture the Redan. He did not know why such men as Kishan Prasad had ever been permitted to visit in Crimea. But they had done so, and Alex was sure that no good would come of it.

Earlier in March he had seen a brief notice in the press, sandwiched casually in between the arrival of the Far Eastern mails and a paragraph relating to the arrival in India of Lord Canning, the new Governor-General, which had stated baldly: *Oudh is to be annexed, with General Outram as Chief Commissioner.* And there had been a longer one a week later: *An army of 16,000 men is now collected at Cawnpore, and in a few days will be pouring toward Lucknow. No resistance is expected, but Lord Dalhousie never leaves opportunities to the disaffected by any mistimed affectation of security. The King will be dismissed with a pension of a lac of rupees a month.*

Recalling that paragraph, Alex had remembered with a renewal of disquiet another night, less than a year ago, when he had stood in the hot shadow of the ancient gateway before the Lunjore Residency and listened, not to guns, but to men who whispered in the moonlight. With such things on his mind he had little attention to spare for the question of Mr. Barton's betrothed.

Alex himself had been equally dismissed from Winter's thoughts, for Cousin Julia, with unexpected kindness, had sent her to the care of a distant relative in London who had been charged with the agreeable task of selecting the young bride's trousseau. England was gay that year. The war was over and the Treaty of Paris was celebrated with illuminations and fireworks. The Queen reviewed her fleet on the Solent and her army at Aldershot. William Palmer, the Rugeley poisoner, was publicly hanged at Stafford before a packed crowd of thousands who had poured into the town to see a fellow creature die, and the wearing of crinolines was attacked by the clergy who pointed out that women "forgot, in loading themselves with such voluminous garments, that the gates of Heaven were narrow."

Lady Adelaide Pike, undeterred by the straightness of that gate, selected Winter's trousseau with wide and ever wider spreading skirts. Ball dresses of tarlatan with five flounces edged with silk fringe and banded with velvet ribbons; of white tulle over white *glacé*, the tulle gathered up in festoons by chains of pearls and bouquets of white camellias; of white muslin barred with silver basketwork; of *moiré* antique in tea rose yellow. Day dresses in muslins, merinos, taffetas and light French *barèges* in delicate hues. Morning dresses of gray cashmere, batiste, poplin and figured jaconet. Gloves of every shade and hue, mittens of black *filet*, absurd evening headdresses of lace, flowers, pearls or ribbon; ravishing chip bonnets of straw or terry velvet trimmed with feathers or blonde, and dozens upon awe-inspiring dozens of petticoats and pantalets and other articles of feminine underwear.

It was an age of lavishness—of enormous meals, enormous families, enormous spreading skirts and an enormous spreading empire. An age of gross living, grinding poverty, inconceivable prudery, insufferable complacency and incomparable enterprise. Those dozens of petticoats and pantalets deemed necessary to the feminine wardrobe were both a symbol of that lavishness and of the sweated labor in the crowded slums where women wore away their fingers and their eyesight and their youth sewing such furbelows for a wage of a few ha'pence.

Julia herself had taken the unprecedented step of traveling to London in order to see her young relative safely bestowed into the care of Mrs. Abuthnot. She had stayed only one night; just long enough to see the cab that contained Sabrina's daughter drive away in the rain toward the docks and the steam packet *Sirius* that was to take her to Alexandria on the first half of her journey toward India.

5

MRS. ABUTHNOT was kind, stout and talkative. She had been barely Winter's age when she had married her George and first set sail for the East, and she was not yet forty. But the long years spent in India, and the birth and death in infancy of five other children, had left their mark on her and she might well have been ten or even twenty years older.

Lottie and Sophie Abuthnot, in contrast to their stout and voluble mamma, were slim and shy and silent, and, it was to be presumed, took after their papa, for they in no way resembled their mother, being small and fair where Mrs. Abuthnot was an ample, though graying brunette.

Sophie, the younger by two years, shared a cabin with her mother, while the eighteen-year-old Lottie was to share an adjoining one with Winter. The cabins were small and cramped and sparsely furnished, and the first days of the voyage had been anything but pleasant.

Lottie, Sophie and Mrs. Abuthnot had retired to their berths while the ship was still in sight of Sheerness, but Winter had returned to the deck to watch the coast of England fade into the wet grayness of that July evening.

The ship rolled and pitched and a sharp hiss of spray stung Winter's cheek. She began to feel distinctly uneasy, but she could not face the prospect of descending once more to the cramped cabin where Lottie Abuthnot, prone upon her berth, had already succumbed to the pangs of seasickness. But presently, as the deck heaved up and sank away again beneath her feet, she realized that she should have retired to her cabin while she still had the strength to do so, for now, quite suddenly, it was impossible to move. Impossible to do anything but cling to the wet rail, oblivious of the driving spray and the fact that the wind had whipped her cloak from her grasp and was billowing it out in imitation of the straining sails above her, or that her bonnet had fallen off and was now attached to her only by its ribbons. Her head appeared to have swollen and to be full of whirling sparks, and she leant on the rail, wet, chilled and racked with nausea.

She did not hear the footsteps behind her, and she would not have cared if she had. She was beyond caring. She only knew that arms were around her, and that she need no longer cling to the rail.

Someone lifted her as easily as though she were a small child, and a man's voice with a hint of a laugh in it said: "I suppose this is included in the duties of a courier." And then she was being carried down into heaving darkness to her cabin.

She was aware of the cabin door being thrown open, and above the creaking pandemonium of the laboring ship she could hear the alternate moans and retching of Lottie Abuthnot. Winter turned her head feebly away from the sound and buried her face against the shoulder of the man who carried her. She heard him say "Good God!" in tones of half-humorous resignation, and then he had closed the door on Lottie's woe and turned abruptly away.

A moment or two later he laid her down and Winter opened her eyes and looked up into Captain Randall's face. He appeared to be amused, and she closed them again, and pressing a hand over her mouth managed with an enormous effort to say in muffled tones: "Please go away. I—I fear I am going to be very unwell."

"I've seen worse things," remarked Captain Randall philosophically, reaching for a basin; and presently it ceased to matter to Winter whether he went or stayed.

It was morning when she awakened. A cold, wet morning in which rain fell steadily and the ship creaked and shuddered and groaned as it thrust its way through the steep, choppy seas, driven onward by a shrill wind.

The small cabin rose and fell alarmingly before Winter's eyes and she shuddered and closed them again quickly. Presently, struck by a sudden thought, she opened them once more. She was in a strange cabin. Captain Randall's, of course. He must have slept elsewhere, probably in the saloon. She could only be surprised that he had bothered to remove!

Winter lay still, remembering the details of yesterday's deplorable collapse with shuddering dismay. How could she have behaved so! Instead of insisting on decent privacy, she had done nothing to prevent Captain Randall from remaining in the cabin and rendering aid, but, if she remembered rightly, had welcomed his assistance. She had a distinct recollection of him holding her head over a basin, and later forcing brandy down her throat with a matter-of-fact competence and a total lack of embarrassment that surprised her.

Winter did not realize that Alex Randall had in his time been called upon to perform a variety of actions in excess of his official duties, including amputating the leg of a man who had been mauled by a wounded tiger, hanging a murderer, acting as midwife to a woman in childbirth, and dragging another one screaming from the pyre that consumed her husband's dead body and on which she had intended—following the custom of her people and in defiance of the Company's new law—to immolate herself. Dealing with a young woman in the throes of seasickness had seemed a comparatively simple matter, and Winter could only be surprised that he had not also thought fit to remove her dress. She moved cautiously and discovered that he had in fact done so. The voluminous folds of her gray batiste traveling dress and the whalebone hoops of her crinoline were flung over a chair back, and the blankets that had been drawn up over her concealed only petticoats and pantalets. Further investigation revealed the horrifying fact that Captain Randall had unlaced her stays! The indignity of this discovery impelled her to sit upright, but it proved an unwise move. The cabin swam unpleasantly before her eyes and she was forced to lean her aching head against the polished wooden boards that formed the wall of the berth.

Someone rapped on the panels of the door and after a momentary pause it opened to disclose Captain Randall himself, looking, thought Winter resentfully, almost offensively well. He encountered her hostile gaze and smiled.

It was a disconcertingly pleasant smile, and the fact that even through a haze of acute physical misery and social embarrassment she could recognize it as such, increased rather than diminished her hostility.

"I've brought you some food," said Captain Randall. "May I come in?"

"It's your cabin," said Winter bitterly. "I cannot prevent you from coming in, but at least you might have sufficient consideration to avoid any mention of food!"

Alex laughed, and entering the cabin closed the door behind him and set down a small tray. "You'll feel a great deal better when you have had something to eat," he assured her. "It's only hot soup and biscuits."

Winter glanced at it and shuddered. The small cabin dipped and rose, tilted, sank and steadied again in an endless sickening rhythm, and the soup in the thick china mug slopped over the rim onto the tray. "Go away!" said Winter in a gasping whisper. "Take it away and go away!"

Alex sat down on the edge of the berth beside her, and presently—she did not quite know how it happened—he was holding her against his shoulder and feeding her with soup and dry biscuits as if she had been a sick child.

The soup was hot and sustaining and, unlikely though it had seemed, she managed to swallow a fair proportion of the biscuit he had brought, and felt considerably better for having done so. Captain Randall's shoulder was strangely comforting to lean an aching head against, and she tried to remind herself that this man was an enemy, a traitor to Conway; that she had once cut him across the face with her riding whip—and deservedly. But it did not seem to matter any longer. She was conscious only of an unfamiliar and inexplicable feeling of being safe; a feeling that she had been a stranger to ever since the day when a small, weeping and bewildered child had been torn from the comforting arms of Juanita and Aziza Begum and the dear familiar walls of the Gulab Mahal. She felt infinitely better, but strangely disinclined to move.

Alex put down the empty cup and said: "It is just as well that your chaperone and every other woman on board is prostrated with seasickness, or I am afraid that I should have damaged your reputation beyond repair. As it is, the ladies have no attention to spare for anything but their own sufferings, so for the moment I think that you can safely stay here."

"I cannot do that," said Winter drowsily. "I must go back to my own cabin."

"I wouldn't advise it," said Alex. "Your cabin companion is showing no signs of recovery as yet."

"How do you know?" inquired Winter, interested. "Have you been looking after them too?"

"I have," admitted Alex with the ghost of a laugh. "I have no doubt that when she is feeling better Mrs. Abuthnot will find it hard to forgive me for it, but at present she is tolerably grateful."

"If you unlaced her stays for her," remarked Winter, "I should not think she would ever forgive you!"

She had spoken without thinking, and the moment the words were out she would have given anything to recall them. She jerked herself away from Captain Randall's supporting arm, her hand to her mouth and a hot wave of color dyeing her throat and white face. How could she have said such a thing! Underclothes were considered an unmentionable subject, and she had spoken of them to a man—and to a strange man at that! Cousin Julia would have swooned with horror.

Captain Randall, however, remained unmoved. The enormity of her observation appeared to have escaped him and he replied to it in all seriousness: "It wasn't necessary. She seemed to have managed it herself."

The sight of Winter's scarlet cheeks and wide, horrified eyes brought home to him for the first time the fact that his proceedings might be considered shockingly unorthodox. A muscle twitched at the corner of his mouth and he said gravely: "May I give you a piece of advice, Condesa? Common sense will nearly always stand you in better stead than a slavish adherence to the conventions. If I had left you to spend the night in wet and uncomfortable clothing it might have saved you some temporary embarrassment, but it would have done no good at all to your health. And in the country to which you are going health is an important thing. You cannot afford to be ill in India."

The shamed color faded from Winter's cheeks and the horror in her eyes was replaced by interest. That common sense was preferable to convention was a point of view so diametrically opposed to all previous teachings that for a moment it seemed almost to smack of heresy. Yet on consideration it was so obviously right, and Winter was conscious of a sudden sense of release from bondage, as though some mental form of tight lacing had suddenly been unloosed. A dimple broke the smooth curve of her grave young cheek and she smiled.

It was the first time that Alex had seen her smile, but he did not answer it. He sat quite still, looking down at her and no longer seeing her as a forlorn child, but as a young woman. The small heart-shaped face was unusually pale, and the shadows under the wide dark eyes made them appear even larger. The crumpled whiteness of petticoat and corset cover served to turn her bare arms and shoulders to a warm shade of ivory, and the loosened hair that tumbled about her in rippling profusion glinted with blue lights in the cold grayness of the small cabin. Looking at her, Alex had a sudden and disturbing vision of the moist, unsteady hands of the Commissioner of Lunjore twining themselves in that soft darkness and sliding over those smooth ivory shoulders. The lines of his face hardened and set and he stood up abruptly, and retrieving the tray said brusquely: "The Captain appears to think that we shall run out of this bad weather by sunset. You had better stay where you are for today at least. I have this cabin to myself as far as Gibraltar."

"But what about you?" asked Winter hesitantly.

"I can manage," said Captain Randall briefly.

The cabin door closed behind him and Winter did not see him again for some considerable time. It was a steward who knocked at her door with a tray of food at midday, and toward the late afternoon she felt sufficiently recovered to resume her discarded dress and find her way to her own cabin. But it proved to be a mistaken move. Ten minutes in the company of Lottie Abuthnot sufficed to bring on a renewal of nausea, and Winter took to her berth where she remained for the next few days.

The Captain's optimistic assertion as to the weather proved incorrect, but a Mrs. Martha Holly, who had recovered her sea legs after a temporary setback of twenty-four hours, had come to the rescue of the Abuthnot party. Mrs. Holly was stout, brisk and motherly, and had once been a nursemaid. She had borne and lost several children in India, but sorrow and adversity did not appear to have dampened her invincible spirits, and after a year spent in England, to which she had returned in the capacity of nurse to the invalid wife and two small sons of a colonel of Native Foot, she was returning to rejoin her husband.

Her energetic ministrations had the desired effect, and when four days later the *Sirius* finally ran out of bad weather and into sunshine and blue seas, even Mrs. Abuthnot was able to appear on deck.

Their fellow passengers included several other ladies, among them a Mrs. Gardener-Smith and her daughter Delia who were also bound for Lunjore, and many officers of all ranks, the majority of them returning to India from leave. These included a Colonel Moulson, whom Alex knew to be a friend of Mr. Barton's, returning to take over command of a regiment of Bengal Infantry stationed at Lunjore, and one other person who was also known to him—a slim, pleasant-mannered Indian who spoke excellent English and was accompanied by several dark-skinned servants. That same Kishan Prasad whom Alex had last seen before Sebastopol.

Kishan Prasad and his retinue had attracted Winter's immediate attention. The sight of the brown-skinned faces and the sound of the swift familiar speech revived memories of her childhood and reminded her not of a foreign land, but of home.

Kishan Prasad had spoken to her one evening. She had been standing under the awning on the poop deck watching the sun sink into the Atlantic while Cape Finisterre showed like a violet shadow on the horizon behind her. The evening breeze had tugged unexpectedly at the light shawl she wore and had tangled its long silk fringe inextricably about a stanchion, and Kishan Prasad, who had been passing, had come to her assistance. She had thanked him prettily and he had been about to turn away when his gaze had fallen upon her left hand. She had been wearing

Conway's ring, the great carved emerald in the curiously wrought setting, and Kishan Prasad had checked at the sight of it and the pupils of his eyes had narrowed like a cat's in the light. He said in his soft voice whose faintly singsong intonation alone betrayed the fact that it was not an Englishman who spoke: "That is a very unusual ring you are wearing. May I be permitted to ask where it came from? It looks as though it were a jewel from my own country—from Rohilkhand."

"Perhaps it is," said Winter holding it out for him to see. "It was sent to me by the man I am going to marry. Mr. Conway Barton."

"Ah!—Mr. Barton. That is very interesting. He is the Commissioner of Lunjore, is he not?"

"Yes. Do you know him?"

"I have some slight acquaintance with Mr. Barton. I own land in Lunjore District."

Among the other passengers was a certain Lieutenant Edward English; a large young man who possessed a generous supply of freckles, red hair and charm. He also possessed a pair of deeply blue and openly admiring eyes, and Lottie Abuthnot's fairness and fragility had made an instant impression upon his susceptible heart. He had lost no time in making her acquaintance, but Mrs. Abuthnot had no intention of allowing any young man to fix his interest with her daughter at such an early stage of the voyage, and she had contrived to keep Mr. English at a safe distance.

There were also, of course, several other young ladies on board; notably Miss Delia Gardener-Smith. Miss Gardener-Smith possessed sufficient pretensions to beauty to cause some slight anxiety in the breast of any mother of other marriageable maidens, and she had early attracted the admiration of several officers, among them Colonel Moulson.

Colonel Frederick Moulson was a bachelor and a lover of women, who fancied himself as a connoisseur of female charms. Advancing years had given him a taste for youth, and no young girl was safe from his ogling eye and the sly pattings and pressures of his fleshy hands. Winter could only be surprised that such an unlikable man should be a friend of Conway's, but for Conway's sake she tried to be as polite as possible to him, and it was an easy enough matter to avoid being left alone in his company, there being a great many other men on board who were only too ready to make themselves agreeable to the young Condesa.

There was indeed only one person who appeared entirely uninterested in her. Captain Randall had not addressed more than a dozen words to her since her emergence from her cabin, and during the succeeding days, although he made himself pleasant to Mrs. Abuthnot and had won golden opinions from that warmhearted lady, he never made one of the group who surrounded Mr. Barton's betrothed, and Winter came to the conclusion that he was deliberately avoiding her.

The discovery filled her with a vague feeling of resentment, and she was forced to remind herself yet again that this man had spoken against Conway, and that had he not kept his distance she herself would have been compelled to avoid his society. Captain Randall had obviously realized this, and therefore kept out of her way, which was understandable. What was not understandable was why she should resent it. She found herself covertly watching Captain Randall and comparing him, to his disadvantage, with Conway.

Alex Randall was slim and deeply tanned and undeniably good looking. His rather hard gray eyes were fringed with black lashes as long as Winter's own, and though he was not much above medium height, his slimness and grace of carriage conveyed an impression of more inches than he possessed. But Conway, blue eyed and blondly handsome, was of a size to make Alex Randall appear insignificant by contrast, and his luxuriant corn-gold mustache enhanced his masculine beauty and compared most favorably with Captain Randall's unfashionably clean-shaven countenance. Conway was also greathearted and the soul of chivalry, and he would have scorned to speak against a man behind his back as Captain Randall had done. Nevertheless that irrational feeling of resentment remained. He might at least speak to her!

She encountered him one evening in the dark passageway that led to the cabins, and he had stood aside to let her pass. Winter drew back her hooped skirts, for the passage was narrow, and was about to pass him when she changed her mind and stopped. Her crinoline, released, brushed the walls of the passage on either side and effectually prevented Captain Randall from moving.

She said hesitantly: "I—I never thanked you for—for your help. It was most kind in you, and—and I would not wish you to think me ungrateful."

Alex bowed but he did not speak. A sudden color tinged Winter's pale cheeks and she said abruptly, her voice unexpectedly breathless: "I am sorry about—striking you with my whip. It was unforgivable of me."

"But entirely understandable," said Alex gravely.

She waited, expecting him to apologize for the words he had said that day; confident, now that she had given him the opening, that he would retract them, or at least admit that he should not have spoken as he had; but he was silent.

The color deepened in Winter's cheeks and her small chin lifted haughtily. She gathered up her wide skirts, and as she did so the ship heeled to a sudden fresh breath of the evening wind that blew off Spain, and threw her against him. For a brief moment his arms held her, and once again she was conscious of that warm sense of safety that she had experienced before on the first morning of the voyage. She lifted her head from his shoulder and saw that his eyes held a glint of something that was uncommonly like anger. Then he had set her on her feet again and walked quickly away.

6

The *Sirius* was to make a short stay at Malta, and the majority of the passengers had arranged to put up at hotels on shore as a welcome change from the cramped conditions on board.

Supper and rooms were in readiness for them at the Imperial Hotel, and at the conclusion of the meal Mrs. Abuthnot had decreed an immediate withdrawal to bed. Once again Winter found herself sharing a room with Lottie, but although it was late she found that she had no desire for sleep. It was wonderful to be on shore again and to feel solid ground under her feet in place of the uneasy decks of the *Sirius*; to smell the scent of flowers and earth instead of the salt winds and the mixed aromas of shipboard. The white moonlight and the very air of the hot, semitropical night called to the southern blood in her, and she made no attempt to prepare for bed.

Their stone-floored room, bare of unnecessary furniture, led out to an arcade that surrounded an open courtyard where tropical plants grew in lush profusion. The outer door stood open onto the black shadow of the arcade and the moonlight beyond, and Winter pushed aside the heavy curtain that hung over it and looked out into the night.

On the far side of the courtyard an orange point of light and a faint smell of cigar smoke betrayed the presence of a tall young man who leant against a stone pillar, the white drill of his suit melting into the moonlight. Winter studied him for a moment or two and then spoke softly over her shoulder:

"Lottie—"

"Yes?"

"How much do you like Mr. English?"

There was a small gasp from Lottie. "Winter!"

"He is out there now. In the courtyard. Watching this room."

There was a swift rustle behind her and Lottie was at her elbow, breathing a little quickly.

Winter said: "I do not think there could be any harm in your going out to . . . to look at the flowers? They are very beautiful."

Lottie said breathlessly: "Oh, no! I could not! It would be shockingly forward and unladylike in me to do so."

Winter did not reply for a moment or two, and then she said reflectively, "Someone only the other day gave me a piece of advice. He—they—said that common sense was nearly always preferable to a slavish regard for the conventions. I am sure it would be most unconventional in you to walk in the courtyard."

She turned her head and looked at Lottie, and then quite suddenly she laughed. A soft gay laugh. "No, Lottie! You are quite right, of course. You should not go. I do not know what can have come over me tonight! I am trying to lead you into temptation, and you should say, 'Get thee behind me, Satan!' and say your prayers and go to bed. And one day you will marry some vastly eligible gentleman of immense fortune and then you will say to yourself, 'Oh, what a narrow escape I had in Malta.'"

"Is that common sense?" inquired Lottie with an answering laugh.

"I am not sure," said Winter soberly.

"But I am," said Lottie. "Quite, *quite* sure." She brushed Winter's cheek with swift warm lips and slipped past her and out into the darkness of the arcade.

Winter saw her move out of the shadows and into the bright moonlight, and saw the tall figure at the far side of the courtyard start forward. Then a tangle of oleanders hid them from her view, and she laughed again, but the laugh broke off in a sigh.

The hot night and the white moonlight called to her with a restless urgency, and on a sudden impulse she pulled up her wide skirts and unfastened her hooped crinoline. It fell to the stone floor with a click of whalebone and she stepped out of it and stood with the folds of her dress trailing on the floor. She was wearing a thin black mourning dress, and there was a black lace shawl among the few belongings that she had brought with her from the ship. She threw it over her head, and gathering up her trailing skirts, tiptoed quietly out into the night.

The arcade was a tunnel of shadow broken at intervals by warm curtained squares of light from other windows and doors that looked out on to it, and there were several stone benches against the walls—at least one of which appeared to be occupied. Winter trusted that Lieutenant English was making good use of his time but she herself did not intend to remain in the courtyard. A few minutes later, having met no one except a few loitering and sleepy servants, she was clear of the hotel and hurrying down a narrow shadow-barred street.

The street gave place to a silent square dotted with trees and overlooked by secretive shuttered houses with covered balconies and flat stone roofs. Winter crossed it, keeping to the shadows and avoiding the occasional late idler, her thin slippers making no sound in the warm dust. A cascade of scented creeper, its color indistinguishable in the moonlight, tumbled over a high wall beyond which she could see the tops of orange trees and two tall cypresses that showed dark against the moon-washed sky. A twisted fig tree leant against the wall in an angle of a buttress, its topmost branches tangled with the trails of creeper. It made an admirable ladder and Winter paused beside it, eying it speculatively. A moment later, laughing and a little breathless, she had reached the broad top of the wall.

There was a garden upon the far side of the wall, evidently belonging to a large private house that lay beyond a line of aloes and a cluster of orange trees on the far side of a wide lawn. Beyond the quiet garden the flat-topped houses fell away to the harbor, and between the treetops and the jostling roofs she could see the shining floor of the Mediterranean. The smells of the East rose up about her and the hot night was still and white and wonderful, and mysterious with the mystery that permeates every Oriental night.

Winter drew a long breath of rapture and settled herself in the shadows of the fig tree, leaning back against a convenient bough that stretched parallel to the coping of the wall, and screened on three sides by broad leaves and a tangle of creeper. Something that had been closed and frozen inside her was awake and stirring, as though a tightly furled bud had felt the first warm breath of summer and was slowly unfurling, its petals breaking open like a white lily in the moonlight. In this warm, scented night the ice of the cold years at Ware was melting from about her heart, and the blood of young Marcos de Ballesteros awoke and sang in his daughter's veins.

The night was strangely silent. So silent that Winter could hear the pattering hoofs of a small herd of goats that wandered across the deserted square, and the soft footsteps of someone who walked quietly toward her on the far side of the wall and stopped almost immediately below her. Presently there was a scraping sound, and a scatter of fading blossoms showered down on her lap as the branch against which she leant shook slightly. Someone was climbing the fig tree as she herself had climbed it.

Winter shrank back into the shelter of the leaves and sat quite still, holding her breath. Her black dress with its powdering of fallen flowers merged with the shadows, and it was evident that the man who swung himself up onto the wall almost within reach of her hand had not seen her. He wore a dark shapeless garment that might have been a closely wrapped cloak, and though she could not see his face she could hear the sound of his quickened breathing. Through the thin screen of leaves that lay between them she saw him drop lightly down into the shelter of a tangle of oleanders and geraniums that grew against the wall, and the bushes rustled briefly as he moved to the left and appeared to melt into the moonlight. But although there were no further sounds, Winter was convinced that he was still somewhere close at hand. There had been something about that silent, swiftly moving figure that had sent a cold tremor down her spine, and she did not move hand or foot for fear that even the slightest movement might attract the hidden man's attention.

A door opened in the house beyond the aloes and the orange trees, and a square of warm light glowed against the hard black and silver of the night. Footsteps approached along a stone-flagged path, and a moment or two later three men moved out of the sharp-pointed shadows of the aloes and advanced across the garden.

They stopped in the full moonlight and spoke together in undertones, their voices pitched so low that despite the silence of the night Winter

could hear only an occasional word. They were speaking in English, but
there was something in the almost inaudible voices that was entirely un-
English and suggested that they spoke in that tongue from necessity,
and because it was the only language they had in common.

A single sentence separated itself from the murmur of speech. A
strange sentence to hear on an island in the Mediterranean: ". . . as
before the rising of the Mahrattas. Only then it was millet. This time
it shall be bread and *bakri!*"

One of the men laughed, a cold, clear little chuckle.

Bakri, thought Winter, remembering the flock of goats who had pattered across the silent square behind her. Who was it who spoke of the
Mahratta invasion and used the Urdu word for "goat"?

One of the men was smoking a cigar and the scent of the tobacco came
clearly across the garden. He was a tall man, bearded and powerfully
built. His beard was either gray or blond, and he dwarfed his two com-
panions, one of whom, a small stout gentleman who wore a long tight-
fitting coat and what appeared to be a round cap, barely came up to his
chest. The third man was slim and of medium height, and Winter presumed that it was he who had climbed the wall, for he wore a dark
cloak. Moreover the big man was too large and the fat man too small to
have been the night prowler.

Winter became aware of the first twinges of cramp, but she did not
move. She was not afraid, for it did not occur to her that there was anything to be afraid of. But the stealthy caution with which the man who
had climbed the fig tree had moved convinced her that he had made his
entry into the garden by this unorthodox route because he wished his
visit to be secret. It followed therefore that she was in the awkward position of eavesdropping on some more than usually private conference, and
her presence had better remain undiscovered.

The tall man said something in a voice that was no longer an undertone,
and which sounded like "*Kogo zakhochet Bog pogubit, togo sperva lishit
razuma,*" but the words made no sense to Winter and she did not recognize
the language in which they were spoken. And then the three men turned
and moved across the open lawn and for a moment she thought that
they had seen her, for they walked directly toward her, their figures dark
against the white expanse of lawn and their black shadows preceding them,
grotesquely elongated.

They stopped not half a dozen yards from where she sat, and it was
only then that she realized that there was a door in the wall, the far side
of which must have been concealed by the shadow of the buttress. She
heard a key turn and the rasp of a bolt being drawn, and then hinges
creaked as the unseen door was opened. She could see the faces of two
of the men quite clearly in the moonlight, but the slim man in the cloak
had his back to her, and it was he who spoke in a soft voice that seemed
vaguely familiar: "We shall want money, a great deal of money."

The tall man laughed shortly. "Money!" he said. "Always money! It

is the same tale everywhere! We, a rich country, remain poor because we
pour out our wealth on others."

"In bribes, my friend," said the fat man softly. "In bribes. You cast
your bread upon the waters, is it not so?"

"But of course!" said the big man with another laugh. "We are not
fools. A year—a hundred years—two hundred years; it is all one. We are
patient. We too can wait. Our bread will return to us. It may be soon—
it may be late."

"But the price goes up," murmured the slim man. "Thirty pieces of
silver are no longer considered sufficient. It is three hundred—and then
three thousand—and then three hundred thousand."

Winter saw the big man scowl and then he laughed again and said:
"Be content that it is paid! In four months time then. *Do Svidānya!*"

The small fat man slipped through the gate and the man in the cloak
sketched an Oriental gesture of farewell and turned to follow him. The
moonlight fell full on his face and Winter recognized a fellow passenger
from the steamship *Sirius*. It was Kishan Prasad.

The hinges creaked again, and a moment later the bolts were shot
home and the key turned in the lock. The big man waited until the soft
sound of retreating footsteps had died away on the far side of the door,
and the scowl was back on his forehead, black and clear in the moonlight.
He cleared his throat and spat on the ground in a violent gesture of
contempt, then turned away and strode quickly back across the lawn,
vanishing among the shadows of the aloes and the orange trees. A minute
or two later the square of yellow light from the open doorway of the
house vanished; a chain rattled briefly, and then the night was silent
again.

Winter drew a deep breath of relief and was about to move when a
sound stopped her. It was a very small sound, but in the stillness of that
moonlit night, painfully audible: a faint rustle of leaves and a sigh
that seemed to echo her own. It came from almost immediately below
her, and she realized with a sudden stab of horror that the man she had
seen climb over the wall had not been Kishan Prasad—and he had not
gone. He had been there all the time, standing motionless among the
oleanders and so near her that she might almost have heard him breathing. The bushes shook as though to a breath of wind and a cloaked figure
detached itself from the shadows and moved into the open.

If he comes back over the wall, thought Winter in alarm, he can't
help seeing me! Perhaps if she could manage to edge round and face the
other way without noise she could jump to the ground—it was not much
more than an eight-foot drop, and once down she could run across the
square and be out of sight before the man could reach the top of the wall.

She moved one foot with extreme caution, but she had not calculated
on the effects of cramp. A sharp, agonizing pain shot through her
numbed foot and wrenched an involuntary gasp from her. The man below

her whirled like a flash and the moonlight glittered on the barrel of a pistol that was suddenly and surprisingly in his hand.

Winter did not wait for explanations. The sight of the weapon had startled her considerably and for the first time that night she was frightened. She struggled to her feet, but she was not quick enough.

The man below her took a short run and leapt, and his hand grasped her ankle. With a gasp of terror she tumbled headlong from the wall, to be caught in a savage hold and fall full length with her captor into the thicket of oleander and geranium.

The man twisted on top of her, holding her in a crushing grip that felt as though it must break her ribs, and with her face pressed hard against his shoulder so that the thick folds of cloth that wrapped him stifled her attempts to scream. She fought him frantically, writhing and twisting, but the weight of his body and the crushing clasp of his arms drove the breath from her lungs and she gave in suddenly and lay still. His grasp slackened a little and she managed to turn her head, gasping for air. If she could only cry out she might be able to attract attention. Summoning up all her forces she opened her mouth to scream.

But the sound died unuttered, for suddenly and inexplicably, and despite the fact that she could not see his face, she knew who it was who held her. She spoke his name instead, gasping and incredulous: "Captain—Randall!"

He wrenched one arm free and brushed his hand swiftly over her face and the tumbled masses of her loosened hair.

"Damnation!" whispered Captain Randall savagely.

The next moment he was on his feet and had swung Winter up in his arms and flung her up onto the wall. She grasped at an overhanging bough of the fig tree with one hand and the coping with the other, kicked violently, heard a smothered expletive behind her and scrambled to safety. Turning, she saw Alex back away, take a run at the wall and leap for the coping. She grasped his shoulders and pulled with all her strength, and half a minute later they had dropped to the ground on the far side and Alex had gripped her arm and they were running swiftly, keeping to the shadow of the wall.

He dragged her across the square and dived down a narrow alleyway between two tall houses, and turning sharply to the right came out on a smaller paved square that was dominated by the wide stone steps and ornately carved façade of a church. Winter's skirts escaped her frantic clutch at last and tangled about her feet, and she tripped and would have fallen but for Alex' hand on her arm. He jerked her upright and she stopped, painfully alive to the uncomfortable constriction of the whaleboned corsets that reduced her small waist to a bare eighteen inches, and said pantingly: "It's no good!—I can't run another step!" Pulling away from his grasp, she walked unsteadily to the steps before the church and sank down upon the warm stone, her back to the carved balustrade. Alex followed and stood above her, frowning down at her. And looking up at him, suddenly and unexpectedly she laughed.

It was a joyous, breathless laugh, gay, courageous and full of the magic of youth and moonlight, and hearing it, Alex was conscious of a swift flash of admiration. He had expected tears or hysteria and possibly both, but not laughter, and it took him completely by surprise. For a long moment he stared down at her incredulously, and then he sat down on the wide step below her and was laughing too. They sat there in the bright moonlight and laughed together, while the sleepy secretive stonework threw back a chuckling echo of their mirth.

It was Alex who stopped first. "What were you doing there?" he demanded.

"Looking at the moon," said Winter.

Alex reached up and his fingers closed about her wrist in a hard grasp. "I want the truth, please."

"But it is the truth," protested Winter, still laughing. "It was so lovely to be on land again and smell the dust and the trees. And—and it was such a beautiful night. I couldn't just go to bed."

Alex released her wrist and the rigid lines of his face relaxed, and Winter said curiously: "Why were *you* there? Were you watching Kishan Prasad?"

Alex made no perceptible movement but she was aware of an indefinable change in him. He said slowly: "Yes. I wanted to know who he had gone to meet."

"What were they doing—those men?"

"Plotting devilry. One is a Russian and another is a Persian. The third, Kishan Prasad, is a man I have known for three years."

"Tell me about him."

"He is a member of one of the great families of Rohilkhand," said Alex. "An exceedingly clever man and an embittered one—always a dangerous combination. He went to one of the better Indian colleges and studied engineering for the Company's service, and passed out as the senior student of his year with higher marks than any European there. But because he was not a European he was nominated only to the rank of jemadar, where he was actually subordinate to a European sergeant—a man who was his inferior in every way, and who was at the same time arrogant, insolent and stupid and who lost no chance to insult him. Kishan Prasad is a proud man and a descendant of princes. He found the position intolerable and resigned from the Company's service. We lost a good man when we allowed that to happen—and gained a dangerous enemy. He went on a tour of Europe a year ago. He saw us fail in the assault on the Redan at Sebastopol, and he met Russian agents. And now he is returning to his own country. . . ."

Alex fell silent, and a wandering breath of wind blew in from the sea and drove a little whirling cloud of dust across the square. It tugged at Winter's lace shawl and ruffled her hair, and she shivered. But it was not the warm wind that made her shiver, but the sudden recollection of the weapon she had seen in Alex Randall's hand. She said with a catch in her voice: "Were you—did you mean to kill him?"

"Kill him?" Alex laughed shortly. "No. Assassination is unfortunately alien to the British temperament. Which must on occasion be a matter for regret."

He came to his feet, the moonlight glinting on the butt of the long-barreled pistol that he carried tucked into the folds of a wide silk waistband, and said: "It is quite time you got back to the hotel. Miss Lottie has probably already raised the alarm, and I can see that I shall have some very complicated explaining to do to your chaperone."

A dimple showed in Winter's cheek. "I do not think that Lottie will have noticed my absence," she observed demurely.

"In that case I can only hope that she will also fail to notice the black eye I shall undoubtedly have by the morning."

"Oh!" said Winter on a gasp. "Did I kick you? I was afraid I had. I am so very sorry!"

"Considering all things, I feel I have escaped lightly," said Alex with a grin. He leant down and pulled her to her feet, and they walked back through the quiet moonlit streets in companionable silence.

The hotel was in darkness and moonlight no longer flooded the courtyard, but a lamp still burned in Winter and Lottie's room and made a faint square of warm light in the blackness. They came to a stop by the entrance to the courtyard and Winter turned to face the shadow that was Alex.

"Captain Randall—"

"Condesa?"

The unfamiliarity of the formal title took her aback and she fell silent, forgetting what it was that she had meant to say.

The night was so still that she could hear the slow murmur of the sea, the sound of Alex' quiet breathing and the beat of her own heart. The scent of jasmine and geraniums filled the shadows with a heady fragrance that was as potent as the sound of distant music, and there was a strange magic in the hot night: a sparkle and an exhilaration, a narcotic and a spell. Winter became aware of an odd breathlessness and a feeling of expectancy, as though she were waiting for something to happen. Quite suddenly it resolved itself into a fantastic, overwhelming impulse. An impulse to reach up and take Alex Randall's dark head between her hands and draw it down to her own. For a long moment it was almost as if she could feel his thick hair under her fingers—the shape of his head and the warm touch of his mouth. . . .

A cock crowed shrilly from somewhere behind the hotel, and the unexpected sound shattered the spell, bringing her back to reality as though from a drugged sleep. A hot tide of incredulous horror engulfed her mind and body in a burning wave of shame, and she whirled round and fled down the dark arcade as though she were pursued by the furies.

Lottie was already in bed asleep, and blowing out the lamp Winter undressed in the dark, shivering with shock and self-loathing.

She could not understand herself! She had no affection for Captain Randall. She did not even like him, for how could she possibly like anyone who had spoken against Conway as he had done? And yet a moment ago if he had made the slightest movement toward her she would have been in his arms. She had betrayed Conway—dear, kind, wonderful Conway—for had she not been told in the course of religious instruction that to think evil was as reprehensible as to commit it? Only a bad woman would have wanted to do such a thing, thought Winter, sick with shame, and remorse.

She buried her face in her pillow and wept.

Alex lay on his back in the hot darkness and thought of India and the unregarded warnings of men like Sir Henry Lawrence. Of the gross stupidities of men like Conway Barton. Of the whispered warnings of spies. Of the sadhu whom he had seen in the Residency gardens at Lunjore, and the face of Kishan Prasad watching with eyes that were avid and intent the shattered men of the British Army flung back from the Redan, stumbling and dying in the mud and blood before Sebastopol.

He thought too of the faces of those men whom he had seen only that night in the moonlit garden. The Peace Treaty had been signed in Paris and there was nothing now to prevent Gregori Sparkov, merchant and noncombatant, from visiting the island of Malta; or Mohammed Rashid, son of a French governess and a Persian princeling, from staying at the house of a Maltese Jew. And no reason why Rao Kishan Prasad, native of India, gentleman of leisure and passenger on the steamship *Sirius*, should not be seen speaking to either or both of them. And yet—

Alex had suspected for a long time that Kishan Prasad was engaged in treasonable activities, and had reported as much to Mr. Barton. The Commissioner had demanded proof which Alex had been unable to supply, and it was shortly after this that the fabulous emerald that he had last seen adorning Winter's small hand had passed into the Commissioner's possession. Which might have been a coincidence, but was probably not.

Kishan Prasad had been permitted to come and go without hindrance; to visit the Crimea and to contact Russian and Persian *agents provocateurs*. And there was little or nothing that Alex could do about it—unless he were prepared to commit murder. Why was it that a man could kill his fellow men in the heat of battle, or by the chill permission of law, and yet not be able to bring himself to shoot down in cold blood a single human being who was as dangerous as a lighted brand in the hand of a lunatic? Because it was the gospel of Violence, and as such it could lead to worse things than the death of the innocent?

As for Kishan Prasad, his actions were treasonable or laudable only according to who was regarding them. The Briton who plotted against the Roman invader was undoubtedly looked upon as a hero by his compatriots

—and hung as a rebel by the Romans. As the Cavalier who spied for King Charles was hunted as a traitor by Cromwell's men. If Kishan Prasad schemed for the overthrow of the Company's Raj, did that make him a traitor—or a patriot?

And why in the name of hell, thought Alex in tired exasperation, can't I stop seeing both sides of a question? Why can't I believe, as Lawrence and Nicholson and Herbert Edwards do, in the divine right of the British to govern? But he could not believe what they believed. He worked for the same end, but for a different reason. Because he believed with a passionate sincerity that it was better for England and for India and for the world that the British rather than the Russians should hold the land of the Moguls.

As a boy of fifteen Alex had traveled in Russia with his father, and the vast, secretive land with its limitless horizons had left an indelible impression on his mind and his imagination. Russia was the Enemy. An enemy to be feared above all others because the very vastness of her territory made her invulnerable to attack, as Napoleon had found to his cost. Russia had only to retreat before an invading army—to withdraw into that silent, brooding land that stretched away and away in endless steppes, forests, forgotten lakes and uncharted mountain ranges—eastward to the Bering Strait and westward to the borders of Poland. Russia, the cold eyed, the patient; consumed by the hidden fires of her belief in her ultimate destiny as the ruler of the world.

Alex had never forgotten that year in Russia, or that beyond the Khyber Pass lay the kingdom of the Cossacks. We have got to hold India! thought Alex. We have got to hold it until it is strong enough to hold out by itself, and not for any of the reasons that gross fools like Barton will hold it for.

For the first time since she had turned and run from him, he thought of Winter de Ballesteros, who was to marry the Commissioner of Lunjore. A girl in a million, thought Alex with a reminiscent grin. She had not shrieked or fainted when he had dragged her headfirst off that wall. She had fought him instead like a young tiger cat. She had helped to pull him back over the wall, had run with him until she could run no longer, and then, instead of treating him to tears or an attack of the vapors, she had laughed.

Perhaps he should have kissed her tonight. Would it have made any difference if he had done so? There had been a brief moment in the darkness of the archway when he had known without any shadow of doubt that he had only to touch her to have her in his arms. He did not know what had held him back. Certainly it had been no feeling of loyalty to the Commissioner of Lunjore. And that lovely, passionate mouth would have been sweet to kiss. Had it been some obscure instinct of self-preservation? A sudden fear of being caught up in some emotion from which there might be no escape?

Alex became aware that the square of sky beyond his window was no longer flecked with stars but was paling to the clear light of a new day, and he turned on his side and slept.

7

THE long, hot days on shipboard passed slowly enough for Winter, but Lottie and her Edward found the time pass all too quickly. Edward had approached Mrs. Abuthnot on the first day out from Malta. It could scarcely have escaped Mrs. Abuthnot's attention, said Edward, that both his admiration and his affections had been deeply engaged by her daughter Lottie, and although their acquaintance was of comparatively short duration, his intentions were of the most honorable. Naturally he could not expect any engagement to be recognized until Calcutta was reached and he had been able to speak to Lottie's father, but he wished to be assured that Mrs. Abuthnot did not regard his pretensions with aversion, and that he might at least have her approval in attempting to fix his interest with the object of his devotion.

Edward had added a diffident but satisfactory account of his financial situation, and had indeed been so earnest and engaging that Mrs. Abuthnot's heart had quite melted, and she had ended by assuring him that she would never oppose the course of true love or stand in the way of her daughter's ultimate happiness. Naturally all that she could permit at present was that Mr. English should not be debarred from Lottie's society—a course which in any case would have been next to impossible, owing to the narrow limitations of shipboard life. The last word must lie with Lottie's papa, but she could see no reason why he should not be brought to look upon Mr. English's suit with a kindly eye.

And indeed, thought Mrs. Abuthnot complacently, although dear Lottie might well have made a more dazzling match, Edward English was of good family and possessed both prospects and adequate means. It might do very well.

The heat became more intense as the ship neared the coast of Egypt, and the passengers were not sorry to leave the *Sirius* at Alexandria, from where they were to proceed to Cairo by train. Winter had seen little of Captain Randall in the days following their departure from Malta, for once again he appeared to avoid her company—a circumstance that she could not be sorry for. He had not traveled in the same compartment as the Abuthnot party on the train, and she had not seen him again until they left Cairo two nights later in a "desert omnibus" drawn by a team of mules and horses. Even then he had not spoken to her. He had sat opposite her, and Winter had studied him by the bright starlight and the glow of an oil lamp that swung beside the driver's seat, aware that as she herself sat in deep shadow he could not return her scrutiny.

In a day when the average male countenance was remarkably hirsute, Alex Randall's clean-shaven face had at first an alien and almost effeminate look. Yet there was nothing in the least weak or effeminate in the hard planes of that face or the line of the obstinate chin. His skin was burnt as brown as an Arab's, but even by that dim light Winter could still see a faint trace of the bruise that her heel had made that night in Malta.

She shut her eyes with determination and thought of Conway. But for some unaccountable reason she found that she could not picture him clearly. Always before, she had been able to conjure him up by a mere effort of will: the Conway who had given an eleven-year-old girl a gold and pearl ring, standing in the Long Walk at Ware with the sun shining on his blond head and his shadow stretching across the velvet turf. Tall, broad shouldered, yellow haired and handsome. A shining knight. Now, for the first time, the vision failed her, and it was no longer a living man that she saw but a picture out of a child's book. A flat, two-dimensional representation, crudely drawn, wooden and unreal. A blank face whose blue eyes were as glassy and as empty of meaning as a doll's, and whose mouth was hidden by a drooping corn-colored mustache so that she could not tell if it were firm or full or weak.

She opened her eyes and found herself looking once more at Alex Randall's relaxed, unguarded face in the pale light of the newly risen moon. Alex' mouth was firm enough, and unexpectedly sensitive. He was Conway's assistant and she supposed that she would see a great deal of him once she was Conway's wife. The reflection disturbed her, and the thought passed through her mind that it would be better—she was not sure for whom—if he were to be transferred to some other district.

Two days later the travelers embarked upon the *Glamorgan Castle* and sailed down the Red Sea, leaving the dust and glare of Suez behind them. And once more the days settled into a pattern of pleasant shipboard monotony, until a storm met them three days out of Aden, the last of the monsoon. It blew itself out after twenty-four hours of tossing discomfort, and on the last evening before they sailed into fine weather they passed the waterlogged wreck of a dismasted ship, its decks swept by the heavy seas.

Captain Ross of the *Glamorgan Castle* had maneuvered his ship as close to it as he dared, and had launched a mailboat in charge of the first officer with a boarding party. They returned wet and exhausted with the news that the vessel had apparently been a troopship bound for China, but there was no one on board and few papers or particulars to be found on her. It was to be presumed that all on board had taken to the boats, for all the boats were gone. The bulkheads of her Captain's cabin had been carried away; the port anchor and the cathead had gone—and from the appearance of the tattered sails and broken spars it was obvious that a sudden squall of hurricane force had carried all away at once. It was unlikely that the men on board would have lived to reach any shore, but there was nothing that could be done about it now, and the *Glamorgan Castle* went on her way in the swiftly gathering twilight.

Winter, who had crept up onto the windy, spray-swept deck, watched the abandoned wreck fade into the stormy dusk, and a cold shiver ran down her spine. The fact that she was actually in the Indian Ocean, and that India itself lay ahead of her at last, had filled her with a sense of glowing happiness. But the sight of that battered and broken ship, drifting and sinking in the lonely wastes of the sea, dimmed the glow and brought with it a chill breath of apprehension and foreboding.

She heard a sigh beside her that was not the wind, and turned quickly. It was Kishan Prasad who stood near her, his eyes fixed on the fast-vanishing wreck. But for once his bland, inscrutable face had dropped its guard, and it was as though a mask had been stripped from it, leaving it naked and exposed. He did not appear to be aware of Winter, and he did not move or speak. But quite suddenly, and as though he had shouted it aloud, she knew his thoughts with a complete and horrified certainty.

He was thinking, with a fierce, gloating pleasure, of the men who had been on that ship. Seeing them in his mind's eye swept away by the savage seas; sinking down into the hungry fathoms, dragged under by the weight of their sodden uniforms; choking and drowning, their struggling bodies torn and ripped by sharks and barracudas. He sighed again, the same long-drawn sign of hatred and satisfaction; and Winter shrank away, and backing from him turned and ran headlong, stumbling down the steep stairs and tripping on her full skirts.

Alex Randall had been coming down the passage toward her and he caught her arm and steadied her: "What's the matter?"

She had forgotten that she had meant to avoid all conversation with Captain Randall outside of social necessity, and she clung to his arm, her eyes wide with shock. "It was Kishan Prasad. He was looking at that ship. And he was glad! He hated them and he wanted them to drown! He was glad that they had been drowned!"

Alex said: "It isn't so surprising. They were soldiers—British troops. If he could have drowned them singly with his own hands he would probably have done so."

"Why? Do they—do they hate us?"

Alex said impatiently: "Did you suppose that they loved us?"

He looked down at Winter's small white face and glimpsed something of the shock this sudden revelation had dealt her. This girl had probably never thought of India as a conquered country. She had imagined herself to be coming home, and the realization that many of the inhabitants of that land could hate all those of British blood with a savage and implacable hatred was like a blow in the face of a trusting child. He wanted to say: "Don't look like that! It isn't safe to be so vulnerable—to expect too much of anything or anyone!"

He said instead, with a kind of exasperated anger: "I warned your cousin Ware that this was no time to send any young woman out to India, but he would not listen! None of them will!" And turning from her he went on down the passage and up onto the wet deck.

But it was only two days later that Kishan Prasad fell overboard, and it was Alex who went after him.

Alex had not known that it was Kishan Prasad who had fallen. Perhaps if he had it might have altered the course of a great many lives.

The day had been hot and still and all that remained of the storm was a long, heaving, barely perceptible swell that swung the cabin doors idly to and fro and made the line of the horizon lift and fall slowly in a leisurely rhythm. The sun blazed down from a cloudless sky so that even under the shade of the awnings the deck planks were uncomfortably hot to the touch, and the sea was blue with the intense midnight blue of the Indian Ocean, and so clear that floating squadrons of jellyfish far below the surface appeared as though embedded like bubbles in blue glass.

It was after four and the decks were comparatively deserted while the passengers changed for dinner, but Lottie had come up early, intending to meet Edward. She had looked up and seen Kishan Prasad standing on the paddle box gazing out to sea, and even as she looked the ship rolled suddenly in the trough of an unexpectedly deep swell, and she saw Kishan Prasad, taken off guard, slip and fall and slide under the rail. The next moment he had vanished, and Lottie shrieked and ran.

Two of the lascars, a ship's officer and Colonel Moulson had also seen him fall, and they ran along the deck shouting. Colonel Moulson, with what he considered to be admirable presence of mind, picked up two deck chairs and heaved them overboard into the creaming wake, where they were joined almost immediately by a hen coop thrown after them by one of the lascars.

"*Man overboard!*" bellowed Colonel Moulson and the ship's officer.

Alex, who had been lying asleep face downward in a patch of shade with his head buried in his arms, woke at Lottie's shriek and came to his feet. She stumbled toward him, her face chalk-white, screaming and pointing, and he turned and raced aft along the deck and caught a brief glimpse of a despairing hand that reached up from the foaming wake.

"It's all right," panted Colonel Moulson. "Only one of those blacks. He'll be drowned by now—they can't swim!"

A sudden flash of pure rage hit Alex with the force of a blow and he kicked off his shoes, and in the next second he had vaulted over the rail and dropped feet first, and the rush of the sea closed over his head.

The water was unexpectedly cold and the churning wake sucked him down and down until the sea felt like a ton weight upon his shoulders. Just when it felt as though his lungs must burst, the weight lifted and he was being shot to the surface like a cork, and there was air again. He gulped deep drafts of it and struck out strongly, aided by the swirl of the

wake. After the sweating heat of the *Glamorgan Castle* the cold rush of
the foaming water was incredibly exhilarating, and he shook his wet hair
out of his eyes and laughed.

It was, he presumed, one of Kishan Prasad's servants who had fallen
overboard, for had it been a member of the crew Moulson would have
said "a lascar." Of all the goddamned, bloody, idiotic things to do! thought
Alex. What the hell is the life of one heathen lackey worth that I have
to make a quixotic exhibition of myself trying to fish the man out?

He saw a dark, struggling shape ahead of him and the next moment it
had disappeared. Alex filled his lungs with air and dived. The man
struggled feebly, and for a minute that seemed like an endless hour they
sank down together through the blue water; and then Alex got a grip on
him and kicked strongly and they were rising once more into light and
air.

Even then he did not realize who it was that he held. He caught the
half-drowned man under the arms and swam toward the heavy wooden
hen coop that was lifting to the swell not twenty yards away. After several
fruitless efforts he managed to heave his limp burden face downward
across the stoutly built coop and hold him there while he trod water.

The swell that had been barely perceptible from the decks of the
Glamorgan Castle was a very different thing when viewed from the level
of the sea itself, and in the trough of it the sea appeared to be empty and
the *Glamorgan Castle* had vanished. The next swell swung them slowly
upward, and far away—miles away, it seemed—the ship showed small
against the blue. It would take a long time for them to heave to and
circle back, thought Alex. They would lower a boat as soon as possible
but it would be a long wait. The distant ship vanished as the burdened
hen coop slid once more into the glassy trough of the swell, and the
Indian coughed, retched, lifted his head and moved feebly.

"Lie still, fool!" said Alex in the vernacular, and saw for the first time
who it was he had rescued.

The two men stared at each other for a long moment and Alex was
conscious of a queer twisting wrench at the pit of his stomach: a helpless,
futile, sick anger against fate and the fatuous, foolish instinct of his kind
that had driven him to leap unthinkingly to the rescue of a drowning man,
and by so doing had betrayed him.

Winter had asked him once if he had meant to kill this man, and he
had replied bitterly that assassination was unfortunately alien to the
British temperament. He knew that he could not bring himself to murder
Kishan Prasad in cold blood, although if he could have proved his suspicions, and so brought him legally to death, he would have done so without a second's hesitation. Yet now that Providence had stepped in and
done its best to put an end to Kishan Prasad, he had risked his neck to
save the man whom he regarded as among the most dangerous enemies to
British supremacy in India.

The salt sea water was bitter in Alex' mouth and he looked into Kishan

Prasad's gray face and laughed. Kishan Prasad's lips drew back from his teeth in an exhausted grin that was a grimace of complete comprehension. He said in a hoarse voice between difficult breaths: "Whom did you think you had saved—*Sahib?*"—the appellation was nearer an insult than a term of respect—"One of your own kind?"

"No," said Alex, treading water. "I thought it was one of your *naukar-log* (servants)."

He saw the flare of astonishment and disbelief in the dark eyes.

"*My servant?*"

"Yes," said Alex shortly. "Had I known it were you—"

"You would have let me drown," finished Kishan Prasad, fighting for each breath.

"Yes," said Alex bluntly. "Do not talk. You will tire yourself and the boat will not reach us for some time yet."

Kishan Prasad was silent for a long while. The slow swell lifted them up lazily, so that at intervals they could see the distant ship and the small speck that was a boat being rowed toward them. Then it would slide them down into a long blue-black hollow and the ship would vanish and there were only two men and a wooden hen coop alone in all those endless leagues of ocean.

Kishan Prasad spoke at long last, and softly, in a voice that despite himself he could not keep quite steady: "You say that had you known it were I who had fallen, you would have left me to my death. But it would seem that death is here now for one of us. Look there—!"

Alex turned his head and his diaphragm seemed to contract and turn to ice.

In the glassy swell beyond them lay a long silvery-brown body, the triangular dorsal fin just clear of the water. Shark! . . .

The sea was darkening below them, and the low sun burned along the water, turning the surface of the swell to gold and outlining the creature with fire. It did not move, but hung motionless like a fly embedded in amber.

Alex seemed to have lost all power of movement. He held on to the edge of the hen coop with one hand and stared back at that small cold eye. It had seen them and was watching them, idly curious.

Kishan Prasad said in a hoarse whisper: "This wooden thing will not bear two upon its surface, and my life is forfeit to thee." He had forgotten to speak in English. He began to slide softly from the coop and Alex said furiously: "Get back onto that! You can't swim."

At the first movement the shark had flicked away, and now they saw its fin cut the water on the far side of them. The swell swung them up once more and they could see the boat, the low sun flashing along the oar blades. But it was still a long way off.

Alex remembered having heard that sharks disliked noise and he beat the water with his cupped hand. The fin sheered away, circled and came back. Kishan Prasad was in the water holding on only with one hand, and

Alex said again: "Get back, you fool!" He grasped the Indian about the waist and heaved, and releasing him, caught his legs and thrust him onto the top of the hen coop where he remained on all fours gripping the edge. It was a perilous and inadequate raft, and now that it bore Kishan Prasad's full weight it lay barely an inch or two out of the water. But at least it held his body clear of the surface.

The fin cut slowly through the water, cruising gently along the flank of a long glassy slope parallel to them, and Alex suffered a spasm of cold, crippling panic. "Oh, God, if only I had a knife!" he said in a whisper, unaware that he had spoken aloud.

"Here," gasped Kishan Prasad. He fumbled among his wet clothes, the flimsy raft rocking dangerously, and drew out a knife with a slim, wicked eight-inch blade which he thrust into Alex' hand. It was an inadequate enough weapon to pit against a fifteen-foot monster who circled warily about them, but the feel of it in his hand gave Alex a sudden surge of hope. It was something. He had read of pearl divers off the coast of Ceylon who fought off sharks with a knife.

He beat the water again and shouted and the creature shot away, hovered and returned. It seemed to hang in the water above him and he realized suddenly that if it came at him while he held to the hen coop, the rush of its great body would overturn that makeshift raft and dislodge Kishan Prasad. He had forgotten that Kishan Prasad was an enemy whose death he would have welcomed, and whom a few short minutes ago he had been passionately regretting that he had not left to die. The man on the raft was a fellow human, and as such they were leagued together against this finny, cold-blooded killer from the deeps beneath them.

He released his hold and swam away at a tangent, his eyes on that cruising dorsal fin. The swell lifted it up and once again the creature seemed to hang in the water above him. It came at him quite slowly, and as it came it turned. Alex avoided it with a superhuman effort, kicking backward with all his strength and twisting again to face it. He heard a hoarse shout of warning from Kishan Prasad and the thought flashed through his mind that the boat had come.

Just in time! thought Alex grimly. And then he saw a flicker of movement to his left. Another fin! There was a second shark—a third. They circled him as though merely curious, and he felt the heave of the water under him as the first shark returned to the attack; and somehow he avoided it. Now they would all rush in.

He beat the water and shouted as Kishan Prasad was doing, but the great creatures were undismayed and the circle closed in. He would not wait for them to come at him, and be torn to bits without a fight. His fingers tightened hard on the haft of the knife and he swam toward the nearest shark.

It was apparently an unexpected movement, for the creature sheered off at lightning speed, hovered and was back. He turned quickly and saw in the slow swell that bore down upon him the swift shape of another coming in. For the flash of a second he saw too, with uncanny vividness, the tiny striped bodies of the pilot fish who raced before and beside it; and then he had dived to meet it, and as it rolled to bring the wicked jaws into play he struck with all his strength.

The knife sliced through a foot of the creature's side and was wrenched from his grasp, and there was a cloud of blood in the water. For a moment the other sharks lay motionless, and then suddenly the water boiled into foam as they rushed in upon their wounded companion, fighting, snapping and tearing like hounds upon a fox. The dark water was red with blood and Alex turned and swam desperately away. He was still swimming when someone grabbed his shoulders and shouted above his head, and then hands were pulling at him and he was dragged over a gunwale to tumble gasping and helpless among the feet of the boat's crew.

"That was a near thing!" said the first mate, beating him on the back. "Here—get down, Mr. Prasad! Holy Moses! Look at the brutes! They'll have us over! Hit with oars—*sumjao!*" The boat rocked dangerously as a ten-foot blue shark, attracted by the taint of blood, rubbed along the keel, and the sea seemed alive with triangular fins and lithe, rolling bodies. And then they were rowing back to the ship into the eye of the setting sun, over a sea that was no longer blue, but black below them and bright gold beyond.

Alex sat up dizzily and grinned at Kishan Prasad, and Kishan Prasad laughed and lifted his hand in a brief gesture of salute. For a moment they were no longer enemies but men who had seen no escape from death —and yet by some miracle had escaped it and were whole and alive. They drank the fiery grog proffered by the first mate and grinned weakly at each other and looked with dazed thankfulness at the clear sky above them while the lascars chattered and tugged at their oars and the *Glamorgan Castle*, its deck rails lined with excited, cheering passengers, grew larger and nearer and at last loomed solid and safe above them.

Alex was aware, as though through a thick fog, of noise and shouting voices and people who shook his hand and thumped his shoulders. He felt absurdly sleepy and rather as if he were very drunk. It was an effort to keep his head erect and his eyes from closing, and he yawned largely in the faces of the congratulatory passengers, and pushing his way through them, stumbled down to his cabin and collapsed onto his berth where the ship's doctor, following him, found him so deeply asleep that he did not even wake when his wet clothes were removed and a blanket thrown over him.

He woke early the following morning feeling refreshed and fitter than he had for many days. The long swim and the violent exertion of the previous evening, followed by almost twelve hours of uninterrupted sleep, had apparently proved more beneficial than the hot, idle days and sweltering sleepless nights that had followed the departure from Malta. Alex lay looking about the small, cramped space and the low ceiling above his head with a strange new appreciation of the miraculous fact of being alive, and presently rolled out of his bunk, and pulling on a pair of trousers went up on deck to breathe the dawn air.

The sun had not yet risen but the sky was already bright, and the decks glittered with the salt water with which a busy group of lascars were washing down the planks as Alex went aft and leant against the rail, idly watching the long white track of the wake. He heard footsteps behind him and turned to see Kishan Prasad. The two men looked at each other for a moment or two in silence and with the cool, narrowed, calculating look of adversaries who measure swords.

Kishan Prasad said slowly: "I wish to thank you—"

"You have nothing to thank me for," interrupted Alex curtly.

"You mean because had you known that it were I you would not have saved me? Is that indeed the truth?"

Alex returned his look with eyes that were hard and level. "I would not have lifted a hand to save you."

Kishan Prasad bowed gravely as though he had received an answer that he both expected and understood. He said: "It is for that reason that I come to thank you. Not for what you did for me, but for what you would have done for one of my servants. There are very few who would have risked their lives for—a black man and the servant of a black man."

"You overrate me," said Alex brusquely. "There was no risk. I am a strong swimmer."

"And the sharks?" said Kishan Prasad gently.

"You force me to admit," said Alex with a grin, "that I had clean forgotten that there might be sharks. If I had remembered it, I give you my word that I should not have jumped! So you see, you owe me nothing."

"Nevertheless," said Kishan Prasad, smiling, "willingly or unwillingly, you gave me back the life that the Gods would have taken from me. In the past I have intrigued against your race—" he saw the sudden flare in Alex' eyes and laughed, lifting a protesting hand. "Oh, no! I tell you nothing that you did not already know! And your Commissioner will not move against me. That I know."

"And I also," said Alex bitterly. "Are you by any chance telling me that you have suffered a change of heart because I risked my neck to pull you out of the sea?"

Kishan Prasad smiled and shook his head. "Alas, no. I have suffered no change of heart. In the name of my country and my people and my Gods I will do all in my power to pull down your Company's Raj."

"And I," said Alex, "will do all in my power to get you hanged or transported—for the sake of my countrymen who govern your country."

"It is good," said Kishan Prasad gravely. "We understand one another, and we are not children."

He turned a small ring that he wore on his right hand and pulling it off held it out to Alex. It was a trumpery thing of little value, fashioned out of twisted silver in a curious design set with three small red stones that might have been flawed rubies. An odd ornament for the hand of such a man as Kishan Prasad. He said: "Will you wear this for me? As a token of my gratitude? It is worth less than ten rupees, but it is a talisman that may one day save you from much evil. If ever the day comes, as I pray it will, that the Company's Raj falls and its charter for robbery and confiscation is destroyed, look on that ring and remember Kishan Prasad. For in that day—who knows?—it may repay a part of my debt."

Alex looked at the outstretched hand with a frown in his eyes and made no attempt to disguise his hesitation. Then he reached out and taking it, slid it onto the little finger of his right hand. He said slowly: "I did not remember that there might be sharks when I went over that rail yesterday, but you would have had me take your place on that damned hen coop when you saw them come. I will wear this because it is the gift of a brave man."

Kishan Prasad put his hands together, the finger tips touching, bowed gravely above them and turned and walked away.

8

WE shall be in Calcutta tomorrow, thought Winter. Only one more day—and then I shall see Conway!

It did not seem possible that the weary waiting that had begun six years ago in the Long Walk at Ware could be over at last; that tomorrow she would see Conway again, and the very next day they would be married.

The *Glamorgan Castle* was anchored off the sandheads awaiting the first light and the turn of the tide when, with the pilot on board, she would begin the slow journey up the Hooghly to Calcutta. Winter turned restlessly in her berth and wondered if Conway would meet her at the mouth of the river or board the ship on her way up. Mrs. Abuthnot seemed to think it possible.

Conway . . . There had been a time during the voyage when she could not picture him clearly and his image had become unreal and lifeless—a shadow without substance. She had, obscurely, placed the blame for this on Captain Randall, though she could not have told herself in what way he was responsible. But at least it had been Captain Randall who had been responsible for reinvesting Conway with all his old glamour, though the way in which he had brought it about was equally involved and quite as impossible of explanation. It had come about through his dramatic rescue of the Indian, Kishan Prasad.

Winter had remembered what Alex had said about Kishan Prasad on that moonlight night in Malta. He had expressed regret that he could not bring himself to murder the man, and appeared to think it a weakness in himself that he could not do so. And yet he had risked his own life to save the life of his enemy. Winter had been filled with a warm, glowing flood of admiration: an admiration that had made her ashamed of the way in which she had behaved to him of late, and that went a long way toward expunging the memory of his disloyal attack on Conway. It had, however, been short lived.

Winter had had no opportunity of speaking to Captain Randall other than in a crowd until halfway through the following morning when, at Mrs. Abuthnot's imperious bidding, he had come to sit on the deck at her feet under the shade of the awning and to answer innumerable questions.

"Of course it was exceedingly noble of you, dear boy," said Mrs. Abuthnot, handing him a skein of embroidery silk to unravel, "but quite inconceivably rash!"

"Mrs. Abuthnot," said Alex, "I cannot masquerade as a hero to you, much as I should enjoy doing so. No one who could swim a stroke could have drowned in a sea like a millpond. As for the sharks, the sight of those creatures gave me the worst shock of my life and I hope I may never have another as bad."

Winter looked up from the embroidery she held in her hands and spoke for the first time: "But you went to the rescue of a man whom you—you had no cause to think well of. That at least was noble!"

Alex regarded her with a distinctly satirical eye. "I am afraid not. You see, I did not know who it was whom I had gone after."

Winter regarded him wide eyed. "But—but if you had known you would not have left him to drown—"

"Oh, yes, I would!" said Alex grimly. "The gesture was a lamentable mistake on my part and one which I deeply regret."

He came to his feet, and handing over the unraveled skein of silk to Mrs. Abuthnot with a bow and a smile, turned away and left them.

"He does not mean a word of it!" said Mrs. Abuthnot comfortably. "He is just being modest. So truly heroic!"

"Oh, no, he is not!" said Winter scornfully, her eyes sparkling with anger. "He means every word of it! And he is quite right—he did nothing in the least heroic."

The reflection that she herself had come close to regarding Captain Randall's exploit with a similar degree of admiration filled her with fury, and the fact that she had been in a fair way to forgiving and forgetting his disloyalty to Conway added immeasurably to her anger. Conway, she thought, would have sprung to the rescue of a drowning man even if he had known the risks! It would have been unthinkable to a man like Conway to stand by and see even an enemy drown. And suddenly, with that conviction, Conway was alive and real again and no longer a thing of pasteboard and straw.

The remainder of the voyage had been uneventful, and now at last they were almost at the end of their long journey. Soon the sun would turn the silt-stained sea to gold, the boatswains' whistles would shrill and there would be a patter of feet on deck and the rattle of the anchor chain. The last day!

Winter had completed her packing on the previous afternoon, except for the last few necessities, for she could not bear to waste a moment of that wonderful day. Every foot of the way—the tangled thickets of bamboo, the thatch-roofed huts surrounded by groves of tamarind, jack fruit and custard apple, the low brown land, the temples and the wide, mud-colored Hooghly—was wonderful and exciting to the girl who had passed that way as a child almost a dozen years ago, held in the arms of Zobeida who had wept as she looked her last on her homeland.

Every approaching craft, every carriage seen upon either bank, might be one that contained Conway. A horseman riding behind a far belt of trees, or a figure carried in a rough palanquin might be he.

Alex Randall, seeing her run to lean over the deck rail as a river launch approached the ship, felt again the same half-angry, half-exasperated desire to tell her that she must not look like that. That she should not let such glowing expectation show on her face for all to see; for before the day was out she would have seen for herself what the years had done to Mr. Commissioner Barton and what kind of man it was whom she had come out to marry, and she would never wear that look again.

The sky was ablaze with sunset by the time the *Glamorgan Castle* reached the Calcutta anchorage, and boat after boat shot out from the shore bringing relatives and friends of those on board or coming to fetch the passengers away. Mrs. Abuthnot, who had informed Lottie only the day before that any public display of affection was not only intolerable but indelicate, abandoned all reserve and cast herself into the arms of a tubby little gentleman with a cherubic face, silver-white hair and mild blue eyes, who proved to be Colonel Abuthnot, and the reunited family retired to shed happy tears in the privacy of the cabin. Only Winter stood apart from the turmoil of welcome and departure, her eyes anxiously scanning every boat. But none contained a familiar face.

She had watched a boat with two rowers bring an Indian wearing an odd sandy-colored uniform out to the ship, and seen Alex Randall go quickly to meet him. The man had saluted stiffly as he reached the deck and then his brown face had creased into a grin of pure pleasure. Winter saw Alex' hand go out and grip the man's shoulder, holding it hard, and saw that he was smiling the same smile. For a moment the two men had looked at each other without words, as brothers might look who meet again after a long separation, with affection and relief in each other's safety. Then Alex' hand had dropped and they had both laughed and turned away together, talking rapidly.

The crowded decks emptied and Winter watched anxiously as boat after boat drew away laden with passengers for the shore; but still Conway did not come. At last someone touched her on the arm and she turned quickly, but it was only Alex Randall. There was a look on his face that was dangerously near pity and it stiffened Winter's small shoulders and brought her chin up with a jerk. Alex said bluntly: "He has not been able to come. My orderly has brought letters from Lunjore."

Winter took the proffered packet with a hand that was not quite steady. Her fingers closed on it so tightly that the stiff paper crackled and she could feel tears prickling behind her eyelids. She said: "Thank you," in a small, cold voice, and as Alex turned away abruptly and left her, she caught at the rail to steady herself. The disappointment was almost too bitter to be borne. Today was to have been the end of a long journey, but the journey had not ended after all. She looked down at the letter she held clenched in her hand, and after a moment broke the seal.

It was a letter that might well have chilled the heart of someone less used to lack of kindness and affection, but she had never received anything that could be called a love letter from Conway Barton and so she saw nothing lacking in the missive she held in her hand.

Pressure of work, wrote Conway, had made it impossible after all for him to meet her in Calcutta. She must know how great a disappointment this was to him. As great, he knew, as it would be to her. But duty must come first and he was persuaded that she would not have him neglect his duty even for her. As he had heard that the Abuthnots, who had so kindly escorted her out, were proceeding to Delhi, she had better remain under their protection and travel to Delhi with them. It was a little out of the way, but he himself would have occasion to go there in the near future and would be staying with the Commissioner, Mr. Simon Fraser, so it would suit very well. They could be married in Delhi and spend their honeymoon in that historic city, visiting the various places of interest with which the ancient Mogul capital abounded. It would mean a delay of a few more weeks, but what were a few more weeks when they had the rest of their lives before them?

The writing was straggling and uneven and the lines ran crookedly across the page. He must have been very tired when he wrote it, thought Winter with loving compassion. Tired and disappointed. It made her own disappointment seem a selfish emotion. It was so noble of Conway—and so like him!—to put duty before personal happiness.

She turned away from the rail and walked steadily down to her cabin with her head high, her face calm and composed and her eyes very dry and bright.

Mrs. Abuthnot was motherly and sympathetic. Dear Alex had already informed her of the state of affairs and had handed her a most charming letter from Mr. Barton. So disappointing! But then life in India was sadly full of such disappointments. One had to learn to bear them. Officers in the service of the Company were not their own masters. India, said Mrs. Abuthnot profoundly, was not England. Naturally dear Winter would remain in her care. It would be delightful to have her!—although she feared that it would mean some delay, as Colonel Abuthnot had official business to transact in Calcutta and Barrackpore which might keep them here for a little time. He had arranged for them to stay with a friend, Mr. Shadwell, a Calcutta merchant; and the Shadwells she knew would be only too pleased to welcome Winter as an additional guest, for Mr. Shadwell had known her uncle Ebenezer well.

The Shadwells' house proved to be a palatial two-storied mansion on Garden Reach, surrounded by lawns and gardens, with wide verandas fronting the river. And to Winter's relief she was given a room to herself. She shut the door behind her and leant tiredly against it, released at last from the necessity of keeping her features composed and her lips smiling, and looked about the huge, high-ceilinged room with its whitewashed walls and long French windows opening onto a deep veranda—a room that was as utterly unlike an English bedroom as the vast slow-moving Hooghly was unlike an English stream. The tight band that had seemed to be tied about her heart relaxed, and the fever of excitement and the leaden weight of disappointed hope both faded.

She walked slowly across the room and out onto the veranda, her wide skirts rustling softly on the matting. Below her, lawns sloped down to the river between thick groves of trees, and the river ran gold in the brief twilight. The evening air was full of sounds, half-forgotten and yet wholly familiar sounds: conches blaring in a temple; the distant throb of a tom-tom; peacocks calling and a jackal pack wailing; the barking of pariah dogs and all the many noises of an Indian city.

The air smelt of sun-baked dust and cow dung fires; of wood smoke and marigolds and jasmine and the rank scent of the river, and Winter leant on the broad veranda rail and drew a long, long breath of happiness. It did not matter any longer that Conway had been unable to come to Calcutta to meet her, or that tomorrow would not after all be her wedding day. She could wait. She had come home.

II

Winter awoke the next morning to a babble of birds—crows, mynas, jays, parrots, *saht bhai* and doves; whistling, screeching and cooing. And to the sight of Lottie clad in a pink cotton peignoir over a cambric night-gown, and with her soft fair curls in tangled disarray. "Did I wake you?" demanded Lottie. "I did not mean to. But—oh, Winter, Edward is to call on Papa today! Mamma has told him all, and Papa has been so kind. And only think!—he knows Edward's uncle! They were at school together. He would not commit himself, but—but he did not look at all displeased."

"What possible objection could he have? Edward is most eligible. And so handsome!" added Winter with a twinkle.

"He is handsome, is he not?" sighed Lottie, accepting the tribute as a simple statement of fact. And indeed to her adoring eyes Edward's blunt-

nosed, blue-eyed, freckled face and flaming red hair embodied all that
was admirable in masculine good looks—although barely two months ago
her mental vision of the ideal male would have been found to resemble
the late Lord Byron, a gentleman who had borne no recognizable likeness
to Lieutenant Edward English.

"You are so lucky, Winter," sighed Lottie. "I do not think that it is
fair. You are a whole year younger than I am, and yet you are going to
be married in a few weeks' time, whereas I shall have to wait for at least
half a year, and probably a great deal longer."

But as it happened, Lottie was to be married within a few weeks of
their arrival in Delhi.

It was Edward who had not only advanced such an unheard-of suggestion, but had actually succeeded in carrying the day against the scandalized opposition of Mrs. Abuthnot.

There was an unauthenticated rumor in Calcutta of tension brewing
between Great Britain and China, and of the possibility of trouble arising
there. Edward had received information—unofficial but believed to be
reliable—that his regiment might be sent to augment Admiral Seymour's
forces in China early in the new year. In the light of this information
he desired to get married as soon as possible in case such a calamity
occurred. And, as he pointed out, he had already known Lottie for two
months, during which time had seen her daily. Surely this could be held
to constitute a long acquaintance, for had they been in England he might
well have seen her at the most once or twice a week, even if they had
been betrothed. This argument, when reinforced by the appeals of senti-
ment, carried the day, for Lottie, upon hearing of the possibility of her
Edward being sent to China, had instantly swooned away, and only the
promise of an early wedding had prevented her—upon being revived with
the aid of burnt feathers and hartshorn—from repeating this affecting gesture.

Mrs. Abuthnot, alarmed by her daughter's pallor and despair, had withdrawn all opposition, and the entire party had repaired to the drawing
room where Mr. Shadwell called for champagne so that all might drink to
the health and happiness of the betrothed pair.

The Abuthnots expected to arrive in Delhi early in October, and the
wedding would take place at the end of that month. "And only think,
Winter!—we may be able to have a double wedding!" exclaimed Lottie
in a pause between the congratulations.

It was at this point that a servant announced Captain Randall, who had
called in order to make his adieus. He regretted that he could not accompany them to Delhi, but he could not delay his return to Lunjore any
longer.

He congratulated the happy pair, swallowed half a glass of champagne
with absent-minded haste, shook hands with the assembled company and
left. Winter heard the rattle of his carriage wheels die away and was
astounded and disturbed to find that the sound brought her a sudden

feeling of being alone and unprotected. And as the slow days dragged by she was surprised to find how much she missed him. Not the man himself, but the feeling he had given her that as long as he was there she was safe. She had not stopped to analyze it, and she would not do so now. But the fact that he had gone, and that it would never again be any part of his duty to see to her comfort and safety, did not bring her any feeling of relief, but rather a vague sensation of insecurity and loss. Which must, she decided, be because he had been a link with Conway.

The days that passed so slowly for Winter were by no means spent in idleness, for cards of invitation to balls and assemblies, including a State Ball at Government House, arrived at the house on Garden Reach in an apparently never-ending stream, and there were shopping expeditions with Mrs. Gardener-Smith and Delia, who were also making a short stay in Calcutta.

Calcutta, as the capital and headquarters of the Governor-General and the Council, and seat of the Supreme Government, had a reputation to keep up in the way of gaiety, and the State Ball had been a revelation to Lottie and Sophie, who had never attended such a function before. Even Winter, accustomed to the almost unrelieved black and white attire of the men who had danced at Ware and in the London ballrooms, imagined for one dazzled instant that the Governor-General was giving a fancy dress ball.

Men in the gorgeous dress uniforms of regiments whose names were rarely heard outside India—regiments of Cavalry, of Irregular Horse, of Bengal Infantry and Artillery—men wearing the pale blue and gold of the Light Cavalry, the canary yellow of Skinner's Horse, the green of the Rifle companies and the scarlet of Infantry regiments, vied with the shimmering silks and frothing tarlatans of feminine ballgowns in richness of color and glitter of gold lace, and outnumbered the women by six to one.

Moving among them in more sober attire, crows among a flock of peacocks, were the rich Calcutta merchants—men such as Mr. Shadwell—or, distinguished by ribbons and orders, the members of the Governor-General's Council and high officers of the East India Company. Indian guests, many of them ablaze with jewels and wearing brightly colored brocades and muslins, their dark faces often no darker than the sunburnt skins above the high tight collars of dress uniforms, mingled with the company but did not dance.

But though the guests were gay, their host Lord Canning was not in the best of spirits. The new Governor-General had hoped for a quiet term in office in succession to the dynamic Dalhousie, whose reforms were said to have launched India on an era of enlightenment and progress. But India was proving a bed of thorns rather than of roses. The annexation of Oudh had been one of the last acts of Lord Dalhousie's reign, but the settling of the province had fallen to Lord Canning. To add to his worries, Wajid Ali, the deposed King of Oudh, had elected to settle in Calcutta, bringing with him a large following of relatives and retainers who lived a life of idleness and occupied themselves with intrigue and the formulating of endless complaints against the behavior of the British officers in Lucknow, who, they alleged, were inflicting disgraceful sufferings and indignities upon the dispossessed nobles of the state, plundering their possessions, turning their women into the streets and using their palaces to house dogs and horses. Wherefore Lord Canning watched his carefree guests dancing the waltz in the ballroom of Government House with an abstracted eye and a mind that was on other matters.

Colonel Abuthnot, also no dancer, had left his wife to gossip among the older women and to keep a watchful eye upon Lottie, Sophie and Winter, and had removed himself to the more congenial company of several like-minded gentlemen who were smoking a quiet cigar in an anteroom some distance from the ballroom, where his appearance was hailed by a portly civilian whose high stock seemed to be in some danger of choking him:

"Hello, Abuthnot!—you're just the man I wanted to see! Fallon here has been talkin' a lot of twaddle about disaffection among some of the regiments around Delhi way. That's your part of the world, ain't it? I tell him he's too credulous by half. The Army's as sound as a bell!"

"Well—there have been rumors of course," admitted Colonel Abuthnot cautiously. "But I have certainly had no trouble with my own men."

Colonel Fallon's bronzed countenance took on a distinct tinge of purple. "Nor I with mine! But I tell you that there are dangerous ideas stirring among the sepoys. Ideas that we have fostered ourselves—or done nothing to prevent. Grievances that we have given insufficient attention to. And then there's all this damned Brahminism. We should have done something to limit it."

A tall handsome man with cold eyes and a marked air of fashion added a languid voice to the discussion:

"Brahminism? Pray enlighten an ignorant globe-trotter, Colonel Fallon. I was not aware that there were political parties in this country."

"It is not a political party, Lord Carlyon. It is an aspect of Hinduism. The Brahmins—the twice-born—are the priestly caste of the Hindus, and as such are held in great reverence by all other castes of Hindus. No Hindu of a lower caste dare offend them for fear of the fearful penalties that would fall upon him not only in this world but the next. And that leads to endless trouble in the ranks, for one Brahmin will not report another, and it is no uncommon thing to see an Indian officer of a lesser caste groveling to a mere sepoy who happens to be a Brahmin. It rots discipline, and we should have put a stop to it long ago: clapped a limit onto the number we recruited, and kept the whole Army on a lower caste level."

"The strong hand, that's what they need!" said Mr. Halliwell, the portly civilian.

"Oh, I agree with you, sir," said Colonel Fallon. "The worst turn anyone ever did the Army was Bentick's folly in abolishing corporal punishment. If anything encouraged weakened discipline, it was that! Our Indian officers were the strongest against it. I had a deputation of 'em who told me that if we abolished corporal punishment the bad elements in the Army would cease to fear, and would one day turn upon us. Yet we continue to flog British troops, and what is more we permit our sepoy soldiers to witness such floggings. We must be mad!"

A bewhiskered gentleman in the pale blue of the Light Cavalry, who had so far taken no part in the discussion, coughed gently and remarked in a diffident voice: "I myself feel that it is the matter of foreign service and the General Services Enlistment Act that has given rise to any uneasiness that may prevail in some regiments. It will pass, of course. But they are bound to regard it with some suspicion to begin with."

Lord Carlyon turned on the speaker. "The General Services Enlistment Act, did you say? And what is that?"

"Service overseas, sir. The Bengal sepoy enlisted on the understanding that he should not be required to cross the sea."

"Caste again," interpolated Colonel Fallon. "The men believe that crossing the sea would deprive them of their caste. They would have to pay heavily to the priests on their return to be cleansed of the defilement, or else be considered as untouchables—the lowest caste of the Hindus whose touch is pollution to all others. But the Governor-General, with the approval of Mr. Halliwell here and his friends in the Council, recently issued a General Order to the effect that no recruit would in future be accepted who would not undertake to go wherever his services might be required. And that means Burma, sir!—or Persia—or China. Is it not understandable that a caste-ridden, bigoted and superstitious people are willing to believe any agitator who whispers that the British plan to destroy their caste and convert them to Christianity in order that they may become willing tools of the Company, prepared to go anywhere and do anything we tell them in order to gratify our lust for conquest?"

"Am I to take it, Colonel Fallon," said Mr. Halliwell contemptuously, "that you consider your own regiment to be a hotbed of sedition and unrest?"

A dark spot of color burned beneath the brick red of Colonel Fallon's sunburnt cheeks and his hand made a small instinctive gesture toward his dress sword, and fell again. He said hotly: "No, sir! I thank God that my own men are loyal. But I am not blind to the attacks that are being made upon both their loyalty and their credulity by agitators and troublemakers. Neither am I blind to the fact that we have done our best to give the sepoy an overweaning sense of his own importance, while at the same time reducing his respect for authority."

A tall man with a thin gray beard and wearing the insignia of a Brigadier General said coldly: "You forget yourself, Colonel."

Colonel Fallon turned quickly and the flush faded from his cheeks as he became aware that he had permitted his temper to lead him into openly expressed criticism of military policy.

"Perhaps, sir. But I do not forget that our native troops number two

hundred and thirty-three thousand men, while the European soldiery
totals barely more than forty-five thousand of all arms. Those are sobering
figures, sir."

"I do not find it so," declared Mr. Halliwell. "It is well known that one
Britisher is a match for fifty Asiatics any day. Are you not agreed, gentlemen?"

There was a chorus of assent and Colonel Fallon said sharply: "That,
if I may say so, is a remark that could only be made by a civilian and a
politician! I will bid you good evening, sir." He bowed stiffly and walked
angrily away as the Governor-General, who had approached unobserved,
took Lord Carlyon's arm and withdrew him from the group.

"You're looking fagged, Charles," observed Lord Carlyon. "Too many
social functions, or too much heat?"

"Too much work," said Lord Canning wryly. "You should try it, Arthur.
I can use someone even as ornamentally useless as yourself."

"My dear Charles! In what capacity? To dance with the ladies who attend
your crushes? It is the most that you will find me capable of!"

"You underrate yourself, Arthur. I know you to be a superlative horseman and a first class shot."

The younger man stopped suddenly and turned to regard his host nar-
rowly. He said slowly: "What exactly is on your Excellency's mind? Do
you too think as that croaking Colonel in there—that there is going to be
trouble?"

"Was Fallon croaking of disaster again?"

"Like a raven!"

Lord Canning shrugged. "Some people enjoy preaching impending
doom. The effects of this prophecy, I suppose. It's quite astonishing how
superstitious even the most level-headed can become."

"What prophecy?" inquired Carlyon, interested.

"Oh, it's an old tale now. It cropped up after Plassey. The Company's
Raj—rule—was to last for a hundred years after the battle that established
it. And Plassey was fought in 1757."

"So the hundred years are up next year," commented Carlyon. "Very
interesting. But you cannot take this seriously?"

"Naturally not! It is just that—well, I would like you to extend your
stay in this country if that is possible. Will you do that?"

"Why?"

The Governor-General looked down upon the crowded ballroom and
spoke in an undertone that was barely audible above the chatter of voices
and the gay music of the fiddles. "It would be of use to me if you were to
decide to go on an extended tour of this country—in an entirely private
capacity of course; as a casual sight-seer only—and give me your impres-
sions. I find that too many people tell the Governor-General only what
they think will please the Governor-General. There is this question of
Oudh. The ex-King and his swarm of hangers-on are here in Calcutta, and

they deafen me with their complaints as to the behavior of our people in Lucknow. I had hoped . . ."

Lord Carlyon allowed his attention to wander. He had no intention of prolonging his stay in the East, and intended to reach England by the new year. He would not have considered visiting India in the first place had it not been that his skill in managing his amours had temporarily deserted him, and a situation had arisen which had made it seem advisable to pay a protracted visit to foreign parts. His languid gaze rested without interest on the dancers, and then suddenly he ceased to lounge, and gripping the balustrade with both hands, leant over to watch someone in the ballroom below. "By Jove!" said Lord Carlyon under his breath, "it *is* the Ugly Duckling!"

He turned to his host with an unwonted gleam of animation in his bored eyes. "Forgive me, Charles. I see an acquaintance of mine below. Perhaps we may continue this conversation some other time." He turned to descend a flower-decked staircase and was lost to view.

The Governor-General sighed a little tiredly, and retreated to his study to wrestle with the contents of a dispatch box, leaving his wife to do the honors. He had emerged in the gray dawn, when lamps and candles were burning low and carriages drawing away laden with yawning men, sleepy dowagers and excited, laughing girls, to find Lord Carlyon escorting a stout matron in a crimson opera mantle across the hall and into a closed carriage. Lord Carlyon handed her into the carriage with a display of affability most unusual in him, and stood back to allow a tubby gentleman in the uniform of a colonel of native infantry to follow her. The carriage drove away and Lord Carlyon turned and walked slowly across the hall between the crowd of gorgeously uniformed servants, to stop at the unexpected sight of his host.

"Ah, Charles—I imagined that you had very sensibly decided to retire to bed."

"Who was that?" inquired Canning without much curiosity.

"No one of interest. A Mrs. Abuthnot." Lord Carlyon glanced down at the wilting flower in his buttonhole, removed it and dropped it onto the polished marble floor. "By the way, Charles," he said softly, "you will be interested to hear that I have decided to take your advice. I intend to extend my stay in India. I shall visit Delhi, and I may even return by way of Oudh."

9

"CAN we take our own road from here?" asked Niaz* Mahomed.

Alex turned away from the window of the sparsely furnished dak bungalow room and dropped the split-cane curtain back into place.

"Is there need?"

"Great need," said Niaz, busy with the straps of a dusty valise. "It was not advisable to speak while there were many to overhear, but now—"

"Here there are also ears," said Alex with a jerk of his head toward the long veranda outside where the shadow of a loitering servant lay upon the sun-warmed stone.

Alex and his orderly had left Calcutta by train. The new railway, one of Lord Dalhousie's most admired strides toward the westernization of his Eastern Empire, now reached as far as Raniganj, a distance of over a hundred and forty miles north of Calcutta. But from this point the remainder of the journey must be accomplished by road.

Alex and Niaz had left the train, hot, dusty and coated with grit and cinders; and having slept the night at Raniganj in company with Colonel Moulson and a varied assortment of troops and travelers moving north, had proceeded for several days' journey toward Benares by dak-*ghari*, a four-wheeled, cablike vehicle drawn by two horses. The roads, as a result of the monsoon, were unspeakably bad; the half-starved ponies made poor time, and Alex' traveling companion, a morose major on his way to rejoin his regiment at Benares, did little or nothing toward improving the discomforts of the journey. On the fourth day the entire *ghari* overturned down the side of an embankment. Its passengers, including the coachman, escaped unhurt, and had made their way to the nearest dak bungalow— happily only a scant mile ahead.

There were several other dak-*gharies* waiting at the bungalow while their passengers partook of such refreshment as its khansamah could provide, and the morose major lost no time in arranging for one of them to take him up. But Niaz suggested that he should procure two horses locally so that he and Alex might dispense with the services of another *ghari*. "When there is work to do it is better to travel alone," said Niaz, his dark face blandly expressionless, "and I have a friend in the village."

Niaz was a Punjabi Mussulman whose home was north of Karnal. He came of a family of well-to-do landowners of some consequences whose daughters would seem to have married far from the family acres, for Niaz appeared to possess blood relations in half the provinces of India. Born in

* Nee-ahz

the same year as Alex Randall, he had served in the same regiment of cavalry and had fought at his side at Moodkee and later at Ferozeshah. Alex' horse had been hamstrung at Moodkee by a wounded Sikh in a charge that silenced the guns of the Khalsa Army, and Niaz had risen in his stirrups and by some miracle of horsemanship had gripped Alex and dragged him clear as the horse fell. A moment later he had slipped to the ground and Alex was in his saddle with Niaz holding the stirrup leather and fighting beside him in the swaying, maddened melee, yelling joyfully as he had yelled in the charge: "*Shahbash, Bhaiyan! Dauro! Dauro!*" ("Well done, brothers! Ride! Ride!")

Four days later, at Ferozeshah, Alex had repaid the debt when Niaz had fallen with a bullet through his chest, and Alex, his own horse killed, bestrode the wounded man and fought above him in the storming of the Sikh entrenchments. Since then Niaz had attached himself to Alex as orderly and body servant, and when Alex had been removed on special duty he had managed, through the judicious use of influence in the right quarters, to gain permission for Niaz to accompany him. Niaz had been granted extended leave during the past year, and Alex had left certain specific and unofficial instructions that he had no doubt at all that Niaz would have carried out.

The dak-*gharies* and the morose major departed in a cloud of dust, and quiet descended upon the bungalow. But the shadow of the loitering servant did not move, and Alex said reflectively: "Bring my gun. There will be quail and partridge in the open country beyond, and I am stiff from jolting in that dak-*ghari*."

Niaz grinned appreciatively and went out to inform the khansamah that the sahib wished to shoot and would return for an evening meal which had better be of the first quality, or he, Niaz, would have something to say on the subject.

Alex strolled down the shallow stone steps of the veranda and walked slowly away through a mango tope that lay to the left of the bungalow. The evening sun thrust shafts of dusty gold between the tree trunks, and a troop of monkeys chattered and quarreled among the thick leaves. Facing the bungalow the jungle through which the road had run swept almost to the compound wall, but behind it and to the left lay comparatively open country; a few fields where crops of maize and sugar cane had been planted, grazing grounds and a glimmer of water that indicated a distant jheel and the probable presence of waterfowl.

The ground in the mango tope was hard and dry and splashed with the droppings of green pigeons, and a warm shaft of sunlight, probing the shadows, illuminated a slab of stone crudely carved with the lingam, the emblem of fertility, that stood propped against the bole of a tree. The obscene thing was daubed with red paint and there were offerings heaped upon the ground before it. Humble offerings: a handful of parched grain, a bunch of marigold flowers, a string of red jungle beads and the remains of a chapatty—the flat cake of unleavened bread that is the staple food of half India.

Alex paused and regarded the crude emblem with some interest. There was nothing at all unusual in the sight, for India was littered with such things. It was the offerings that surprised him. The flowers were unfaded and the grain and the cake of unleavened bread must have been placed here comparatively recently, for birds and squirrels would make short work of them. Yet he had seen no one go near the mango tope, and it was unusual for villagers to bring offerings to a shrine at such an hour.

There was a light step behind him and Alex turned to see Niaz, who carried a shotgun and a bag of cartridges. Niaz glanced at the red-daubed emblem of Mahadeo and said cheerfully: "Misbegotten unbelievers!" He spat on the ground and jerked a thumb over his shoulder in the direction of the bungalow: "The driver of the dak-*ghari*, brought the offerings. There was, I think, a message also, but it has gone. See there in the dust—"

The hard, dry ground of the mango tope did not hold the print of footmarks well, but the day was windless and dust, twigs and fallen leaves betrayed a well-worn track from the bungalow to the shrine, while beyond it the print of unshod feet showed where a single man had approached from the direction of the grazing grounds and the open plain, and returned again.

Niaz moved slowly out of the shadows of the tope, his eyes on the ground. Presently he said: "Here he turns aside and returns to the village. It is an old trick to thrust a message into a chapatty and bake it so that it is well hid. But the driver of that *ghari* was a Mussulman and no Hindu."

Alex nodded without speaking and turned to look out across the plain, his eyes screwed up against the low sunlight. A black partridge was calling, and he held out his hand for the gun. He was an excellent shot, and Niaz was carrying half a dozen limp feathered forms by the time they reached the edge of the jheel—a shallow stretch of water fringed with straggling rushes, stray clumps of elephant grass and a few scanty palms that stood up against the bright evening sky like worn broomsticks.

Alex sat down on a tussock of dry grass with his back to the open water at the end of a narrow arm of stony ground that reached out into the jheel. He pulled a packet of paper and a pouch of tobacco out of his pocket and rolled two cigarettes—a habit he had acquired in the Crimea—and tossed one over to Niaz who squatted beside him.

Niaz struck a sulphur match on the sole of his shoe, and having lit the cigarettes blew the flame out carefully and flicked the spent match into the placid water. "There are no ears here," he remarked approvingly, "and none can approach by the water. We need watch the landward only."

He drew the tobacco smoke deep into his lungs and expelled it slowly through his nostrils. The evening was warm and very still. So still that they could hear the leap of a little fish a dozen yards away, the quack of

water birds far out on the jheel and the rustle of a small snake that slid
through the grass stems.

Alex had learned patience with much else in the East, and he knew
that Niaz would speak when he wished to—and not before. Meanwhile
it was pleasant to sit here and smell the familiar scents of an Indian
evening, while the sky behind the ragged palm trees blazed with the
spectacular glories of a sunset unimaginable to those who live only in
Western latitudes.

Presently Niaz said reflectively: "I did as thou asked. I took my leave
and went on horseback, as befits one of the risala (cavalry) to visit those
of my relatives in Oudh and Rohilkhand and Jhansi, and from them I
heard much. And when that was done I went on foot, and no longer as
Niaz Mahomed Khan of the Company's risala, but as Rahim, a man of
no consequence. From Ludhiana of the Sikhs to the north of my own
ilaqua, to Benares of the Unbelievers, and further south to Burdwan went
I, listening to much talk in the twilight and hearing many things in the
bazaars and by the way."

He turned his eyes on Alex and said: "Thou wert right, my brother.
There is devil's work toward, and this time it is not a plague that will
break out in one spot only and may thereby be kept from others. This
runs north and south, and the infection is carried by many and to all
men. Even by such as the drivers of these dak-*gharies!* There are also
many tales told of signs and wonders, and the prophecy of the Hundred
Years is spoken in every village throughout Hind."

"There is always talk," said Alex laconically, his eyes on a high-flying
wedge of garganey teal that cut a thin dark pattern against the quiet sky.

"That I know. But this time it is more than talk. There is a grievance
among the sepoys on account of pay, and so the old grievances, that have
never slept, are spoken of once more—that the Company desires to destroy
all caste, and that the rail-*ghari* and the telegraph, the jails and hospitals
are weapons for the destruction of caste. The foolish talk of missionary-
log adds fuel to that fire, for they and many of the Company's officers
tell the people of Hind that their customs and practices are evil and must
be abolished. Perhaps this is so; I do not know. But these customs are
as a tree that is deep rooted, and if the trunk be cut down, there are still
the roots. . . ."

He paused, but Alex made no comment, and sat silent, waiting.

"It has long been a custom of Hind," said Niaz slowly, "for a man who
has no heir to adopt one who shall succeed him. For the son, say the
Unbelievers, delivers his father from the hell called *Pat*, and if there be no
son to perform the funeral rites, they believe that there can be no resur-
rection to eternal bliss. Therefore their priests and lawgivers have permitted the adoption of sons where the male line has failed. Comes the
order of the Company saying that where there is no male heir of the
blood the lands and titles of a prince shall not pass to any adoptive son,
but pass instead into the possession of the Company, and that that man's

line shall die out and cease. Thus many states, by right of lapse, have
been swallowed up into the maw of the Company and their ancient names
have become as dust—Satara, Nagpur, Sambalpur, Jhansi—their greatness
has departed."

Alex said softly: "These be Hindus, O follower of the Prophet!"

"That is so. But now there is Oudh also, and therefore Hindu and
Mussulman, Unbelievers and the Elect of God plot together in fear and
hatred, and the word goes up and down the land."

"And what is that word?"

"That the Feringis (foreigners) are few and their councils are divided,
and that the men of the North, the Russ-*log*, have made so great a
slaughter of their armies that there are none left to come to the aid of
those in Hind. The head and the heart of this evil lies in Oudh, for it
is from thence that the whisper goes forth, carried into the towns and
villages by a hundred different ways. It runs from pulton (regiment) to
pulton—from risala to risala. It is carried by men on pilgrimage to the
shrines of Kashi and Haramuk; by merchants, mulvis, sadhus; Mussulman, Brahmin, Sikh and Jain. They spill the powder, and when the train
is laid it will need but a spark to ignite it.

"But that spark must be something that touches Mussulman and Hindu
alike, for if one should rise without the other the Company, few and
weak as they have become, may still triumph. Therefore they seek dili-
gently. Are thy people blind or mad, or both, that they cannot see what
is toward?"

"Neither," said Alex. "It is a national conceit. They—we—can only see
ourselves as benefactors whom such as thou"—he grinned maliciously at
Niaz—"must perforce regard only with admiration and gratitude."

"And do they never learn?" inquired Niaz scornfully.

Alex shrugged. The swift tropic twilight was almost gone and he could
no longer see Niaz's face clearly. He said abruptly: "All this is talk. Have
you proof?"

"Proof!" said Niaz and laughed shortly. "Spoken like a sahib—*Sahib!*"
He gave that title the same scornful emphasis that Kishan Prasad had
once done.

"Niaz," said Alex gently, "were it not that thou art my brother in all
but blood, I would throw thee into the jheel for that word!"

Niaz threw up a hand in mock appeal: "*Marf karo* (have mercy),
Sahib!"

Alex caught the upflung hand about the wrist and bent it backward,
and for a moment the two men wrestled silently, hand against hand.

"Is it to be the jheel, then?" inquired Alex.

"Nay, it is enough! *Marf karo—bhai!* (brother)."

"That is better," said Alex, releasing him.

Niaz rubbed his wrist and grinned. "At least thy sojourn in Belait has
not softened thee! Well, thou shalt have thy proof, though small good
will it give thee."

"Ah!" said Alex, his eyes suddenly bright. "I thought that there was something more. Tell me swiftly, and let us have no more of this talk that runs in circles."

Niaz glanced uneasily over his shoulder as though to make sure that there could be no third person near by, and despite the fact that nothing larger than a jackal could possibly have approached within fifty yards of them without being seen, he lowered his voice until it was barely audible.

"I have learned," whispered Niaz, "that there is to be a meeting of certain men in a place near Khanwai that lies to the north of Bithaur within the borders of Oudh. It is dangerous knowledge and known only to a few. Perhaps a hundred in all Hind. No more. It is set for a night but twelve days hence, when there is a fair at Khanwai. Those who know will attend—for the frolic, or so it will seem—and by night these will walk apart from the press and steal away to the jungle near by where there is the place of meeting. I have been to spy out the land. The place is a ruin; no more than a handful of stones and a broken wall which the jungle has swallowed. A foolish place for such talk, but these men are assuredly bitten with madness. There is but one path to it, for the jungle grows thick behind it, and the path leads through a deep nullah where was once a gateway that has fallen. Only one man at a time can pass through, and each as they pass must say a word. That word I have."

Once again he paused to peer into the gathering dusk, and in the silence they heard from somewhere far out across the darkening plains a jackal howling at the evening star. Niaz's gaze returned to Alex and even the green dusk could not disguise the glitter of his eyes and the flash of his teeth.

"You old devil!" said Alex in English—the same glitter in his own eyes. "Was the overturning of that dak-*ghari* thy work?"

Niaz waved a deprecatory hand. "I judged it to be necessary," he said airily. "Also the driver was an unfriend of mine. I owed him somewhat in the matter of repayment for certain insolence that he had spoken. He was an eater of opium and he dozed upon the box. A twitch of the reins, and the thing was done. It was necessary that we should separate ourselves from those others who traveled by the road. Do we go to Khanwai?"

"Assuredly," said Alex, and laughed. It was a laugh that men hear sometimes in the heat of battle or as the order is given for a cavalry charge, and that no woman would recognize. Niaz recognized it and his own laugh answered and echoed it. "It is well!" he said. "Come, give me the gun. It is time that we returned."

10

TEN days later an itinerant toy seller, his pack laden with crudely painted plaster trifles, trudged down the dusty road that led from Cawnpore into Oudh. He had no assistant, but he was of a cheerful and gregarious disposition and always ready to enter into conversation with fellow travelers upon the road and at the wayside halts. At one of these he had attached himself to a party of jugglers who were proceeding to the fair at Khanwai, a small village on the borders of Oudh, not far from Bithaur.

His ready wit and the quick-fire patter with which he accompanied the sale of his gimcrack toys appealed to the leader of the troop, and after some haggling it was agreed that the man, Jatu by name, should act as barker to the jugglers in the intervals of pursuing his own trade. In return for which the troop would provide him with food and, if profits allowed, a small percentage of the takings; an arrangement that appeared highly satisfactory to all.

From the opposite direction, that of Fathigarh, a slim, wiry Pathan, sitting astride a bony and bad-tempered down-country stallion and trailed by two sorry-looking hacks on a lead rein, was also riding toward the fair at Khanwai. His dress and speech, and the hard, light-colored eyes in the brown face, proclaimed him as a son of the border tribe of the Usafzai, and he too was of a cheerful disposition, for he sang the songs of the border—the more questionable ones—as he rode, and was always ready to fall into talk with any he met upon the road.

His cousin Assad Ali, he explained to any who were interested, had brought a string of horses down from the north, hoping to sell them for greater profit in the Punjab and Rohilkhand, and had done well with his string. But he had died of cholera at a village on the outskirts of Delhi, and the horse boys, fearing the disease, had run away, taking with them the greater part of the profits. Wherefore he, Sher Dil, with only three unsalable hacks picked up at Karnal, had been forced to take the road alone, hoping to dispose of them farther south. He had heard talk of a fair at Khanwai, and intended to try his luck there. He carried a long Pathan knife in his broad waist belt, and an antiquated but service-able jezail slung over his shoulder, together with a well-stocked cartridge belt, and he took for preference the center of the road. Alex had always been a believer in the old saying that it is darkest under the lamp.

The town of Khanwai was little more than a village, and distinguished only by the annual fair which was held in honor of a treaty between two warring clans who, centuries ago, had endeavored to exterminate each other for reasons long lost sight of in the mists of time. It was a humble affair and not to be compared with such things in larger cities, but it attracted its crowds and provided a yearly excuse for gaiety for the neighboring villages.

The fairground was surrounded by the booths of sweetmeat sellers, toy makers and hucksters, and there was plenty to entertain the idle. Jugglers, acrobats, fire-eaters, a sad and ragged performing bear, snake charmers and fortunetellers; and when night fell a troop of fireworks makers brightened the sky with a display of their wares and frightened the timorous with the crash of exploding rockets. But as the fireworks flared, dyeing the awed faces of the spectators red, green and amber by turns, it might have been noted, had any been interested in such a thing, that sundry men were drifting away from the fairground by ones and twos and making their way through the fields beyond the village to the uncultivated land and the dark barrier of the jungle that backed on the grazing grounds.

Sher Dil of the Usafzai, following the same path, caught his garments on an unseen branch of thorn tree and swore softly and fluently in Pushto as he freed himself, and a shadow that followed noiselessly on his heels lengthened its stride and spoke in a whisper: "Hai! thou from the north" —Alex checked and his hand went to the knife in his belt—"what dost thou here? Thou art a Pathan and no man of Hind."

"I come that I may carry the word to those who wait beyond the border," replied Alex in whispered Urdu. "And thou?"

"I likewise, but to Bengal go I. To Berhampore by Murshidabad. Of what pulton art thou?"

"Of none. But my cousin's brother is a duffarder in the Guides," said Alex mendaciously. "He too is like-minded with us. And thy regiment?"

"The 19th Bengal Infantry." He was a Purbeah sepoy on leave; a lance naik, and a man of some influence in his regiment. He hurried on ahead and was lost in the shadows.

The flare of the fireworks from the fairground lit the path with intermittent flashes of light, and in these brief glimpses Alex could see that there were men ahead and behind him hurrying forward down the narrow track that wound between thickets of thorn, bamboos, dhak trees and elephant grass, and keeping a safe distance from each other. Niaz had studied the ground with the eye of a general, and a map that he had drawn in the dust of the roadside, though crude, had been remarkably accurate, so that even by night and on strange ground Alex could guess the lay of the land and knew what to expect.

The path—it was little more than a goat track—having wandered with apparent aimlessness between tall clumps of grass, descended a sandy slope into a dry nullah. To the right the nullah ran straight on into the darkness, but to the left it narrowed and appeared to be blocked by a fall of rock. The sepoy could not have been half a dozen yards ahead, but he had vanished, and Alex, turning unhesitatingly to the left, was once again grateful for the care with which Niaz had reconnoitered the ground. There was a space between two huge slabs of fallen rock that would have been invisible to one who was not aware of it, for the rocks overlapped each other and were overgrown with creepers and the roots of a tree, and only a close inspection by full daylight would have discovered the gap.

It was barely wide enough to allow one at a time to enter it, and behind it—Niaz had told him—lay a narrow, walled tunnel; for this had once been the outer gateway of a fortress whose walls ran back to left and right, hidden and overgrown by the trees and creepers of the jungle. Alex heard feet slither on the path behind him as another conspirator entered the nullah, and he set his teeth and walked between the rocks.

He had taken no more than four steps in the blackness when his outstretched hands touched the shaft of a spear that barred his way. It dropped instantly and after a moment's pause he moved forward again and heard it lift once more behind him and heard too a man's quick breathing. Making sure we go through one at a time, thought Alex grimly. He could see no glimmer of light and his hands brushed against rough stonework. Niaz had said that the tunnel of the ruined gateway was no more than eight fair paces in length; that meant that there was something or someone blocking the far end of it. And then he saw a glimpse of grayness and something touched his chest—an ironbound lathee such as nightwatchmen carry—and a voice almost in his ear whispered: "Give the word."

"A goat for Kali."

"Pass, brother." The lathee dropped and Alex moved on into the open air.

The sides of the nullah were steeper and narrower here than on the far side of the concealed entrance, and the jungle arched above it and excluded the moonlight so that the place was almost as dark as the tunnel behind. Then the darkness thinned and torchlight glowed through the undergrowth ahead, and presently the track ran out into a clearing before the ruins of a long-forgotten fort or palace.

The starlight and a half-moon, the flaming torches and the occasional flare of a rocket, illuminated roofless walls and fallen pillars half hidden by weeds and creepers. A giant peepul tree split the stones of what might once have been a hall of audience, and in the uncertain light it was difficult to tell which were fallen pillars and which the roots of the great tree. India is full of such ruins; relics of cities and dynasties that have passed away and been forgotten; the haunt of snakes, foxes and monkeys, and the lair of the wild boar.

It seemed to Alex an odd spot to choose for a meeting of malcontents, except that there was little doubt that the place had a certain eerie atmosphere about it, and though it lay less than half a mile from Khanwai and the beaten track, its presence would never have been suspected by the casual passer-by. He could see now that the clearing was not a natural one but the remains of what had once been a large, stone-paved courtyard open to the sky. Thornbushes and the tough jungle grass had thrust their way between the sandstone blocks, but the jungle had been unable to obliterate it and stood back from it, walling it about with impenetrable vegetation.

The open space was crowded with shadowy figures and sibilant with whispering voices, and Alex stood still, the lance naik of the 19th breathing heavily beside him. At the far side of the square, before the ruined entrance to a roofless hall, stood two men holding torches—flaring countrymade things of dried grass, branches and pitch. They stood as though waiting, and the orange light flickered weirdly on the rolling eyeballs of the shifting, whispering crowd and threw grotesque shadows on the wall of the watching jungle.

Presently there was a stir among the men at Alex' back and the crowd drew aside, Alex with them, as half a dozen men muffled in dark cloaks entered the clearing by way of the nullah. It seemed that they had been expected, for the crowd made a lane for them, parting to left and right, and they passed quickly through and came to a stop before the torchbearers. They stood for a few moments talking in undertones with a small group of men who had apparently been waiting for them, while the crowd ceased its whispering to listen.

Alex was too far away to hear what was said, and it is doubtful if any but a handful heard them, for at that point the fireworks on the distant fairground let off a very fusillade of rockets. This is too easy, thought Alex, waiting for them to mount the ruined steps behind them from which he imagined that they would harangue the crowd. There must be a catch in it somewhere. A line from a nursery rhyme drifted through his brain: " 'Will you walk into my parlor?' said the spider to the fly." It had been easy enough to walk in. Would it be as easy to walk out again?

The group of men by the torchbearers turned, but they did not mount the steps behind them as Alex had half expected. They walked between the torches and simply disappeared as though the ground itself had opened and swallowed them up.

From where Alex stood the illusion was so complete that he heard the men about him gasp and shrink back, and saw the sepoy put up a hand to clutch at some hidden amulet he wore concealed under his shirt. Then the crowd began to move slowly forward and Alex realized suddenly that the torchbearers stood on either side of a shaft that descended into the ground. There was a chamber, then, that lay beneath the ruined hall, an underground vault for the storage of grain or treasure. As he drew nearer he saw that the two men with the torches scrutinized the faces of all who went past them. A hand touched Alex in the press and he turned to see Jatu, the seller of toys.

"They will never let thee pass. Try the ring!" The words were barely a breath against his ear, and then the man had melted into the darkness and was gone.

Alex moved forward, a step at a time. He was conscious of a cold, tingling sensation between his shoulder blades and was aware that his mouth was dry. For a fleeting moment he wondered what would happen if the ring meant nothing to the guardians of the shaft? Would they let him stand to one side and wait as others were waiting, or would they?— The light of the torches flared full in his face and his nerves tightened and leapt, but the hand he held out was entirely steady.

The three small stones in Kishan Prasad's ring gleamed redly in the torchlight, and the ring appeared a small and insignificant thing; but the men who held the torches evidently recognized it. One of them, bending forward to stare at it, muttered something that Alex did not catch, and salaamed low, and Alex walked between them and down a steep, narrow flight of steps, aware that the palms of his hands were wet and that there were drops of cold sweat on his forehead.

The entrance to the shaft had been concealed by a huge flagstone that had been drawn up with ropes, and it must have taken at least two men to move it. The walls of the shaft were smooth and dry and the worn steps so steep and narrow that only one man at a time could possibly have descended them. They went down farther into the ground than Alex would have believed possible, and once again he had the sensation of walking into a trap. A bat flew up past him, its leathery wings brushing his cheek—proof at least that there was some other entrance—and then he had reached the foot of the steps at last and was standing in a vaulted chamber, the roof of which was supported by crude stone pillars.

It was impossible to gauge the full extent of the underground room, for the walls beyond the pillars were lost in darkness and the only illumination was supplied by a single brazier, supported on an iron tripod that stood at the far end of the vault, in which an uneasy flame burned flickeringly. The stone floor and the pillars were slimy to the touch, and not dry as were the walls of the stair shaft, and in the faint light of the brazier Alex could see tree roots that had thrust down between the curved slabs of the vaulted ceiling. That accounted for the bats and the fact that the air was breathable. Perhaps this underground room had once held the hoarded treasures of a king, or been used as a torture chamber, or for some dark priestly purpose. Possibly the latter, for there appeared to be carvings on the wall behind the brazier.

There seemed to be between thirty or forty men squatting on the stone floor between the pillars, but it was difficult to tell in that uncertain light whether there were yet more of them whom Alex could not see. He edged his way toward a pillar and squatted down by it, Indian fashion, keeping his back to the stone. He could hear hard breathing all about him and smell the rank smell of unwashed human bodies, and as his eyes became accustomed to the dimness he saw that many of those present were sadhus—holy men of all sects and persuasions; wild eyed and ash smeared, naked or wearing the ill-cured skins of animals, their long hair matted and hideous—Bairagis, Sannyasis, Bikshus, Paryrajakas; Aghoris whose custom it is to steal and eat the flesh of corpses; devil worshipers, mendicants and mystics.

Alex shuddered and felt his skin crawl, and was grateful for the feel of the dank stone at his back. But it was not the presence of the Hindu ascetics that made him afraid. It was the unbelievable, impossible fact that there were others in that ill-lit underground vault. Not only Sikhs, but Mussulmans also; followers of the Prophet to whom all Hindus were dogs of unbelievers. Yet they were here too; crouching side by side with the worshipers of Shiva the Destroyer, of Vishnu and Brahma and Ganesh of the elephant head; of many-armed Mother Kali the drinker of blood, and of a hundred other gods and godlings. It was true, then. Mussulman and Hindu were prepared to combine against the men of John Company —against the white-faced foreign conquerors whose dominion had lasted for a hundred years. Nothing but a common cause and a common hatred could have brought about this weird gathering.

A man stood up at the far end of the chamber, towering above the crouching figures that filled the aisle between the stone pillars. His back was to the fitful flame of the brazier and Alex could not see his face, but the voice and dress told him much.

The man was a Mussulman and probably from Oudh. A tall man with a silver tongue. He spoke quietly and with a curious suggestion of a chant; the voice of a priest or a storyteller. And the tale he told was the story of a conquered people; trampled, cheated, robbed and exploited by the men from the West—from the land beyond the Black Water. He spoke of kings and princes who had died fighting the Company, or been defrauded of their rights. Of great names and great houses that had become as the blown sands of the deserts of Bikaner. Of cherished laws and customs and religious freedoms that had been curtailed or put aside. Of sheltered zenana women, queens and princesses in their own right, forced to beg their bread in the streets. His voice rose and sank and the men before him swayed and groaned in unison as though they were so many puppets pulled upon a single string.

Even Alex found himself stirred to anger or intolerably moved by that wild, bitter, sorrowful saga, and he could not have told for how long the man spoke—it might have been for an hour, or two hours, or three. The flame in the brazier flickered and danced, and the shadow of the speaker leapt and shrank and leapt again across that motley mob of listening men with an effect as hypnotic as the remarkable voice. The man ended with an impassioned plea for unity: "They of the Company be few! A handful only, scattered up and down the land. We of Hind have risen against them many times, but the risings have always failed. They have failed because we of this land were divided one against the other. But it is well known that ten men with one heart are equal to a hundred men with different hearts, and it needs only this—that we hold together with one heart—and we are rid of them forever. Let us put aside our differences and strike as one!"

He flung up his arms with a wild gesture and the crowd gasped and shrank back, for a green fire seemed to run up his arms and leap for a moment from his spread fingers. But the spell had snapped for Alex. He had seen that trick performed by an illusionist at a London theater, and sanity returned to him; and with it an icy sense of danger. If this man could sway others as he had swayed this bigoted, caste-ridden, creed-divided assembly tonight, he was more dangerous to the Company than anything that had as yet risen against them.

Another man was speaking. A Hindu this time. His theme was the same but his shrill, impassioned oratory lacked the almost hypnotic appeal of the previous speaker, and Alex allowed his attention to wander and concentrated instead on trying to memorize the members of the audience and file their features away for future use. It was no easy task in that wavering light, but there were several faces that he thought he would recognize again.

The talk went on and on and Alex shifted restlessly. During his first years in India, when he and Niaz would take leave together and go off shooting, he had taught himself to squat, native fashion, on his heels. Although Alex' gray eyes had made it impossible for him to pass as any but a hillman or a northerner, it had amused him to study and copy the habits and customs and speech of many kinds of men; a game which Niaz, who was a natural mimic, had entered into with enthusiasm. But he had spent the last year and more in Europe and his muscles had grown unused to the treatment they were receiving. They ached abominably, and he wondered how much longer this performance was going to last.

Yet another man was speaking. A sadhu this time. His message was less general and more specific. Spread the word! Carry it into every town and every village. Tell every man to be ready; to procure arms and secrete them; to steal them if necessary! To sharpen his sword, his ax or his knife and to tip his lathee with iron. The coming year was the Year of the Prophecy in which the Hundred Years of Subjection would be accomplished. Man, woman and child, the oppressors would be slain, so that not one would remain to carry the tale to the West.

"Carry the word! Carry the word!" The hoarse, hysterical voice rang and echoed uncannily under the vaulted stone. "See—now we prepare a sign as in the old days, so that all men may know!"

A shaven priest arose and threw something on the brazier, and the flame flared up with a sudden intolerable brightness that for a brief moment threw the avid faces into harsh relief. It died again and in the near darkness that followed a second priest began a chant that was taken up by other voices.

The light flickered up again, though dimly, as the two priests moved about it, coming and going, and the crowd craned their necks to see. Alex would have given much to stand upright and look over the heads and backs that obscured his view, but he did not dare to draw attention to himself by doing so. He could catch only glimpses between the silhouetted heads. Something was being poured onto a platter; it appeared to be *ata* —the coarse-ground flour of the villages—and a man squatting near the brazier began to beat on a small drum, softly at first, so that it was barely more than a rhythmic accompaniment to the chant, but growing slowly louder and more insistent. Gradually the chant changed its note and became a frenzied incantation, and Alex recognized it as a hymn to Kali:

"*Kali! Kali! O dreadful-toothed Goddess! Devour, cut, destroy all the malignant—cut with an ax! Bind, bind, seize! Drink blood! Secure, secure! Salutation to Kali!*"

The ranks of half-seen men began to jerk and sway and once more one of the two priests flung something on the brazier; but this time the brief flare of the flame was followed by a dense smoke that whirled upward and filled the darkness with a choking smell akin to incense. A heady, stupefying smell that drugged and yet exhilarated. The other priest who had moved back into the shadows returned dragging something that struggled feebly and gave a small bleating cry. A sacrifice, of course, thought Alex. A white goat for Kali. They would cut the creature's throat with suitable ritual.

He saw the light glint on the long blade of a knife, and the men nearest the priests and the brazier drew back and caught their breath in a harsh and simultaneous gasp that was clearly audible above the thudding beat of the drum. A shudder swept back through the crowd as a wave sweeps in from the open sea, so that even those who could not see felt the surge of that savage emotion, and Alex was seized with a sudden sick horror, inexplicable and paralyzing. A horror that crisped his hair and dried his mouth and brought the cold sweat out on his forehead.

He would have moved then, but he could not. His muscles would not obey him, for he was helplessly afraid with a fear that he had never known before. A primitive, primeval fear; not of death, but of Evil. . . . He could hear the harsh, panting breath of the men about him and it seemed to him as though they breathed as a pack of wolves might breathe, avidly, tongues lolling, circling about a wounded buck.

The smoke from the brazier faded and the flame leapt clear, and as it did so a man near it sprang to his feet with a hoarse cry. It was, thought Alex, the tall man who had first spoken, and for a moment his face showed clear in the leaping light. A harsh, hawk-nosed face whose deep-set eyes were white ringed with horror. He called out something that Alex did not hear, for the drum beat louder and the chant rose to a frenzy. Someone in the crowd pulled the man back, and the knife flashed and fell. There was a bubbling, agonized cry, shrill and high and almost instantly drowned in the concerted groaning howl of the crowd. But it had not been an animal's cry, and Alex stumbled to his feet and stood pressed against the slimy stone of the pillar, and saw what it was that had cried out.

It was not the body of a white goat that lay on the slab of stained and reeking stone below the flickering brazier, but the naked body of a child. A white child. Alex caught a momentary glimpse of yellow hair and a

small mouth that gaped from that last shriek of terror above the gaping
scarlet gash of the severed throat. It was a boy of no more than three or
four years of age, his small body startlingly white against the dark stone
and the bright blood.

A blind, killing rage laid hold of Alex, blotting out reason and any
thought of caution. His hand fumbled in the breast of the flowing Pathan
shirt and closed upon the warm metal of the pistol he carried hidden
there. At that range he could not miss the priest who stood above the
child's body. He would kill him and his fellow priest who held the bowl,
and three others. And after that there was still his knife—

He jerked out the pistol and leveled it, and as he did so the man immediately in front of him rose, momentarily blocking his view, and turned
to grope his way into the blackness beyond the line of pillars. But that
moment had been enough. Sanity returned to Alex and the red fog of
rage cleared from his brain. There were more important things at stake
than avenging the slaughter of a child. The lives and safety of other children and of countless men and women might hang upon his ability to
leave that underground den alive. It would do no good to anyone were he
to die too, even though he were to take a dozen of that evil company with
him to the grave. The thing was too big. It would go forward and spread,
and there would be one less to raise a warning voice. Niaz too would not
live to carry a warning, for he too would fight.

Alex slid the pistol back into hiding and wiped the sweat out of his
eyes. The horrible ritual of the sacrifice had drawn all eyes and there had
been no one watching him. He sank down again onto his heels and found
that he was shivering violently. The man who had stolen away into the
darkness had left him a clearer field of vision, and once more someone
threw a substance on the brazier which hissed and flared and burnt with a
bright flame, throwing the faces nearest to it into strong relief. One face
in particular caught Alex' attention. A dark, gloating face, contorted with
hate and excitement, the eyes wide and glittering and avid. Red stones—
rubies from their color—adorned his ears and flashed upon his quivering
hands. I shall know that man again, at least, thought Alex.

There was some ritual being performed that he could see but not
understand, and then he realized that the fresh blood was being mixed
with the flour on the platter. He caught the familiar movements of knead-
ing that he had seen a thousand times before in the lines and beside
campfires and in the bazaars. They were making a chapatty, the daily
bread of India. To the droning accompaniment of strange incantations
and the ceaseless, maddening thud of the drum the cake was kneaded,
shaped, flattened and baked on a metal platter laid across the glowing
brazier. And all the while, to the sound of that chanting, the rows of
watching men swayed and bowed and groveled on the ground in a state
of half-hypnotic frenzy.

At last the platter was lifted off the fire and the priests of Kali broke
up the cake that smoked upon it, mumbling and grunting invocations to

gods and devils—invocations as old and as evil as those chanted in the temples of Moloch. The man with the ruby earrings was handed a square of silk by someone behind him, and laying it across his hands he received the broken pieces of the chapatty from the priests.

"Let the token be sent forth!" howled the tallest of the priests, tossing his arms above his head. "Let it go up and down the land. From the north to the south, from the east to the west! And where it passes, there shall men's hearts be turned to hatred of the oppressors. For this is the pestilence—this is the evil—this is the blood of the British!" His eyeballs rolled in his head and there was froth on his lips. "Hear me, Kali! Hear me, O drinker of blood! From the north to the south! From the east to the west!"

He fell to the ground and writhed upon the stone floor as the second priest flung oil into the brazier and a crackling flame leapt upward to roof, blazed furiously for a moment and died. The drum crashed and was still. The chanting ceased on a long, wailing note and the vault was plunged into darkness and silence—a darkness in which only the red coals of the brazier gleamed like a single malignant eye.

A voice spoke softly into that silence. "This that ye have witnessed shall be binding upon all; for were it known, there is not one here whom the Feringis would not hang at a rope's end for this night's work. In the eyes of the Company's government all who have seen it would be held guilty of the blood that has been shed, and it were well to remember that, lest any be tempted to speak unwisely." The voice ceased, and presently man after man rose noiselessly and groped their way to the stair shaft to pass up it and out into the clean night air.

Once there, they did not linger but seemed anxious to avoid each other's company, emerging from the shaft like ants debouching from a hole in the ground, to hurry furtively away into the darkness.

The torchbearers had gone and the stone-paved square with its surrounding wall of jungle was shadowy under the starlight and the waning moon. Alex made his way down the black length of the nullah, guided by a spark of light that proved to be a single *chirag*—a tiny earthenware saucer filled with oil in which a wisp of cotton did duty as a wick—which had been left on a ledge by the narrow cleft of the gateway. He saw the spark vanish briefly as the man ahead of him passed in front of it and entered the tunnel, and then he himself had reached it.

11

THREE minutes later Alex was climbing the goat track on the far side of the nullah, and then he was among the high grass at the edge of the plain.

A hand touched his arm as he passed under the black shadow of a thorn tree, and a voice whispered: "It is I, brother!"

"Back!" said Alex softly. He caught Niaz by the wrist and dragged him swiftly back into the high grass beside the path, and they flattened themselves against the dry, warm ground and lay still as man after man climbed out of the nullah and hurried silently along the narrow goat track toward the distant village, each man keeping his distance from the next and each one glancing furtively from left to right and quickly over his shoulder. Sadhus, sepoys, merchants, townsmen and zamindars; followers of the Prophet or wearers of the sacred thread, disciples of Baba Nanak and worshipers of Kali.

'Divide and rule,' thought Alex watching them as they passed, their feet almost noiseless on the dusty goat track and their breathing loud in the warm silence of the late September night. As long as these people were divided by their castes and their creeds into antagonistic factions they would always be at the mercy of a conqueror, but if they once combined they could stand against any from sheer weight of numbers.

Niaz jerked at his sleeve and whispered: "Why do we linger here? Let us go."

"There is a debt to pay," said Alex softly. "When these have gone we go back. There are some few who will remain, and the priests will leave last, for there is work to do. They cannot leave the dead unburied."

"Has there been killing, then?"

"Yes. Quiet—here is another—"

Two men this time. One, tall and turbaned, his hawk nose clear cut against the starlight, did not walk furtively as the others had done. He strode past, brushing against the grasses, careless of noise, and although he spoke in an undertone his words were clearly audible:

"Dogs and devil worshipers!" said the tall man furiously. "Must they stoop to such filth to insure that none shall betray them for gain? Now are all our heads forfeit for this night's work! Let the *Angrezis* (British) but hear of this killing and they will hunt us down like mad dogs—each one of us. Dogs and devil worshipers!—" The sound of their voices faded as they disappeared into the darkness.

"That is Ahmed Ullah, a Tulakdar of Faizabad," whispered Niaz. "He is one who goes up and down the land speaking against the Company's Raj. They call him the Mulvi of Faizabad."

At last the steady procession of shadowy figures ceased, and for a full ten minutes no one passed along the narrow path. "Thirty-seven," said Niaz. "There should be some few more, but not all came this way. Some came northward along the nullah."

Alex stood up with infinite caution and remained for a further minute or two, listening intently. But the night was silent and nothing moved. Presently he turned to look up at the moon where it hung low in the sky like a pallid wedge of sweet lime above the dark tangle of cane brake and kikar trees.

"It is foolishness to go back into the tiger's lair, having once escaped," said Niaz. "Forgo thy revenge and come away. There is more in this than one life."

"It was a child," said Alex. "An *Angrezi* child."

"Ah!" said Niaz. "Let us go back, then."

They regained the path and crept back along it, pausing every few paces to listen. When he had first passed that way it had seemed to Alex as though he had moved with an almost complete lack of sound, but then there had been others on the path, both ahead of him and behind him. Now that these were no longer there his progress appeared alarmingly audible, and every rustle of grass or crack of a dried thorn twig underfoot seemed magnified out of all proportion by the silence.

There was no other way of reaching the ruined fort except by the way they had taken before, and they crept down the steep, sandy slope that led down into the nullah, their nerves tensing to each rattle of a dislodged pebble or slither of dry earth crumbling beneath their feet.

The huge stone-paved courtyard lay bathed in starlight in which the clumps of coarse grass, thorn and stunted saplings that had thrust up here and there between the paving stones took on the appearance of crouching men; but nothing moved except a breath of night wind in the grasses. The two men stole forward silently, moving from one clump of shadow to the next, and reached the shelter of the peepul tree that straddled the entrance to the roofless hall.

The block of stone that closed the shaft still leant upright against the lowest step of the ruined stair that rose behind it, and from the shaft itself came a faint light and a murmur of voices. Alex left the shelter of the peepul tree and, creeping forward until he was directly above it, knelt listening. A voice that was faintly familiar was speaking in tones of cold scorn:

"—so all are endangered!"

"Nay, all are now bound one to another!" replied another voice, a shrill, hysterical voice. "None now dare betray us, for all are guilty of the blood —as thou thyself hast said! And was not this thing thine own scheme? a ruse—an excellent ruse!—for the unsettling of men's minds? And for such things a sacrifice is necessary—yes, necessary!"

"A goat!" snapped the first voice. "Had I known that ought else were planned—"

"Of what use to Mother Kali is the blood of one starveling *bukri* when we may offer her the blood of a thousand—nay, a hundred thousand Feringis?"

"But to slaughter a defenseless babe in this fashion is an abomination before gods and men!" There was a brief silence and then the first speaker continued: "Well, it is done now and it cannot be undone. But though this may do well enough for the villages, it will not serve for the sepoys. For them it must be something that strikes deeper and that touches every man. They are already as tinder, but there is as yet no spark. No matter; we will find it."

Alex felt a touch on his arm and Niaz whispered in his ear: "Let us let down the stone. I do not think they will lift it from below. They will be trapped like rats and die slowly."

Alex' eyes gleamed in the starlight and he rose to his feet, and then checked and shook his head. "No. They could, I think, find a way out. There are bats in that place, and where a bat can enter, the tree roots may have loosened the stones so that men might burrow a way out. We will wait. They must come up one by one."

Niaz nodded and eased his knife from its sheath, and then quite suddenly his head came round with a jerk and he stiffened like a pointer, listening. "Back!" said Niaz in a harsh whisper. "There are others here!" They turned from the stair shaft and a moment later were once again among the shadows of the peepul tree, crouched down among the twisted roots.

Niaz's ears had not deceived him. There was someone approaching from the dense jungle behind the ruined walls. A branch cracked and grasses rustled, and presently they heard the sound of shod feet on stone. Two men emerged from the blackness beyond a crumbling archway, and passing under the shadow of the peepul tree stopped by the entrance to the stair shaft. In the clear starlight they were little more than dark silhouettes against the paler expanse of the open courtyard; shadows who carried something in their hands; something that looked in the uncertain light like short-handled axes. A nightjar called in the jungle away to the right, and a moment later, from the opposite side, an owl hooted. One of the shadows spoke:

"The *Philao* and the *Thiboa* both! The omens are auspicious, though they come late. And the *bhil* is well hidden."

There was a chink of metal striking against stone as one man rested the thing he carried, and Alex felt Niaz shiver and was aware with a sense of shock that he was frightened. He had never known Niaz show fear before and had thought him a stranger to it. But now he could feel it shudder through the body whose shoulder touched his, and he knew that Niaz was sweating and shivering in the grip of a similar horror to the one he himself had experienced in the vault that lay beneath their feet.

The man who had spoken bent down and called softly down the shaft:

"*Ohé, thakur*—it is done." He was answered from below, and a moment later a head appeared above the hole in the paving. Alex' muscles tensed involuntarily but Niaz's fingers clamped down upon his arm and checked him as four men, one after another, emerged from the shaft. The light from the vault below glimmered redly on the rubies that one of them wore in his ears. The men conferred together in whispers and he of the earrings said querulously: "It is late, and I have far to go before morning. The two down there can close the stair. Let us go." It was the same voice that Alex had heard screaming hysterically of death.

One of the men turned and called down the shaft: "We go now. Close the stone when all is finished." The faint light from below brightened for a brief moment as though more fuel had been thrown in the brazier, and for an instant the speaker's face showed clear against the surrounding darkness. It was Kishan Prasad. The next moment the group by the stair shaft had turned away and vanished as quietly as they had come, and the night was silent again.

The two who crouched in the shadow of the peepul tree did not move for a full five minutes after the last faint rustle had died away, and then at last Niaz released his grip on Alex' arm and put up an unsteady hand to wipe the sweat from his forehead.

"My father's uncle spoke truth," said Niaz in a shaking whisper. "They are *not* all dead!"

"Who are not dead?"

"Those two were Lughais—the diggers of the *bhil*, the buriers of the slain! Didst thou not see that they carried the *khussee*? They are Phansigers, Thugs—the followers of Bhowani. The Stranglers!" Niaz's voice shook and Alex heard his teeth chatter. "Now do I know that this is an evil thing that must be stamped out, else will the old evils arise again. Two score years ago my uncle aided Sleeman Sahib in the hunting down of the Stranglers, and he has told me—" the words broke off in a shiver. "Let us go from here. Let us go quickly!"

"In a little while," whispered Alex. "There are only two below."

He rose and moved away from the peepul tree and after a moment Niaz followed him, and they crouched down on either side of the tilted slab of stone and waited, listening to the faint sounds from below, while the shrunken moon sank below the horizon and the sky darkened.

At last the light below was extinguished, and presently feet groped on the stairs and a man's head lifted out the black well of the stair shaft. Alex waited until his shoulders were clear of the shaft and then he reached out and took him round the throat. The man uttered one choking gasp and then he was struggling frantically, his hands clawing the air. But Alex was behind him and the man's clutching hands could not reach him. His bare feet beat a tattoo against the steep stone steps, and Alex lifted him clear with one savage heave as though he had been of no more weight than a sack of vegetables.

"What is it? Hast thou fallen?" said a voice from the darkness below, and a second head appeared above the pavement. Niaz's lean fingers closed about the fat throat and he jerked the man up and backward across the rim of the shaft and brought his head down upon the stone with a sharp sound like the cracking of an egg. It was enough.

Alex let the limp thing drop in a huddled heap at his feet. His hands were wet and sticky with the blood that had burst from the man's mouth and nostrils, and he stooped, panting, and wiped them on the priestly robes.

"What now?" asked Niaz.

"Throw them back. If any raise the stone to seek for them, they shall find them waiting."

They tumbled the bodies back into the shaft and lowered the stone above it. They could not see how the thing had been raised or on what principle the two dead priests would have lowered it into place, and they had no time to discover the trick of it. They put their shoulders to it and discovered that it took the last ounce of their combined strength to send it crashing into place. The noise of its fall broke the silence of the night as though it had been the crash of a cannon, and awoke a hundred echoes from the ruined walls.

"Quick," gasped Niaz. "If there be any within earshot they may return."

They ran together across the wide, ruined courtyard and plunged into the blackness of the nullah. Once there they paused to listen, but the rustling of the night breeze in the jungle that leant above them drowned out all other sounds and they could not afford to wait. They met no one in the nullah and there was no one on the far side of the rocks that hid the ruined gateway, and ten minutes later they had reached the edge of the grazing grounds and the open plain. They did not go toward Khanwai but turned right, and skirting the fringe of the jungle came at last to a grove of trees where Alex had tethered the horses.

"Where now?" whispered Niaz, mounting a fidgeting horse with an ease that consorted ill with the character of Jatu the toy seller. "We should not ride together."

"Lunjore. I go by Pari."

By first light they were no more than a dozen miles from Khanwai, for the roads were rough and now that the moon had set the darkness made it necessary for them to keep the horses to a walk. As the dawn broke and the morning mists turned from silver-gray to rose and saffron, Niaz fell behind and Alex rode on alone through open country where peacocks screamed from the standing crops and the dew diamonds on every blade and twig glittered in the first rays of the rising sun. It was barely more than a hundred miles from Khanwai to Lunjore; less as the crow flies. But the horse would need rest, and the thought of any halt oppressed him, for his instinct was to keep going with all possible speed. He could not rid himself of the thought that at any hour the word might go out to look for Sher Dil of the Usafzai who had stood in the full glare of the torchlight and shown Kishan Prasad's ring.

Alex looked down at the ring now, and dropping the reins wrenched the thing off in a sudden spasm of loathing as though it had been something unclean. It had been useful once and it might be so again. On the other hand it might by now be a very dangerous thing to possess. He flung the thing away into the rank grass by the roadside, and wondered how long it would be before Kishan Prasad learned that someone had used that ring to gain admittance to a secret meeting that had ended by placing every man present at it in the shadow of the gallows.

It had been Kishan Prasad whose voice Alex had heard in the vault protesting against the murder, but Kishan Prasad, whether he had condoned it or not, had convened that unholy coven, and as the instigator of it he could be held to account for all that had happened there and summarily hanged for his part in the night's work. Alex scowled down at his bloodstained hands. There must not be a rising! It must be prevented at all costs, for if such a thing were to occur, and the blood lust that he had witnessed last night were to be let loose, the British, who would do little now for the sake of reason, would do much under the spur of blind rage. The retribution that would follow an armed rising would be both harsh and horrible, engulfing innocent and guilty alike. It must not happen! thought Alex desperately. If it does it will leave a legacy of hatred and suspicion that will go on and on into the future.

Shortly after midday he led his horse off the track and tethering it some hundred yards within the borders of the surrounding jungle, he lay down and slept while Niaz, an hour later, ambled past in company with a party of armed men whose acquaintance he had made on the road.

The low sun was shining gold between the grass stems and the bamboo canes when Alex awoke, and he made considerably better time over the next twenty miles or so, for the horse appeared to have benefited from its rest, but it was late and the road was white in the moonlight as he neared the little town of Pari. He had covered over eighty miles since he had left Khanwai before dawn that day, and only a matter of some six or seven more separated him from the river that formed the border between Oudh and Lunjore. Once across the river, an hour's ride would bring him to the cantonment and Lunjore City that lay barely ten miles from the border.

The road ahead of him dipped into a deep dry gulley that was a stream in the rainy season, and rising out of it passed near a high outcrop of rock. Something moved in the black patch of shadow that it cast and Alex reined in hard as Niaz moved out into the moonlight and catching the mare's bridle, turned her off the road. He was breathing quickly and the flanks of his own weary beast were white with foam and heaving as though it had been ridden to exhaustion.

"Thou canst not go forward," said Niaz speaking in a whisper as though even in that wide plain he feared to be overheard. "The word has gone out against thee. There were men in Pari asking if any had seen a Pathan horse dealer—one Sher Dil, a man of the Usafzai. I rode on through the town and circled back two *koss* through the crops and the grazing grounds so that none should see me. They will look for thee to enter the town. We will ride on for half a *koss* and then turn away from the road and make a circle through the fields. It is on the far side that we shall find it difficult, for there is only one place where the river may be crossed; by the bridge of boats into Lunjore, and that will be watched."

"We will deal with that when we have the town behind us," said Alex.

Leaving the road, they moved at a foot's pace, the horses picking their way wearily between rocks and tussocks of grass, and presently they were skirting the cultivated land to the south of Pari. A pariah dog barked at them as they crossed a shallow irrigation ditch where Niaz's horse stumbled and all but threw him, and a watchman perched in a ramshackle *machan* in a mulberry tree to scare the deer and wild pig from the crops, shouted hoarsely and discharged an ancient fowling piece. The pellets rattled through the leaves and something like a red-hot knife sliced into Alex' arm, and he felt the warm blood pour down it and wet the fingers of his left hand. Then water glimmered in the moonlight and presently the path narrowed and ran along the marshy margin of a jheel that stretched away and to the left.

Niaz glanced over his shoulder, and drawing rein in the shadows, slid to the ground. "Art thou hit?"

"It is only a flesh wound," said Alex, and dismounted awkwardly.

A raw-edged fragment of the scrap iron with which the watchman's gun had been loaded had plowed through the fleshy part of the arm midway between shoulder and elbow, making an ugly jagged tear that bled freely, and Niaz ripped two strips of cloth from his turban, and making a pad of the first bound the wound skillfully.

The brief pause appeared to have benefited the jaded horses, and an hour's riding brought them the smell of the river. There was a square mud tollhouse where the road ended, and behind it, screened by plantains and bamboo, lay a meager huddle of huts that housed the family of the tollkeeper and the bridge guard. The tollhouse was in darkness, but Alex and Niaz kept to the shelter of the trees on the far side of the road, and gave it a wide berth.

The near bank of the river was low and fringed with casurina scrub, and the white sands and wandering shallows stretched far out into the moonlight. A raised stone causeway ran from the Oudh bank to the edge of the deep water, where a bridge of boats spanned the main arm of the river. But the bridge that night appeared to be unguarded. There was no sign of life on or near it, and it lay open and innocent in the waning moonlight, creaking to the sluggish pull of the slow-moving current.

"They are on the other side," muttered Niaz.

Alex nodded, frowning. He knew the far bank of the river well. The jungle that clothed it was so dense as to be almost impenetrable. A horse could not force its way through that tangle of trees and scrub and high grass, and it was no easy task for a man, for there were no paths except those made by animals. The only road was the one which wound for almost ten miles from the river to Lunjore, walled in by the jungle. And even if they could swim the horses across there was no point for several miles, either up or down stream, where they could get them ashore, for the current ran strongly on the far side and had worn away the bank until it overhung the river. They would have to leave the horses.

"We must swim," said Alex slowly.

Niaz did not speak but he pointed silently, and Alex, looking along his raised arm as a man sights along the barrels of a rifle, saw a long gray object at the water's edge; something that might have been a log washed down by the river, and which lay at the exact angle that such a log would have grounded. Mugger: the blunt-nosed, man-eating crocodile of the Indian rivers.

"If I die, I will die on land," said Niaz, "and not in the belly of such as that, for—" He checked suddenly, listening, and Alex, following his example, heard a faint and distant sound. There were carts approaching the bridge; a long line of creaking, bullock-drawn country carts of the kind that might be met with on any Indian road at any time of the night.

Niaz drew a breath of relief and jerked his head in the direction of the distant sound. He said: "Let us turn the horses loose. We shall not need them again. I do not think that we shall die tonight, for these will take us across."

They left the weary horses to graze in the jungle and ran back along the road toward the carts, keeping to the shadows. There were five carts rumbling and creaking down the moonlit road, moving as slowly as crawling beetles, the torpid bullocks lumbering through the dust in a ruminative trance, noses almost to the ground and horns swaying, while their drivers crouched upon the cart poles, miraculously preserving their balance, and slept. A flickering oil lantern swung from the leading cart, and the moonlight showed that two of the carts were piled high with sugar cane while three carried sacks of bhoosa. Alex and Niaz slipped across the road between the carts, and Niaz, walking behind one of them, dragged out several of the light, bulging sacks and flung them away, while Alex watched the man on the cart immediately behind for fear that he should wake.

"In!" whispered Niaz, and Alex swung up onto the cart and wriggled into the cave that Niaz had made among the sacks. The plodding bullocks did not slow their crawling pace by a step at the additional weight, and Niaz thrust two sacks on top of Alex and dropped back to burrow his way into the heart of a pile of sugar cane with the celerity of a grass snake.

Left alone in the dusty, sweet-smelling darkness Alex shifted the sack beneath him and worked his way down and farther forward into the pile, until he lay in the center of the stifling load. The carts rocked and squeaked and rumbled forward on the rutted, dusty road and presently, as the wheels met the dry sand near the river bank and a sleepy voice called from the tollhouse, they jolted to a stop. The carters, jerked abruptly into wakefulness, entered into surly argument with the yawning tollkeeper, and after some delay the carts started forward once more, and with shoutings, tail twistings and belaborings, jolted down the sandy slope onto the causeway. One by one they rolled out onto the bridge which swayed and groaned beneath the rumbling wheels, and one by one, as the bullocks grunted and strained under the hail of blows and shrill yells of encouragement, they breasted the slope on the far side and were on the road again.

Alex did not catch the shouted orders that checked the carts, for the creaking and rumbling had deafened him and the close-packed sacks muffled all other sounds, but the wheels ground to a halt and there were men all about the carts and hoarse angry voices.

"What is this? Yet another toll?" called one of the carters. "A Pathan? Nay, we have seen no Pathans. . . . Look then and see! . . . We carry fodder and such stuff to Barowli village. Are you strangers that you do not know this?"

There was another burst of angry shouting and a man's voice said: "Any fool would have known that the bridge would be watched once the word had gone out, and this man we seek is no fool. He will have doubled back to the Ganges."

A torch flared as men passed along the carts prodding and peering, but the task of unloading and reloading each cart was clearly impossible.

"Thrust with thy spear!" growled a voice.

"And who is to pay me for my sacks?" shrilled the carter furiously.

A voice farther down the line said angrily that there was no spear made that could be stabbed down through sugar cane. The wrangling voices passed down the line and presently someone climbed upon the sacks that concealed Alex, crushing them down stiflingly upon him, and then something jabbed down, ripping through sacking and bhoosa. It missed Alex by a millimeter, but it caught the edge of the bandage that Niaz had tied about his arm and ripped it away. The blood had clotted and dried, but the wrench tore open the wound again and he could feel the fresh blood well out once more. But either the spear had been pulled back in the fractional second before the blood flowed again, or the bhoosa and the sacking had cleaned any traces from the metal, for the man jumped down upon the road again and passed on to the next cart.

Alex pressed his wounded arm against a yielding sack and tried to get his right hand across to cover it. If blood should drip upon the white dust of the road it would be seen when the carts moved on again. He managed to clench his fingers over it, but the blood continued to flow in a warm sticky tide. And then after what seemed an eternity the carts jerked forward again, and it was over—and they were through. The dusty, airless darkness closed in upon him, and he was still asleep when Niaz pulled him out from among the bloodstained sacks in the yellow dawn.

Three hours later, bathed, shaved and fed, and clothed once more in his own clothes, with his wound probed, cleaned and bound and his arm in a sling, Alex presented himself at the Residency.

The Commissioner was engaged with a visitor and sent out word asking Captain Randall to wait; he would not, he said, be above half an hour.

Alex sat down in a veranda chair and stretching his legs out before him prepared himself to wait. It was over thirty hours since he had left Khanwai, and an hour's more delay could make little difference one way or another. After a time the gorgeously uniformed chuprassy who squatted farther down the veranda by one of the outer doors of the living room, sprang to his feet and held aside the split-cane curtain that hung in front of it, and Alex could hear the Commissioner's voice raised in affable farewell. A man, an Indian, came out past the salaaming chuprassy and turned and walked down the length of the veranda. It was Kishan Prasad.

Alex did not move and not a muscle in his face quivered; nor was there any alteration in his lounging pose to betray the shock that the sight of Kishan Prasad had given him. Kishan Prasad, walking softly, came to a stop in front of him and bowed. Alex looked up at him with eyes that were as cold and hard and passionless as gray granite, and smiled.

Kishan Prasad drew back involuntarily, and for a fractional moment some of his assurance seemed to drop from him and the lines about his mouth and jaw were suddenly accentuated. Then he had recovered himself and his voice was smoothly urbane.

"Ah, Captain Randall! This is an unexpected pleasure. The Commissioner was telling me that he did not expect you back until next week. I am sorry to see that you have suffered an injury to your arm. Nothing serious, I hope?"

"No, nothing serious," said Alex from behind that cold smile. "It was kind of you to come here. It will save me the trouble of sending an escort to bring you in."

"To bring me in where?" inquired Kishan Prasad affecting polite surprise.

"To the jail—and the gallows."

"My dear Captain Randall! I must admit that I do not understand you. Is it some English joke?"

"You understand me perfectly," said Alex softly. "Murder has always been a capital offense."

"Murder?"

"What else? '*This that ye have witnessed shall be binding upon you all, for were it known, there is not one here whom they would not hang at a rope's end for this night's work,*'" quoted Alex in the vernacular. He saw Kishan Prasad's pupils widen and said, "Yes, you were right. I am the man whom your cutthroats are hunting through Oudh. You should be more careful whom you admit to your meetings. I had heard many tales, but until two nights ago I had no proof. Now I have it; and your life and the life of every man who was there is twice forfeit—for sedition and for murder."

Kishan Prasad released his breath in an audible sigh and after a moment he said very softly: "That killing was by no will of mine. I do not war on babes, and had I known what was planned I should have prevented it. I am no ignorant worshiper of devils to dabble in such foulness! As for the rest, I have told you before that I desire to pull down your Company's Raj, and to that end I will use any and every means that lie to my hand. But you cannot hang me, for this proof that you have is no proof. If you send men now to Khanwai there will be nothing found to support your tale. As for me, a hundred witnesses can prove that I was elsewhere than at Khanwai two nights ago."

Alex said grimly: "I think you will find, Rao Sahib, that my word will be taken against a hundred thousand of your witnesses."

"Even when one of those witnesses is the Commissioner of Lunjore?" inquired Kishan Prasad softly.

Alex' face stiffened and there were suddenly two white patches at the corners of his mouth.

"He does not know that he lies," said Kishan Prasad. "You see there was a—a little party that night at the house of a mutual friend, and the Commissioner perhaps indulged too freely in perfumed brandy. He does not remember very much of what occurred, and he is convinced that I also was present. He was good enough to admire a trinket that I had brought back from France; an ingenious toy that he was pleased to accept. He has even mentioned it to Colonel Moulson who is with him now. So you see—"

Kishan Prasad sketched a deprecatory gesture with one slim brown hand, and Alex saw—saw with a complete and bitter understanding. Kishan Prasad had made full use of both Mr. Barton's drunkenness and his vanity. It must have been so easy—so fatally easy. A prearranged party at the house of one of the more disreputable noblemen; drink and dancing girls, champagne laced with brandy and probably opium. A man—any man with a superficial resemblance to Kishan Prasad—and his name repeated until it was impressed upon a fuddled brain, and a gift accepted.

"They will say that you must have been mistaken," said Kishan Prasad softly. "As for this meeting you will tell them of, they will say it was a mere gathering of malcontents. Talk—but no more than talk. Shall I tell you why they will not believe? Because they do not wish to! The colonels who command the sepoy regiments here suspect that their regiments are rank with sedition. Their Indian officers are insolent in many small ways. But for shame's sake they will not admit it and each cries louder than the other that all is well." He looked at Alex' rigid face and he lowered his voice until it was barely a whisper: "You know that you cannot win this fight. The Company is only a handful of men and its power is an illusion. I have seen the slaughter at Sebastopol and I know that your Queen has no more regiments to send. Do not fight us. Join us! It will not be the first time that men from the West have risen to greatness in the armies of Hind. There have been many—Avitable, George Thomas, Ventura, Potter, Gardiner—"

Alex laughed and the laugh brought a sudden flush into Kishan Prasad's olive cheeks. His hand dropped and he stepped back. Then: "I am sorry," he said gravely. "That was a foolish thing to say."

"Very," agreed Alex.

Kishan Prasad smiled. "I am sorry too that our blood makes us enemies. Perhaps in your next life it may be that you will be born a Hindu."

"Perhaps," said Alex, "when I have hung you in this one."

"That too may come about," said Kishan Prasad. "But the time is not yet."

He saluted Alex with grave courtesy and turning, walked down the shallow flight of steps into the bright sunlight of the garden and was driven away in an open carriage, his servants running beside it.

But the hours that followed, and the days that followed those hours, bore out all that he had said. Mr. Barton listened with entire incredulity to Alex' story. Alex had made a mistake—a very natural one. All niggers looked as like as two peas when in a crowd. The suggestion that he himself might have been mistaken drove him to blustering and apoplectic indignation. Why, the Rao Sahib had actually shown him a toy that he had bought in Paris—a musical box ornamented with a naked dancer who contorted her waxen limbs in time to the tinny little tune. There it was, standing on the table to prove his words! Kishan Prasad had begged his acceptance of the trifle and had called only that morning in order to bring the duplicate key—a very sensible idea; these fiddling things were so easily lost.

Alex had brought him remorselessly back to the subject under discussion and Mr. Barton had been horrified and disbelieving. It was obvious, he said, that Alex had happened upon some queer religious rite; it never did to pry into such things—leave 'em to wallow was his motto. At such ceremonies the blacks were bound to get above themselves and talk a lot of inflammatory nonsense. It meant nothing. As for Alex' assertion that an English child had been murdered in cold blood, he could only suggest that Alex had been carried away. Of course it had been a young goat that he had seen killed! A very common form of sacrifice. And if Alex took his advice he would refrain in future from play-acting in native dress and mixing himself up in such affairs. It did not consort well with the dignity of a Company's officer, and might lead to a deal of trouble. That wounded arm should be a lesson to him!

And now that that matter was settled, Mr. Barton would like to know what news Alex had brought of the Condesa? He hoped that she was well? No beauty, what?—but looks were not everything. It was a thousand pities that he had found himself unable to travel to Calcutta, but he had not been well. A bout of fever. It was inconvenient, this journeying to Delhi, but he had known of no one else who was proceeding to Lunjore at this time, and as he would be visiting Delhi shortly on official business, it would do very well.

The past year had done nothing toward improving either Mr. Barton's health or his appearance. He had, it is true, intended to take both in

hand, and by abstaining from overindulgence in the matter of wine and
women, and taking daily exercise, to have effected a considerable improve-
ment. But on consideration he had come to the conclusion that such a
course was entirely unnecessary. This was his last year of freedom and he
would make the most of it. After this he would have a mewling, puking,
scrawny and ill-favored girl forever about the house, who would doubtless
kick up a fuss at all his amusements, and might, if he overstepped the
mark, rouse her influential relatives to protest on her behalf. Not that that
would make much odds once he had his hands on the girl's money.
Still, life would not be the same and so he would enjoy himself for this
last year. Having reasoned thus, Mr. Barton abandoned all ideas of ab-
stinence and exercise with a thankful sigh, and the result was the obese,
balding, slack-lipped figure who now confronted Alex Randall with a glass
clutched in one unsteady hand and his mustache and chin all slopped with
brandy.

The Commissioner's opinion of the meeting at Khanwai was endorsed
by Colonels Moulson and Packer, commanding two of the three regiments
of Native Infantry stationed at Lunjore, and by Major Beckwith, in temporary command of the third in the absence of Colonel Gardener-Smith.
Alex asked for a week's extension of leave on account of his wounded
arm and rode to Agra to see Mr. John Colvin, Lieutenant-Governor of
the North-West Provinces. But the mission had proved abortive. The
Lieutenant-Governor too thought that Captain Randall must have been
mistaken, and that he was surely exaggerating the dangers of the situation.
He too suggested that it was hardly suitable for an officer of the Company
to take such investigations upon himself. There were paid spies among the
native population who were entirely trustworthy, and better qualified for
the work on account of their dark skins. He would, of course, pass on the
information Captain Randall had given him to the proper authorities, but
in the meantime . . .

Alex had set his teeth and listened with a gathering sense of frustration
and bitterness. He had thought that if he could produce proof he must be
believed. But it seemed that the evidence of his eyes was not proof and,
as Kishan Prasad had so truly said, the great majority did not wish to believe. They found it more comfortable to close their eyes and look the
other way in the hope that if they ignored its existence the danger would
pass. To take any form of preventive action, they reasoned, would be to
advertise a lamentable want of confidence, and possibly precipitate thereby
the very dangers whose existence they refused to admit.

The most that Alex could gain was permission to take six sowars and
three British officers to see if any concrete evidence could be brought back
of the murder that he professed to have witnessed. There had been a report of the disappearance of a child a week earlier, admitted Mr. Colvin
reluctantly. The three-year-old son of a private in a British regiment stationed in Cawnpore; and it was always possible, though hardly credi-
ble . . .

Alex had ridden back to Khanwai with six troopers and three skeptical but enthusiastic officers. They had found exactly nothing. The stair shaft leading to the underground chamber was open to the sky and choked with fallen debris that had the appearance of being there for some considerable time. There had been a heavy and recent fall of earth and stonework from the spot where the roots of the peepul tree had forced their way downward, and the vault appeared to be in too dangerous a state to encourage a thorough search.

Ten paces within the jungle behind the ruined fort they uncovered a grave, but it contained only the rotting carcass of a white goat.

Conway

12

JOURNEYING northward from Calcutta to Delhi, the Abuthnots had received four unexpected additions to their party in the persons of Lord Carlyon and the Gardener-Smiths. The Gardener-Smiths had decided to leave Calcutta with the Abuthnots, while Lord Carlyon, it seemed, had taken a fancy to visit the old Mogul capital of Delhi, and had requested permission—with what the fluttered Mrs. Abuthnot could only describe as distinguished affability—to avail himself of the pleasure of their company on what he must otherwise find to be a singularly tedious journey.

To the majority of travelers the protracted journey was an unavoidable discomfort that must be endured, but Winter found interest and enchantment in every mile of the road. Each dawn that broke over the plain or the jungle in a wash of saffron yellow, each evening when the red ball of the sun would plunge to its rest in a dusty glow of gold and rose and amber, leaving the moon like a silver nutmeg in the sky—the silver nutmeg that a king of Spain's daughter had traveled far to see—was to her a thing of delight. But there was one aspect of the journey to Delhi which she did not find pleasant. The presence of Lord Carlyon.

Winter had not been favorably impressed by Carlyon on the occasion of their first meeting at Sybella's Summer Ball at Ware, and although his manner toward her since their meeting in Calcutta had been outwardly unexceptionable, she was uneasily aware of hidden undercurrents.

Carlyon's languid gaze had a way of resting on her with a look of insolently comprehensive appraisal, as though she had been a slave girl on the block, or a blood horse whose purchase he contemplated. His words too, though apparently superficial, frequently contained the same underlying suggestiveness, and he took every opportunity to touch her—gestures that she found hard to avoid without appearing ungracious or childishly rude. The pressure of those lingering hands, as white and well kept as a woman's despite their efficiency with reins or gun, would send a shrinking shiver of dislike and apprehension through her.

Carlyon was aware of that shiver, and he misinterpreted it. He was an egotistical and self-centered man whose languidly disdainful manner and cold eyes disguised a sensual appetite that had never yet had to go unsatisfied. Wealth and position, combined with handsome features and excellent physical proportions, had brought him all that he demanded of life. His amours had been many but he had avoided matrimony or any entanglement of a serious nature with the same practiced skill with which he shot, rode across country or seduced another man's wife, and he had always considered the *droit du seigneur* an admirable institution, and regretted that it could no longer be enforced. It would do no harm—and should prove quite delightful—to give this delicious young creature an advance course of instruction in the pleasanter aspects of matrimony, and she would enjoy the subsequent embraces of the nonentity she intended to marry all the more for having been introduced to the delights of passion by an expert. A girl with such a mouth and so sweetly seductive a figure could not, he was convinced, prove anything but an apt pupil in the art of love. A journey of several weeks had seemed to offer endless opportunities for sentimental dalliance by the way, but however carefully he maneuvered he found it impossible to speak to the little de Ballesteros alone.

As day succeeded day and the travelers drew nearer to Delhi, Winter remained as cool as her name and tantalizingly out of reach, and Lord Carlyon, angry, frustrated and piqued, ended by doing what he had always pronounced to be the very height of folly. He fell in love.

As his desire for her changed its quality, Winter's initial dislike of him changed in turn to something that bordered upon fear. Young and inexperienced as she was, she yet had a vague awareness of the dangers inherent in a temperament that combined egotism and sensuality with a belief in the divine rights of Birth and Wealth to live by standards not admissible to those of the middle and lower classes. It would not occur to Carlyon that he could be denied anything that he had set his mind and his strong appetites on acquiring, and the fact that his attentions were unwelcome would not deter him in the least.

Thus the days that had been a delight ended by becoming a torment of embarrassment and strain, and Carlyon was the only member of the party who was not inexpressibly relieved at the sight of the rose-red walls of Delhi.

The Abuthnots' bungalow was situated in the cantonments on the stony ridge some four miles outside the walled city, where the Gardener-Smiths were also staying with friends. Carlyon had had no difficulty in obtaining an invitation to stay with the Abuthnots, and although before the journey was over Mrs. Abuthnot would have given much to get out of it, she consoled herself with the reflection that the Commissioner of Lunjore, who had been apprised of the date of their arrival, would certainly be in Delhi to meet his bride, and that the wedding could be counted upon to take place within a few days.

What a relief it would be to see Mr. Barton! He would be staying until the wedding at Ludlow Castle with Mr. Simon Fraser, the Commissioner of Delhi, and would be sure to present himself at their bungalow on the very first evening. She did hope that he would allow dear Winter sufficient time to bathe and change her dress before making his appearance. The child would wish to look her best for such a momentous meeting.

There were no less than seven letters awaiting Lottie at the bungalow: fat, sealed packets, each as large, as Sophie remarked teasingly, as one of Mrs. Heyman's novels, and all of them from Edward English. But there was neither letter nor message for the Condesa de los Aguilares.

Of course there would be none, thought Winter, comforting herself. There was no longer any need for letters when Conway himself was at Ludlow Castle only a mile or so from the cantonments. In an hour—perhaps less—she would see him! She must hurry and change into her prettiest dress. Her hair was dull from the dust of the roads and there was dust too on her long lashes and at the corners of her nose and mouth. She must wash and change quickly—quickly!

An hour later she took a last anxious look at herself in the looking glass, and crossing the hall went into the drawing room to wait for Conway. The servants were already laying dinner and it must be nearly five o'clock. Surely he would come soon! Someone entered the room behind her and closed the door, and she turned, expecting to see Mrs. Abuthnot.

"Who are you waiting for?" asked Carlyon. "The tardy lover?"

Winter stood quite still. Her dark eyes widened a little and a pulse beat at the base of her throat, for it needed only one look to see that Carlyon had been drinking. He was far from drunk, but his flushed face and overbright eyes, and the slight slurring of his drawling voice were sufficient indication that he was not entirely sober.

She said in a cool, steady voice: "I am expecting Mr. Barton. I will wait in the garden, I think. It is quite pleasantly cool out there now that the sun is so low." She pressed back the wide flounces of her crinoline and walked quietly toward the door.

Carlyon waited until she was almost level with him and then moved with unexpected swiftness, blocking her way. "I think not. I haven't had a chance like this before. Do you know that I have never once been alone with you?—even for a moment? Why do you behave like this? Do you do it to pique me, Winter? No! don't go! I won't let you."

She had tried to pass him and he had moved again, keeping between her and the door. Winter said a little breathlessly: "Lord Carlyon, please let me pass. I—I think I hear Mrs. Abuthnot in the hall—"

"No, you don't. And my name is Arthur. Do I have to tell you that? Do I have to tell you that you are the loveliest and most desirable creature that I have ever known? That I—"

"Lord Carlyon, you must not speak to me like this," said Winter desperately. "You know that I am to be married shortly and—"

"And to some clod of a commissioner? What ridiculous, damned non-

sense! You know it's nonsense, don't you, my snow maiden? Shall I melt
that snow and teach you to be as warm as summer instead of as cold as
your name? Shall I? shall I—"

Above his soft, slurred voice Winter could hear horses' hoofs on the
drive. *Conway!* She tried again to pass Lord Carlyon and he reached out
and caught her wrist. The touch of those hot fingers sent a sudden shock
of revulsion through her but she knew that it would be fatal to struggle.
In a moment—only a moment, surely—the door would open and they would
come looking for her. She could hear voices on the veranda. She must not
let Conway find her struggling degradingly in the arms of another man!

She said quite steadily: "If you do not let me go I shall call out."

Carlyon laughed. "No, you won't! It would make a vulgar scandal, and
this is no moment for a vulgar scandal if this is your chosen clod arriving.
So as time is short—"

Before she realized what he meant to do he had jerked her to him and
caught her close, pinning her arms to her sides in a grip that was agonizingly painful, and kissing her with a bruising violence that deprived her
of breath. She struggled wildly and soundlessly, anger and disgust swamp-
ing out thought as the greedy mouth moved to her throat, kissing its cool
whiteness with a savage intensity and traveling downward to the warm
hollows of neck and shoulder.

And then the door into the hall opened, and at the sound of it the
arms that had held her dropped and she leapt back, one hand to her
bruised throat and the other clutching desperately at a chair back. But
it was not Conway who stood there. It was, astonishingly, Captain Randall.

"*Alex!*" The word was a gasping breath and she was unaware that she
had called him by his given name.

Carlyon turned. He was entirely self-possessed, and it did not seem possible that this was the same man who only a moment ago had been gripping her in a paroxysm of greedy physical desire. "Ah," said Lord Carlyon
blandly, "Mr. Barton, I presume?"

Alex' hard gray eyes took in Lord Carlyon from head to foot in one
coldly speculative glance, and he raised his brows. "No, sir. Am I to take
it that you were expecting him?"

A sudden flush burnt in Carlyon's cheeks and his lips tightened. He
drew himself up to his full height and said in his coldest drawl: "You
have mistaken the room, sir. You may find Colonel Abuthnot in his office,
I think."

"Very likely," said Alex, strolling forward into the room. "But I did not
come to see Colonel Abuthnot. I am charged with a message to the Condesa de los Aguilares."

"Then pray deliver it, sir, and go," snapped Lord Carlyon. "You interrupt us."

"So I observe," said Alex, his gaze dwelling lazily on the red blotches
that disfigured Winter's white neck and shoulders. "The message, however, is of a somewhat personal nature, and when I tell you that it is

from this lady's future husband, I feel sure that you will permit me to deliver it in private. I shall not keep you above a moment."

He walked over to the door and holding it open smiled at Lord Carlyon. Alex' acquaintances would have recognized that smile. Carlyon did not. The fury died out of his face and contempt took its place. He looked at Winter and said: "For the moment then, my dear," and walked past her into the hall. Alex closed the door upon him and Winter sat down very suddenly on the ottoman, feeling ridiculously weak at the knees and seized with an absurd desire to cry.

"Who was that?" inquired Alex without interest.

Winter looked away from him and said in a difficult voice: "Lord Carlyon. He—accompanied us from Calcutta and is staying here. But you must not think—"

She looked up quickly, the hot color in her cheeks, and said, "I know that it must look most peculiar to you, but—" And then she saw for the first time that Alex carried his left arm in a sling, and cried out: "You are hurt! What has happened?"

"A shooting accident," said Alex indifferently.

"An accident?" A sudden recollection of stories of risings and the murder of men in outlying districts drove the blood from her face, and she stood up quickly. "Has there been trouble in Lunjore? Is that what you have come to tell me? Is anything the matter with Conway? Is he ill?"

"Not so far as I know," said Alex in a completely expressionless voice.

"Then why are you here?"

"The Commissioner found himself unable to come to Delhi after all. He asked me to explain the matter to you, and to arrange if possible for you to travel to Lunjore with the Gardener-Smiths who will be going there shortly."

"But—" Winter put out a small hand and clutched at a chair back as though for support—"but they are not going for nearly three weeks!"

"I know. I am sorry. But there appears to be no one else going there at present, and you cannot travel alone."

"Why can't I go with you?"

"The Commissioner does not consider it would be suitable," said Alex dryly. "Besides, I do not go myself for at least two weeks. I have some business here that the Commissioner wishes cleared up."

Winter sat down slowly, the apple-green flounces that had been intended to please Conway foaming about her. She looked very small and forlorn, and Alex found himself reflecting, not for the first time, that strangling was probably too good for Mr. Barton.

And yet was this slender young thing quite as unsophisticated as she appeared? It would be interesting to know just what was behind that scene that he had interrupted. Young ladies—particularly young ladies who were engaged to be married—did not normally indulge in tête-à-têtes with unwelcome admirers, and if she had not wished to be alone with

Lord Carlyon she had only to call out. The bungalow appeared to be swarming with servants, not to mention four Abuthnots.

Lord Carlyon, decided Alex dispassionately, appeared to be a strikingly handsome man of a type who might be expected to exercise a considerable appeal to women of all ages. If he had traveled from Calcutta to Delhi with the Abuthnots it would not be surprising if he had succeeded in making an impression upon the Commissioner's betrothed. And if he had done so Alex could not feel sorry for it. Almost anyone would be preferable to Mr. Barton as a husband for the Condesa.

Alex looked down at the bent head and the small hands that were clasped together so tightly among the absurd apple-green ruffles, and frowned impatiently, thinking again that India was really no place for young women, and that if there ever should be a rising on a serious scale they were going to be a devilish responsibility.

Winter, looking up at this point in his reflections, caught that look of frowning irritation, and it brought back her courage and a sudden spark of anger. She rose, straight backed, and said in a cool, composed voice: "It has been very kind of you to trouble yourself on my behalf. I hope you will not think me ungrateful. Did Mr. Barton not send a letter?"

"There was no time. The alteration in plan came at the last moment and I myself left at less than half an hour's notice," said Alex curtly. He considered it unnecessary to explain that the Commissioner had been in no condition to stand upright, let alone write a legible line, when he had last seen him.

If the truth were known, Mr. Barton, faced with the journey to Delhi, had once again been attacked by the fears that had kept him from sailing to England to claim his bride. Supposing that when she saw him again she did not like what she saw? There was still time to draw back. Better perhaps to bring her to Lunjore where she would be in the society of strangers (he did not count Moulson and the Gardener-Smiths), for once there she would have no friends to turn to, and no chance of changing her mind. He would see to that!

He had celebrated this decision by getting exceedingly drunk and been barely able, on the morning on which he had originally intended to set out, to do more than mumble a few directions to Captain Randall, the gist of which had been that Alex must deal with that Delhi business, and make his excuses to Winter. He was damned if he could go chasin' to Delhi to get married. She must come to Lunjore with the Gardener-Smiths. Mountain t' Mahomet! Alex must arrange it.

A description of this scene would, Alex considered, only lead to further misunderstanding, and if the Commissioner's betrothed had indeed found herself growing attached to Lord Carlyon the problem would probably solve itself without any further interference on his part. He could only hope so, for if the girl did not marry either Carlyon or Barton he could see himself being landed with the unwelcome task of finding a suitable chaperone to escort her back to Ware.

Lottie was to be married at St. James's Church in Delhi on the twenty-sixth of the month, and preparation for the wedding kept the ladies of the household in a constant ferment over silks and muslins and the mysteries of feminine underwear. There were also expeditions and picnics, parties and balls, and Carlyon received a flattering amount of attention from the garrison, and was even asked to call upon the ragged old ghost who lived surrounded by a tatterdemalion court in the Palace within the Red Fort of Delhi—Bahardur Shah, descendant of the House of Timur, and last of the Moguls.

But Winter remained as elusive as ever and Carlyon's exasperation mounted daily. His temper was not improved by the frequent addition of Captain Randall to the party, and he found that his first and instant dislike of the man increased with every sight of him. But Alex appeared to be entirely uninterested in Lord Carlyon and his proceedings. Nor did he seem particularly interested in the social gaieties of the Delhi season, and Carlyon was frequently puzzled to know why he troubled to accept invitations to affairs that he so obviously found uninteresting.

Alex would have found it hard to explain this himself. The business that was occupying him in Delhi consisted mainly of the collecting, correlating and checking of evidence in a contested case of accession of territory by lapse, and the bulk of the documentary evidence was being dealt with by the clerks of Mr. Fraser and Sir Theophilus Metcalf. He found himself with a fair amount of time on his hands and the Abuthnots were pressing with their invitations, but he had previously experienced no difficulty in refusing equally pressing invitations and he was not entirely sure why he did not refuse these.

Perhaps it was largely on account of an irksome feeling of responsibility toward Winter that he could not rid himself of, for he was aware, without quite knowing why, that she was frightened and unhappy. She certainly gave no outward signs of being either, but there was a difference in her that had not escaped him. She had lost that look of expectation, and was once again the withdrawn, wary child of the early spring. The girl who had seemed to him to possess something of the stillness and caution of a wild creature who freezes into immobility at the approach of danger, hoping to be overlooked among the protective coloring of its surroundings. He sensed that in some way—perhaps because she looked upon him as a link between herself and Conway Barton?—his presence reassured her.

In this he was partly right. Winter had understood and forgiven Conway's failure to meet her at Calcutta, but she could not help feeling that just this once he might have arranged things so that he could have left his desk for a few days to come for her in Delhi. If he had been in ill health she could have understood it better, but Captain Randall had denied that he was ill, and in a letter that had arrived a few days later Conway had mentioned only pressure of work. He was, he explained, anxious to clear up the more pressing business of the district so as to enable him to take a really adequate spell of leave for their honeymoon. The letter was a more affectionate one than Conway usually wrote and it had dispelled some of her unhappiness.

Winter was not unaware that Captain Randall was inclined to regard her as a somewhat tiresome responsibility, but she could not help feeling grateful for his continued presence in Delhi, if only because it protected her from Lord Carlyon's more than unwelcome attentions. When Alex was there she could forget about Carlyon and relax from the strain of being perpetually upon her guard.

That she was not being coy was gradually borne in upon Carlyon, and he began to realize that vanity and self-assurance had led him into making a grave tactical error. Far from awakening Winter to the delights of dalliance he had only disgusted and frightened her, and if he were not careful he would lose her to the nonentity after all. But he could not make his apologies and set himself right with her in the presence of others, and it seemed as though he were never to see her alone.

His opportunity came at a ball when he stood up with her for a waltz that she had been unable, in the interests of politeness, to refuse him, and he made the most of it. He attributed his unforgivable conduct on the day of their arrival to the brandy and laudanum drops which, he explained, he had taken as a precaution against a suspected bout of fever. He abased himself and begged for forgiveness, employing all his considerable charm and facility of address. Having received it, he proceeded with confidence to make her a proposal of marriage.

He was fully aware, said Carlyon, of the impropriety of addressing such a proposal to an engaged lady, but he must beg her to make allowances for a man deeply in love. The fact that she had not seen her betrothed since she was a child had given him grounds for hoping that she might bring herself at least to postpone the wedding, in order to allow him time in which to make her change her mind.

He had received an unqualified refusal. The music had ceased, and Winter had not granted him a second dance. She had been touched by the humility of Carlyon's apology, and disagreeably surprised by his subsequent proposal. But having left him in no doubt as to her feelings she had expected him to leave the Abuthnots' house and Delhi more or less immediately. Carlyon however had not removed. Instead he had written her a carefully worded letter, delivered to her by his bearer, in which he had assured her that he had not intended to distress her, promised never to mention the subject again or enact her any more tragedies, but hoped that he might be honored at least by her friendship though he must be denied that nearer relationship he had so ardently desired. If he could at any time be of any service to her, his life was at her disposal. He remained—etc.

Winter could not help feeling that she had misjudged Lord Carlyon, and she had smiled at him shyly when they next met. What she failed to realize was that Carlyon was in an exceedingly dangerous mood, and that he had written that letter with no other motive than the hope that by so doing he might prevent the little de Ballesteros from pressing for his removal from Delhi. He had every intention of removing shortly, but he had made up his mind to take her with him.

His plan was quite a simple one. Make his peace with Winter, and having made a few necessary arrangements, carry her off and compromise her so that she would be glad to marry him.

13

A MOONLIGHT picnic on the walls of Delhi had been arranged by some of the livelier young officers from the cantonments, but on the evening of the picnic there were clouds along the horizon, and Mrs. Abuthnot had regarded them with some anxiety. She had been with difficulty restrained from bringing an assortment of capes and umbrellas and ordering the closed carriage, but Alex had assured her that their presence merely indicated rain somewhere in the foothills; adding that if it had been raining up north he might well find himself being held up on his way back to Lunjore, but that they stood in no danger of a wetting that night.

The setting sun bathed the walls of the ancient city in warm splendor and dazzled the eyes of the earlier arrivals who strolled upon the broad battlements that lay between the Kashmir Gate and the Water Bastion, overlooking the green tangle of the Kudsia Bagh.

Carlyon, Winter and Alex had ridden to the picnic, while Mrs. Abuthnot and her daughters had driven in the carriage. The ride had been a pleasant one, though a trifle dusty, and Carlyon had behaved in an exemplary manner. He could be excellent company when he chose and this evening he had exerted himself to please, so that by the time they arrived at the Kashmir Gate Winter was feeling quite in charity with him. They rode in under the massive arch of the gate, and dismounting before the Main Guard, left their horses to the care of the attendant syces and walked up the sloping stone ramp to the battlements.

Alex had not accompanied them there. He had been hailed by a man on horseback who was approaching the gate from the direction of St. James's Church.

"Alex, by God!" The man had spurred forward and leaning down from the saddle had smitten Captain Randall between the shoulder blades. "When did you get back? I haven't had so much as a word from you in half a year, you ingrate!"

Alex had turned swiftly and gripped the proffered hand. "William! What the devil are you doing here? They told me you were in Dagshai." "So I am—officially."

Alex said: "Get down off that horse and join us. Condesa, may I introduce Lieutenant Hodson. William, the Condesa de los Aguilares and Lord Carlyon."

Lieutenant Hodson had reached down a hand to Winter and said: "Will you forgive me if I do not dismount? I have been suffering from a dislocated ankle and can do little more than hobble when on the ground."

He was a slim, wiry man, as slim as Alex though taller and looked to be a few years older; but where Alex was dark haired and deeply sunburned this man was of an almost Nordic fairness. The Indian suns that had apparently had no power to tan his intensely white skin had bleached his blond hair and long cavalry mustache to a yellow so pale as to be almost white, and only his eyes were dark. They were remarkable eyes, of so deep a blue as to appear black at first sight; large enough to have graced a girl, but hard and fierce and as glittering as a hawk's.

Winter and Lord Carlyon continued on their way and joined the remainder of the party on the ramparts, and Alex said: "William, your manners are as abominable as ever!"

"Nonsense! You cannot expect me to waste time talking social inanities when I have not seen you for close on two years. Ride with me; I cannot talk with you here."

Alex swung himself back into the saddle, and the two men rode out through the gate and turned right along the far side of the deep ditch that formed a wide, dry moat between the walls and the open country and jungle-like greenery of the Kudsia Bagh.

"Who was the Spanish beauty?" demanded Hodson, "and what are you doing in such company?"

"Acting as duenna," said Alex with a grin. "The Spanish beauty has come out to marry my respected chief, and I have had the thankless task of seeing to her safety during the journey."

"What!" Hodson threw back his head and shouted with laughter. "Now I have seen everything!"

"It has its humorous side," admitted Alex with a somewhat wry smile. "But then I admit I had not visualized, when I joined the Bengal Army, finding myself called upon to act in almost every civil capacity from magistrate to midwife. Being required to bring out brides for senior officials should be no surprise."

"My God, yes! The tasks we are called upon to perform in this service would raise the hairs on the heads of any Horse Guards officer! Who was the lordling? Do not tell me that you have been press-ganged into bearleading the globe-trotting nobility in addition to nursemaiding your unspeakable chief's betrothed?"

"Not yet. Though I daresay I shall come to it! Lord Carlyon is merely visiting in Delhi."

"Dangerous look in his eye," commented Hodson. "What have you done to your arm? Riding accident? or did someone put a bullet through you?"

"The latter," said Alex drawing rein among the scrub and the grasses that fringed the banks of the Jumna River. "But the sling is merely a façade. I could have discarded it some days ago, but I find it useful."

He smiled; and Hodson, who unlike Lord Carlyon had reason to know that particular smile, said accusingly: "What devilry are you up to, Alex?"

Alex laughed. "No devilry I assure you, Will. But one cannot insult a man who appears incapable of repaying the insult with a blow, and while I carry my arm in a sling his lordship can hardly be as offensive as he would wish. He has influential friends, and I have no desire to be involved in a brawl at this particular juncture. Get down, if you can hobble as far as that tree. I have more to say to you than can comfortably be said in the saddle."

He offered a hand, and having tethered the horses the two men moved off between the tussocks of grass and seated themselves on the river bank, looking out across the placid Jumna that lay all pearl pink and glinting in the evening light. Hodson put up an impatient hand and pulling off the peaked pith helmet that he wore, tossed it away into a clump of grass and ran his fingers through his yellow hair, and Alex said: "You have not yet told me what you are doing here. Have you taken French leave?"

"More or less. I came because I heard that a friend of yours was expected in Delhi—Sparkov."

"Gregori!"

"The same."

"Then he must have moved quickly. I saw him in Malta not so long ago—"

Alex recounted the incident, and Hodson said: "Very interesting. It's something to know that Kishan Prasad is one of Gregori's contacts! A clever devil, and likable. And a bosom friend of your delightful Commissioner Barton, I gather!"

"That too." Alex' voice was edged with bitterness. Hodson reached out and gripping his uninjured arm, gave it a little shake.

"I know how it is. God—don't I know! If only we could sweep out some of these obese fools what an empire this would be! But it takes more than a hundred good men to undo the harm that one Barton can create. One day we are going to find that out."

"Probably sooner than we think!" said Alex grimly.

The hard blue eyes were suddenly intent. "Why do you say that?"

Alex told him. And by the time he had finished, the shadows that the setting sun had thrown long and blue on the sands at their feet lay black behind them in the full blaze of the risen moon. A jackal scuttled out across the silver sands to feed on the rotting remains of a half-burned corpse that had stranded in shoal water, and a peacock called harshly from among the canebrakes of the Kudsia Bagh. The tethered horses stamped uneasily and Alex' mare whinnied softly.

"That will be Niaz," said Alex glancing over his shoulder. He stood up, and reaching down his hand helped Hodson to his feet. "I shall have to go back and do my social duty. Join us, Will."

"Not a chance. I must be in Dagshai tomorrow."

"Tomorrow! Are you mad? William, you cannot do it!—not with a bad ankle. Why must you always ride hell-for-leather?"

"Prefer it. And it may come in useful one day. As for the ankle, I've got it strapped into splints for the occasion. That's why I'm so lame. Damnably painful, but entirely serviceable." He limped over to his horse and called out: "Holla, Niaz Mahomed. Is it thou?"

Niaz rode forward into the moonlight and slipping from his horse gave the salute that is only given to elders of high rank.

"*Salaam Aleikum*. Is it well with thee, Hodson Bahadur?"

"Nay; ill. My star has fallen."

"That I have heard," said Niaz gravely. "No matter, it will rise again." He held the stirrup for Hodson to mount, and Alex said: "If you really mean to ride for Dagshai tonight, William, I shall not be seeing you for some time. I'm for Lunjore on Monday."

"Then this is good-by, Alex." He leaned from the saddle and their hands met in a brief, hard grip, and then he had touched his spur to his horse's flank and galloped away into the moonlight while Niaz stood stiffly to the salute.

"What does Hodson Bahadur do here?" inquired Niaz as they rode back to the Kashmir Gate.

"He sees a friend in the city."

"Does he so!" said Niaz thoughtfully. "Dost thou remember how, in the year following the taking of the Punjab, an astrologer in Amritsar cast his horoscope and foretold that in seven years his star would arise and burn bright among much blood? Those years be all but sped, and it may be that he smells that blood!"

He took the reins as Alex dismounted by the Main Guard and walked up the ramp to the battlements into a babel of voices and laughter and the clink of glasses and silver.

The picnickers were grouped about a long white cloth that had been spread over a carpet on the warm stone. The older ladies were seated in wicker chairs while the younger ones sat on cushions, their wide skirts spread about them like full-blown roses, and the men sat cross legged beside them or leant against the embrasures of the battlements. White-clad servants handed round an impressive selection of cold foods and drink by the light of the full moon—that Indian moon whose light is as clear and as bright as many a spring evening in the West.

"My dear Alex, we had quite given you up! Where have you been?" Mrs. Abuthnot edged her chair back a little and pulled aside her ample skirts, and Alex came over and subsided onto the carpet at her feet.

"I am sorry. I met a friend whom I had not seen for over two years and who leaves Delhi tonight." He accepted a plate of cold food and ate it abstractedly, his mind still on his conversation with William, but presently he became aware that someone had addressed him by name, and rousing himself he turned to find that it was Winter who sat on his left.

Winter had kept close to Mrs. Abuthnot since her arrival, for although Carlyon had made no effort to single her out for attention she was conscious of a feeling of tension and uneasiness that had been heightened by her discovery that Captain Randall had not joined the party on the battlements. If Alex did not mean to attend the picnic she would have to ride home alone with Carlyon! He had no right to leave her like this! Conway expected him to protect her from annoyance and alarm, and he should not ride off with strangers and leave her to the care of men like Carlyon!

Carlyon, however, had kept his distance and had taken his place between Delia Gardener-Smith and a Miss Jennings, daughter of the Chaplain of Delhi. A shy young lieutenant of the Bengal Artillery, George Willoughby, was seated on Winter's left, and Mrs. Abuthnot's voluminous skirts effectively protected her right.

The party was a gay one, but, try as she would, Winter could not bring herself to share in the universal high spirits. Every woman there was loved and protected. Only she, Winter de Ballesteros, belonged to no one. To no one except Conway, who could not come to Delhi to marry her! Once again a cold shiver of apprehension chilled her. Supposing when he saw her he did not want to marry her? He would do so, of course—he could hardly draw back now. But to marry without love—

And then Alex had materialized out of the moonlight and sat down at Mrs. Abuthnot's feet, and some of the tension and fear and doubt had faded. There was something about Alex that was instantly reassuring, and she fought down a sudden and childish desire to reach out her hand and clutch at his sleeve and hold it tightly. Instead she turned to him and said: "Who was the man whom you introduced us to, Captain Randall? Is he stationed in Delhi?"

Alex turned toward her with something like a frown, and then his face cleared and he said: "Oh, it's you. I'm sorry; I was not attending. What did you say?"

Winter repeated the question and Alex said: "William Hodson. No. He was only here for a day. His regiment is at present in the Simla Hills. I rather think that he has taken French leave."

"You mean left without permission? Are officers allowed to do that?"

"No. But William is a law unto himself—which has caused him a great deal of trouble in the past and will probably cause him more in the future! But if ever we get into another war in this country, I would rather have William at my back than a whole army corps. Not that he'd be at one's back! He'd be twenty paces ahead."

Winter said: "You are fond of him, aren't you?"

"Yes," said Alex briefly.

"Tell me about him."

Somewhat to his surprise Alex found himself complying with the request and telling her something of William—how he had worked under the object of their mutual admiration, Sir Henry Lawrence; acted as secretary, overseer and a hundred other roles; assisted in raising the Corps

of Guides, fought with them through the Sikh War and risen to command.
Of how the promotion of a young officer to so coveted a position, and Hodson's unorthodox methods, had aroused the enmity and spite of lesser men
whose jealousy had led to his removal from command, while official indolence had pigeonholed and suppressed the findings of the court of
inquiry that had exonerated him.

"And now he has been sent to kick his heels doing a subaltern job in
Dagshai—and this at a time when we need his kind of man more than we
have ever needed them before! My only consolation is that if there ever
is any serious trouble no one will be able to hold him!"

Alex had forgotten that he was talking to the promised wife of Mr.
Commissioner Barton who had caused him a great deal of inconvenience
and irritation. He had been talking, as he had talked once before in the
Malta moonlight, to someone with whom he was entirely at ease, and he
looked down at her now and frowned, realizing suddenly that he had been
talking uninterruptedly through three courses, and as though the two of
them had been alone. Looking away again he caught a smoldering glance
that momentarily held his own. So Carlyon at least had noticed that he
had been monopolizing the little de Ballesteros! Alex looked thoughtfully
back at Winter and then reached out and removed the empty plate that
she held in her hands.

He said: "What a subject for a moonlight picnic! Have I bored you?"

"No."

A swift and appreciative smile lit Alex' eyes. He found the brief monosyllable, shorn of the polite protestations with which a more socially experienced young lady would have adorned it, curiously touching. Alex,
himself a man who did not trouble to say "Yes" or "No" unless he meant
it, appreciated not only its obvious sincerity but the fact that the speaker
was as yet sufficiently unversed in social small talk to say exactly what she
meant and no more. He said: "Why were you interested in him?"

But this time the answer took him completely by surprise, for Winter
said simply: "Because he was a friend of yours."

Alex looked up, startled. "You see," said Winter slowly, and as though
she were explaining something to herself as much as to Alex, "I do not
really know very much about you, but one gets to know a little more
about people when you know something of their friends."

"And do you know more about me now?" inquired Alex with an odd
note in his voice.

"I think so." She looked away from him and traced a small aimless
pattern with one finger on the close pile of the Persian rug before her.
"Alex—"

"Yes?"

"Why could not Conway come to Delhi? Was there—any other reason?"

Alex did not answer and Winter said: "Other than his work I mean?"

Damnation! thought Alex, taken off guard and completely at a loss.
How did one answer a question like that at a time like this? And what

was the good of answering it? He had told her once and been slashed across the face for his pains. Now that she knew him better would she take it from him and believe it? or—I cannot throw it into her face in the middle of this bloody picnic party! thought Alex. It will have to wait—

"Was there?" persisted Winter.

"No," said Alex shortly. "That is—no. I—"

He was interrupted by Mrs. Abuthnot who leant forward and tapped him upon the shoulder with her fan. "Alex, dear boy, you are sitting on my flounce and I wish to move. Thank you—" She rose and shook out her skirts. "Winter, my love, Mrs. De Tessier tells me that we are to remove for a while so that the gentlemen may finish their wine. Come, dear. Come, Lottie."

There was a ruffle and a rustle of silks and muslins as the crinolines ceased to be flattened circles and their owners drifted away in the moonlight like a flight of enormous bubbles blown along by a light breeze.

By the time they returned, the debris of the picnic had been cleared away. Only the carpets and cushions remained, and an officer possessed of impressive whiskers and a luxuriant mustache was playing a sentimental ballad on a guitar. Winter was relieved to see Carlyon attach himself to Delia and lead her away to look at the view across the river; a proceeding that drew only a complacent smile from Mrs. Gardener-Smith. She could see no sign of Alex and wondered uneasily if he had gone home, but Sophie informed her that he had walked along the wall toward the Water Bastion. Why had he looked so disconcerted when she had asked him about Conway? He had looked—guilty.

"Winter, my love," said Mrs. Abuthnot, bearing down upon her accompanied by an unknown gentleman, "here is someone whom I am sure you must be pleased to meet. Only fancy! Mr. Carroll here passed through Lunjore less than a week ago and stayed the night with Colonel Moulson —you remember Colonel Moulson, do you not, dear?—and they both dined with Mr. Barton, so that he can give you the latest news of him. Mr. Carroll, this is the lady who is shortly to marry Mr. Barton. The Condesa de los Aguilares."

Mr. Carroll, a large man with a red face, stared at Winter and muttered that he was honored to meet her, and in reply to her eager questions said that he had indeed seen the Commissioner at the previous week end. Mr. Barton had in fact been kind enough to urge him to stay on and keep him company, there being little to occupy him at present, but though the Commissioner of Lunjore might find time hanging heavily on his hands, he himself had too many calls upon his time to allow him to—

Mr. Carroll became aware of the amazement and shock reflected on the faces of Mrs. Abuthnot, her daughters and the young Condesa, and stopped, disconcerted and alarmed.

"But that is absurd!" said Mrs. Abuthnot sharply. "Perhaps you did not know that we expected Mr. Barton in Delhi, but pressure of work did not permit him to leave Lunjore. You must be mistaken."

"Oh—er—yes," said Mr. Carroll unhappily. "I must have misunderstood. Yes, of course. I—"

Winter broke in upon his flounderings. "Mr. Carroll, please tell me. Why could my—the Commissioner—not come to Delhi? Is he—is he not well?"

Mr. Carroll, embarrassed and distressed, caught at the excuse with the fervor of a drowning man snatching at a passing straw, and overplayed his hand:

"Yes. Yes, I am afraid that is it. He—er—did not wish to distress you."

"But—but why did he not tell me?" said Winter, her hands gripped tightly together.

Mr. Carroll gulped, groped wildly for a suitable answer and was visited by inspiration: "Would not mention it, of course, for fear that you might consider it your duty to proceed immediately to his side. Sickroom no place for a delicately nurtured lady. Fever, you know—er—" Mr. Carroll had a momentary vision of the corpulent, bloated face of the Commissioner of Lunjore, and improvised glibly: "—a swelling fever. No, no, nothing serious I assure you. Merely—er—disfiguring. Not catching. But no man of sensibility would wish to meet his betrothed looking so."

"Oh, the poor, dear man!" exclaimed Mrs. Abuthnot, touched. "How well I understand! How could he wish to allow you to see him in such a sad state? Perhaps that is also why he could not come to Calcutta?"

Winter said in an eager, breathless voice: "Is that so, Mr. Carroll? How long has he been ill?"

Mr. Carroll looked unhappily at the small, tense face. He had roistered with Mr. Barton on more than one occasion and considered him a bad man with a bottle or with women. But he could not tell this white-faced young woman the truth.

"Er—not above six weeks," said Mr. Carroll. "Or it may be a little more. Slow business. He hopes to be recovered shortly. On the mend now. You will not let him know that I have told upon him? He—he did not wish you to suffer any anxiety on his account."

"No," said Winter unsteadily. "No, I will not tell him. But I am so very glad to know—and to know that he is better. Thank you, Mr. Carroll. I am truly grateful to you."

She caught up the short train of her riding habit, and turning from them went quickly away down the long stretch of the moonlit rampart toward the Water Bastion.

There were few people strolling now upon the broad ramparts, for most of them had returned to join the party. There was still, however, a lone gentleman who remained seated in an embrasure of the battlements overlooking the river, the end of his cigar making a small, warm pin point of light in the blue and black and silver of the night.

Alex had no wish for company. He was feeling angry and irritable and irrationally guilty. He had hoped that he need do no more in the way of warning off Mr. Barton's betrothed. Once she reached Lunjore and saw the man the whole affair—apart from arranging for her return to England —would be over. And what was more to the point, the breaking of the engagement would have nothing whatever to do with him, Alex Randall, and therefore it would not lead to the Commissioner having him removed from Lunjore and sent to eat his heart out—as William was doing—in some useless and junior appointment.

He heard a sound of quick, light footsteps and the rustle of a woman's dress that came to a stop beside him, and tossing the end of his cigar over the battlements he turned and rose to his feet.

Winter's small face appeared drained of all color in the white moonlight and she breathed unevenly as though she had been running. The close-fitting pearl-gray habit she wore in place of a crinoline molded the lovely lines of her figure and lent her an illusion of maturity and height. But she could not control the childish trembling of her lips or keep the hurt and anger from her eyes, and Alex, looking at her in the full moonlight with his own face in shadow, felt an odd tug at his heart, and a hurt and anger that matched her own.

She said in a quick, breathless voice that she tried to keep steady: "You knew what was the matter with Conway, didn't you? You knew all the time! You could have told me even if he did not want me to know. I had a right to know! And all these weeks I've thought—I've thought—"

Her voice broke and Alex said curtly: "I did try and tell you once, but you would not listen."

"You never told me! I asked you if there was anything the matter with him and you said there was not."

"I'm sorry," repeated Alex, relief and pity submerging that inexplicable anger. The fact that she had trusted him to tell her the truth touched and at the same time exasperated him.

Winter said: "You knew the reason why he did not come to meet me in Calcutta. You had a letter from him too. He must have told you in that."

Alex' brows twitched together in a sudden frown. "Told me what?"

"Oh, I know that he did not want me to know! Mr. Carroll told me so. He thought it would distress me and—and he wished to spare me anxiety. And I know he cannot have wished me to see him looking—"

Alex cut harshly across the sentence: "We seem to be at cross-purposes. I find I have not the remotest idea what you are talking about. What is it that Mr. Carroll has told you?"

"He told me the truth! That Conway has been ill."

"Ill?"

Winter's small chin came up with a jerk. "I hope you do not mean to deny having had any knowledge of it?"

"I most certainly do!" said Alex. "I suppose it is just possible to describe his condition in such a term, though it is not the one I would have used myself. Perhaps you will be good enough to tell me just exactly what Mr. Carroll had to say?"

Winter told him, her voice quick with indignation and reproach. "I—I suppose you meant it for the best," she finished. "But you should have known that I would prefer to be told the truth. I did not think it of you. I thought that you—"

She stopped and bit her lip and Alex said curtly: "You are right. I should have told you the truth. Will you hear it now?"

"I know it now."

"Oh, no, you do not. No—" His hand shot out and grasped her wrist as she made a move to leave him. "This time you are not going until I have said what I have to say."

Winter tugged furiously at her imprisoned wrist but Alex' lean fingers were hard and unyielding, and realizing that she could not free herself without an undignified struggle, she capitulated. "Very well. I will listen."

He released her and she snatched her hand away and stood rubbing it, her breath coming unevenly. There was doubt, and something else in her face—a dawning apprehension.

Alex said: "Mr. Barton is not ill. Not in the accepted sense of the word."

"What—what do you mean?" The words were barely a whisper.

"I mean," said Alex with brutal clarity, "that Mr. Barton suffers from overindulgence in drink, drugs and women."

Winter caught her breath in a harsh gasp and turned swiftly, but again Alex was too quick for her. He caught her by the arm and jerked her round to face him.

"I'm sorry, but you are going to hear me out. I told you once before that Barton was not a fit person for you to have anything to do with, let alone marry. I meant it. A libertine and a drunkard is hardly a suitable husband for such a woman as yourself—or for any woman for that matter. He would not come to England to marry you because he must have been well aware that, should he do so, one look at what he had become would have been enough to insure that the engagement was broken. I do not know why he did not meet you in Calcutta. Probably for the same reason. I do know, however, that the aftereffects of a debauch, if nothing else, prevented him from leaving for Delhi. He was incapable of standing upright when I left him."

He let her go, but Winter did not move. She stood quite still, her eyes wide and frightened, and once again Alex was conscious of that queer tug at his heart. He said harshly: "Well, now that you know the truth, I can only suggest that you return to Calcutta and sail for England as soon as there is a passage available."

She did not answer him, and the moment seemed to stretch out interminably. Someone at the far end of the wall was singing *Where are the flowers we gathered at morning?* and the tender, plaintive melody filled the moonlit silence with a sweet nostalgic sadness.

Winter stretched out a small groping hand in a gesture that begged for reassurance, and as it touched him something as vivid and as elemental as a flicker of lightning seemed to shiver between them. The next instant his arm was about her and he was holding her hard and close. For a brief moment she resisted him violently, her body taut with shock. And then his mouth came down on hers, and all at once the rigidity and resistance left her and the ground was no longer solid under her feet.

Her skin smelt faintly of lavender and her body was soft and sweet and fragrant in his embrace; as soft and sweet and fragrant as her lips and her closed eyelids and her shining hair. Alex' mouth was not hot and greedy as Carlyon's had been. His lips were cool and firm and his slow-moving kisses were a warm, drugging wonder that deprived her of all power of thought or movement and narrowed the night and the moonlight, the wide world and the wider sky, down to nothing more than the close circle of his arm.

She felt him free his left arm from the sling, and then his fingers were on the nape of her neck, pressing upward slowly and caressingly through the thick soft waves of hair; fondling the curve of her head and holding it as closely and possessively as his right arm held her body. His mouth moved from hers at last, and his cheek was cool and harsh against her smooth warm one.

"*Darling* . . . *darling* . . ." His voice was no more than a breathed caress, but at the sound of it the passionate spell broke and dissolved before the cold inrush of reality. Winter tore herself free and backed away from him, shaking with rage and shame and the shock of a sudden revelation.

"So *that's* why you hate him! . . ."

Her voice was low and breathless and edged with scorn: "You're jealous of Conway, and so you made it all up! You haven't even enough honor and—decency to prevent you from making love to his future wife! Conway is ill—and because you are jealous of him you do your best to blacken him to me so that you can make love to me behind his back! I hope—I hope I never have to see you again!"

Her voice broke on a sob, and then she had whirled about and had run from him, and he heard the sound of her flying feet die out along the wall and lose itself in the sound of the distant singing.

Alex lifted an uncertain hand and rubbed it dazedly across his forehead, and sitting down slowly in the embrasure, felt mechanically in his pockets for tobacco and matches. He rolled a cigarette with careful concentration and struck a match against the worn stonework. It burnt out slowly between his fingers and he dropped it with a quick grimace of pain, and removing the cigarette from his mouth, he flicked it away into the shadows.

"*Hell!*" said Alex aloud and softly, addressing the moonlight, the ancient city of Delhi, and all India.

14

CARLYON could have echoed Captain Randall's expletive, though with more violence. In pursuance of the policy of lulling Winter's fears he had seated himself as far away from her as possible, but this had not prevented him from observing that Randall had held her in conversation for the greater part of the meal, and the unusual animation on Randall's face and the interest on Winter's had both infuriated and alarmed him.

Carlyon looked across the laden cloth at Winter, trying to decide what it was about her that had become such a fever in his blood. He had known many beautiful women; women far lovelier than this slender young creature whose wideset eyes were full of a sweet unsureness that gave the lie to that full-lipped passionate mouth. Perhaps it was that—the youth and unsureness and the unawakened passion—that attracted him. To a palate jaded by experience, inexperience alone had a charm that was strangely and sharply new.

Later that evening, when the singing had begun, he had not failed to mark that neither Winter nor Randall were present; and judging from the direction of Sophie's anxious gaze he had little doubts as to where they were. As the minutes slipped by and they did not return, his jealous rage had increased until it had suddenly become past bearing, and he had risen and walked quickly away in the direction of the Water Bastion.

Halfway down the stretch of wall the shadow of a huge neem tree lay across his path, and as he reached it he heard a sound of running footsteps and someone ran into him and would have fallen but for his arms.

"Oh, it's you—" Winter's voice was breathless and sobbing and she had forgotten that she disliked this man. She had forgotten everything but the fact that Alex had betrayed her—lied to her—shamed her. "Take me home! Please take me home. I cannot stay here!"

Carlyon drew her out of the shadows and into the bright moonlight and looking down at the small distorted face saw that it was wet with tears. He said furiously: "What has he done to you? I'll go back and break his damned neck for you!"

"No—no, please." Winter's fingers clung to his arm. "I want to go back to the bungalow. Please take me back."

"Of course. But had you not better compose yourself first?" He proffered a handkerchief and presently she said in a more rational voice: "You are very kind."

"No, I am not!" There was an unexpected bitterness and sincerity in his voice and Winter looked up, startled. Carlyon recovered himself swiftly. "I told you, did I not, that if I could serve you in any way it would give me great happiness to do so. I meant it, you know."

Quite suddenly she found herself telling him everything. Conway's illness—Alex Randall's perfidy—her own fears and doubts when Conway had failed to come to Delhi. . . . "I must go to him at once. I cannot wait another week in Delhi! If he is ill he needs me. Will you—would you help me to go to him?"

Carlyon looked down into the wide, appealing eyes and saw that she was shivering violently. He knew nothing of this man that the little Condesa was to marry, but what he had seen of Captain Randall led him to suppose that Captain Randall's revelations concerning his chief were probably correct. Randall did not give him the impression of a man given to that particular form of lying. On the other hand, in making advances to his superior officer's future wife he had played his, Carlyon's, game for him, by providing him with an opportunity that appeared to be little less than a gift from the gods.

He said: "I will take you to Lunjore myself. You cannot go unescorted."

Winter drew a quick breath, her hands clasping and unclasping against her gray habit. "Would you? Would you really?"

"Of course. It is a piece of the greatest good luck that I have just purchased a carriage. There is only one thing—" He paused, frowning, and Winter said anxiously, "What is it?"

"I think perhaps it would be well if you did not mention the matter to the Abuthnots." He saw that he had startled her and said quickly: "I am sure that they would sympathize with your intentions, but they would not consider it at all suitable for you to travel alone or in my care, and I do not imagine that Mrs. Gardener-Smith could be prevailed upon to put forward the date of her departure."

"No," said Winter slowly. "No, she would not. And you are right about the Abuthnots. But I will not wait. When can we leave? Tomorrow?"

"I could arrange it."

"You are very kind. I will speak to Mrs. Abuthnot tonight and tell her that I wish to leave immediately for Lunjore. I must do that. If she will assist me then I will not have to trouble you. But if she will not, then—then I think it will be better if we leave as early as possible."

Carlyon said gravely: "You are quite right of course. Perhaps she may assist you."

He had no qualms on that score, for he was quite certain that the Abuthnots would do no such thing. He offered his arm to Winter and said: "Shall we go now? I will tell Mrs. Abuthnot that you have a headache. I do not think, you know, that you had better leave without her. It would be remarked."

Winter had returned in the carriage with Mrs. Abuthnot who, alarmed by the girl's looks, had hurried her into bed and prescribed hot milk and chlorodyne drops. Her solicitude provided the opportunity Winter had needed to beg permission and approval for an immediate departure to

Lunjore, but Mrs. Abuthnot, although deeply sympathetic, would not hear of it. Such a plan was out of the question.

"After waiting for so long, dear, you can surely wait another eight days! Only think of poor Mr. Barton's chagrin if you were to see him after all these years when he is not in looks!"

She had turned out the light and left the room, and Winter had lain awake in the darkness and made her own decision. Alex would be leaving Delhi on Monday, and if she left tomorrow she would be in Lunjore by then: married to Conway and safe from him. She did not know why she had to be safe from Alex, or stop to realize that a part of the driving impulse to get to Lunjore and to Conway arose from a panic desire to escape from him.

Conway would have to get rid of Alex. He must arrange for him to be sent to some other appointment, and until that happened she at least need not see him again. As for Carlyon, she had forgotten both her dislike and distrust of the man and thought of him as no more than a means to an end.

She groped for matches and having found and lit a candle, slipped out of bed and wrote a brief note to Carlyon. The ayah should deliver it first thing in the morning. She wrote a second and longer one to Mrs. Abuthnot, sealed it with a wafer, addressed it and put it away. Her trunks would have to be sent after her. To be packing trunks would not do at all. Lighting a second candle she made a selection of garments and other necessities, and packed them in a small valise and a capacious carpetbag. Carlyon would have to devise some means of smuggling them into the carriage. Struck by another thought she scribbled a hurried and loving note to Lottie. Lottie at least would understand! That done, she blew out the candles and fell at last into an uneasy sleep.

Mrs. Abuthnot had evidently given the question of Winter's proceeding immediately to Lunjore no further thought, for she did not refer to it on the following morning, but was full of plans for prewedding festivities, from which she was only interrupted by Carlyon inquiring of Winter if she would care to drive out with him that morning to try the new carriage?

As they drove away, Mrs. Abuthnot was surprised to see that Carlyon did not intend to sit in the carriage with his guest, but to ride beside it. The hood of the carriage had been raised against the morning sun and Mrs. Abuthnot did not leave the shade of the veranda. Winter kissed her with unusual affection, and Mrs. Abuthnot, unsuspicious by nature, was touched.

The carriage rolled out of the drive under the shadows of the pepper trees, and shortly afterward, happening to look out of her bedroom window, Mrs. Abuthnot saw Carlyon's down-country bearer and two of his syces riding out of the side gate that led from the stables, and taking with them the two spare carriage horses. She supposed that they must have had their orders, but it seemed to her an odd time of day to exercise horses and she could only imagine that it was Carlyon's ignorance of the country that had led him to order them out in the hottest part of the day.

Twelve o'clock brought no sign of the carriage, and by one o'clock Mrs. Abuthnot was seriously disturbed. Neither Winter nor Carlyon, she was persuaded, would be so thoughtlessly inconsiderate as to hold up luncheon to this extent. There could be only one explanation. The carriage must have broken down, or—horrifying thought!—the horses had bolted with it!

"Mamma," said Sophie thoughtfully, "you do not suppose that they can have eloped?"

Mrs. Abuthnot uttered a small shriek. "Sophie! How can you suggest such a thing!"

"I am sorry, Mamma, but you will own it is a little strange that all Lord Carlyon's servants and his horses have left, and none of them returned. And anyone could see that he admires Winter."

"Dear Winter would never—" began Mrs. Abuthnot, and stopped. She had suddenly recalled the kiss that Winter had given her before setting out that morning. She had imagined at the time that it was intended in part as an apology for her outbreak on the previous night when she had pleaded to be allowed to leave immediately for Lunjore. *Lunjore—!* Mrs. Abuthnot fell back in her chair with a groan that brought Lottie and Sophie running to her side.

"Oh, no!" gasped Mrs. Abuthnot pressing her plump hands to her ample bosom. "Oh, no! She *could* not do such a thing! She would at *least* have left a letter!"

Lottie flew for the hartshorn while Sophie, more practical, departed in the direction of Winter's bedroom. She returned a few minutes later with the two letters that she had found propped up on the chimney piece where they could not fail to catch the eye of the first comer.

Colonel Abuthnot, summoned from the lines by an entirely unintelligible missive from his wife and requested to pursue the runaways, had replied with an unqualified refusal. He was far too busy a man to go tearing about the country after a young chit who was old enough to know better.

"If anyone is to go in pursuit of her it had better be Captain Randall. The girl is betrothed to *his* superior officer, not mine. And he is a deal younger than I am; he might even overtake 'em. I should not."

"*Alex!*" exclaimed Mrs. Abuthnot frantically. "*Why* did I not think of that before?"

She had hurried away to dash off a brief note requesting Alex' immediate presence, and this missive had been dispatched posthaste to Ludlow Castle, with instructions to the bearer of it that it must be delivered into the Captain Sahib's own hand. But Alex had been out, and the bearer of the letter, whose instructions had not included scouring Delhi for the Captain Sahib, had settled down to sleep away the afternoon in a con-

venient patch of shade in the compound until such time as the sahib
should return.

Alex had arrived back barely half an hour before sunset and in no very
good humor. He had not been pleased to receive Mrs. Abuthnot's agitated
summons, and he was entirely unprepared for the announcement with
which the tearful lady greeted him. She saw the color leave his face and a
white line show about his mouth. He said: "What time did they leave?"

"Quite early," sobbed Mrs. Abuthnot dabbing her eyes with a handkerchief. "Ten o'clock, I think."

"Good God, ma'am," said Alex violently, "could you not have sent for
me before?"

"But we did not realize what had occurred until Sophie found this
letter—" She held it out and Alex read it with eyes that were almost black
with anger, and crushing it into a ball, thrust it into his pocket.

Colonel Abuthnot nodded gloomily at Alex. "What do you propose to
do about it, my boy?"

"Bring her back," said Alex tersely.

"Too late for that now. She'll have been out all night with that fellow
Carlyon before you can catch up with her. Probably ruined her by now."

He caught Alex' eye and took an involuntary step backward, saying
hastily: "No, no! I don't expect he'd do such a thing. But as far as her
reputation is concerned—"

Alex cut him short. "May I take it that you would be willing to allow
her to remain here when I bring her back, Mrs. Abuthnot?"

"Of course I should! I know only too well that the dear child means no
harm. It was only that she was upset by the news of Mr. Barton's illness
and wished to go to his side without loss of time. One can understand
that so well. The *best* of motives! But she may not wish to come back."

"Her wishes," said Alex through shut teeth, "have nothing whatever to
do with the matter. I shall hope to be back at a tolerably early hour tomorrow, and if this matter has not been mentioned outside the house I see
no reason why it should become known."

"You need have no fear on that score, my boy," said Colonel Abuthnot
firmly. "And if you take my advice you'll let her press on for Lunjore.
I daresay Barton may be persuaded to take a lenient view of the matter
once he has her safe, and if you don't try fetching her back it's he who'll
have the handling of her."

Alex, who had turned to leave the room, stopped with his hand on the
doorknob and looked back. "It is precisely on that account," he said savagely, "that I intend to bring her back. Lord Carlyon can go to the devil!"

The door slammed behind him, and Colonel Abuthnot, who had been
giving the matter thought, said reflectively: "Damme if I don't believe
he's in love with the girl himself! Now there'll be the devil to pay!"

Alex had stopped at Ludlow Castle barely long enough to inform his
host that he would be unavoidably absent, and to collect Niaz, a third

horse and his revolver. He had proffered no explanation for his actions and had left, riding at a breakneck speed that had taken them far on the road by the time the moon was high. He knew that the carriage could not travel at any great speed owing to the poor state of the roads, and he imagined that it would halt at some dak bungalow for the night, so that he calculated, with luck, on being able to come up with it well before midnight.

He had not given much thought to Carlyon—beyond considering him a more suitable husband for Winter de Ballesteros than the Commissioner of Lunjore—and the murderous rage that had taken possession of him at the news of their flight had been almost entirely on account of Mr. Barton.

If Winter had gone to Lunjore in the care of the Gardener-Smiths they could not have refused to shelter her and assist her to return to Delhi or Calcutta when she discovered, as she must almost immediately do, the impossibility of marrying Mr. Barton. But if she were to arrive in Lunjore alone, with no one to turn to, there was no knowing what might happen. In all probability Mr. Barton would see to it that any return was made impossible, and Alex had turned sick at the thought. Even Colonel Abuthnot's reference to Carlyon's ruining the girl had done little more at the time than add to his fury. But now he remembered it again, and a cold fear took the place of that fury as he remembered also the scene he had interrupted on the evening of Winter's arrival in Delhi, and the look he had seen in Carlyon's eyes only last night; and setting his teeth he bent far forward in the saddle, riding as though he rode in a race, and with a recklessness that startled Niaz. But he had forgotten the ford at Jathghat and the unseasonable clouds that Mrs. Abuthnot had commented upon the previous evening.

There had been rain in the foothills and on the plains beyond Moradabad and Rampur, and now, twenty-four hours and more later, the river had risen and was still rising. It had been dangerously high, but still just fordable, when Winter and Carlyon had reached it some four hours earlier. But what had then been a ford of no more than fifty yards in length was now a brown, turgid torrent measuring a quarter of a mile from bank to bank, and swirling sullenly past in the moonlight with an ominous chuckling gurgle that spoke of whirlpools and hidden currents.

Alex had been riding at a hand gallop and paying little attention to the road, and he reined in hard at Niaz's shout of warning and stared at the ugly stretch of water in blank dismay. He knew that road only too well, and knew too that when the river ran high there was nothing to do but wait for it to fall again, for the nearest alternative route meant a detour of fifty miles and over such a country as to make it a matter of less delay to wait for the floodwater to pass.

There was only one hope: that the flood had also prevented Carlyon's party from crossing. But an interview with a sleepy villager, aroused by Niaz, destroyed it within ten minutes. The river had risen to its present height only during the past three hours, and a carriage with a mem-sahib in it and a sahib riding beside it had crossed the ford less than half an hour before it became impassable. How long would the flood last? Who could say! Perchance until daylight. Perchance for a day—or two days. It had seldom lasted longer than two days except during the monsoon, when travelers went by the eastern road which took three days longer.

For the remainder of that long night Alex ranged the bank trying to find a boat that would take them across, but without success. The current was too strong and the whirlpools too dangerous to allow them to swim the horses, and to cross without them would have been worse than useless.

The dawn broke in a blaze of green and gold and saffron. Parrots shrieked, jays chattered, well wheels creaked and the smoke of early morning fires drifted blue along the level plains—and the river ran as wild and wide as it had by moonlight. By midday it showed no signs of falling, and Alex, his face harsh and haggard in the hot sunlight, swung himself back into the saddle and turned north on the long detour to the nearest bridge.

Half an hour later a small python who had recently sloughed his skin slithered across the narrow and little-used track almost under the hoofs of the horse that galloped down upon it. Shalini shied wildly, and the low branch of a kikar tree slammed against Alex' wounded arm.

He hit the ground with the point of his shoulder, and in the fractional second before his head struck against the rocks by the roadside, heard his collarbone snap as he went down into darkness.

15

WINTER lay back in a corner of the carriage and closed her eyes. The setting sun shone in under the heavy leather hood above her with a golden glare, and the surface of the road was unbelievably bad. The carriage wheels jolted into ruts and out again, and every jolt threw her body sideways or jerked it back against the squabs, and her head began to ache dully.

She told herself again that she was going to Conway and that in four days' time—less, if the roads improved—she would be with him at last. No more waiting. No more doubts or fears or loneliness. But the spell had begun to lose some of its first potent charm.

Perhaps it had first failed a little at the ford. The horses had jibbed at the swirling brown water and the coachman had looked frightened and had protested that it would be better to turn back or to wait until the water fell. But the villagers had assured them that the river was rising, and though the ford was still passable it would not be so for much longer.

For one inexplicable moment Winter had experienced a feeling of over-whelming relief. They would have to go back! The next second shame at such cowardice had stiffened her resolution and she had feverishly sec-onded Carlyon's decision to cross.

They had rested a while on the far bank and had watched the river rise steadily, inch by inch. "No more will pass that way for some days," remarked a villager who had crossed with them, and Winter had looked back at the swirling water and thought, Now there is no going back. Now, whatever happens, we must go on. The thought had been oddly frighten-ing. She did not want to go back; of course she did not want to go back! But now, even if she had wanted to do so, the road was barred behind her and the flooded river lay between her and Alex.

The road on the far side of the river had been almost worse than the one they had traveled since leaving Delhi, but Carlyon had handed the reins of his horse to one of the syces and joined Winter in the carriage. She had had little speech with him since they had started out, for it had been impossible to carry on a conversation with anyone riding beside the carriage. But now that the river had been crossed, and lay impassable be-hind them, his manner had undergone a noticeable change, and she found that she could not look up without finding his eyes upon her in that same slow appraising gaze that had so often disturbed her on the journey from Calcutta.

As the sun sank behind the trees and the carriage began to fill with shadow she asked that the hood might be lowered so that they could get the benefit of the cooler air, and Carlyon, although he had stopped the carriage and complied with her request, had laughed and said: "Why? Are you afraid of what I might do?"

There had been no possible answer to that, and Winter had forced herself to meet his gaze calmly and with a faint touch of disdain that had aroused his admiration. Despite her youth and inexperience this was no vaporish miss who would fall into a swoon and capitulate to a show of masculine force. She would be a wife worth having. His gaze rested upon her with possessive appreciation and it crossed his mind that he must re-member to see that none of the horses were left unattended and within her reach.

There was apparently a dak bungalow some few miles farther on, which they should reach before darkness fell. Winter had wished to travel by night, but Carlyon had been able to make her see the impracticability of such a course. He had not thought it necessary to explain that he had no intention of traveling farther than this particular dak bungalow. It would in all probability be no better, and possibly worse, than any they met with on the long journey from Calcutta. But it would serve. They would spend a brief, premature honeymoon under its roof. A wedding night that would only anticipate the wedding by a few days. They might even, if the sur-roundings were not too sordid and the ford remained impassable, remain there for several days. Days that would be made idyllic by the possession of a loved and desired object that he had come to covet beyond reason. And when the river fell they would return to Delhi and be married quietly and without fuss, and leave immediately for Bombay, from where they would take ship for England.

Winter would be frightened at first, but she would give way to the inevitable. Carlyon had a shrewd suspicion that the young Condesa possessed little knowledge, if any, of the physical aspects of marriage. So much the better. She would be the more easily brought to realize, in the shock of the discovery, that marriage with any other man was now quite impossible. And he had no fear whatsoever that he could not eventually make her love him.

He was surprised to discover that he wanted her love almost as much as he desired her body. Perhaps the first would take a little longer to obtain, for that he could not gain by force. But it would come to him in the end. Too many women had loved him for him to have any doubts on that score.

His annoyance on finding that the dak bungalow, when they reached it just before moonrise, was already sheltering what looked to be a large party, was considerable. It had not occurred to him that they might have company, and for a moment fury at such a disruption of his plans made him consider giving a reckless order to drive on. But both horses and riders were tired and the next dak bungalow was twelve miles ahead. As he hesitated his Calcutta bearer, who spoke sufficient English to make himself understood by his master, returned with the information that it was only an Indian lady and her servants who had broken her journey at the dak bungalow; there were rooms in plenty for himself and the miss-sahib. Carlyon, who regarded all Indians with less interest than he would the furniture of a room, drew a sigh of relief and helped Winter to alight.

They ate a tolerable meal in the main room of the bungalow while the moon rose over the plain and someone—the khansamah said it was the Mohammedan lady in the room at the far end of the veranda—played a tinkling tune on a stringed instrument.

It was a haunting thread of sound, oddly familiar, and Winter found herself listening to it with a feeling that she had heard that particular plaintive tune before. She was tired, and anxious to get to her own room and be free of Carlyon's disturbing gaze and the necessity to appear calm and composed and to make some effort at conversation, and the meal seemed interminable. She had excused herself as soon as it was over, and stepping out into the veranda had seen a *ruth*, a closed, double-domed cart, to which a pair of trotting bullocks were being harnassed.

"It is the Begum Sahiba," said one of the bungalow servants in reply to Winter's question. "She stopped only on account of a broken wheel which has now been repaired. She stays the night at a village farther on the road. She is from Oudh and returns to her home."

Winter walked slowly to the door of her room, her wide skirts rustling on the dusty stone of the veranda. I am from Oudh, she thought, and

I too am returning home. The thought gave her fresh courage and she turned and gave her hand to Carlyon, who had followed her out into the moonlit veranda, thanking him once more for his help and escort and bidding him good night.

Carlyon took her hand but he did not release it. He held it in a hard grasp with fingers that were feverishly hot and unsteady, and lifting it suddenly to his lips, he kissed it.

It was not a light gesture of gallantry, but a kiss as greedily passionate as the kisses he had forced on her once before, and which the shock of Mr. Carroll's revelations, Alex' perfidy and her own frantic desire to escape to Conway had driven into the background of her mind. She tried to drag her hand away but he held it hard, kissing it again and again, moving his hot, hungry mouth against its cool softness, and when he lifted his head at last and looked at her in the moonlight his cold eyes were cold no longer, but as hot and avid as his mouth had been. He stared at her for a long moment, breathing hard and unevenly, a dark flush on his cheeks and his eyes bright with a feverish excitement that was as inexplicable to Winter as it was terrifying. Her body shrank and turned cold with a primitive fear and a misty comprehension that the passion she had aroused in him was beyond her control—and his.

She had been disgusted and shocked and furiously angry when he had kissed her that day in the Abuthnots' drawing room. But she had not been frightened. She was frightened now. So frightened that for an appalling moment she thought that she was going to be physically sick from the fear that cramped her stomach and dried her mouth. Then Carlyon had released her hand at last and Winter turned and stumbled through the open doorway of her room.

She closed the door behind her with trembling hands and leant her weight against it as though to keep him out, while disjointed thoughts whirled round in her brain as helplessly and as frantically as the moths that battered their wings against the smoky glass of the oil lamp . . .

She should have known—she *must* have known!—that it was madness to accept Lord Carlyon's offer to escort her to Lunjore! What had possessed her to set off with him, alone and unchaperoned, or allowed her to forget —or at least excuse—his behavior on the day of their arrival in Delhi? How could she have been so foolish as to imagine that she could use him to further her own ends? Now, for the first time, she began to wonder if he had ever intended to take her to Lunjore, and even if he did so, what Conway would think of this escapade? Would it damage his position as Commissioner of Lunjore to marry a woman who had behaved in so improper a manner? Why had she never thought of that before! Well, there was only one thing she could do now; and that was to remove instantly from the dak bungalow. If she were to go at once— But how could she leave and where was she to go? The road back to Delhi was closed by the swollen ford, and she could not ask Lord Carlyon to permit her to proceed to Lunjore alone. Supposing he were to refuse? Supposing he—

A sound of wrangling voices and laughter from the compound outside cut across her despairing thoughts, and her ear caught the jingle of bells as one of the bullocks tossed its horns. The other travelers! Why, of course! She would beg help of the lady from Oudh. Surely another woman would not refuse to help her?

Winter straightened herself resolutely, and remembering the size of the Indian lady's conveyance she pulled up the spreading yards of chintz-flowered balzarine that had seemed suitable for a short drive in a carriage, and unfastened her crinoline. The hooped underskirt fell to the ground with a rustle and a click, and she stepped out of it and ran to fetch the carpetbag. The valise would have to be abandoned.

The hinges squeaked protestingly as she eased open the door, but the veranda was deserted. A flare of torches and oil lamps and a babel of voices came from the compound where the tinseled *ruth* stood, and a square of light from the window of the end room showed that the Indian lady had not yet left. Winter gathered up her trailing skirts in one hand and the carpetbag in the other and ran lightly down the moonlit veranda. The door was not locked and she could hear a woman talking on the other side of it. She pushed it open and went in.

There were three women in the room. A young and strikingly beautiful woman wearing the silk tunic and full trousers of a Mohammedan lady of family, and two older women who were obviously servants, the younger of whom uttered a small scream of alarm at the sudden appearance of a stranger.

Winter put a finger to her lips in a gesture that implored silence and spoke in a quick, breathless whisper, explaining what little she could of her predicament and begging that they would take her with them. The Indian girl—she could not have been very many years older than Winter —listened in wide-eyed astonishment and when she had finished clapped her hands like a child and said: "But it is wonderful!" She turned to the elderly serving maid: "Is it not wonderful to hear a Feringi speak as one of us? Who art thou? What is thy name?"

"Winter. Winter de Ballesteros. If the Begum Sahiba would be so kind as—"

"*What?* What is that you say?" said the girl sharply. She snatched up the oil lamp that stood on the floor and held it so that the light fell full on Winter's face.

Winter blinked at the sudden blaze and the girl stared in silence, moving the lamp so that it lit first one side of Winter's face and then the other; lifting it so that the light poured down upon the black waves of hair.

"It is!" said the girl. "*Allah Kerimast!* It is so. Little sister, do you not know me?"

"I—I do not think—" began Winter breathlessly.

"Ameera!—does thou not remember Ameera? Hast thou indeed forgotten the Gulab Mahal and my mother Juanita Begum, and the tales that *nani* told us on the rooftop?"

The older serving woman, a stout, gray-haired old lady, threw up her arms with a little wailing cry: "*Aie! Aie!* It is the *Chota Moti!* It is Zobeida's baba whom I nursed as a babe!"

Winter's eyes widened until they were dark pools in her white face and she looked from the elderly woman to the girl who had called herself Ameera.

"*Anne Marie!*" All at once there were tears in Winter's eyes, and her voice was a shaken whisper: "It is Anne Marie!"

And then quite suddenly they were in each other's arms, laughing and crying and pulling away to look at each other and clinging together again.

The soft silk; the smell of sandalwood and attar of roses; the liquid Eastern vowels—the touch and the scent and the sound of home!

A sudden tumult from the compound outside brought Winter back from the past to the recollection of her present position. She pulled away, listening, her face once more strained with alarm.

"Quick, Anne Marie—quick! Take me with you! If he should find that I am gone—"

"Hush, hush," said Ameera, granddaughter of Anne Marie de Lazencourt who had also been Condesa de los Aguilares. "None shall harm thee now, little sister. Those are my servants out there, and they shall protect thee."

"No!" said Winter urgently. "There must not be fighting! He has guns. Let us go quickly before he finds that I am not in my room."

"As thou wilt," said Ameera. "Is it thy husband from whom thou wouldst escape?"

"No. It is someone who—Anne Marie, I cannot go out there! There are lights, and his servants might see me go. Cannot the *ruth* be brought nearer?"

Ameera laughed. "No one shall see thee, Little Pearl. See, we will put Hamida's *bourqa* upon thee, thus!" She snatched up a voluminous white cotton garment that lay on the floor and dropped it over Winter's head. It was a long, full, tentlike cloak that shrouded her from head to foot, leaving only an inset of coarse net over the upper part of the face that allowed the wearer to breathe and see, but not be seen. "There!" said Ameera triumphantly. "Hamida must cover her face with her chudder if she fears that men will attack her for the sake of her beauty!"

The elderly waiting woman who had been the infant Winter's wet nurse mopped the tears from her wrinkled face and chuckled like a parrot. "I will go out by the back way, lest any of the *naukar-log* should see four women go out where but three came in."

"That is well thought of," said Ameera, donning her own *bourqa*. "Come now. We are ready."

"No—wait!" said Winter suddenly. "I must leave a message. If I do not he will think me lost and rouse the country looking for me, or go to the police. He could not just leave me and go back. Hast thou paper and ink?"

"Paper and ink? No. But Atiya here shall fetch some from the khansamah. Quick, Atiya—run!"

Ameera gave the girl a push, and she scuttled away, looking like a Halloween ghost, to return breathing hard a few minutes later and bearing a soft sheet of native paper, a bowl of black and gritty ink and a quill pen. Winter threw back the folds of the *bourqa* and wrote swiftly, Ameera holding the lamp. She thanked Lord Carlyon for his kind assistance, but she had met with a relative, a cousin, and so need put him to no further trouble on her behalf. He need be in no anxiety about her as she would be quite safe, and was continuing her journey immediately.

She held the paper above the lamp to dry the ink, her hands shaking with nervous haste, and folding it, begged Atiya to take it to her room and leave it there, but to make no sound that might attract attention. The girl had slipped out again and Winter had waited in a fever of impatience and dread until she had returned, giggling reassuringly and, to Winter's amazement, carrying the small valise. "No need to leave thy gear," said Atiya. "We will cover it with a chudder, so, and it will pass unnoticed."

They hurried down the veranda steps and out into the night, and a moment later they were in the dark, close-curtained *ruth*. There was a startled ejaculation from one of the entourage, and a fierce request to be silent from Hamida, as a fourth figure crept into the *ruth*. "That son of an owl will ruin all!" muttered Hamida angrily. The man who had exclaimed at the sight of four women, where he had expected three, inquired anxiously if all were well? "All is well, Fateh Ali," said Ameera. "Drive on. It is late."

The driver of the *ruth* shouted, the bullocks grunted and the *ruth* jolted forward and precipitated Winter into Ameera's lap, and the pent-up strains and anxieties and emotions of the last twenty-four hours found relief in a gale of laughter. She clung to Ameera and laughed and Ameera and the two serving women laughed with her, so that the driver and the four elderly mounted retainers who accompanied the *ruth* stared at each other in bewilderment and ended by chuckling in sympathy with that joyous sound.

"And now," said Ameera, drawing breath and dabbing her eyes with the edge of her veil, "tell me all! How dost thou come to be here? Art thou not yet wed? And who is this Feringi from whom we escape?"

She received no answer. Winter's head was still against her shoulder, but she had fallen asleep.

Carlyon had waited until the sound of quarreling voices and the wheels of the Indian woman's equipage had been swallowed up by the night. He had heard the khansamah and others of the dak bungalow servants pass along the veranda, and had waited until the voices from the stables and the servants' quarters at the back of the house sank to a murmur and there was silence at last.

He adjusted his long silk dressing gown to his satisfaction, ran a hand over his hair, and smiling a little, went out into the deserted veranda. The light still burned in Winter's room and he pushed the door open and went in. The room was empty, which meant that she must be in the bathroom. She had evidently prepared for bed, for her discarded crinoline was lying on the floor. He closed the door softly behind him and crossing the room sat down on the bed to wait. It was not until several minutes later when, disburbed by the silence, his eye fell upon a paper that bore his name.

Less than a minute later he was on the veranda shouting for horses, servants and lights. He dressed with desperate, raging haste, but he had allowed too much time to elapse and he did not know of the narrow side lane that led off the road to the house where Ameera was to pass the night, and down which the *ruth* and its escort had turned less than five minutes before he galloped past it.

An hour later he was forced to realize that Winter had escaped him, and he turned back, rage contending with fear for her safety, and headed for the ford on the chance that Winter's letter had been a blind and that she had, after all, turned back to Delhi. But morning showed a raging torrent where the ford had been and Carlyon had returned, white with fury, to the dak bungalow, admitting to himself at last that Winter had tricked him. He had spent two appalling days of enforced idleness at the bungalow, and on the morning of the third day, having heard that the river had fallen, he had returned to Delhi.

For Winter de Ballesteros, journeying toward her wedding in Ameera's *ruth*, it was the happiest time that she had known since the long-ago days of the Gulab Mahal. She had found a friend and a companion of her own age, and here once more was all the warmth and wonder of the old happy memories coming alive again. She told Ameera all that had happened to her, and heard in return all the news of the Gulab Mahal.

There were, Ameera said, few left in the Rose Palace who would remember the Little Pearl, for cholera had taken a heavy toll. Dasim, son of old Ali Shah's brother, was now an elderly gentleman whose wife, a soured and shrewish woman from Faizabad—Ameera pulled her laughing face into an expression of mock malice—was the senior lady of the household, though Dasim had acquired two junior wives and now possessed the three permitted by the Prophet. Ameera's sister, a baby who had been born in the fateful January that had seen the retreat from Kabul and the disastrous end of the First Afghan War, had died too of the cholera, as had the son who had been born in the same year as Winter. Ameera herself had married her second cousin Walayat Shah, a petty nobleman who had occupied one of the numerous hereditary and lucrative sinecures at the dissolute court of the King of Oudh. The annexation had dispossessed him of employment and livelihood and he and his family lived now at the Gulab Mahal. The loss of power, privilege and revenue had enraged Walayat Shah against the Feringis, and it would be better for Winter not to visit the Gulab Mahal just yet.

Men, explained Ameera regretfully, were apt to get hot and angry. They had less patience than women, and although she herself considered that the action of the Company had been highhanded and unnecessary—for were there not others of the royal line to replace Wajid Ali if he had offended?—she was happy to be back in the Gulab Mahal and had no wish to kill and burn. She had her children's safety to think of, and for their sake would be content to live quietly in the Gulab Mahal under any government who could be trusted to keep order.

"Your children!" exclaimed Winter, instantly diverted from politics to the personal. "Have you children? How lovely! How many?"

"I have two sons," said Ameera proudly. One was four years old and the other three. There had been a daughter, but she had died at birth. The little boys had been left in the care of her husband's mother while she had been away on a visit to attend the wedding of a near relative, and Ameera could not wait to get back to them.

"When thou art married and have sons of thine own thou wilt know how it is with me."

Ameera's road lay through Lunjore and across the bridge of boats. But when some five days later they neared the outskirts of the city, she would not come to the Residency, but stopped the *ruth* and sent one of her servants to fetch a hired carriage. "I have thought," said Ameera lovingly, "that it were better if thou didst not arrive at thy bridegroom's house with a cousin who is not of thy own race. I have heard that there are those among the sahib-*log* who do not look kindly on such things. But we will meet again. Surely, surely we will meet again! And now, as thou hast no woman of thine own to attend thee, Hamida here will go with thee. Nay, nay, we arranged it all last night whilst thou wert asleep! It is not seemly for thee to go to thy husband with no woman to attend thee. If he has procured another for thee, then she can return."

The two young women embraced, and Hamida collected her own and Winter's belongings and followed her out into the road. A moment later the gaily decorated *ruth* with its mounted escort had rumbled away down the long, tree-shaded road. A slim hand waved briefly between the embroidered curtains, and Ameera was gone.

Winter stood by the side of the road looking after the dust cloud that hid the *ruth*, and blinking back tears from her eyes, until Hamida, scandalized by the staring crowd of countryfolk who had paused to gape at the sight of a strange mem-sahib, hurried her into the hired carriage, and they were driven away through the hot sunlight toward the cantonments and the Residency.

16

THE Residency was a rambling, single-storied house that had once been part of the palace of a local princeling, and which had been acquired, altered and added to by a former East India Company official. It stood in extensive grounds on the edge of the jungle that was separated from it by a deep nullah that formed a natural moat on three sides, while the fourth side was protected by a high wall of whitewashed brick in which only the massive stone gateway remained to mark the fact that this had once been a royal residence.

The carriage drew up under a stone porch festooned with flowering creeper, and a startled chuprassy gaped at the girl in the close-fitting riding habit who descended from it.

Yes, agreed Durga Charan the head chuprassy cautiously, straightening his turban with an agitated hand, the Commissioner Sahib was at home. But he could see no one. He was indisposed—far too sick to receive visitors.

"I know," said Winter. "That is why I have come. I will see the sahib at once. Show me to his room."

The head chuprassy, bewildered by this young white woman who showed such an unexpected command of his own language, made an ineffectual attempt to stop her, but Winter swept past him and into the wide hall.

Conway's bedroom was darkened by curtains drawn across the windows and it smelt unpleasantly. There was a woman in it. A plump native woman dressed in brightly colored spangled muslin who crouched on the floor beside the bed and waved a palm-leaf fan. The woman looked up, startled by Winter's entrance, and rose with a clash of anklets and jewelry. She was fat and past her first youth, but in a bold, florid manner, not unbeautiful. She had been chewing pan and the smell of it, as well as the musk with which she was scented, almost overpowered the stench of sickness and brandy. She stared at Winter in indignation and hostility, her kohl-blackened eyes enormous in her plump dark face.

"The sahib is not well!" said the woman in a shrill, angry voice. "He can see no one. No one!"

"He will see me," said Winter, and walked past her to the bed.

The heap on the bed moaned, grunted and stirred, and said in a thick voice: "Wha's that? Wha's that? Shurrup, can't you! Filthy din—"

It turned over on its back and groaned aloud, and Winter looked down at a bloated, unrecognizable face. Was this—could this be Conway? She had expected to find a worn, haggard man, wasted by fever, and the fat, bloated face, yellow in the dim light of the curtained room, was entirely and unexpectedly shocking. A reek of stale spirits and foul breath made her draw back sharply. They had been dosing him with brandy! Surely that could not be a good thing for fever?

And then suddenly she remembered what Mr. Carroll had said. "A swelling fever." Of course! No wonder he had not wished her to see him like this! No wonder, not knowing her well enough to trust in her devotion to him, he had feared the effect it might have upon her! Pity and love choked her and her eyes filled with compassionate tears. She leant over him and laid a cool hand on his forehead.

Conway grunted and opened his eyes with an effort. He stared up at her for a long time, trying to focus her; half shutting one eye and then the other, and forcing them open again, completely at a loss. Must have been drunker than he had thought last night—or was it the opium? God, what a head he had! Tongue like a roll of dusty matting! He'd seen things before, but they had been strange, spotted things that had crawled or hopped. Not young and beautiful women. Couldn't be the brandy. Must be the opium. The creature was speaking. He wished that she would stop speaking and go away. He liked women, but not after a thick night. At the moment, noise—any noise—hurt his head abominably.

". . . Winter! Conway, it's Winter. Conway dear, don't you know me? I have come to look after you. You will be well soon, dearest. I am here—"

At long last, through the thick, sick, agonizing torment that filled his head and stomach, the sense of the words penetrated. . . . *Winter!* This was the fortune that he was going to marry. The ugly, skinny, dark-eyed creature from Ware. She was here! Surely he could not have collapsed from the effects of a debauch and been unconscious for weeks? What did it matter anyway? The girl was here. Must get rid of her. He was going to be sick again any minute, and that would finish it. Must get rid of her—

He was sick. Exceedingly sick. But in the more lucid interval that followed he discovered with amazement that she was holding his head and bathing his forehead with cold water, whispering endearments and telling him that he would soon be well. Fatima, standing by in stunned fury, began to protest, and Conway turned his head slowly—he could not turn his eyes—and spoke a single virulent word of dismissal.

The small, cool hands pressed his head back upon the pillow and he lay still with closed eyes, trying to think; dimly aware of disaster and the need for action. Presently he opened his eyes a little, peering at her under puffy, half-closed lids, and said thickly: "Didn't expect you. Good of you t'come. Call Ismail, there's a good girl. M'bearer."

The portly bearer, who had been hovering outside the door with a whispering and curious crowd of servants, hurried to his master's side, and after a brief and muttered colloquy turned to Winter and salaamed deeply. If the miss-sahib would follow him he would show her to her room, and refreshments would be brought. The Huzoor wished Ismail to attend upon him.

"Go with him," said Conway, forcing the words with an effort. "Y' can come back later."

When the door had closed upon her he crawled out of bed and dragged himself to the bathroom. The water in the earthenware *gurra* was cold from the cool night, and he took a tin dipper and sloshed it over his head and shoulders, shuddering at the shock of the chilly cataract on his hot, sweating body and coldly sweating head. Ismail, returning, applied a variety of well-tried remedies, and the Commissioner groaned and staggered back to his bedroom to subside heavily into a chair and demand brandy and the meaning of his future wife's premature arrival. Damn the girl! What had possessed her to come gallivanting off on her own? He would not have had this happen for the world! He had intended to arrange for the wedding to take place within an hour or two of her arrival, so as to allow her no time to change her mind. And now she had arrived unexpectedly, and alone, to find him suffering from the after-effects of a debauch, in a house stinking of spirits and the sandalwood and essence of the five nautch girls from the city who, with Fatima, had entertained his guests at a bachelor party he had given on the previous night. Had she heard rumors, and wished to catch him out unawares?

"The miss-sahib, hearing that the Huzoor was suffering from illness, hurried from Delhi in her haste to care for him," said Ismail, laying out clean linen.

Illness! She had said something to that effect, so she had. Why, of course! An innocent creature like that could have had no experience of drunkenness. She had imagined him to be suffering from some illness. . . .

The way opened before him with such surprising simplicity that he would have laughed aloud if such a physical effort had not been too painful. She was here alone and unattended. There was no one she knew in Lunjore and she could not stay the night in his house unless she were married to him. It was all going to be quite easy after all. He would send for the padre and explain that, in order to protect the young bride's reputation, the wedding must be performed immediately. And until the knot was tied he must keep up the fiction that he had been suffering from fever. It could not be better!

Revived and invigorated by the prospect, he stumbled back to bed and ordered Ismail to send a message instantly to the padre sahib requesting his immediate presence, and another to Colonel Moulson to say that he wished to see him. "And send in the barber to me, and get this room cleaned up, and open all the windows and clear the air a bit—no, don't draw the curtains, you black bastard! Oh—and keep the miss-sahib out of here, d'you hear? Tell her I'm asleep—in my bath—anything! But keep her out. Now *hut jao*—and *jeldi!*"

The padre, a thin young man suffering from weak eyes and incipient malaria, listened with an attempt at concentration to the explanation of the young Condesa's unexpected arrival and unprotected state, and agreed,

shivering with ague, that immediate marriage seemed the best solution to
the difficulty, and that as the bridegroom was unfortunately in poor health
the ceremony could be performed in the house. He would make the necessary arrangements, but the Commissioner must procure two witnesses.

Three hours later, in the drawing room of the Lunjore Residency, Sabrina's daughter stood before a makeshift altar and was married to the
nephew of Sir Ebenezer and Lady Emily Barton. She wore the pale
gray riding habit in which she had arrived, and carried a bunch of the
white jasmine that grew by the porch, and Hamida had tucked jasmine
blossoms into her black hair.

Hamida was uneasy. She had no knowledge of the ways of white men,
but the Commissioner's servants appeared to hold him in scant respect
behind his back, and half an hour in the house had left her under no
delusions as to what type of woman it was who occupied the *bibigurh*—
the small detached set of rooms that lay behind the main building and
was screened from it by a discreet hedge of poinsettia and a cluster of
pepper trees. It had been no unusual thing in the past for the sahibs to
install Indian women in their compounds, and there had been a time
when such a practice was encouraged. Not only because the lack of white
women drove men to consort with prostitutes—and therefore to take a
morganatic wife or a mistress from among the women of the country was
considered preferable—but because close association with such women
taught them more of the country, and gave them a better understanding
of the men under their command. Many had married Indian women, and
Lady Wheeler, wife of the British General commanding at Cawnpore,
was known to be an Indian lady of good family. But with the arrival of
more and more white women in the country these relationships became
fewer, and Hamida considered that out of respect to his bride the Commissioner Sahib should have pensioned off the occupant of the *bibigurh*
before her arrival. Hamida viewed the situation with suspicion and took an
instant dislike to the Commissioner's servants, whom she considered lax
and insolent.

But if Hamida had qualms, Winter had none. Her only anxiety was
on the score of Conway's health, and she was alarmed at hearing of his
intention to leave his bed for the ceremony. Supposing he should suffer a
relapse? Conway had, however, assured her that her arrival had already
worked such wonders on his spirits that he felt himself to be a new man,
and as he was already on the mend such a small exertion on so happy an
occasion could do him no harm.

That had been in the course of a brief interview in the darkened bedroom where the curtains had still been drawn against the strong sunlight.
Winter had not seen Conway again until Colonel Moulson had appeared
to lead her to the drawing room. The sight of Colonel Moulson, whom
she had never liked, was a shock to her. She had forgotten that he would
be in Lunjore, and she had not expected him to be on such intimate
terms with her betrothed as to warrant his being asked to give away the

bride. She would rather have had anyone but Colonel Moulson give her away, even Alex. . . .

Alex . . . She had a momentary and disturbing vision of Alex' face, as real and as sharply defined as though for a fractional moment he were standing between her and Colonel Moulson. Alex who had lied to her and tried to prevent her from marrying Conway. Well, he had not prevented her! She thrust the thought of him away from her, her mind recoiling from it with something oddly like panic. She would not let herself think of him at all. He did not matter any more.

Winter looked at Colonel Moulson, her pale cheeks pink, her eyes very bright and young and a little frightened; not seeing him at all, but seeing instead the old, familiar picture of Conway—golden haired, blue eyed, wearing bright armor and standing between her and Cousin Julia and unhappiness. That picture did not fade when she looked at the gross, ageing man with the pale, protuberant eyes, graying hair and slack, twitching mouth who stood or knelt beside her, and whose damp, fleshy fingers were so unsteady that it was only with difficulty that he managed to put the ring upon her finger.

There was nothing about this bulky stranger that was familiar. But he was Conway, and he had been ill. She looked down at the ring that was too loose for her finger, as the first ring that he had given her had been, and her eyes were suddenly full of happy tears.

The Rev. Chillingham had left immediately after the ceremony, but to Winter's distress Conway had refused to return to his bed.

"Nonsense! Nonsense! Never felt better in my life! Told you I was on the mend! Don't get married every day of the week. I've sent out to tell some of my friends, and they'll soon be over. They'll want to see the bride. You're the Commissioner's Lady now, m'dear. You'll have to learn to do the honors. Have some champagne! Capital stuff for putting life into yer! You'll find we keep a good cellar. Hey there, Rassul, bring another bottle!"

He toasted Winter and looked her over with considerable approval. Between pain and nausea, he had been able to spare little attention for her personal appearance. Now, however, secure in triumph, he took stock of his bride and decided that Fate had indeed been kind to him.

Who could have believed that the plain, skinny, owl-eyed child whom he had last seen six years ago would have turned out so well? She was not precisely in his style—there were enough dark-haired women in India, and when it came to Europeans he preferred 'em blond—but she was well enough. Those eyes were magnificent and if he knew anything of women that mouth promised a very pleasant wedding night. As for her figure, if her riding habit did not lie, it left little to be desired.

He put an arm about Winter's slim waist and squeezed it, and the champagne slopped over and splashed down his waistcoat.

Winter said anxiously: "Conway, please sit down. I am sure that you

cannot be strong enough to stand. Colonel Moulson, please persuade him
to return to his bed."

"Persuade him to go to bed?" exclaimed Colonel Moulson, who had
been lacing his champagne with brandy. "You shouldn't have any difficulty about gettin' him there! If I were in his place, the difficulty would
be in holdin' me back from it—the lucky dog!"

Winter had not fully understood the allusion, but the coarseness of the
laugh which accompanied it had made her color hotly and her slim body
stiffened with disgust. But Conway had only laughed and said: "Time and
to spare for that, Fred—time and to spare!" And then carriages and men
on horseback had begun to arrive and the room had filled with noisy
strangers.

There had not been many of them; perhaps a dozen in all; and only
two of them had been women. These were neither of them of the kind
whom Winter would ever have felt drawn toward, and now they made
her feel young and stiff and gauche. They were both considerably older
than she and they appeared to know Conway well, for they addressed
him—and every other man in the room—by his given name, so that Winter
had some difficulty in deciding which were their husbands.

Mrs. Wilkinson was small, plump and pretty, and made no secret of
the fact that she used rouge. She jangled a great many bracelets, smelt
strongly of violet essence and had rolling blue eyes and a high-pitched
laugh.

Mrs. Cottar was tall and thin, red haired, green eyed and ugly. She
was dressed with extreme smartness, though in a somewhat *outré* style,
and she appeared to be a general favorite with the gentlemen. Her remarks were invariably greeted with a burst of laughter and applause, but
as they were mostly delivered *sotto voce* Winter heard few of them, and
those she did hear conveyed nothing to her.

Winter herself stood silent, a small rigid smile on her face and her
anxious eyes fixed on Conway. Once, when a particularly uproarious burst
of laughter had greeted one of Mrs. Cottar's more audible sallies, he had
observed that his bride had failed to join in the general mirth, and had
urged her in rousing tones not to be such a little innocent.

"She ain't likely to remain one long; not in your company, Con!" observed Colonel Moulson with a hiccup. "Not like you to take to milk and
water after years of champagne and country-brewed brandy, eh, what!"

"But then I do not suppose that he will be putting down his cellar,"
said Mrs. Cottar softly.

There was another burst of laughter in which the Commissioner
joined uproariously, and Mrs. Cottar looked from the bridegroom's face
to the bride's, and frowned.

Lucy Cottar possessed a caustic and malicious wit and little kindness
toward her own sex, but despite her lack of beauty many men found
her attractive as well as entertaining. Mrs. Cottar enjoyed playing with
fire and had no conscience in the matter of other women's husbands, but

something in Winter's bewildered eyes gave her a momentary twinge of compunction.

"Con," said Mrs. Cottar in an undertone, "you shouldn't have done it. It isn't decent."

"What ain't decent?" demanded Mr. Barton.

"You aren't! What possessed that child's family to send her out to you? Why, it's no better than rape! Didn't they know you?"

"I took dam' good care that they didn't!" said Mr. Barton, and shouted with laughter. He was feeling lightheaded with triumph. All over—all the waiting! All the work! He'd married the fortune. He was a rich man. A rich man and a dam' clever one! He'd planned it all, and it had all come about just as he had planned it. Not a hitch. Clever!

Mrs. Cottar left him and addressed herself to his wife: "You must find so many strangers a little bewildering at first. But I hope you will not expect Lunjore to be as gay as Calcutta or Delhi, or you will find yourself sadly disappointed in us!"

"Oh, but I never expected it to be gay," Winter hastened to assure her, "and I know that Conway—Mr. Barton—will be far too overworked, once he is well again, to have much time for entertainments."

"Has he been ill?" inquired Mrs. Cottar in some surprise. "I did not know. But then I have not seen him for above a week. You must know that that is most unusual, for we all meet a great deal. Your husband has been used to giving a small party as a regular thing each Tuesday night for his special cronies—in addition to any official entertaining and his bachelor parties. But I had a migraine last week and could not attend, although Josh went—the selfish creature."

She saw that Winter was looking at her with a stunned bewilderment and said in explanation: "Josh—Joshua—is my husband. The large dark one by the door." She pointed with her fan.

Winter said slowly and as if she found it difficult to articulate: "But—but Conway—Mr. Barton, has been ill, you know. Since—since late August."

"Ill? Feathers! Did he tell you that? He was joking. Perhaps he meant you to believe that he was sick for love!"

"But Mr. Carroll told me—"

"Carroll? Do you mean Jack Carroll? Oh, that would be just his way of saying that Con gave one of his bachelor parties when Jack was last here, and they were all in a melancholy way the next morning. I know Josh was! I am afraid that the men will sadly miss those parties now that Con is married, but I hope that you do not mean to discontinue our Tuesday sociables? We gamble, you know. Not very heavy stakes, but enough to make it exciting. Do you play cards?"

"No," said Winter. "No, I—I have never . . ."

"We must teach you. And you need not be afraid that Con will be too overworked to enter into our few entertainments. Why, he is the idlest of creatures! He lets Alex Randall do all the work while he takes all the credit. Quite shocking—is it not, Con?"

"What's shockin' about that?" demanded Mr. Barton, coming to anchor beside them. "Randall likes work. *I've* better use f' my time, m'dear, but Alex is a cold fish."

"Oh, no, he is not," said Mrs. Cottar with a twisted smile. "You're out there, Con!"

"Speakin' from personal experience, Lou?"

"No, alas!"

"Which means that you tried your lures on him, eh?"

"But of course! Any woman of spirit would have done the same. But he does not mix business with pleasure, and Lunjore is business. Such a pity."

"Not for me!" said the Commissioner, holding out his glass to be refilled by an obsequious khidmatgar. "He deals with the business while I take care of the pleasure. Very satisfactory arrangement, Lou, my love!" He drank deeply and looked down at his wife's white, rigid face. "Mustn't forget I'm a married man now. Have to watch m'self. Eh, m'dear?" He pinched his wife's chin and slopped a quantity of brandy down her dress.

The rest of the evening was a nightmare to Winter. A dreadful, feverish dream of babel and noise and the clink of glasses. She sat on a sofa with her back straight and her head high and a small social smile frozen on her face. She answered when she was spoken to, but her voice did not seem to belong to her any more.

The sun sank and the room filled with shadows. Lamps and candles were lit and the *chiks* rolled up to let in the cool night air, but still the noise went on and still no one left. Hours later—or so it seemed—a meal was served in the big dining room, and Winter sat beside her bridegroom at the head of the table, white faced and dry eyed, smiling with stiff lips and trying to force herself to eat the food that was placed before her. Toasts were drunk and speeches were made, and still she sat there as if she were held in a strange trance in which her body had turned into some inanimate jointed thing and her mind had ceased to function.

It was midnight before the guests departed, and they would not have gone then but for a Major Mottisham, who, suddenly recollecting that this was a wedding party and not a carouse, made a short and garbled speech full of distressingly broad allusions, and herded the wedding guests into the hall.

Winter stood on the porch steps beside her husband with her hands hanging at her sides and her face still wearing that frozen smile, while carriage wheels rolled away and horses' hoofs scattered the gravel. They had gone at last, and the house was quiet.

The garden was full of moonlight and in the drawing room the servants were stacking glasses and removing cigar stubs, turning out lamps and blowing out candles. "Well, we may not have had a full-dress weddin'," said Conway, "but we cer'nly had a capital celebration! Don't get married every day of your life, s'just as well to enjoy it. Eat, drink an' ge' married! That's it, ain't it, m'dear?"

He appeared to expect some reply and Winter said in a stiff, expressionless voice: "I am very tired. I think if you do not mind that I will go to bed."

"Tha's right. You go to bed. I won't keep y' waiting." He laughed uproariously and Winter turned away and walked slowly and unsteadily to her room, as though it were she and not Conway who was drunk.

Hamida was waiting for her, and the sight of the girl's white face and dazed eyes filled her with clucking alarm. But Winter paid no attention to her words and did not even hear them. She allowed herself to be undressed and bathed, clad in a cambric nightgown, her hair brushed out and tied with a ribbon, and put to bed as though she were not even a child but a large doll. Her world—the dream world that she had built up for years and planned for and longed and lived for—was in ruins about her, but she could not even think.

At least it was quiet at last. The noise and the babel, the meaningless talk, the incomprehensible jests, the shouts of laughter and the clink of glasses had stopped, and she was alone, for now even Hamida was gone. Now perhaps she could think again—could cry, to ease the terrible pain in her heart. And then the door opened and Conway was there.

Winter sat up swiftly, pulling the sheets up about her, wondering dully what he wished to say to her so late at night. She watched stupidly while he came toward her, weaving a little in his walk, and put his candle down upon the bedside table and began to remove his dressing gown. And then, quite suddenly, the numbness left her and gave place to sheer panic and horror.

This man—this gross, repulsive, drunken stranger—was going to get into the same bed with her! To lie down beside her—touch her—kiss her! She dragged the sheets up to her chin and her eyes widened until they were enormous in her small face.

"Please go away at once!" Her voice was hoarse with fear and loathing. "You cannot sleep here tonight—not tonight. Go away!"

Conway gave a drunken chuckle of approval. "Coy, are you, my shy little virgin? That's as it should be! But yer a wife now." He looked down at her and his red-rimmed eyes lit with a look that she had seen before. A look that had been in Carlyon's eyes. . . .

"By gad, yer a beauty after all!" The thick voice held a note of awe. "It would a' been worth marryin' any ugly wench with that fortune, but to get a beauty into the bargain—!"

He reached out an unsteady hand and lifted a long tress of the black unbound hair, and Winter struck at his hand in fury and terror.

"Don't touch me!"

Conway lunged toward her across the bed and she flung aside the sheets and leapt out, in the grip of the same frantic, shuddering panic that she had experienced when Carlyon had looked at her by the door of her room at the dak bungalow beyond the ford. But her husband's clutching hands were on her hair and they gripped it and jerked it brutally, so that she fell back and was caught. And this time there was no escape.

17

ALEX was both strong and healthy, and Niaz had sufficient knowledge of such matters as concussion and broken collarbones to deal more than adequately with the situation. Having assured himself that the injury was not serious, he had eased off Alex' coat and set the collarbone, binding it securely with his puggree, retrieved Shalini, who had stopped a hundred yards further on and was peacefully cropping grass.

Leaving Alex lying in the shade, Niaz had ridden back to a small village they had recently passed. There he had procured a ramshackle palanquin and bearers to carry it, and an hour later Alex had been installed in the hut of the village headman and under the care of a wrinkled crone well versed in the use of healing herbs.

He had not recovered consciousness until a little before dawn on the following day, and all through that day, while Niaz held him down so that he should do no further injury to his arm and shoulder, he had talked, sometimes in English, sometimes in Urdu or Pashto, muttering and raving. Once he spoke in a strange tongue. An odd sentence, twice repeated: "*Kogo zakhochet Bog pogubit, sperva lishit razuma,*" and Niaz did not know that he spoke in Russian: "Whom the Gods would destroy, they first make mad."

Toward sunset he became quieter and lay still at last, talking to Winter, his hoarse, exhausted voice barely a whisper. But it was not until the morning of the sixth day that, awakening to the first brilliant rays of the sun and the squeaking of a well wheel, he remembered Delhi and all that had happened there.

It had taken him some time to realize how many days had elapsed since he had ridden in pursuit of Winter and Carlyon, and when he had done so he had propped himself on his unwounded arm and cursed Niaz with a savage, concentrated fury for having let him lie there; for having given him drugs and for not having put him on his horse and taken him on to Lunjore.

"Had I done so, it had gone ill with thee," said Niaz, unmoved. "I sent word to Fraser Sahib in Delhi, and also to Barton Sahib, that thou hadst met with an accident and would be delayed. Tomorrow we will go on to Lunjore."

"We will go today, and within the hour," said Alex.

Niaz observed him with a thoughtful eye and said in a noncommittal voice: "I sent a man to get news at the ford. The river fell three days back, and the Lord Sahib returned with the carriage and horses and his *naukar-log*. They go to Delhi."

Alex looked at him for a long moment. Then he said: "Was the Lady Sahib with him?"

"No. But the man spoke with one of the syces, and it was said that she had met with friends upon the road and had gone forward with them to Lunjore."

Alex lay back slowly on the string bed and stared up at the smoke-blackened ceiling above his head. He was silent for so long that at last Niaz cleared his throat and said carefully: "Do we ride today?"

"No." Alex closed his eyes, and turning his face to the wall did not speak again.

If Winter had indeed met with friends upon the road she would have reached Lunjore days ago, and there was nothing more that he could do about that. She would have learned by now what sort of a man Conway Barton was, and would probably be staying with these friends until she could arrange to return to England. If he should see her again, would he try and stop her from returning home, or would he let her go? He did not know. Barely more than a week ago he would have been thankful to see her go. But that had been before he had kissed her. Alex had kissed other women, and forgotten them; but he could still feel that warm, rounded slenderness in his arms and the way in which, for a long moment, she had seemed to melt against him and become so much a part of him that her every nerve and pulse and breath and heartbeat had been as though it were his own.

Her mind could deceive her with the pretty pictures that it made up and hugged for comfort during the past six years, and her tongue could talk of her love for Conway; but her body had betrayed her. If she had known anything of love—if her love for Conway Barton had gone deeper than a lonely child's romantic attachment and hero worship—Alex' arms and his kisses would have been unendurable to her. But they had not been; for a long, long moment they had not been. . . .

She had better go home—and soon. He would not see her again, and for all he knew she might already have left Lunjore. He should have refused point-blank to have anything to do with bringing her out to this country. But if he had quarreled with the Commissioner . . .

He was back again in the old, infuriating impasse. To come into direct conflict with the Commissioner would mean, without a shadow of doubt, that he would end up by being sent to some useless and nonessential post where he could do neither harm nor good, and to Alex, pupil and disciple of Sir Henry Lawrence, the necessity of doing to the best of his

ability the work that lay to his hand, no matter how many obstacles official-
dom placed in his way, took precedence over every other consideration.

That evening when the cooking fires were lit, the headman and some
of the village elders, finding that Alex was sufficiently recovered to sit
up and eat, came to squat by the door, smoke their hookahs and converse
with him.

Their talk was a talk that Alex understood and had listened to on
many occasions—the all-important problems of village life. Crops and
harvesting, the drying up of a well, the damage done by deer and wild
pig, the failure of certain crops owing to a poor monsoon, a dispute over
a marriage dowry—half of which had not been paid—and a vexed question
of grazing rights. This was the India that he knew and loved and which,
as far as any European may understand the mind of India, he understood.

India to Alex was the land. The cultivator and the herdsman and the
hundreds of thousands of small, humble village communities whose way
of life had not changed in the slow centuries since Alexander of Mace-
donia and his warriors had poured through the passes to conquer the unknown land that had been old when Greece was young. It was the cities
that spawned dirt, disease and dissention. The villagers had their failings:
their methods of cultivation did not change; they never learned better
and they did not wish to; what was good enough for their forefathers
was good enough for them, and so they lived always with the specter of
starvation grinning at their shoulder. But they toiled hard and they were
kindly people and Alex, listening to them now, felt more relaxed and at
peace than he had for many days.

The following day he and Niaz had left for Lunjore in the cool brightness of the early morning, to a courteous chorus of good wishes; the headman and some others escorting them a mile upon their way.

Alex took the remainder of the journey by easier stages than he would
normally have done, and Winter had been married almost a week by the
time he rode down the long dusty road that led past the Residency and
his own bungalow. He had ridden less than thirty miles that day, but he
was intolerably tired and impatient with himself for being so. His bungalow was pleasantly cool after the heat of the sun-baked roads, and Alam
Din, who combined the offices of butler and bearer, had prepared a meal
—Niaz having sent forward word of their arrival.

Alex had meant to go straight to bed and merely send word to the
Commissioner of his arrival, reporting to him on the following morning,
but the Commissioner had sent over to say that he wished to see him
that evening, and so he walked over to the Residency in the warm starlight
and was ushered into the Commissioner's drawing room.

The big room was brightly lit and empty, and there was something unusual about it. It was no longer the untidy and somewhat raffish apartment with which he was familiar. The furniture had been rearranged
and the place was clean, and there were no less than three vases of flowers.
Alex was frowning abstractedly at an arrangement of orange lilies and

yellow jasmine, when a door at the far end of the room opened and he looked up and saw Winter.

He should have been prepared for it, but he was not. He was neither prepared for the sight of her nor for what it did to him.

They stood quite still and looked at each other, their faces white and drawn with shock, their eyes wide and fixed and unbelieving. There was a clock in the room, a massive affair of marble and gilt. The pendulum swung to and fro counting the ticking seconds into the silence, and the sound of them seemed to grow louder and louder in the stillness. Alex put out a hand with the groping gesture of a blind man and caught the back of a chair and held it, and Winter saw his knuckles shine white, and saw too that there were bright beads of sweat on his forehead.

Her own fingers tightened about the doorknob, gripping it desperately as she fought with a tide of shame and despair that equaled the shame and desperation of her wedding night.

Alex said harshly: "Did you marry him?"

"Yes." The word was barely a breath.

"Why?"

Winter moved her head in a slight, helpless gesture that was less a refusal to answer than hopelessness.

Something in that small despairing movement hurt Alex with savage pain that was as entirely physical as the touch of a hot iron. "Was it because you had no one else to go to? You could have—" He stopped abruptly, aware of the futility of questions or answers. The thing was done. His head was aching abominably and it was suddenly an effort to stand erect. He said in a curiously formal voice that somehow gave the impression that he was a little drunk: "Will you make my excuses to your husband? He sent for me, but I have had a somewhat tiring day and I feel sure he will forgive me if I postpone the interview until the morning. Good night."

He turned on his heel, and Winter heard him stumble as he went down the porch steps, and then the sound of his footsteps died away into the silence until there was only the clock ticking again, louder and louder, and presently a muffled bellow of laughter from the direction of the dining room where Conway and his friends were finishing the port.

Alex had gone. She had let him go, though she could have stopped him. Even now, if she ran after him, he might help her. He could not dissolve her marriage; that was irrevocable; but he would not refuse to help her. He would do something—she did not know what, but something! Yet how could she possibly appeal to him after what had occurred in Delhi— after the insults she had hurled at him? She could only hope that she need not see him again. And there was no one else she could appeal to, for even Hamida had gone.

The morning after her wedding day Winter had awakened from the deep sleep of utter mental and physical exhaustion to the full and despairing realization of what she had done. There had been a heavy out-

flung arm lying across her, its inert weight hurting her breasts, and beside
her, his mouth open, her bridegroom snored in sodden slumber. He had
groaned and rolled his head on the pillow when she had moved, but he
had not awakened, and Winter had crept shuddering from under that
arm and from the bed, dizzy, bruised, sick with loathing and despair,
and huddling a shawl about her had stumbled into the dressing room and
bolted the door behind her.

Hamida had been there, waiting for her, and Winter had clung to her,
shivering, dry eyed and desperate. Hamida had crooned over her and
petted her, but it was obvious that she considered that these things were
but a normal part of life. She herself, said Hamida, had been many years
younger than Winter when she had been wed, and her husband had been
a lusty man—a bear!—so that Hamida too had screamed in terror on her
wedding night and had wept and shivered for many days afterward. But
in time she had come to love her husband and to welcome his embraces,
and she had borne him five sons of whom four still lived, so that her
grandsons were many. Husbands, said Hamida, were often rough and
brutal in the marriage bed, but wives must bear such things and learn
to please their lords, lest their lords turned to light women. Winter's
hysterical assertion that she intended to leave Lunjore immediately was
received with scandalized horror. Such a thing was impossible—unthinkable! Wives did not behave thus. They had their duties and their responsibilities, and to run away because they found a bridegroom not
entirely to their taste was unheard of! She was married now, and she
could not run away from it.

But within a week Hamida had gone. It was the plump, painted woman
whom Winter had found sitting beside Conway's bed on the morning of
her arrival who was responsible. Fatima Bai, the woman who lived in the
bibigurh behind the scarlet poinsettias and the feathery screen of pepper
trees with her sister and her own serving women. Fatima Bai had recognized an enemy in Hamida and had taken steps to remove her. Conway
had told his wife that she must dismiss the woman she had brought with
her, as he had already made arrangements for an ayah, and an outsider
would only cause trouble among the other servants.

Winter had refused flatly to part with Hamida, and Conway, to his
wrath, had found that he could do nothing to alter her decision. He had
lost his temper and had said things that had stripped the last rags of her
illusions from her. She had not given way, but the next day Hamida had
been taken ill, and had whispered to Winter that her food had been
poisoned. "Do not fear, child. I ate only a little, and tomorrow I shall be
well again. But after this I must buy all my own food and cook it apart,
letting no one near, so that they cannot try again."

But Winter would not hear of it. She would not risk Hamida's life and
she sent her away, sending gifts and messages by her to Ameera. And
with Hamida went her only link with the outside world.

There remained Mrs. Gardener-Smith, who had called upon her on the afternoon of her arrival in Lunjore. But Mrs. Gardener-Smith's views on young wives and their duties toward husbands—especially husbands as senior and affable as the Commissioner of Lunjore—appeared to be much the same as Hamida's. She had not only been unsympathetic, she had been scandalized. Of course all men drank, and on occasions drank too much and behaved accordingly. But ladies did not mention such things! They looked the other way. As for the suggestion that she, Mrs. Gardener-Smith, should assist Winter to leave her husband, she would have nothing whatever to do with such a preposterous proposal! Such a course could only involve her in unpleasantness with the Commissioner, and on those grounds alone she would not think of it. But even if Winter *should* be mad enough to run away, she would not get far, for the law would be on Mr. Barton's side and could force her to return. Dear Winter must remember that she was no longer a heedless girl but a married woman, and marriage entailed responsibilities. . . .

Winter watched her drive away down the dusty, shadow-barred roads of the cantonment with her last hope gone. Mrs. Gardener-Smith had been right, as Hamida had been right. She had married Conway and she could not run away; because there was nowhere to run to, and because however far she ran it would not be far enough. The law would send her back to her lawful husband. She had indeed made her bed and now she must lie on it.

She had not thought it was possible to experience more humiliation or more despair, until on the evening of that same day she had opened the door into the drawing room and had seen Alex Randall, and known that she was wrong.

In the slow days and weeks that followed she had seen Alex only rarely, and never to speak to. He had not left Lunjore, and Winter, who had once meant to influence Conway to send him away, had grown to be almost glad of it. The fact that he was there, even if she did not speak to him or see him, was curiously comforting; the one strong link in a rotted and rusty chain. If ever life and living became more than she could endure, there was Alex. He at least would not refuse to help her. He knew Conway.

Alex spent a large part of his time in the outlying areas of the district, but when he was not on tour he was often in the Commissioner's office, and Winter would hear the murmur of his level voice that always seemed to her, when he was addressing her husband, to hold something of the deliberate restraint of an adult explaining a problem patiently and tactfully to a backward and fractious child. The truth of Mrs. Cottar's flippant remark that Captain Randall did the work while Mr. Commissioner Barton took the credit was soon patently obvious to her.

There was a rumor that the Governor-General was contemplating an extensive tour, which would include Lunjore, in the following year, and the Commissioner scented a possible knighthood. The prospect of being able to retire not only as a wealthy man but as "Sir Conway," appealed strongly to his vanity, and he therefore decided to postpone his resignation for a year, and also to make that year as pleasant as possible. He ceased to take even a casual interest in the affairs of Lunjore, and Alex' work was greatly simplified thereby, though it meant that he spent more time in Lunjore itself and less out in the district.

Secure now in the possession of large wealth the Commissioner entertained lavishly and the Residency was always full of guests. He ordered new furniture and furnishings from Calcutta, so that his house should be fit to entertain the Governor-General and his Staff in, and talked of building a new wing. He was proud of his wife's looks and poise and of the way in which she ordered his house and played hostess to his guests. He could see that her dresses, her jewels and her youthful dignity made an impression on them, but he had early tired of her as a woman. She had never again screamed and wept and fought him, but the passive, rigid disgust with which she had endured his subsequent embraces had soon robbed them of any pleasure, and he had returned to the coarser and more co-operative Fatima for his entertainment.

18

CONWAY did not allow the fact that he was now married to alter his way of life to any great extent, and his more raffish friends were frequent visitors at the Residency. Mrs. Cottar, acidly witty, and Mrs. Wilkinson, plump, pouting and feline, were often to be seen there, with or without their husbands, and the Tuesday parties of which Mrs. Cottar had spoken were not discontinued. Winter played hostess at any of the Commissioner's parties that might be considered official entertaining, but she had refused to preside at the long sessions of gambling and drinking that constituted these particular entertainments, and on Tuesdays she would retire early to bed with the plea of a headache.

She made no friends among the British community in Lunjore. She had been too frozen with misery, and too occupied with the strain of concealing it from a horde of interested, curious and congratulatory strangers, to appear as anything but quiet, pleasant, but cold. Neither did she like the Residency servants, in particular her ayah Johara, the sister of the woman in the *bibigurh* who, so Conway had informed her—his eyes sliding away from hers—was the wife of his butler Iman Bux, whom he had permitted to occupy the quarter. But she was given no opportunity to dismiss them.

Mrs. Gardener-Smith claimed that her daughter Delia was Mrs. Commissioner Barton's greatest friend, and indeed Delia went often to the Residency. But if the truth were known she went there more on Colonel

Moulson's account than on Winter's, and Winter had been surprised and disturbed to find that Delia was becoming one of the "Tuesday Crowd." She had not thought that Mrs. Gardener-Smith would permit it, and she felt sure that Colonel Gardener-Smith—a silent, elderly, earnest man— would not wish his daughter to attend such affairs.

But Delia's father had other things on his mind. With the laudable intention of improving the lot of his sepoys' families he had provided them with a school and a medical center, but their response to both had been disappointing. He had recently discovered that they regarded his philanthropic venture as being a subtle method of destroying their caste, and he had no hesitation in laying the blame for this attitude at the door of Colonel Packer, the commanding officer of the 105th Bengal Infantry Regiment.

Colonel Packer, a bigoted Christian, felt that his duty toward his God impelled him to make every effort to convert his entire regiment to Christianity—a proceeding that the majority of the British officers and every sepoy in Lunjore viewed with the utmost hostility and dismay—and Colonel Gardener-Smith, attributing the suspicions aroused by his own schemes to Colonel Packer's proselytizing, did not despair of popularizing both school and medical center, and his absorption in the welfare of his beloved regiment left him with little attention to spare for the social activities of his wife and daughter.

Winter had endeavored to warn Delia's mamma of the style of the Tuesday parties. "You see, I—I do not attend them myself, and I would prefer them not to be held in my house. But they were established before —before I married Mr. Barton, and he wished to continue them."

But Mrs. Gardener-Smith had been either genuinely or intentionally obtuse, and had continued to permit her daughter to attend these functions, and Winter had made no further attempt to interfere.

She had made one friend within the walls of the Residency. Zeb-un-Nissa, the nine-year-old granddaughter of Akbar Khan, the gatekeeper. Nissa was a frail little creature whose enormous dark eyes had a curiously blind look, as though they looked through people and not at them. She was reported to be subject to fits and to have second sight, and the servants were afraid of her.

She was a solitary child, and spent much of her time among the roots of the big banyan tree near the Residency gate, watching the birds and squirrels who appeared to have no fear of her, and would feed from her hand and take grain from between her lips. Winter would often join her there, and the two had become fast friends.

As the weeks passed, Winter became less actively unhappy. There was still India, and that alone, in the ruin of her dreams, had not betrayed her. She would ride out every evening and in the early morning before the sun rose; galloping across the plain and along the banks of the distant river, or riding through the dew-wet crops where the peafowl screamed at the dawn and skeins of wild geese, who had been feeding among the plowed lands, honked overhead on their way to the jheels of Hazrat Bagh and Pari. The glory of the sunrise over the limitless plains and the wide, winding river; the quiet beauty of the evenings when the sun sank with incredible swiftness, dyeing the river and the long silver sandbanks to a warm, glowing apricot; the swift, opal twilight, and night unfolding like a peacock's tail—green and blue and violet, flecked with the last gold of the day and spangled with stars—these were the things that comforted Winter and held for her a never-failing enchantment, daily renewed.

There was a fatalism too about the East that appealed to her, and the filth and squalor and cruelty that everywhere underlay the beauty did not in any way lessen her love for the land. The city was ugly and fetid and full of sights that were unbelievably horrible to Western eyes, and Winter's eyes did not miss them. But she loved the city despite it: loved the heaped colors of fruits and vegetables and grain in the bazaar. The rich smell of mustard oil and *masala*, of musk and spices and of ghee. The shops of the potter and the silversmith. The stalls that sold glass bangles, fine and light as silk and as fragile as a dried leaf, in glittering, sparkling, burning colors—red and blue and gold and grass-green. The silk shops with their gay bales piled high in the shadows. The drifting, jostling crowds and the great, lazy Brahmany bulls, sacred to Shiva, who shouldered through the narrow streets taking toll of the baskets of the vegetable sellers.

White women were seldom to be seen in the city, and on the rare occasions on which they went there they went in carriages and were escorted by white men. But Winter would go with only Yusaf, the syce, and at first the crowds would collect to giggle and stare and follow her, peering and whispering; but she went so often that they became used to her, and to the fact that she spoke their language with an idiomatic fluency that they had rarely met with in others of the sahib-*log*. She came to have many friends and acquaintances in the city. Unexpected friends and strange acquaintances who would have horrified and disgusted her husband had he known of it. But Conway took little interest in his wife's doings, and he did not know or care where she went.

Alex knew, and though it had at first disturbed him, he had come to the conclusion that her greatest safety might one day lie in such friendships, and he had withdrawn the watch he had set on her. He seldom saw her, and then only at a distance when he rode abroad, and he might never have spoken to her again—or, indeed, to anyone else!—had it not been for a sudden drop in temperature on a night early in the new year.

The unexpected cold had awakened Winter who slept alone in the wide bed, for Conway had moved back into his own room once more and seldom visited her. The moon rode high and shone into the windows of her room, and Winter sat up and reached for the quilt that normally lay folded at the foot of her bed. But it was not there, and she remembered that she had taken it into the dressing room earlier that evening.

She slipped out of bed, shivering, and pulling a light cashmere shawl about her shoulders, crossed the room and pushed open the door of the dressing room. She had left the quilt on the couch by the bathroom door, and her hand was upon it when she became aware of the whispers, and stood still, listening.

The sibilant sound held something of the faint, hollow clarity of an echo and seemed to come from the bathroom, the door into which had been left open. Winter stood clutching the quilt, shivering and a little frightened, until quite suddenly she realized that the voices were speaking in Urdu and that the ghostly echoing quality was accounted for by the wide stone sluice pipe that carried off the bath water.

Someone was squatting on the far side of the bathroom wall. Winter heard the bubbling sound of a hookah, and supposed that it must be Dunde Khan, the night watchman, whiling away the long hours with a wakeful friend from the servants' quarters. She had a sudden childish impulse to creep into the bathroom and wail down the sluice pipe. Such a sound, coming out of nothingness, would startle old Dunde Khan considerably.

She tiptoed through the open door, smiling at the thought, and then dismissed it reluctantly, visualizing the household aroused by a piercing yell of panic. She was turning away when the soft, disembodied voice whispered again in the silence: "He will be riding Chytuc or Shalini, for the Eagle has cast a shoe; and either will show up far against the crops—"

Winter stood still, her attention suddenly arrested. Those were Captain Randall's horses. Then a second voice spoke, less distinctly this time but still audible: "But what of Niaz Mahomed? It is seldom that Randall Sahib rides without him."

"That has been arranged. By now I think he will be suffering from a little sickness—enough to keep him to his bed tomorrow. And the syce has a poisoned hand. I think the sahib will ride alone."

Yet another voice spoke, but this time the speaker must have been farther away, for Winter could not catch the whispered words. She found that she was shivering again, but not with cold, and crept forward into the darkness, feeling for each step, and with a hand outstretched before her. She crouched down so that her head was nearer the level of the pipe, and started as a voice appeared to speak almost in her ear: "And what if he does not ride by way of Chunwar?"

"He will. There is a report that the canal bank has been breached by Mahomed Afzal for his fields, and sitting by the office door I heard him tell the Commissioner Sahib that he would go on the morrow, when he rides at dawn, to see if the report were true. And as all know, to ride to Chunwar he must cross the nullah near the dhak trees. There is no other way for a horseman. Mehan Lall will be waiting there. It will be thought an accident, and afterward there will be witnesses to tell that the sahib's horse took fright—which all will believe, for did not he fall from his horse not three months agone, and lie sick with a cracked head? When a man has been dragged by a foot that is caught in the stirrup of a bolting horse it is difficult to tell which injury caused his death."

There was a pause in which the hookah bubbled again, and a faint scent of tobacco smoke drifted into the cold blackness of the bathroom. Winter heard a man clear his throat and spit, and then a voice said: "Why is this necessary? It is but one sahib, and there are many."

"There be many fools to one wise man," grunted the first speaker. "Up by Peshawar way they say that there are many sahibs—but only one Nikel Seyn! It is the same everywhere and with all men. If those who see where others are blind be removed from the path, the matter is thereby made easier."

"But—but this is a good man"—another voice, farther away and almost inaudible—"He knows our ways, and though at times he is hot and very angry, he is just."

"*Fool!*"—the epithet echoed hollowly in the cold room—"it is not those who spit upon us and treat us as dogs and slaves who are of danger to us! Those do but light a fire for their own burning. But men such as Randall Sahib, who speak our tongues as one of us, and who have many friends amongst us and are seen to do justice to all men, are a stumbling block in the path, for many of our people will listen to their words and many more follow them to the death, taking up arms even against those of their own blood. It is these who must first be slain!"

There was a murmur of agreement and again the purr and bubble of the hookah. Winter's teeth began to chatter with cold but she clenched them tightly and continued to crouch in the darkness, straining her ears to listen. But something had evidently startled the group outside, for she heard sounds of hurried movements and an unintelligible mutter, and after that for a long time there was silence and she did not know if the men had gone or were still crouching against the wall.

She waited for perhaps a quarter of an hour longer, huddled in her shawl and numb with cold, but she heard no more voices. Presently she stood up stiffly and crept back to bed, closing the dressing room door softly behind her. She had forgotten about the quilt and she did not go to sleep, but dragged the blankets up about her and sat with her chin on her knees, shivering and thinking and waiting for the dawn.

Chunwar—that was a village to the south of the city. The nullah that the man had spoken of cut diagonally across the plain a mile or so short of the village, which lay behind a thick belt of trees. It was more a wide, steep-sided ravine, and riding to Chunwar from the direction of the cantonments there was only one practicable place where it might be crossed—where the narrow, rutted cart track ran. The ravine was full of trees and scrub and high grass, and someone—perhaps several men—would be waiting there for Captain Randall to pass. It would be easy to un-horse a man in such a place. And when they had dragged him off and stunned him his foot would be jammed into the stirrup and his horse lashed forward to drag him at a gallop across the sharp, stony plain.

Winter had a sudden vision of Alex Randall's brown, clean-cut face torn and battered into a shapeless mass of blood and dirt, and she shuddered as she stared into the darkness. The hours crawled past and the moonlight left the window and then the veranda beyond, and the room was dark and very cold, but she dared not sleep for fear that she should awake too late and not be in time to stop Alex from riding to his death.

At long last a hint of gray crept into the blackness and a cock crowed from somewhere behind the servants' quarters at the far side of the compound. Winter lit a candle and began to dress herself hurriedly, her fingers clumsy from cold and weariness and a sudden fear that perhaps after all she might be too late. The thought terrified her and she ran through the quiet house and shook awake the sheeted, corpselike figure of one of the house servants who slept in the hall at night, and told him to tell her syce that she wished her horse brought round immediately.

The members of the household were by now too accustomed to her early rising for the man to feel any surprise, and barely fifteen minutes later she was cantering down the long drive in the gray, aqueous light of the early morning.

She had never been to Captain Randall's bungalow, but she had passed it almost daily. There was a light burning in one of the rooms and a groom was walking a restive horse up and down in front of the veranda. Then he had not yet left! Furiante was feeling fresh and above himself and did not relish being kept to a gentle canter, but Winter reined him in and made him walk sedately down a narrow lane under a feathery canopy of tamarisk boughs while she listened for the sound of Chytuc's hoofs behind her.

The lane came out upon an open stretch of ground beyond which lay a mango tope and a deep belt of cropland. To the right lay the city and the river, while half a mile to the left lay the maidan and the rifle range. Winter drew rein a little beyond the mouth of the lane as though undecided which way to turn. She heard Yusaf's horse Shiraz fidgeting behind her, and then the sound that she had been waiting for, and she turned, as though in surprise, swinging Furiante so that Alex had no choice but to stop. He pulled up, and Winter saw that he was alone. So they had been right in that at least!

She said on a note of surprise, and for the benefit of Yusaf: "Captain Randall! How fortunate that I should have met you. I have been wishing to see you. May I ride with you?"

It was the first time that she had met or spoken to him since the night of his arrival in Lunjore almost three months previously, but if Alex was in any way surprised at being thus accosted, he gave no sign of it. He bowed slightly and said in his most expressionless voice: "Certainly, Mrs. Barton, if you wish. But I am riding to Chunwar this morning and I am afraid that you would not find it very amusing. The going is rather rough."

"Then perhaps you will ride with me to the maidan instead," said

Winter, turning her horse's head. "You can ride to Chunwar some other morning."

"I am sorry to sound disobliging," began Alex, "but—"

Winter looked over her shoulder at him with raised brows, letting the reins lie loose, and under cover of her long habit she used her spur on Furiante. Furiante needed no second invitation. He had been sidling and snorting and seething with impatience for the past quarter of an hour, and he responded to the spur with all the outraged velocity of an exploding rocket.

Winter screamed once for Captain Randall's benefit, and thereafter concentrated on remaining in the saddle without making the smallest attempt to arrest Furiante's headlong flight. She was not, if the truth be known, in the least sure that she could do so if she had wished, for Furiante had the bit between his teeth and was galloping as though he were pursued by seven devils.

Mercifully the ground was level, and once they were through the trees the vast stretch of the maidan lay ahead. The path through the trees was a narrow one and branches whipped at Winter's skirt; her hat fell off and her hair streamed out behind her like a black silk flag, and then they were racing across the open maidan. She could hear Chytuc's hoofs behind her and Alex' voice shouting "Left!—pull left!" and remembered then the wide ditch that bounded the far side of the ground. She pulled on the near-side rein with all her strength, but she could not turn the maddened horse. And then Alex was gaining on her and she saw Chytuc's black head and laid-back ears draw level with her, and Alex had caught her bridle and turned Furiante, still galloping at full stretch but tiring at last, away from the ditch and toward the open country. Two minutes later he had brought them to a stop.

Winter bowed over Furiante's neck in sudden weakness and felt Alex' hard fingers grip her shoulder and heard him say: "Are you all right?"

She lifted her head and looked at him—and saw the sudden comprehension in his face as he met that look. His hand dropped and he said incredulously: "Did you do that on purpose?"

Winter straightened up and drew a deep breath to steady herself. "I—I had to. I'm sorry. But I had to talk to you. Tell Yusaf to keep behind."

Alex looked at her for a long moment. His eyes were black with anger and his mouth had closed in a hard, unpleasant line. He threw a curt word of command over his shoulder, and touched Chytuc with his heel, and the two horses moved forward at a sober pace, Yusaf following at a discreet distance.

Alex said curtly: "You had better do something about your hair. Give me the reins."

He watched her as she attempted to gather up and reroll the shining mass into some sort of order, and the anger went out of his face. He smiled a little crookedly. "Don't look so tragic! What is it?"

Winter said abruptly: "Why did you ride alone today? Doesn't your orderly usually ride with you?"

"He is ill," said Alex briefly. "Why do you ask?"

Winter drew a little gasping breath. "Because—because that means it is true—that I didn't imagine it all."

Alex looked at her, frowning. "What is true? What is all this?"

"They were going to kill you," said Winter. "In the ravine on the road to Chunwar. I heard them talking last night, and I had to stop you. But—but I did not want them to know that I knew, so when you would not come with me I had to do something to make you—"

Alex said: "Wait a minute. Begin at the beginning. Who are 'they'?"

"I don't know. I only heard voices—" She told him of those voices, and Alex listened without interruption. When she had finished he was silent for a moment or two and then he asked if she had recognized any voice. Winter shook her head.

"No names?"

"Only one. A man named Mehan Lall would be waiting in the ravine. There is no one of that name among the servants."

"But there is among my acquaintances," said Alex grimly.

He snapped his fingers at the level of his shoulder without turning his head. It was a brief and almost inaudible gesture, but Yusaf, twenty yards behind, saw it and spurred forward. "Huzoor?"

"Hast thou a pistol?"

Yusaf thrust a hand into the bosom of his coat and produced a small five-chambered Colt pistol, a surprising item of equipment for a syce. Alex held out his hand for it and slid it into his own pocket, and said: "I may have need of two. Take the mem-sahib home by way of the cantonments, and keep a still tongue in thy head."

He noticed Winter's startled face and smiled; a smile that did not quite reach his eyes. "It's all right. Yusaf is one of my own men. I did not think that you should ride so far afield without a trustworthy escort."

He made as though to turn Chytuc and Winter snatched at his rein.

"No! Alex, no!" Her voice was sharp with panic.

Alex looked down at her white frightened face and the harsh lines of his own face softened. He dropped his hand over hers for a brief moment and gripped it hard and reassuringly.

"I shall be all right. I promise you. Forewarned is forearmed, you know."

But Winter's fingers still clung to the bridle. "What are you going to do?" she demanded breathlessly.

Alex grinned unexpectedly. "To tell the truth, I am not sure. But I do not like being gunned for, and I intend to discourage it. There is a deal of difference between falling into an ambush and walking into one with your eyes open."

"Alex—"

Alex wrenched her hand from the bridle and said suddenly and savagely: "For God's sake don't look at me like that!" He saw her flinch as though he had struck her, and said with harsh impatience: "I'm sorry. I am very grateful to you for warning me. Now get on—go back to the house."

He wheeled Chytuc and was gone, galloping back across the open ground toward the distant belt of trees, and Winter turned her horse's head and sat watching him grow smaller and smaller across the colorless plain until at last the trees swallowed him up. It was less than an hour since she had left the Residency, but it seemed as though hours had passed—or years. As though she were not even the same person who had ridden out under that gate.

Why had she not known before that she loved Alex Randall? Why was it only now, when he was riding away from her, perhaps to his death, that she should realize how much he meant to her? She had loved him for so long and been too obsessed with her childish, foolish, pasteboard and tinsel image of Conway to recognize it. Once, in Malta, she had wanted him to kiss her, and been horrified at herself—because of Conway. And when he had kissed her at Delhi she had been shamed and startled by her own instinctive response, because it had seemed a betrayal of Conway and she had hated herself for it.

She had been blind and stupid and stubborn. She had refused even to think of him; had shied away from any thought of him, like Furiante shying at a shadow; and it was only now, facing the possibility of his death, that all the mixed and unmanageable emotions had suddenly sorted themselves out and left only the one fact—that she loved Alex. But whether he lived or died, it was too late, because she had married Conway Barton.

Winter straightened her slim shoulders and lifted her small chin in the familiar gesture of her childhood when she had braced herself to meet reproof or hurt or humiliation and to endure it in silence, and turning Furiante she rode back through the brightening dawn to her husband's home. But she did not enter the house. She dismounted within the gate, and dismissing Yusaf and the horses she went across to the great banyan tree to sit silent among the roots and watch Akbar Khan's little granddaughter share her morning meal with the birds. The sight of the small, still figure with its slow, unhurried movements, surrounded by a host of friendly birds and squirrels, was always a soothing one to Winter. But today the creatures appeared wilder than usual, and would barely come to Zeb-un-Nissa's soft, wordless call.

"It is because they know that thou art afraid," said Nissa. She turned her enormous unfocused eyes on Winter and smiled her sweet vague smile. "There is no need. He will come to no harm."

The words were spoken with entire conviction, and though she could only have been referring to a bird or a squirrel, Winter was suddenly and strangely reassured. The terror and the tension ebbed away from her, and a bold blue jay, its plumage glinting like a handful of jewels in the morning sunlight, swooped down to take a fragrant of bread from Nissa's small palm.

19

THE sun was still below the horizon when Alex left the green croplands behind him and gave Chytuc his head across the wide stretch of the open plain. A rough cart track idled across the plain toward the ravine and Chunwar, but the heavy dew and the rain of the previous day had laid the dust, and the prints of Chytuc's hoofs lay clear on a surface that showed that no cart and only two men on foot had passed within the last few hours. Alex noted the fact, but without optimism. There was no reason to suppose that reinforcements had not entered the ravine from the opposite side, and he could only hope that there were not more than three—or at the most four—men lying in wait for him. Experience had taught him that out of four there is generally one who will run away; and out of three, one who gets in the way of his allies.

Mehan Lall! Yes, he remembered Mehan Lall, and he had a fairly clear idea as to why the man had been selected to carry out this particular form of assassination. Mehan Lall possessed an unusual accomplishment, and Alex had once seen him use it to bring down a galloping leopard that had broken cover during a partridge shoot. The creature had bounded across an open stretch of ground, and Mehan Lall had swung and released a weighted silken rope with unbelievable swiftness and accuracy. The rope, swung by its weights, had whipped about the leopard's forepaws and brought it to a rolling, snarling stop. It was said of Mehan Lall that he could bring down anything from a galloping horse to a long-legged heron with his weighted rope, and Alex did not doubt it.

He slowed Chytuc to a canter as the clump of dhak trees loomed larger and the tops of the scrub and trees and cane that choked the ravine showed as a dark line above the level of the plain. As he neared it he reined in to a walk, and drew out the slim skinning knife that he carried under the saddle flap. It was an item of equipment that was useful on long rides in rough country, and had in its day been put to a multitude of uses. Niaz kept the blade sharpened to a razorlike edge and Alex ran his thumb lightly along it and grinned appreciatively to see the blood start at its touch. He held the knife with the blade uppermost against his sleeve and touched Chytuc with his heel, and they passed by the dhak trees and down over the rim of the ravine.

Chytuc's hoofs slipped a little on the slope and Alex spoke softly. He was riding loosely in the saddle, and there was nothing about him to betray the fact that every nerve and faculty was tense and alert. He heard a faint rustle to one side of the track, and the whistle of the weighted rope; and because he had been waiting for it he pulled back on the rein and brought up his left hand in the same movement.

The rope whipped about him like a thing with a life of its own, but instead of pinning his arms to his sides, his arm was raised to meet it. The knife blade shored upward, and Chytuc, reined in savagely on the slope, had backed instead of plunging forward.

Almost simultaneously a man rose from the high grass by the track and clawed at Alex' boot, but Alex had dropped the reins after that one savage jerk and there was a pistol in his right hand. The explosion and the howl of pain sent Chytuc rearing wildly on the narrow track, and the slashing blow of an iron-tipped lathee from the opposite side missed its mark and caught the horse on the flank, raising a long, vicious weal. Alex dropped the knife and fired again as with a squeal of rage Chytuc reared up with flaying hoofs. The next moment horse and rider had burst out of the ravine and onto the level plain with the speed and violence of a thunderbolt.

Alex made no attempt to check the infuriated horse, but let him have his head until his pain and panic had subsided. They rode into Chunwar by way of the canal bank and Alex noted that the report that it had been illegally breached was correct, but that it was another cultivator, and not Mahomed Latif, whose fields had reaped the benefit. He called upon the Kotwal—the village headman—and having dealt with the matter he rode back to the ravine accompanied by the Kotwal and some of the more responsible villagers.

A man who gave his name as Sobha Chand was discovered hiding in the thickets a quarter of a mile above the track. It had not been difficult to trace him, for he had a bullet through the shoulder and was suffering from severe loss of blood. He appeared to imagine that he was either dead or dying. Mehan Lall had not gone so far. A smashed knee is a painful thing, and he crouched in the tall grass by the path and groaned. There had been a third man, but he had fled.

Alex had seen the two wounded men loaded into a bullock cart, their wounds roughly bandaged, and had ridden slowly back to the cantonments in the wake of the cart, where having handed the groaning pair of would-be assassins over to the care of the police, he had returned to his bungalow for breakfast. He hoped that the morning's work might act as a deterrent to others interested in his removal, for the average native of the country, though for the most part careless of death, possessed a disproportionate fear of being painfully wounded.

Having breakfasted, he walked over to the Commissioner's office and paid particular attention, without appearing to do so, to the demeanor of every servant whom he met with. No face expressed any surprise at his appearance, but he noted with interest that although Durga Charan, the head chuprassy, could control both his face and his bland, unwinking eyes, he could not prevent his hands from quivering. Alex dropped his gaze to those unsteady hands and allowed it to linger on them thoughtfully.

"Durga Charan," said Alex softly, "I think that I have heard some talk of *taklif* (trouble) in thy village. It may be that thou shouldst take leave and see that all is well with thy house—while thy health permits." He had passed on, and the man had said nothing, but two hours later he had asked the Commissioner for leave to go to his home.

Winter had heard Alex' footsteps and his quiet voice, and she had gone to her bedroom and locked the door behind her and wept for the first time since that night in Malta; weeping with relief and thankfulness as she never wept for the loss of her illusions.

It had been a Tuesday, and that evening the "Tuesday Crowd" were to dine as usual at the Residency. Winter had agreed to dine with them on the understanding that she could retire immediately afterward. Provided she sat at his table, said Conway, he had not the smallest objection to her feigning a headache and retiring at the conclusion of the meal. In fact he would appreciate it, by God he would! She cast a damned damper on such parties, and they would do very well without her.

He looked at her with scowling irritation, wondering how he could ever have imagined, even for so short a time, that she had grown into a beauty? She had lost a lot of weight and was looking remarkably sallow. A pity. He disliked skinny women. And her eyes were too big. He had thought them amazingly fine when she had first arrived in Lunjore. The most speaking eyes he had ever seen in a woman's head. But now there was a blankness about them and they seemed to look round him or through him, but never at him, and there were blue shadows beneath them like bruises.

He said a little uneasily: "You are not looking at all the thing, my dear. Are you not feeling well? Lunjore is not held to be a good station for women. The climate is not all it could be. Perhaps it might be a good thing if you were to go away on a short visit, to set you up before the hot weather? We might consider sending you to Lucknow. You will like to see your father's house—our house. What do you say to that?"

He saw the bright, transient color flood up into his wife's pale face and her eyes lose their blankness and become brilliant again, and thought with baffled amazement: Why, damnit, she *is* a beauty!

Winter said with a tremor in her voice: "Could I really go to Lucknow? I have wanted to so much! Could I really?"

The Commissioner patted her shoulder with condescending affection and said, well, well, they would see about it. It might not be a bad idea at all. He might even come with her. The Casa de Ballesteros—he believed that it had once been called something fanciful to do with peacocks—was really a very fine house. He had stayed there once or twice when inspecting the property on behalf of her guardian.

Pleased with that momentary flicker of beauty and his own magnanimity, he had put an arm about her waist, and pulling her against him had planted a wetly alcoholic kiss upon her cheek. She had done nothing to avoid his embrace, but had stood quite still, enduring it with closed eyes, wishing with a sudden passionate intensity that it was Alex who held her. She heard footsteps in the hall and Iman Bux' murmured "Huzoor," and realizing that in the next moment a visitor would be ushered into the drawing room, attempted to free herself: "Conway— please. Someone is coming in—"

Winter's arms had been hanging stiffly at her sides, but now she put her hands up and caught at his coat sleeves in an endeavor to thrust him away, so that for a moment it appeared as though she were returning her husband's embrace. She heard the door open and found herself looking into Alex Randall's expressionless face.

It was a sudden and nightmare repetition of the day at Delhi when he had walked in and found her in Carlyon's arms. A nightmare with a cruel twist to it, because then she had been so afraid that it would be Conway who would find her in that degrading position. But it had been Alex. And now it was Conway who held her, and again it was Alex. But it was Alex whom she loved.

Conway released her and turned. "Hullo, Alex m'boy. Walked right in on the turtledoves, dammit! Have a drink. Make yerself at home. Nothin' urgent, is it? Because I ain't got the time to look to it now. Here's Mrs. Barton already dressed, and I still to have a bath and change."

He shouted for drinks to be brought, took one himself and moved to the door. "M'wife'll look after yer. Why don't yer stay t'dinner? Good party on tonight. Time you got yourself out of a rut. Shall expect you."

"I am afraid, sir—" began Alex, and stopped. He looked at Winter's small rigid face, and after a perceptible pause said quite deliberately, and as though he had intended to finish the sentence that way—"that I have been neglecting my social duties of late. I should be glad to."

The Commissioner removed himself, and Winter said stiffly: "I am sorry that you should find Mr. Barton unable to attend to you, but we are expecting guests within the hour."

Alex strolled across the room and came to a stop before her. He was feeling angrier than he had ever felt in his life: an entirely illogical anger, for surely he should be glad that she was not as unhappy in her marriage as he had supposed? He said: "I did not come here to see Mr. Barton. I came to pay my debts."

"Your debts?"

"Let us say, my thanks. I am afraid that I cannot have appeared particularly grateful to you this morning. But I am. I think I owe you my life, and the least I can do is to thank you properly for the gift."

Winter took a quick step backward, bewildered by the derisive note in his voice. She said curtly: "You have nothing to thank me for, Captain Randall. I did nothing that anyone else would not have done in the same circumstances." Moving to a chair she seated herself with her wide skirts spreading crisply about her and said: "You have not yet told me what occurred. Was there no one in the ravine?"

Alex gave her an edited and colorless version of the ambush, and passed on to other topics, inquiring if Winter had had any news of Lottie. Winter had in fact received a long and rapturous letter from Lottie by the last dak, but its only really important item of news—that Lottie had begun to cherish hopes of a child who would be born in midsummer—could not be imparted, for such subjects were unmentionable before gentlemen.

Captain Randall finished his drink and excused himself, saying that if he were to dine at the Residency that night he would have to change into more formal wear, and Winter rose with a rustle of yellow *gros de chine*. She had not looked directly at him during the past ten minutes or so, but she looked at him now. "Why did you change your mind about dining here tonight, when you had meant to refuse?" she demanded abruptly.

"What makes you think I meant to refuse?"

"Well—you have never accepted any previous invitation to dine."

"That was churlish of me," said Alex gravely. "But it will be remedied tonight." He bowed and went away, leaving her question unanswered.

He had returned some thirty minutes later, and Winter had had the doubtful felicity of observing that he appeared entirely at his ease among the inner circle of the Commissioner's friends. Mrs. Cottar addressed him familiarly by his Christian name and devoted a large part of her attention to him, and her conversation had seemed to afford him considerable amusement. He had made himself unusually pleasant to Delia Gardener-Smith, while at the same time blandly refusing to be drawn into any argument with Colonel Moulson, who regarded him with a hostile eye.

At the conclusion of the meal the guests had repaired to the drawing room, where the furniture had been moved to allow for a long table covered with a baize cloth, on which cards and dice were laid out. There were several Indian guests present: rich landowners and noblemen, or their sons, who gambled heavily, and were on that account on easy terms with the Commissioner and his more raffish friends. Those who were Hindus, and whose caste raised difficulties in the matter of eating, usually arrived after dinner, and tonight they were joined by Kishan Prasad, whom Winter had not seen since the day of her arrival at Calcutta.

She had been about to excuse herself on the plea of a headache, but two things had made her change her mind. The arrival of Kishan Prasad and something that had been in Alex' face when he had seen him. It seemed to her as though there was a glint of satisfaction in his eyes, as though he had bet on the turn of a card and won, and she had been suddenly sure that he had known Kishan Prasad would be present that evening, and that it was for this reason that he had accepted her husband's invitation to dine.

Kishan Prasad, having greeted several acquaintances, had drawn up a chair beside the sofa on which Winter had seated herself and addressed her in his own tongue. She was well aware of his proficiency in English, and appreciated the compliment. He talked well, and she found herself conversing with him with more interest and ease than she had as yet experienced since her arrival in Lunjore.

He inquired presently where she intended to spend the summer months, and on hearing that she would not be removing to the hills, advised her earnestly to do so. She would, he assured her, find Lunjore unpleasantly hot from mid-April until the monsoon broke, as it had a bad reputation in the matter of high temperatures during May and June. At this point, they had been joined by Delia and Colonel Moulson, and the conversation had turned to the forthcoming duck shoot at Hazrat Bagh, a jheel which lay some fifteen miles to the west of the cantonments.

Hazrat Bagh—the "Grove of a Thousand Trees"—had once been the site of a hunting park of some forgotten king, but nothing remained of it but the lonely stretches of water and the intersecting bunds on which the "thousand trees"—kikar and an occasional peepul tree—stood among high grass and reeds and provided excellent cover for sportsmen. There were no villages near the jheel, and the waterfowl came there by the thousand. The shoot was being arranged by some of the local Tulakdars, and food and beaters on an elaborate scale were being provided for the guests, who included most of the British officers stationed in Lunjore. Those ladies who had been invited to attend as spectators would watch the battue from the tree-lined bunds or from an artificial "hide" to one side of the jheel. Several hundred sepoys were to be lent for the occasion to keep the birds from settling on outlying jheels and inaccessible stretches of water, and a kutcha (rough) road was in progress of construction so that the ladies would be able to drive there in their carriages, for the jheel lay far from any made road and was at present difficult to reach even on horseback.

"I hope that we are to have the pleasure of seeing you there, Mrs. Barton?" said Kishan Prasad. "I am to be one of the hosts, you know."

"No, I did not know," confessed Winter. "But I shall certainly be there. I have never been out on a big shoot yet."

"You must let me arrange a tiger shoot later on," said Kishan Prasad. "One may shoot duck in Europe, but a tiger shoot is something that you will see only in the East."

"For my part, I could not endure to attend such a thing!" declared Delia Gardener-Smith. "I am sure I cannot conceive how any lady could do so!"

"Why?" inquired Kishan Prasad. "Would it distress you to see so beautiful a creature shot? But tigers are vermin, you know. They prey upon the herds of the villagers, and in their old age they often take to killing men, while the duck you will see shot do no harm."

"Oh, but I did not mean that!" said Delia, opening her eyes at him. "I meant the danger of course. There can be no danger in a duck shoot, but a tiger shoot cannot help but be dangerous."

"That is why it is exciting," said Kishan Prasad with a smile. "No sport is worthy of the name that does not include an element of risk."

"Is that a creed, or merely an opinion?" inquired a pleasant voice behind them. "Good evening, Rao Sahib. When did you arrive in Lunjore?"

None of them had observed Alex approach, and Winter saw Kishan Prasad's slight involuntary start at the sound of that voice; but he turned a bland countenance and his voice was as pleasant as Alex' own.

"A creed of course, Captain Randall. I seldom advance opinions. I arrived at midday."

"In good time for the obsequies in fact," said Alex with a grin. "I am sorry to have had to disappoint you."

"Yes?" Kishan Prasad's slim brows rose and he looked puzzled though polite, as though he imagined Alex to have attempted some Western joke, the point of which had escaped him.

Winter looked sharply from one face to the other, for Alex' apparently pointless remark was entirely clear to her. *Had* Kishan Prasad known that there was to have been an attempt to kill him? No, that was absurd, for Alex had saved the man's life! But she could not be sure; and because she was not, she was all at once afraid.

Alex laughed, but did not explain himself. He said instead: "I hope you mean to invite me to this tiger shoot. When is it to be?"

Kishan Prasad met his gaze blandly, holding it for a long moment, and then said gently: "Sometime in the hot weather, shall we say? They are always easier to deal with in the hot months, for instead of ranging at large they are forced to keep near water, and are less active."

"That is not a thing that I should care to count on," said Alex regarding him under drooping eyelids.

Kishan Prasad shrugged his shoulders. "Perhaps. In any event I do not imagine that Mrs. Barton will be with us then, for I feel sure that she will have removed to some hill station to escape the worst of the heat. I have just been warning the ladies that Lunjore can be a veritable furnace in the months before the monsoon breaks, but coming from Europe they have as yet little idea of how fierce our Indian hot weathers can be."

"I shall do my best to impress it upon them," said Alex.

"I am sure you will, Captain Randall," said Kishan Prasad with a smile, "though I fear your warnings are doomed to be disregarded. You will find that those ladies who have not yet experienced a hot weather will be sure that you are grossly exaggerating the discomforts, while those who have will have forgotten just how bad they can be. So you see I am really quite safe in playing traitor to the climate of my native land."

Both Alex and Kishan Prasad laughed, and their laughs contained a disturbing and identical note of grimness. It was almost, thought Winter uneasily, as though their casual conversation had possessed two separate and distinct meanings, but that each knew exactly what the other had meant. She looked at the two men, and for a fleeting moment it seemed to her that there was a strange likeness between them. A likeness that had nothing to do with coloring or feature, but that went deeper than externals.

Winter had not, after all, left the party early that night. She had stayed for the first time, watching Alex and watching Kishan Prasad, and telling herself that there was nothing there—nothing! That Kishan Prasad had not blandly presented Alex with some obscure piece of information or warning, or that Alex recognized it as such.

The Commissioner had as usual drunk too much, and had eventually abandoned cards in favor of lolling upon a sofa at the far end of the room with his arm about Mrs. Wilkinson's waist, fondling her plump bare shoulder and whispering something in her ear that sent her off into peals of laughter. Winter knew that she should not remain and lend her countenance to such proceedings. But she did not go.

She could not leave, because Alex was there, and it was suddenly enough to be in the same room with him: to be able to watch his face and to hear his voice and his laugh. To realize, having visualized him dead, that he was alive and safe and real, and to feel the ache of loving him tug at her heart. Tomorrow, or the next day or the next, he might meet with another carefully planned accident, or die of cholera or typhus or black-water fever, or any one of the deadly diseases that ravaged India. Life was cheap in such a country, and a face seen laughing across a luncheon table one day might well lie slackmouthed in death less than twenty-four hours later, to be hidden under six feet of earth before another sun had set.

Kishan Prasad left at midnight, but his departure had not been the signal for any of the other guests to leave. The Tuesday parties seldom ended before three and sometimes four o'clock in the morning, but shortly before one o'clock the Commissioner, who had passed successively through the convivial, the amorous, the quarrelsome and the maudlin stages of intoxication, finally arrived at the unconscious, and as though he had been waiting for that, Alex put down his unfinished drink, flung his cards face upward on the table and rose.

"Where are you going, Alex?" demanded Mrs. Cottar.

"Bed," said Alex briefly. "And so are the rest of you."

Unbelievably, he had managed to get rid of them. Winter did not know how he had done it, but within a quarter of an hour the last carriage had rolled away down the drive and only Alex remained. He had looked thoughtfully at the Commissioner's snoring bulk and then at Winter and said: "Do you need any help?"

Winter had not been entirely certain as to what he had meant by that question, but she had chosen to put the obvious interpretation upon it and had said a little stiffly: "You need not trouble. Ismail will help him to bed."

Alex shrugged his shoulders very slightly and had been turning to go when she had stopped him.

"Captain Randall—"

Alex turned back. "Mrs. Barton?"

Winter said: "Did you know that the Rao Sahib would be coming to the house tonight?"

"I had heard that he might be."

"Is that why you were here tonight?"

"Perhaps. Why do you ask?"

"Why did you want to see him?"

Alex' lazy glance dwelt reflectively on her for a moment or two and then he said: "Because there is a reason for everything that Kishan Prasad does, and it is always the same reason. He is a man with only one idea."

"What idea?"

"My dear girl," said Alex with sudden impatience, "you know as well as I do! You saw him that night at Malta, and you once saw his face in the raw when we passed the wreck of that transport. He has only one aim in life—to throw off the rule of the Company. And to achieve it he would, if it were necessary, be prepared to cut the throat of every white man in this country with his own hands—with one possible exception. Myself. He will not deliberately take my life, or plot to take it, because I once made the grave mistake of saving his. But if someone else should do it, that would be quite a different matter."

Winter sat down again a little abruptly. She said, looking up at him, "What were you talking about? It sounded just like ordinary talk, but it wasn't, was it?"

Alex subsided onto the couch opposite her and drove his hands into his pockets. He said slowly: "Not exactly. I think that he intended to do you a service—or me—and that he is sufficiently sure of himself to be able to afford to do so. Perhaps he is right."

Winter said: "I don't understand," and Alex looked at her under lowered lashes.

"That may be just as well. Are you going to the hills this summer?"

"No. I do not think that I shall mind the heat so much. Why are you changing the subject?"

"I'm not. I think you should go, and I shall do all that I can to see that you do. Are you so particularly anxious to stay?" His gaze wandered to the sofa on the far side of the room where her husband lay and snored.

"Yes," said Winter, watching the turn of his head against the lamplight. Had that been what Kishan Prasad meant? Had he been hinting that there might be trouble in Lunjore in the coming months? But if that were so, how could she go to the hills, knowing that Alex would still be in Lunjore?

She said almost inaudibly: "There are times when—when one would so much rather not be sent away."

Alex misinterpreted the hesitant words. He turned sharply, his mouth suddenly white. "Are you going to have a child?" he inquired bluntly.

Winter did not move, but he saw her face set in a dreadful silent stare and felt the shudder that went through her body as clearly as though she had been touching him instead of separated from him by a full two paces.

The abrupt and unexpected question had faced her with something that filled her with sick horror, as though she had been a sleepwalker waking to find herself balanced on the lip of a yawning gulf. She had not thought of this, and the color drained out of her face, leaving it pinched and sallow.

Alex said: "Are you?" The harshness of his own voice surprised him.

Winter steadied her white lips with an effort, too shaken to resent the question. "No."

Alex stood up abruptly and went across to the table that was still littered with cards and dice, and picked up his unfinished drink. The brandy burned his throat and he drank it as though he were parched with thirst, and refilling the glass at a side table by the door, came back with it in his hand and stood looking down at her.

"I'm sorry. I thought that was what you meant, and it seemed to make it even more necessary that you should remove from Lunjore for the hot weather."

Winter did not look at him. She said: "I only meant that I will not run away—from anything."

"No," said Alex thoughtfully, "I don't believe you will."

He sat down again, stretching his legs out before him, and leant his head against the back of the sofa. He did not speak again for a long time, and the silence lengthened and drew out and filled slowly with small sounds; the Commissioner's stertorous breathing, the ticking of the clock, the chirrup of a gecko lizard and the monotonous fluttering of a large moth that had found its way in from the night and was battering its wings against the glass of the large oil lamp, throwing whirling, wavering shadows across the walls and the high white ceiling.

Winter sat motionless, looking not at Alex' face but at the hand that held his glass: a brown, thin, long-fingered, nervous hand, possessed of unexpected strength and equally unexpected gentleness. She seemed to see beside it the damp, fleshy, unsteady fingers of the man she had married, she knew then that she must not bear children to Conway. To do so would be the ultimate indecency. She would go to Lucknow as Conway had suggested. Not to the house that had been her father's, but to the one that had been her only home. To the Gulab Mahal. If she could only get back to the Gulab Mahal she might be able to see things clearer; to stand back and get them into some sort of perspective. She could not do that while Alex was here and her need for him was so great: while Conway was here and her shuddering aversion for him filled her with such sick despair. She would go home. . . .

Alex was still silent, but it was a silence devoid of tension, and gradually her own tension lessened. Looking at his abstracted face she was surprised that this should be so, for surely now that she had discovered that she loved him she should feel embarrassed or shy or ashamed in his presence? She was a married woman, and it was shockingly improper of her to allow herself to fall in love with another man. She should by rights be overcome with shame. But then she had not allowed herself to fall in love with Alex Randall. She had only discovered the fact when it was far too late to do anything about it. The drawing room smelt stalely of cigar smoke and spirits, fading roses and the heavy violet scent affected by Mrs. Wilkinson. It looked as cluttered and untidy and forlorn as any room when a party is over and the guests are gone, but all at once it was curiously peaceful, and watching Alex she wondered what he was thinking of.

Alex was not thinking of Winter. There were too many other things to think about. Too much that needed to be done, and always too little time in which to do it . . . He was thinking of Kishan Prasad. Kishan Prasad who never did anything without a reason, and who was to be one of the hosts at the duck shoot. What, then, was behind this shoot at Hazrat Bagh? It would of course insure that for the best part of a day the cantonments would be practically denuded of British officers, as the majority of them were attending the shoot. Had anything been planned to take place in their absence? The armory—the magazine—?

No, that was absurd. Kishan Prasad had said the hot weather, and he would not have troubled to say that if it had not been true. The real hot weather did not officially start until the end of April or the first week of May.

Sepoys . . . They had asked for sepoys to help put up the birds. Why, when there were so many villagers and coolies that they could call upon? Was there anything in that? *This may do well enough for the villages, but it will not serve for the sepoys. For them it must be something that strikes deeper and touches every man. They are already as tinder, but there is as yet no spark.* Had Kishan Prasad found a spark? What had made him sure enough of himself to give that warning? For it *had* been a warning. . . .

I must see Moulson and Packer and Gardener-Smith in the morning, thought Alex, though they will none of them believe a word of it. What the devil is behind this damned duck shoot? . . .

The clock on the chimney piece struck two and Alex removed his abstracted gaze from the ceiling and turned his head to look at Winter. He said slowly: "I didn't mean to keep you up so late. I'm sorry. . . . Riding this morning?"

"Yes."

"Where?"

"Anywhere. To Parry's mound?"

"All right. Six o'clock, then." They smiled at each other, their faces dim and peaceful.

Alex finished his drink and stood up, and Winter rose with a rustle of silk and walked beside him into the hall, where he turned to her and held out his hand. He seemed about to say something, but he changed his mind and was silent for a moment or two, looking down at her and not quite smiling; the line of his mouth unexpectedly tender. Then he lifted the hand he held, and turning it palm upward, kissed it lightly and deliberately; folded her fingers upon the kiss, and released it.

There had been nothing in the least passionate in the gesture: it might have been either a wordless apology or a comforting caress given to a child. He had turned then and gone out into the night; and Winter had heard him speak to a servant on the porch, and had waited, standing in the silent hall, until the sound of his footsteps died away into the darkness.

20

Less than four hours later she had found Alex waiting for her on the Residency Road, and they had ridden out through the quiet cantonments and across the rifle range to the open country beyond, Niaz and Yusaf riding behind them.

The rifle range was hard and level and the horses were fresh, so they did not talk much. But beyond the range the ground became broken, and they slowed to a walk, threading their way between rough tussocks of grass, kikar trees and thornbushes, feathery clumps of pampas and out-crops of rock. They drew rein on the crest of a lonely knoll that was crowned by a banyan tree and the weather-worn slab of an ancient grave whose inscription was still faintly legible: *Here lyes the body of Ezra Parry of the Honourable Company of Merchants of London trading to the East Indies, the son of Thos. Parry and Susanna, who departed this lyfe the eleventh of October 1666.*

The sun rose as they reached it, and they sat looking out across the country beyond while every blade and spear of grass flashed and glittered with dewdrops, and the morning mists lifted in veil after veil so that the land appeared to unroll itself, stretching back and back into limitless dis-tance. Doves cooed among the branches of the banyan tree, and a flight of wild duck whistled overhead making for the jheel that lay ten miles to the northward.

"That is Hazrat Bagh out there, isn't it," said Winter, turning in the saddle to watch them. "Is that the new road?" She pointed with her riding crop.

"Yes. That's a temporary track so that the ladies of the garrison can all drive out in comfort to watch the duck shoot. No expense is being spared to impress upon your husband and the garrison how friendly and co-operative our local landowners are. I wonder . . ."

He did not finish the sentence, but screwing up his eyes against the dazzle of the newly risen sun, said, "Listen to those partridges calling! I must bring a gun out here one evening."

"Have you brought a pistol with you?" inquired Winter.

Alex nodded, and after a moment Winter said abruptly: "Would you give me one?"

Alex turned sharply. "A pistol? Why? What for?"

"I should feel—safer," said Winter lightly, affecting an interest in a pair of weaverbirds who were fluttering anxiously about their dangling nest in a thorn tree below.

Alex surveyed her with narrowed eyes and inquired if she had ever used firearms before.

Winter shook her head. "No. But I do not suppose it is very difficult, is it?"

"Try." Alex dismounted and pulling the Eagle's reins over his head whistled to Niaz and turned to help Winter from the saddle. The sunlight glinted on the barrel of the small Tranter revolver as he explained its mechanism.

"Is it loaded?" inquired Winter.

"My dear girl," said Alex impatiently, "do you really imagine that I should carry one that wasn't? Here—take it. No, don't aim as low as that. Fire it in the air."

The report sent Furiante dancing and snorting indignantly.

"Well done," said Alex approvingly. "You didn't jump; but you must allow for the recoil."

"Show me how."

There was a bright blue jay's feather caught among the thorns of a kikar tree less than a dozen yards away, and he jerked up his hand and fired. The feather vanished and Niaz, behind them, gave a grunt of approval.

Winter said: "Is that really the way to do it? Not taking aim?"

"No," admitted Alex with a grin. "That was just showing off. I apologize. I'll do it slowly for you this time. Stand behind my shoulder and look along the barrel."

He leveled the revolver and fired.

Winter took the weapon less gingerly, selected a mark and pulled the trigger. Her slim wrist jerked to the kick of the discharge and the bullet went high of the mark. Alex made her fire the remaining rounds and then remarked: "Not bad. You can keep it."

"Thank you," said Winter gravely. She held it out to him and said: "Will you reload it for me, please."

Alex shook his head. "No. Not until I've taught you how to use it. For the present it is safer unloaded. And probably just as effective a deterrent."

He saw the hot color rise in a wave from her throat to the roots of her hair, and had a sudden startled suspicion as to why she had asked for a pistol. Winter thrust the weapon into the pocket of her riding habit and turned away to where Yusaf held the indignant Furiante, and Alex, following her, helped her to the saddle and stood holding her stirrup leather and looking up at her under frowning brows. Winter did not return his look. The bright color was fading from her face and her expression gave nothing away, and after a moment he dropped his hand without speaking.

Alex had asked no further questions as to why she had wanted a weapon, and he did not know that three days after he had given it to her she had used it, unloaded but with, as he had predicted, a satisfactorily deterrent effect, against his superior officer.

Conway rarely visited his wife's room, but he had done so on the night following the Tuesday party and had found it locked against him. He had created a scene, which availed him nothing. The next night, finding it still locked, he had decided to teach his wife a lesson, and on the following evening he had walked in upon her as she was dressing for dinner. He had been tolerably sober and therefore more dangerous, and had bellowed at Johara to get out and stay out.

"Now, my dear wife," said Conway unpleasantly, his pale eyes red-rimmed with rage and brandy, "you will find that there are other times of day when I can demand your obedience. You can take that dress off again. You won't need it."

Winter had opened a drawer of her dressing table and turned toward him with the revolver in her hand. She had been perfectly polite and quite definite. He had not married her for love, but for money, and he had got what he wanted and must be content with that. She would fulfill her duties as his wife in every way but this, and if he ever attempted to force his attentions upon her again she would shoot him.

"Not to kill you, Conway. I shall stop short of murder. But just to hurt you painfully enough to insure that such a thing does not occur again. I hope you realize that I mean it?"

If she had screamed or raged Conway might not have believed it. Because she did neither, but faced him with white-lipped calm, he had blustered and shouted and called her unprintable names, but he had backed out of her room and had not attempted to enter it again. The revolver had served its purpose, but Winter continued to take instruction in how to fire it. Partly because it amused her, but largely because it gave her an excuse to see Alex.

Alex had taught her with a grim, unsmiling efficiency, making her load and fire, reload and fire again until her wrist ached. "You never know when it may come in useful," was all he would say.

One day he had brought a rifle with him on the morning ride, and had told her to fire it. It was, he said, one of the new issue: the Enfield rifle that was to replace the old-fashioned infantry musket—the famous 'Brown Bess'—that had long outlived its usefulness.

He had made her lie down to fire it, holding the heavy weapon as though she had been on the range, and had lain beside her on the dew-wet ground explaining the method and mechanism and exhorting her not to hold it as though it were made of glass. The recoil had bruised her cheek and shoulder badly, and the bullet had gone far wide of the towering anthill, over two hundred yards distant, at which she had been aiming.

Alex had refused to let her fire it again. He had fired it himself, and Niaz, seeing the distant explosion of dust, sucked in his breath and said "Wah!" in an awed voice. Both Niaz and Yusaf had regarded the rifle with considerable interest.

"It is true, then, that these things will fire a ball many times the distance of the old ones," said Niaz. "But how is it done?"

"They have grooved bores," said Alex.

"They will be difficult to load, especially when they are fouled," commented Niaz, squinting down the barrel.

Alex shook his head. "No, for the cartridge papers are greased." He took one out of the pocket of his riding coat and biting off the end, rammed it down the barrel to demonstrate, and fired again.

"May I try?"

Alex handed over the gun and another cartridge and Niaz bit off the end and spat it out upon the ground. "*Pah!*" he said with a grimace. "With what is that greased?" He lay down, cuddling the butt against his cheek, sighted carefully and fired. A fluff of dust showed that the bullet had chipped the anthill, and Niaz laughed.

"May a man buy such a gun for his own use?" inquired Yusaf, his eyes sparkling.

Alex did not answer. He was staring down at the small scrap of greased paper that Niaz had spat out upon the ground, and there was an odd, still look on his face. He drew another cartridge from his pocket and stood looking at it, turning it over in his hand and rubbing the ball of his thumb slowly across the greased paper wrapping, until Winter said sharply: "What is it?"

"Hmm?" He turned toward her, but his eyes were blank and unfocused and they looked past her as though she were not there.

Yusaf said: "Huzoor, may I too try the gun?"

Alex' eyes narrowed suddenly. The abstraction left them and his hand clenched hard over the cartridge that he held. "Assuredly." He turned slowly and held out the cartridge, and Winter, watching him as she always watched him when he was not looking at her, was all at once aware that behind that casual gesture his nerves were tense and alert as if he were waiting for something to happen; for some expected, or unexpected, action. As if, perhaps, Yusaf might recoil from the thing he held in his hand. Yusaf took the cartridge, and having bitten it, rubbed his mouth with the back of his hand as Niaz had done, and a curious light leapt to life in Alex' eyes. He turned away and stood looking out across the plain with his hands in his pockets, and after a moment or two Winter heard him say something under his breath that sounded like "—and furnish the pretense."

"What is it?" she asked again, unaccountably disturbed.

Alex looked round at her with a faint frown as though he had forgotten that she was there: "I was thinking of some lines of Dryden's. '*When churls rebel against their native prince, I arm their hands and furnish the pretense, and housing in the lion's hateful sign, bought senates and deserting troops are mine.'* It seemed remarkably appropriate."

He turned on his heel, and although it was still early they rode no farther that day, but turned back to the cantonments—Alex riding with a speed and recklessness that he had never shown before when he had been out with Winter. He left her abruptly at the Residency gate, and fifteen minutes later he had been ushered into Colonel Gardener-Smith's office.

"Well, Captain Randall," said the Colonel shortly, "what is it now?"

Alex walked over to the table, and tossing a small object down upon it said without preamble: "That is one of the cartridges for the new Enfield, sir. Can you tell me what they are greased with?"

The Colonel had stared, considerably taken aback both by the question and the tone in which it was uttered. He had picked the thing up, examined it and dropped it, and had marked his displeasure by seating himself behind his desk and keeping Alex standing.

He said coldly: "I have no idea. And I hardly think that the composition of cartridge grease lies within your province."

Alex said: "Perhaps not, sir, but it must be within yours. Those cartridge papers have to be bitten, and if there is any doubt as to the composition of that grease, it is a thing that will affect the caste of every sepoy in the Army. A grievance that will unite men of every regiment. A common denominator—"

The Colonel cast a startled glance at the innocent-seeming object that Alex had thrown down on his desk. He looked at it for a minute or two in silence and then looked up again at Alex' grim face and thought fleetingly that Randall appeared to have aged a lot recently. He said slowly: "You mean, if it were animal fat—?"

"If it should contain any lard or animal fat," said Alex harshly, "no sepoy should be asked to touch it, let alone bite it. The pig is an unclean animal to a Mussulman and the cow a sacred animal to the Hindu, while the fat of any dead creature is an abomination to both. But no one knows that better than you, sir."

Colonel Gardener-Smith's worried gaze returned to the cartridge and he frowned at it, pulling at his lip. He said uneasily, but without conviction: "That is a point that cannot have escaped the attention of the responsible authorities."

"Why not? The method and manufacture of these things was worked out in England, not India, and the men responsible for it are not likely to possess any special knowledge of the caste system that prevails here."

"I do not believe—" began the Colonel unhappily; and then a sense of irritation and frustration came over him. He too had lately been aware of a changing atmosphere and a lack of that sympathy and close co-operation between officers and men that had obtained in earlier and more troublous days. He could feel it in the air and sense it in the very faces and voices of his men, and he did not like it. But it was the New Order, that was all. New methods. New men. A new outlook. The lack of large-scale wars

and operations to keep the troops occupied. This restlessness in the ranks
—it meant nothing. It would pass. If only men like Randall would stop
croaking of disaster life would be a much pleasanter affair. His men were
all right. They were his own men and he could handle them. They would
follow him anywhere: hadn't he proved that? He wished Randall would
leave well alone and stop this continual harrying . . .

He banged the table suddenly with his clenched fist and said violently:
"What do you expect me to do about it anyway? It's none of my business
—or yours! I'm not Master General of the Ordnance! These things will be
issued to every regiment in India shortly."

"I know," said Alex tiredly. He reached out a hand and picked up the
cartridge, and his face was suddenly bleak. "But at least it can do no harm
to ask for the official analysis of this stuff, and in the meantime it might
be possible to manufacture our own wrapping papers here in Lunjore,
where the men can see for themselves what is used."

"That would be impossible!" said Colonel Gardener-Smith shortly.

"Nothing is impossible now," said Alex slowly. "Not even a mutiny of
the Bengal Army."

Colonel Gardener-Smith stood up abruptly and pushed his chair back
with unnecessary violence. "If that is all you wished to see me about, I
must ask you to excuse me, as I have a great many calls upon my time.
I will bear in mind what you have said, and write at once to inquire
into the composition of the lubrication which is being used. But you may
be quite confident—as I am—that your fears will be proved groundless."

"Thank you, sir," said Alex in a colorless voice, and went out into the
bright blaze of the midmorning sunlight.

He rode less with Winter after that and he did not again take out the
Enfield rifle.

Winter missed those early morning rides in his company, and did not
know that the reason for their curtailment was the fact that Alex spent a
great many of his nights in unexpected places, listening, watching, and
occasionally—very occasionally—asking questions. It was an easier matter
by night to pass unnoticed in the crowded bazaars and alleyways of the
city, and he had sources of information there whose usefulness would
have been severely reduced had they been observed coming to his house.

Niaz too spent much of his time similarly occupied, but he did not
frequent the city. Niaz had friends among the sepoys and was often to be
found visiting the lines. Much of his information tallied with Alex',
and none of it was in any way reassuring.

"It is said," reported Niaz, "that it is the purpose of the government
to convert all men, by force or fraud, to be Christians. But they say that
as the Feringis are few, to force their faith upon all in Hind would be
difficult, and therefore they will accomplish it by fraud."

"With what purpose?"

"So that they may use the sepoys to conquer all the world for them.

When the sepoys go on ships, and to far countries, they become sick and do not fight so well. But it is not so with the sahib-*log*, and this, it is said, is because of the food that the sahibs eat. Therefore if the army were all of one caste—Christians—they too would eat the same food and be as strong, and as slaves of the sahib-*log* would fight their battles in a hundred countries. There is even now a tale that to this end the Company have ground up the bones of pigs and cattle and mixed that dust with the flour and with the grain, so that all who eat of it will thereby lose their caste, and being casteless will have to become Christians. What do they say in the city?"

"They have refused the last consignment of government flour," said Alex. "It lies still unloaded in the carts. I have sent for grain from Deesa, so that they may grind it for themselves."

He had brought up the question of the refusal of the bazaars to accept or handle the flour at a general conference earlier that day, and the Commissioner had merely observed that if they didn't like it they could go without. Colonel Packer had given it as his opinion that it was merely a trick on the part of the local farmers to force up the price of their own grain, and Colonel Gardener-Smith had said that a few words of calm explanation would soon put his own regiment to rights on the matter, while Colonel Moulson had remarked unpleasantly that he did not know what the garrison was coming to when members of it allowed themselves to be panicked by every petty rumor in the bazaars.

Alex had glanced down at his hands in the shadow of the table and had been surprised to see that they were comparatively steady when he felt physically sick with rage and exasperation.

The windy, unconstructive debate had dawdled to an indecisive close, and Alex had flung out into the sunlight in a fury and had taken his own measures to deal with the situation without consulting the Commissioner or anyone else.

He had been dining out that evening, and it was long after midnight before he got back to his bungalow. The sleepy syce deposited him in the porch and drove the trap round to the stable, and Alex walked stiffly up the veranda steps, tugging at the fastening of the high, braided mess collar and throwing it open with a sense of relief.

There was a lamp burning in his room, and two shadows rose to their feet from the far side of the soft square of orange light that lay across the matting of the veranda. One of them moved forward and lifted the *chik* that hung over the doorway to allow him to pass in.

"Who have you there?" asked Alex in an undertone.

"It is the Kotwal of Jalodri," said Niaz. "He missed thee by less than a moment and would have gone away, saying that he would come again in the morning; but I constrained him to stay, for he has news that concerns thee somewhat."

"Send him in," said Alex.

The man slipped in under the lifted *chik* and stood blinking nervously in the yellow lamplight. Alex greeted him gravely and offered an apology for his having been kept so late. "What is the trouble with thee, Chuman Lal?"

"I do not know," whispered the Kotwal, and his eyes rolled and started like those of a frightened horse. "It is a thing I do not understand, and therefore I brought one to thee, and by night. If there be some evil charm in this, it may be that thou canst draw it out."

The man looked back quickly over his shoulder, but there was only Niaz behind him, and thrusting a trembling hand into the folds of his garments he drew out a chapatty.

Alex' expression did not alter, but it was a moment or two before he spoke.

"What evil is there in that?"

"I do not know," whispered the Kotwal, shuddering. "It was brought to me last night by a runner from Chumri, which is four *koss* to the north. He brought with him five of these things, together with a fragment of goat's flesh, and told me that I must prepare five more, breaking one of these which he had brought and mixing a little with the new five. These I must dispatch by a runner to the next village, sending also a portion of goat's flesh, to be given into the hand of the watchman of that village, saying to him that he must do likewise, and send in turn to the next village. And with it must also be said certain words that the runner from Jalodri had spoken to me:—'From the north to the south, and from the east to the west.' Then did I know that it was a charm."

Alex stretched out his hand and took the small flat cake of coarse ground flour and stood looking down at it with the smile that he had taught himself to wear when his face was being watched by tense or frightened men for a clue to his thoughts.

Here it comes, thought Alex. The fiery cross. This is what he spoke of in Malta; ". . . as before the Mahratta rising." But it had been cakes and millet that were distributed through the villages then. This was the fruit of that devildom at Khanwai. "*It will do well enough for the villages, but it will not serve for the sepoys. . . .*"

He handed the chapatty back to the Kotwal and said: "And what hast thou done?"

"I did as it was told me," said the Kotwal. "Five I prepared and had sent by runner. Those that I received, saving only this one, I have wrapped in a cloth and buried deep. Huzoor, what is the meaning of this thing? I am a poor man and ignorant, and I fear that it may bring misfortune upon my house and my fields."

"There is nothing to fear," said Alex quietly. "It is only, as thou knowest, that last year the rains failed and many of the crops failed also. That thing in thy hand is the food of all, and if it be a charm it is one that is sent for good, in propitiation, so that this year the rains will not fail and the crops of every village through which the chapatties pass may be good."

"Ah," said the Kotwal gratefully. "That is good talk. I will tell the village, for they feared greatly, wondering what evil this might portend. I will strew these things about the fields, and then surely my crops will prosper. And the goat's flesh? What is the meaning of that? Tara Chund, whose fields lie by mine, said that it foretold the fall of the Company's government, for is it not said that—" The Kotwal stopped abruptly and coughed a small dry cough of embarrassment.

"—that he who kills an Englishman sacrifices a goat to Kali," finished Alex grimly. "So I also have heard. But the goat's flesh that was sent thee is but a sign that the flocks and herds shall increase, for in a good year there is grass and water for many. Tell them this in the villages, that they may know that it is a sign for good."

The Kotwal salaamed deeply, and stowing the crumbling chapatty with reverent care among the folds of the blanket he wore wound about him, he backed out of the room, and they heard his feet patter away on the matting of the veranda.

Alex wrote a report on the mysterious distribution of the chapatties the following morning and sent it across in triplicate to the Commissioner, who was pleased to be facetious on the subject that evening.

"Damned if I don't think Fred Moulson is right about you, Alex. Megrims and the vapors! Yes, yes, yes!—I know y' had a wild tale last year about some hocus-pocus at Khanwai. But as I told yer then, it's a mistake to go pokin' about in that side of native life. Probably no connection with this at all! Far more likely that this is only some local bigwig propitiating the gods by a distribution of cakes; it ain't unusual—you should know that! And if you think I'm going to forward such a farrago of nonsense to the Governor, y' *must* be mad! Fiery cross indeed! Tell you what, you should relax. Yer gettin' a sight too fidgety. Get a woman instead!—do you all the good in the world! Comin' on this shoot tomorrow? Good, good. Day in the open will blow some of these cobwebs away."

Alex, who spent the larger part of his day in the open dealing less with paperwork than with people, and who had recently spent half his nights there as well, forbore to comment. He would have to go more often to the villages and talk with the headmen and the elders, and see what he could do toward allaying any panic that the distribution of the chapatties might have caused.

Did the things also carry any specific message? Or were they merely a means of creating an atmosphere of suspicion and alarm, and thus providing a fruitful breeding ground for deeper and more savage hates and fears? Five . . . Did that mean anything? Alex knew the Indian custom of sending a message by means of a handful of oddments—flowers, leaves, fruits, bangles; things that each carried its own meaning in the language of signs and were in common use as messages between lovers. In that language any object appearing in duplicate stood for a number indicating time, unless it were accompanied by a pinch of saffron or incense, in which case it stood for place. Five chapatties . . . The fifth month? That would be May, and Kishan Prasad had said "in the hot weather."

An open carriage passed him bearing Captain and Mrs. Hossack, their four children and an ayah, and Alex thought with sudden vehemence: Thank God I'm not married! At least I have not that fear to face! And thought instantly: I must get him to send her to the hills. She will have to go if he orders her. After all he is her husband.

But he was not thinking of Mrs. Hossack.

Moonrise

21

THE duck shoot at Hazrat Bagh was timed to begin soon after eight o'clock in the morning, to allow the guns and the guests to assemble and breakfast to be eaten on a prepared ground half a mile from the jheel.

The temporary road proved remarkably good, and the carriages that had started from Lunjore as the dawn was breaking had reached the rendezvous in ample time for breakfast. To Winter's surprise, many of the guests proved to be strangers to her, and she found on inquiry that they were officers and officials from Suthragunj, a large cantonment town beyond the borders of Lunjore.

As the crow flies Suthragunj lay less than thirty miles from the Lunjore cantonments, but the main road ran far to the southward for more than double that distance before a branch road to Suthragunj added yet another fifteen miles to the score. Although there were various small footpaths and side tracks that wandered between the villages, none were capable of taking a carriage, and so the British residents of Suthragunj and Lunjore seldom met. Now however, the kutcha road had been extended beyond the jheel so that guests from both garrisons might attend.

The jheel was not in the least as Winter had pictured it. She had imagined a mile-long lake fringed with reeds, but the narrow bunds divided the shallow water into numerous squares and triangles, few of which were more than a hundred yards across. Kikar trees and high grass grew thickly along the bunds; reeds and red water weed fringed them, and the sportsmen with their loaders and beaters took up their positions at intervals of fifty to a hundred yards apart, under the thin shade of the kikar trees, with the reeds screening them ahead.

Winter seated herself on the hard ground with her back to a tree trunk, a few yards from where her husband had taken up his stand behind a tussock of tall grass, and taking off her wide-brimmed hat she let the faint breeze ruffle her hair. There was a continuous coming and going among the thousands of waterfowl who blackened the open water, and the noise of quacking and quarreling birds and the ruffle of wings made a soothing and monotonous music.

The first shot broke the drowsy, murmurous tranquillity of the morning with a shattering impact, and instantly the day was no longer peaceful, but full of noise and violence, for the shot was followed by a crashing fusillade and a sound that Winter had never heard before—the slow, rushing roar of a hundred thousand birds rising off the water. The quiet air was ripped by wings and deafening explosions that crashed and echoed and crashed again as the panic-stricken birds whirled toward the bunds, banked and rose, wheeled and broke, to sweep up over the treetops and rise higher and higher in dark, lacy patterns against the high blue sky.

Winter stood up, backed against the rough bark of the tree and pressed her hands over her ears to keep out the noise of the shots and the shouting; closing her eyes in shuddering horror against the falling birds and their helpless dying flurries as they strove to dive and could not do so, or threshed upon the water with broken wings, striving to evade the men who waded in to retrieve them, but whose caste forbade them to put a dying creature out of its misery.

And then something crashed through the thin branches and struck against her, and she opened her eyes to see a huge goose struggling on the ground at her feet. It dragged itself away, one wing trailing and its beak wide as though it gasped from fear or for air.

"Good shot, that!" commented Conway lumbering up. "Better wring its neck, or it'll get away. Surprising how tough these birds are."

He stooped, but Winter was before him. She caught the great bird in her arms, her face white with all the accumulated pain and horror and panic of the last months, and backed away from him, her mouth open in a soundless scream.

"Here, give it to me," said Conway. "Can't kill it yourself. You'll find it takes a deal of doing."

"Don't touch it!" the words were almost a scream. "It isn't going to die. You shan't kill it!"

Conway stared, his pale eyes bulging with anger. "Don't be a fool! Put it down at once, d'you hear me!"

He lurched toward her and Winter evaded him with a frantic leap, and turning, fled down the bund clutching the wounded bird to her breast, its warm neck across her shoulder and one huge helpless wing almost brushing the ground as she ran.

The bund bent at a right angle less than fifty yards from where her husband had taken up his position, and high grass closed in about it, reaching up to the lower branches of the thorn trees. Winter ran blindly, in the grip of a breathless, reasonless, gasping panic, and she did not see Alex until she had run into him.

He caught her by the shoulders and held them in a hard grasp, staring down into the wide, panic-stricken eyes. For a moment she had tried to wrench herself free, and then she had seen who it was who held her.

"*Alex!*—Alex, don't let him kill it! Don't let him—" She thrust the warm heavy body at him, and as she did so the soft feathered neck slid down from her shoulder and hung limp.

"It's dead, dear," said Alex quietly, and took it from her.

Her dress was splotched and spattered with bright scarlet drops and a wide patch of blood stained the breast of the gray habit as though it were she who had been shot, and not the bird; and at the sight of it a savage wave of fear lashed at Alex as though something had struck him over the heart.

He let the bird slip to the grass, and Winter caught at his arm as though she would have snatched it from him. And then quite suddenly she dropped her head against him and wept.

Alex stood very still, holding her, feeling the shuddering of the slim warm body under his hands. Her hair smelt faintly of lavender as it had on the walls of Delhi, and he held her quite gently because he wanted so much to hold her hard against him—because he wanted so much to thrust her away from him. The sound of that helpless, broken sobbing tore at his heart, and his face above her bent head was twisted with pain and scored with harsh lines that had not been there before. At last he heard the choking, shuddering sobs quiet and cease, and he put her gently away from him.

She made no attempt to turn away, but sat down on a tree stump, facing him, her black lashes sticking wetly together and her face streaked with tears, and groped in the pocket of her habit for a handkerchief. It was a flimsy enough affair and stained too with the blood that had run down the great wing. Alex produced his own and handed it over. His nostrils were pinched and there was a white shade about his mouth, but he spoke quite pleasantly: "Try this one," he advised. "It's larger and a good deal cleaner."

He watched her with a wrenching tenderness as she dried her eyes and blew her small nose with a complete lack of self-consciousness, and wondered how many women would have been sufficiently oblivious of their own looks as to face his direct gaze instead of turning away to repair the ravages of tear stains and disheveled hair.

Winter folded his handkerchief into a careful square and drew a deep breath. "I'm sorry," she said, her voice under control once more. "I don't know why I should have behaved so stupidly. The goose came down on top of me, and it was hurt. Conway wounded it—he wanted to kill it, and—"

"I wounded it," said Alex.

"You?" She looked up at him, startled, frowning a little.

"Yes. I saw it fall and I was coming to get it."

"Oh." She was silent for a moment or two, and Alex, watching her, said gently: "Does that make a difference?"

Her gaze came back to him and she said thoughtfully: "Yes. But I don't know why it should."

"Better?—or worse?"

She did not answer him and Alex lifted a hand that was not quite steady and brushed his fingers lightly across her forehead: "Don't frown, dear. It can't matter as much as all that. As a matter of fact I dislike these large-scale battues myself. I prefer to do my shooting on my own or with one or two people at most, instead of indulging in this type of mass slaughter."

"Then why did you come—if you knew what it would be like?" inquired Winter.

"Curiosity," said Alex with leisurely promptitude. "I wanted to see if I could find out why Kishan Prasad and his friends had arranged this elaborate shoot."

"And have you found out?"

"Yes."

He subsided on to the ground at her feet and Winter pulled a grass stem and bit it thoughtfully, watching his brown profile against the sharp crisscross lines of sunlight that fell between the branches of the kikar trees and the tall spears of dry grass. Presently she said: "Why do you think that they gave this duck shoot?"

"It isn't a duck shoot," said Alex, his eyes on the glittering expanse of water. "It is merely a means to an end. And also, possibly, a rehearsal."

"A rehearsal? What are they rehearsing for?"

"They aren't. We are very kindly doing it for them."

He stretched out at full length and turned, lying on the warm ground and facing her. "It was quite simple really. Lunjore lies across one of the main roadways into Oudh, and that road crosses an iron bridge ten miles to the south. If there was a rising in the Punjab, or Delhi way, we could hold that bridge; or if the worst came to the worst, blow it up and not only isolate ourselves from rebel troops, but prevent them using this route into Oudh, which is at the moment a hotbed of disaffection. There is an arsenal at Suthragunj. A very large one which is, in my opinion at least, inadequately protected against the possibility of a large-scale rising. Some of our local Tulakdars have not missed that point, and under cover of this lavish and well-organized entertainment, they have constructed a very adequate road that avoids the bridge and brings Suthragunj within roughly twenty miles of us. We have very kindly tested it for them, both from the point of surface and timing, by driving a variety of carriages along it, and where a carriage can go, guns and ammunition wagons can follow."

Alex rolled over on his back with his hands linked behind his head and Winter said a little uncertainly: "Are you—do you really think that there is going to be trouble?"

"Not trouble. A rising. Yes, I do. I've thought so for about five years. We've been asking for it. But we cherish a theory that to listen to warnings, or act upon them, is a sign of panic and shows loss of confidence, and we would rather lose our lives any day than be accused of either."

"What will happen?" asked Winter.

Alex was silent for a moment or two, and when he spoke his voice held a savage bitterness that startled her.

"We shall see the ruin, in one day or in twenty days, of what might have been the finest army in the world! We shall build it up again, but it will never be quite the same. We shall turn half the army against its fellows, and play off Sikh against Mussulman and Mussulman against Hindu, and Gurkhas against both. There will be atrocities on both sides—all sides—for the East drops straight into barbarism when it is frightened or enraged, and we shall follow its example, and call it revenge. It will leave a legacy of hatred that will be handed down to future generations—from father to son and from mother to daughter. We shall forget; but they will not."

"Is that why you wanted me to go to the hills?—and taught me to shoot?" inquired Winter, leaping woman-like from the general to the personal.

"Yes," said Alex briefly.

Winter stood up and shook out the gray folds of her skirt. She said quite lightly: "I will think about it," and was turning away when she remembered the goose. She hesitated for a moment and then said a little diffidently: "The—that goose. Conway thought that he had shot it. Can I take it back? Then perhaps he will not be so—"

She stopped, flushing painfully, and bit her lip, suddenly ashamed of her desire to placate her husband in this unworthy manner.

Alex was watching a flight of mallard who were approaching from the open water, too high to allow them to pass within range. He said: "Of course," without turning his head.

He did not look round as she went away, but he heard the tall grass rustle behind her and he stood quite still, listening, until he could hear it no longer; his face drawn and bleak in the harsh sunlight.

Later that afternoon he had spoken bluntly to Kishan Prasad, telling him that British regiments would be sent out to take over the country if the Company fell: "For if there is a rising, there will be women of ours—and children also—who will be murdered: you will not be able to prevent it, and it is the one thing that my countrymen will not forgive. England—not John Company—will go on sending out troops until she has avenged them. A day may come when we will stomach such an affront and turn from a fight; but it is not yet—not now."

"Then I will wait for that day," said Kishan Prasad softly. "And if I am dead, then my son's son will be ready—or if it be not him, then his son's son; or the son of that son! Would you yourself not do likewise?"

Alex did not answer and Kishan Prasad repeated the question in Urdu, using the familiar title: "Tell me, Sahib, wouldst thou not do likewise wert thou of my blood and this thine own land?"

Alex stared at him, his eyes hot with a helpless anger that was as much against himself as Kishan Prasad, and he said violently and as though the

words were wrenched from him: "Yes—God damn you!" and turning on
his heel he walked blindly away without once looking back to where Kishan
Prasad followed more slowly behind him.

The carriages and the ladies had left Hazrat Bagh early so as to get
home before dark, but the men had remained to shoot once more on
the jheel and had ridden back three hours later, by the light of a half-
moon, to attend a large party given by the Commissioner to round off
the day's festivities.

The gathering at the Residency had included the members of a self-
styled Italian opera company, who had sung excerpts from a number of
light operas and followed them by a selection of popular songs.

Alex, who had attended the party, had arrived in a singularly unpleasant
frame of mind, and for perhaps the first time in his life had deliberately
set himself to drink too much. The Commissioner's port, wine and brandy
were of the best obtainable, but they had little effect upon Alex beyond his
increasing his ill temper, and the sight of Mr. Barton openly making
amorous advances to the auburn-haired ornament of the opera company, in
complete disregard of his wife's presence, did nothing to mitigate it.

He had put down his glass, walked across the room and calmly removed
the Signorina from the Commissioner's orbit. Alex could be charming
enough when he chose, and he chose now. He had blandly ignored the
glowering indignation of his chief, the hostility of Colonel Moulson and
the momentary shock he had seen on Winter's face, and had taken the
lady away—ostensibly to view the garden by moonlight.

They had not returned, though the majority of the guests had remained
until well after two o'clock, and the Commissioner had been crudely out-
spoken on the subject of Captain Randall's behavior. He had ended by
observing that Lou Cottar had been right about the man, by God!—he was
a dark horse, and they were always the worst with women. Lou had said
that Randall was no cold fish, and he'd certainly taken home a hot enough
piece to keep him warm tonight. It was only he, Conway Barton, who
had a cursed cold fish on his hands.

Winter had gone to her room and had sat for a long time on the edge
of her bed, staring before her and thinking of Alex: Alex with his hard,
nervous fingers caressing another woman's hair. Alex' slow kisses on another woman's mouth, and his dark head lying pillowed on that opulent
powdered breast or buried in the suspicious brightness of those auburn
curls.

I must go away, thought Winter, as she had thought on that day when
she had first discovered that she loved Alex. I will go home to the Gulab
Mahal. If only I can get back there, I shall be safe again—safe from everything! And she thought, as she had thought so often, of the rose-pink
walls and the brilliant flowers, and of the brightly colored birds who had
been so tame that they had allowed her to touch them.

She had fallen asleep at last, fully clothed, and she had not ridden that day, either in the morning or the evening, because she had been afraid of seeing Alex.

She had not seen him again for some considerable time. Alex had seen to that. The night he had spent in the arms of the Signorina had resolved nothing and solved no problems. It had not even made him forget, as he held her, the feel of Winter's slim body in his arms. In the cold gray light of the early morning the auburn-haired singer had looked blowzy and coarse—the lip rouge with which she had deepened the red of her pouting mouth smeared and ugly, and the blacking from her lashes smudging her cheeks. She smelt faintly of perspiration and rice powder, and overpoweringly of patchouli, and Alex had looked at her with impatience and pity and a twinge of disgust, and thought of Winter sobbing jerkily against his shoulder for the death of a wild bird. And had found that his anger had not evaporated with the morning but was still a hard, hot stone in his breast.

He had attended no more parties at the Residency, and he spent more and more of his time in the outlying villages of his district. The villagers respected Alex, and many of them liked him; but he was a Feringi—a foreigner: they saw similar things by different lights and weighed them by different standards. "Is there a meeting point?" thought Alex. "Is there any real neutral ground?" But there was Niaz, who was as much his friend as William. How did one explain his strong kinship for this man who had turned from his own race to serve one of alien blood?

He had asked Niaz that question one evening, and Niaz had replied lightly: "I have eaten the Company's salt."

"That is no answer," said Alex. "Many have done that; but the bread that is eaten is soon forgotten."

Niaz shrugged. "We are brothers, thou and I. Who can say why?"

"And if it come to bloodshed, as it may come, wilt thou stay with me against thy own kin?"

"*Beshak!* I owe thee my life, Sikandar Dulkhan (Alexander the Great) —and thine is forfeit to me. That alone were a rope that is hard to cut. I will fight at thy side and take thy orders when the bloodshed begins— and I do not say 'if it begin'!—but I too would gladly see a Mussulman rule once more in Delhi, and were it not for thee I myself might well cry *Deen! Deen!* for the Faith."

It was Niaz who brought Alex a copy of a pamphlet that was being circulated in the city calling upon all Mohammedans to prepare for a Jehad—a Holy War.

"Who is behind this thing that comes?" asked Alex. "Is it the Hindus or the Mussulmans? Or is it the work of foreigners—Russians and Persians?"

Niaz laughed and made a gesture of negation with his hand. "No. This that will come is the Rising of the Moon," he said with Oriental imagery. "We who were once great in the land have lost almost all that we had of power, and revolt may serve us where peace will not. This will be a Jehad. And I think it comes soon!"

Alex too was aware of an ominous feeling of expectant stillness. But it was a stillness that was not to last long, and the first warning mutter came from faraway Bengal.

On that same January morning on which the garrison of Lunjore had ridden gaily out to shoot duck at Hazrat Bagh, a man of low caste, a lascar who worked in the ammunition factory at Dum-Dum near Calcutta, had stopped a high-caste sepoy and begged a drink from his lota—the brass waterpot carried by every caste Hindu and religiously preserved from defilement. The sepoy had answered, less in anger than astonishment, to the outrageous request: "How can that be, fool? I am a Brahmin, and my caste forbids it."

"Caste? What is caste?" grinned the lascar. "The cartridges that we prepare here are defiled with the fat of hogs and cattle, and soon ye will be as one—casteless together—when the new guns are given out to the pultons and ye bite the cartridges daily."

"What is that?" said the sepoy thickly. "Tell again!"

The lascar had done so, with embellishments, and the sepoy had not waited for him to finish, but had run to his comrades in the lines. Here was proof at last of the duplicity of the Feringis! The hated policies of Annexation and Lapse, the suppression of suttee, the seizure of land, the deposing of kings and the curtailment of pay and power and privilege were as nothing to this; for this struck at the deepest beliefs of men, in that it destroyed their souls.

Hindu and Mohammedan together recoiled in horror from sacrilege and defilement. Panic spread through the lines, and from there, with the incredible swiftness that fear lends to evil tidings, it swept out across India, its progress sped and fanned by those who had been ready and waiting for such an opportunity, and who made the best use of this brand that had been given into their hands.

A hundred men—a hundred thousand—picked up the panic whisper and passed it on: "It is an order from Belait, from the Queen and her Council, that by means of these cartridges all sepoys, both Mussulman and Hindu, be defiled—as are all men in the towns and cities by the eating of bone dust in their flour—so that being made casteless they shall do the will of the sahib-*log* as slaves forever! We are betrayed by the Feringis who have stolen our country and now wish to steal our souls!"

It was then that the nocturnal fires started. Suddenly in the night the thatch of an officer's bungalow would catch fire, set alight, more often than not, by a blazing arrow shot by some unseen hand. The telegraph station of the big cantonment of Barrackpore burned to the ground, and night after night, despite guards and sentries, flames would glow bright in the darkness, creeping up northward from Calcutta and Barrackpore. The news that the 19th Regiment of Native Infantry at Berhampore, a hundred miles to the north of Calcutta, had broken out into mutiny spread upward through India and fanned the panic.

But that mutiny, which had flared up so suddenly, died out, and without violence. An inquiry into the question of the greased cartridges was instituted and proceeded upon its ponderous way, and officers who had begun to eye the men under their command with an anxiety they would not own to, relaxed again.

The rumors died down, and the Commissioner of Lunjore, who had consistently pooh-poohed the possibility of any serious trouble arising, remarked complacently that he had always known it was a mere tempest in a teapot, and there was too much panic about among fellows who ought to know better. Why, he had even heard some preposterous story of a manifesto being circulated to all Mohammedans, calling for a Jehad! All nonsense of course! There hadn't been any such thing circulated in *his* district.

"About eight hundred of them, I think, sir," said Alex expressionlessly.

"*What's that?*" The Commissioner's voice had cracked with angry amazement. "You're telling me we've had 'em in Lunjore? Then why the devil wasn't I told!"

"You were, sir. I sent in a full report—in triplicate. It will be somewhere in the files."

"Oh," said the Commissioner, disconcerted. He glowered angrily for a moment or two and then observed sulkily that he hadn't the time to read every damned, panicky paper that came into the office.

Relieved by the passing of the temporary uneasiness caused by the cartridge scare and the abortive mutiny of the 19th N.I., he turned his attention to the question of leave and a visit to the Casa de Ballesteros in Lucknow.

22

THERE was nothing in Winter's first sight of the beautiful, barbaric city of Lucknow that awoke even an echo of memory, and her father's house was as unfamiliar to her as the city had been. But the golden ghost of Sabrina would have found little changed, for the years had been kind to the House of the Peacocks. The groves of lemon and orange and pomegranate still scented the twilight, and the fountains still made a splashing, tinkling music in the patios. The peacocks cried at dusk and dawn, and often Winter would find a glittering gold-powdered tail feather lying on the grass or the stone flags of the river terrace. The servants would collect the fallen feathers, and tying them together would use the gorgeous things to dust the carved furniture and the dark, magnificent portraits that her grandfather, Don Ramon, had brought from Spain.

Many of the servants remembered her parents, and they had pressed about her with smiles and tears and garlands, and she had been touched, but a little sad because she could not remember even one face among all those faces. There was only one face that Winter wanted to see in Lucknow—Ameera's. And only one place. The Gulab Mahal.

Ameera had arrived at dusk one evening in a palanquin with tinseled curtains borne by bearers in shabby finery; and by good fortune Conway had been out. She had embraced Winter with tears in her eyes, and they had walked together on the river terrace in the cool twilight while Hamida and two of the grizzled retainers from the Gulab Mahal kept watch.

They had talked of many things, but the news that Ameera brought had been a bitter blow, for it meant no less than this—Winter must not come to the Rose Palace. Someday, promised Ameera, but not at this time. And she had sighed, thinking of her husband Walayat Shah, and the hatred that had soured him since the Company's government had deposed the King of Oudh, and thereby deprived him, and many like him, of employment, privilege and power.

Walayat Shah, brooding on present calamity and past glory, listened to the words of those who preached a Jehad, and dreamed the Mohammedan Dream. For now a Jehad meant more than the spreading of the Faith and the slaying of Unbelievers. It meant revenge—and perhaps, once more, an empire.

"He is changed even toward me, his wife, because my mother was a Feringi," said Ameera sadly, "and therefore I cannot ask thee to enter the Gulab Mahal. Someday, surely. But for the present it were better to keep away."

Winter had come back at last to Lucknow, but not to that charmed and peaceful starting point from where she had hoped to draw strength and find a meaning and a purpose in the pattern of her life. She had seemed within reach of it at last, but she might not stretch out her hand and grasp it. The door was barred against her.

Sir Henry Lawrence, perhaps the best-loved man in India, had arrived in Lucknow late in March to take over the administration of Oudh. He was aged by grief and disappointment, and in failing health, but no one knew better than the man who had settled the conquered Punjab and won the respect and affection of the defeated Sikhs, what unavoidable tragedies resulted from such a change in government, or how best to soften and mitigate the hardships and heartaches and hopelessness that inevitably followed in its wake. The news of his appointment sent a sigh of relief through half India. If anyone could tame the sulky, suspicious, wild-eyed stallion that was Oudh, it was Henry Lawrence.

The Conway Bartons had been invited to dine at the Residency, and

Winter had had her first sight of the man whom Alex had spoken of as men speak of a god or a hero.

He was a tall man, thin to emaciation, and his gray hair and thin, straggling beard were already turning white. His haggard, hollow-cheeked face was scored with the lines of weariness and anxiety and the unending strain of sorrow for his wife Honaria, who had died three years before. But the gray, deep-set eyes were quiet and farseeing, and they could still glow with the same fire and fervor and enthusiasm with which he had faced his task as a young man newly come to India.

The Residency was always full of guests these days, for the newly appointed Chief Commissioner kept open house for the nobles, landowners and gentry of the district as one method of inspiring confidence and getting in touch with the opinions prevailing in Oudh.

The Bartons attended several functions there, and Winter had made friends with Mrs. Daly, who had been acting as hostess and housekeeper for Sir Henry. Mrs. Daly, her little son and her husband Captain Harry Daly, who had just been appointed to command of the Corps of Guides, were staying as guests at the Residency, and Mrs. Daly had temporarily taken on the management of the vast, scantily furnished house. She had taken a great fancy to young Mrs. Barton, and a few days before her departure with her husband and child to Hoti Mardan on the North-West Frontier, where the Guides were stationed, she had asked if she might invite Winter to spend a few nights at the Residency.

Conway had produced no objection, for it had occurred to him that his wife's absence would provide an excellent opportunity to arrange a few entertainments of his own at the Casa de Ballesteros. He had given the scheme his cordial approval, and having seen Winter off to the Residency he had settled down with a large glass of brandy and water to plan a week of pleasurable and unrestricted amusement.

The Lucknow Residency was a large, three-storied building whose deep verandas and pillared porticoes looked out over the beautiful city and the winding river, and Winter had been happier there than she had been for months past. The relief of being free of Conway's society was itself immeasurable, and she had been charmed both by the atmosphere that prevailed at the Residency and the casualness and complete lack of ceremony shown by its host. But her peace of mind did not survive the arrival of an unexpected visitor who walked in on a breakfast party on the last day of her stay. The house party had been animatedly discussing the rival merits of Buddha and Confucius as religious teachers, when a caller was announced, and Captain Daly had looked up and jumped to his feet.

"Alex—by all that's wonderful!"

Winter had been peeling an orange and her hands were suddenly still. As still as her heart.

Alex' voice spoke behind her: "Hello, Harry. I hadn't heard you were here. I hope you may forgive me for walking in on you like this, Sir

Henry? I arrived an hour or so ago, but Mr. Barton cannot see me until later, so I thought—"

"You know that you need no apology for walking in on me at any hour, Alex," said Sir Henry, and smiled.

Winter laid the orange down very carefully on her plate and turned slowly, but Alex was not looking at her. He was not even aware that she was present. He was looking at his old chief, and Winter was seized by a helpless, foolish pang of pure jealousy. A resentment, as keen as it was ridiculous, because neither she nor any woman would ever be able to bring that look to Alex' face, or to any man's face.

"Had any breakfast?" inquired Sir Henry.

"At about five o'clock this morning, sir."

"Then you can do with another one now. *Hazri lao Sahib kerwasti*, Ahmed Ali. What are you doing in Lucknow, Alex?"

"The Commissioner sent for me, sir."

Alex' voice was entirely expressionless but Sir Henry regarded him with a twinkling eye in which there was a good deal of comprehension: "Called up to explain yourself, eh?"

Alex laughed. "You are too acute, sir."

"And entirely mannerless, for I have not yet made you known to my guests. But then you know all of them except Dr. Ogilvie, I think. Mrs. Barton is staying with us for a few days to keep Mrs. Daly company."

Alex looked round with a sudden startled frown in his eyes. "I'm sorry, Mrs. Barton. I did not see you were there."

"How long will you be staying?" inquired Sir Henry.

"Not above a day I imagine, sir. It depends on the Commissioner."

"Only one night? That is not long. You'll stay here of course."

"I would like to, sir, if you are sure—"

"Oh, Mrs. Daly will arrange it. You need not worry. She is in charge just now, and I cannot think what I am going to do when her husband selfishly removes her on the thirteenth. Daly is off to command the Guides."

Alex turned quickly. "Is that true? Congratulations, Harry. You always were a lucky devil. Pleased?"

"Who wouldn't be! But I could wish it had come at any other time. It is hard to leave Lucknow just as Sir Henry arrives."

Sir Henry smiled. "My dear Harry, don't think that I do not appreciate the compliment; but you could hardly refuse the finest appointment open to a soldier."

Alex said: "You wouldn't try pulling a few strings, sir, so that he can stay on here and I could go instead?"

Sir Henry looked at him reflectively. "I might try, though it would not have a particle of effect. Would you really go if I could?"

Alex returned the look, and his mouth twisted in a wry smile: "No, sir."

There was an odd note of bitterness in his voice, and Sir Henry nodded understandingly. "I did not think so. Not at this time." He pushed back his chair and stood up. "Well, if you will all excuse me, I must go. I'll see you later, Alex—when you have had your wigging!"

The conversation had become general after his departure, but although Alex had borne a part in it he had appeared distrait, and Winter found that he did not even glance in her direction. Looking at him across the wide table she was filled with despair. Nothing had changed. She might just as well have never come to Lucknow—have never left Lunjore. She had found no solution to her problems or her unhappiness or her love for Alex. Perhaps there was no solution—and no answer except fortitude.

Alex had left at the conclusion of the meal, and she did not see him again until that night, when he entered the crowded drawing room just before dinner. She thought that he looked tired and cross, and she would have given much to be able to go to him and run her fingers over his forehead to smooth away the frown lines, as he had done to her at Hazrat Bagh.

There had been a large dinner party at the Residency that night, and when the last carriage had driven away shortly after eleven o'clock the house party dispersed to their own rooms, leaving Sir Henry and Captain Randall in the cool darkness of the high veranda whose tall, supporting pillars stood black against the moon-flooded garden.

"Well, Alex?" inquired Sir Henry after a moment or two of silence.

Alex turned from his contemplation of the white lawns and the tree shadows. "Far from it, sir. Will you forgive me if I omit the reasons for my visit here? I do not feel capable at present of discussing them in a rational manner."

"In fact," said Sir Henry softly, "if anyone were now to offer you command of the Guides, you would return a different answer to the one you gave me this morning!"

Alex gave a short laugh. "If anyone were to offer me any post whatsoever that would enable me to return to regimental duty, I would accept it!"

"Oh, no, you would not," said Sir Henry placidly. "If you think that, you know less about yourself than I do. I have been wanting to see you for some weeks past. Colvin gave me news of you when I stayed with him in Agra on my way here. It seems that you saw him in October. Tell me the story that you told him then. I imagine that your version differs somewhat from his."

Alex propped his shoulders against the nearest pillar and told again the story that he had told in the previous autumn to Mr. Colvin, Lieutenant-Governor of the North-West Provinces. He told it all, beginning with a moonlight night in Malta and ending with his second visit to the ruins near Khanwai, and when he had finished Sir Henry asked only one question.

"Who," said Sir Henry, "was the man with the ruby earrings? Did you ever find out?"

"No, sir. I should recognize him again if I saw him, but that's the most
I can say."

"A pity. It is a help to know for certain who are one's enemies. Have
you come up against any serious signs of disaffection in your district?"

"One, at least. The building of a kutcha road between Lunjore and
Suthragunj." Alex gave details and Sir Henry listened and nodded.

"What do you think is going to happen, sir?"

"*Khuda ke malum!* (God knows!)," said Sir Henry. "Let us have your
views. I am on the bench tonight, and I should like to hear what you
think."

Alex frowned abstractedly at the contents of his glass. "I think it is the
Army that we have to fear, sir."

"A mutiny." The word was a confirmation rather than a query.

"Yes, sir. Not a spontaneous outbreak, but a planned one, set to take
place simultaneously in every cantonment in India on a given date. A
few months ago I would not have believed such a thing possible, because
to achieve it there would have to have been some exceedingly strong
grievance that was common to both Mussulmans and Hindus—strong
enough to unite them against us. We have, however, very thoughtfully
provided that common bond in the greased cartridges. That was all that
was needed. Having armed their hands we have furnished the pretense."

Sir Henry was silent for a moment or two, stroking his beard, and
presently he said gently: "Any evidence, Alex?"

Alex told him, repeating the words that Kishan Prasad had spoken in
the drawing room of the Residency at Lunjore.

"In the hot weather," said Sir Henry thoughtfully. "Why are you so
sure that he was presenting you with the truth in this oblique manner?"

"I saved his life once," said Alex shortly. "And there is another thing
that seems to suggest he was speaking the truth. That road, if I am right
about it, will have to be used before the monsoon breaks, for it will be
useless afterwards. Which limits it to this side of mid-June."

Sir Henry nodded and leant forward in his chair, his clasped hands on
his knees and his head silvered by the moonlight. He said slowly: "I am
in agreement with you. In fact I am so much in accord with your views
that I will tell you something that few people are aware of. I have already
begun to prepare the Residency to stand a siege."

"Then you think—"

"I hope!" interrupted Sir Henry. "And I will go on hoping until the
last possible moment! But I am also doing what I can to prepare, in case
that hope fails me. Given time I believe I may be able to hold Oudh quiet
even if the rest of India rises. But it is *time* we need! Oh, a hundred other
things as well—tolerance for one!—but time most of all. And that is a
thing which God and the government may not grant me. The sands are
running out, Alex! That Barrackpore affair was the Writing on the Wall."

He was silent for a moment or two, and presently Alex said restlessly:
"How the devil do they get their information, sir? The telegraph doesn't

account for it, for we aren't on the line at Lunjore, and have to get our news by runner. We didn't get word of the Barrackpore business for a full week, but the city knew it all within two days."

"It's the same everywhere," said Sir Henry. "I don't pretend to account for it, but if I were a superstitious man I'd say that in times like these the very wind carries bad news. I believe that it is done with drums in Africa, but here one would almost say that they are able to transfer their thoughts from one agitator to another."

"Talking of agitators," said Alex, "I saw Hodson some months ago, and he told me that he had heard a rumor that Gregori Sparkov was expected in Delhi. If he's there, I imagine he is in the palace, where he'll be safe enough, as it can't be searched. Intriguing with the King, I suppose."

"More likely to be the Queen," said Sir Henry. "The old Padishah is too enfeebled and futile a personage to be of much danger except as a lay figure to prop up on a throne. But Zeenut Mahal is a very different matter. She has brains and drive and fury, and she is burnt up with hate and ambition. I imagine it is she who is the focus of this Russian-Persian intrigue."

"Do you suppose there is much in it, sir?"

"A certain amount. Russia has always wanted India. She has always wanted the whole world! but particularly the East. She can't get it while we are here, and she knows it. But if she can help to get us out she may crawl in through a hundred cracks and crannies and rot it from top to bottom until it falls into her hand like an overripe pear. Naturally she's doing all she can to fan the flames. That was only to be expected. But Russia is not the villain of this present drama. We have relieved her of that responsibility by casting ourselves in the role."

He turned to look at Alex and smiled his tired, charming smile. "I am taking a dreary view of the future tonight, am I not? But though I can feel the wind and hear the thunder I do not despair of averting the storm. And if it comes—it comes! And I shall look to you to hold the western road for me, so that if you should be right, and the regiments at Suthragunj mutiny and seize the arsenal, they will not reach Oudh by Kishan Prasad's road!"

"I will do my best, sir. You know that."

"Even if you were offered command of the Guides tomorrow?"

Alex threw up his hand in the gesture of a swordsman acknowledging a hit, and laughed; but this time without bitterness. "You could offer me no greater inducement, sir. But I will content myself with trying to hold the western road for you."

They talked of other things for a space, and then at last Sir Henry rose and held out his hand.

"If you are making an early start I shall not be seeing you again before you go. Good luck to you. God bless you and—" He hesitated for a moment, and then said thoughtfully and as though the word was not a light one—"good-by." His thin fingers gripped Alex' hand for a brief moment, and then he turned away, and Alex had a last glimpse of his tall figure outlined against the lighted square of the open doorway as he passed through it and was gone.

I shall not see him again, thought Alex with sudden conviction; and in spite of the windless warmth of the night he shivered as though he were cold, and could not rid himself of a sense of foreboding.

It was late, and in a few hours' time he would have to start for Lunjore again. He knew that he should get what sleep he could, but he had seldom felt less like sleeping. The house was hot and it was too warm even in the shadows of the veranda, but the garden looked cool and inviting.

Alex strolled across the wide lawns, his footsteps inaudible on the grass that the gardeners had watered at sunset, and came by chance to a line of flowering trees whose shadows lay velvet-black in the moonlight. There was someone standing at the far edge of that belt of soft darkness, her wide, pale skirts luminous in the shadows, and despite the fact that her outline was barely distinguishable and that she had her back to him, he knew that it was Winter.

Something in the pose of her dimly seen figure arrested his attention: she was watching something, and there was a suggestion of alertness in the tilt of her head that even the deep shadows could not disguise. Curiosity overcame discretion and he went forward and came to stand beside her.

She heard the quiet footsteps and turned her head, but she made no movement of surprise or alarm and seemed as instantly aware of his identity as he had been of hers. She might almost have been waiting for him, though for once she had not even been thinking of him. But it seemed entirely natural to her that he should be there. Standing beside her, Alex could see the pale outline of her profile against the massed darkness of the leaves, and smell the clean, cool scent of lavender that he had come to associate with her, and despite the shadows he could make out the curving line of the long lashes, the faint, puzzled crease between her brows and a stray tendril of black hair that curved childishly above her ear.

Winter did not appear to be aware of his gaze and presently she inquired in a whisper: "What are they doing?"

Alex looked away from her, and for the first time became aware of what it was that had caught her interest. There were things moving across the open ground between the sharp-edged shadows of buildings that lay within the precincts of the Residency. Things that moved in complete silence, keeping for the most part to the shadows and flitting noiselessly across the moonlit spaces like a frieze of trolls; bowed, hunchbacked and grotesque, silhouetted briefly against the silver-washed grass or the wall of a house, lost again in shadow and emerging only to be swallowed up by the ground.

It took him a moment or two to realize that they were men carrying heavy loads, shouldering sacks or bent under weighted boxes, and stowing them away in the underground cellars that lay beneath some of the Residency buildings. He said lightly enough: "They are only men laying in supplies for the summer. Grain and—"

"And ammunition," finished Winter. "Why? And why are they doing it by night? They were doing it last night too. And the night before. They cannot need so many supplies unless—unless they think this place might be besieged. Is it that?"

Alex did not answer. "Is there really going to be a rising?" persisted Winter. "Ameera says—"

She stopped and after a moment Alex said: "What does Ameera say? And who is Ameera?"

Winter turned to look at him in surprise. It seemed absurd that Alex should not know about Ameera. Then she remembered that he did not even know the story of how she had come to Lunjore. She told him something of it now, and of Juanita and Aziza Begum and the Gulab Mahal. . . .

"I think Ameera is afraid. She said that the city was full of strange rumors, but she would not say what they were. Only—only she said that I must go to the hills, and not stay in Lunjore."

Alex said dryly: "I seem to remember saying that myself."

"I know you did. But there are twenty or thirty other women in Lunjore, and—" She broke off abruptly, wishing that she had not spoken. The inference was so obvious; and what did she expect Alex to say? That she was the only one whose safety he cared about? She drew back from him involuntarily. But Alex' voice was clipped and cool.

"I am aware of it. And if I had the authority to do so, I would have every one of you sent to the nearest hill station where there are British troops, while there is still time. Not for your safety, but for ours."

"For yours?" said Winter uncertainly. "I don't understand—"

"Don't you? I should have thought it was obvious," said Alex brutally. "Because men are sentimental over women they will throw away military advantages, and hesitate and weigh the chances of failure when attack is their best or only hope, and lose their opportunity because they have to think of the women and children. Men who would not otherwise dream of surrendering will make terms with an enemy in return for the safety of a handful of women. If a man is killed, it is an accident of war; but if a woman or a child is killed, it is a barbarous murder and a hundred lives—or a thousand—are sacrificed to avenge it. It is only a man like John Nicholson who has the courage to write—and mean it—that the safety of women and children in some crises is such a very minor consideration that it ceases to be a consideration at all. If only more men thought like that, you could all stay in Lunjore and be damned to you!"

There was exasperation and bitterness in his voice, as though some prophetic vision of the future had risen before him in all its tragic futility. And then a dry leaf crunched behind them and he turned quickly to see

George Lawrence standing in the moonlight beyond the rim of the tree shadows.

"Who is it?" George Lawrence spoke softly but sharply, and as Alex moved out into the moonlight he said with undisguised relief: "Oh, it's you, Alex. I thought—" He checked at the sight of Winter. "Mrs. Barton!"

His eyebrows twitched together in a sudden frown and Winter said: "I'm sorry, Mr. Lawrence. Did we startle you? I came down to walk in the garden because I couldn't sleep, and Captain Randall found me here."

The Chief Commissioner's nephew said sharply, as though Winter were not there: "How much has she seen?"

"Quite enough," said Alex laconically. "But she won't talk."

"I promise," said Winter. "I didn't mean to spy on you, and I won't speak of it to anyone. Word of honor!" She smiled at him and his set face relaxed in an answering smile.

He turned to Alex and said a little stiffly: "I thought that you were intending to make a five o'clock start, Alex? It is nearly two o'clock already. Had you not better be getting some sleep? I will see Mrs. Barton to her room."

Alex regarded him with a good deal of sardonic comprehension in his gaze. So George considered that he had been gravely imperiling young Mrs. Barton's reputation by being found talking to her in the garden at two o'clock in the morning, did he? He wondered what impression would be gained by anyone who might happen to see Mr. Lawrence escorting Mrs. Barton to her bedroom at that hour? George would not have thought of that. He said gravely: "I am sure I could leave her in no better hands. Good night, Mrs. Barton. Good-by, George; I hear you return to Sikora soon. Good luck to you."

"Thank you," said George Lawrence soberly. "I may need it."

Alex lifted his hand in a brief gesture of farewell, and turning on his heel he walked away across the moonlit lawn and was swallowed up by the foreshortened shadow of the Residency tower.

23

THE Dalys had left shortly after twelve o'clock on the following day, and an hour after their departure Winter drove back in Sir Henry's barouche to the Casa de Ballesteros.

Her husband, she was informed, was still abed. There had been a party last night. Not a large one. Half a dozen sahibs in all. But they had stayed until the small hours.

Despite the lateness of the season every door and window in the big drawing room stood wide, but the hot air of midday and the scent of fresh-cut flowers could not disguise the stale reek of cigar smoke and spilled brandy. There was another smell too that reminded Winter of Hazrat Bagh and there was something in the room that had not been there before: a large square of faded velvet that she recognized as a bedspread from one of the upstairs rooms, and which hung neatly over the Goya portrait of Don Cristobal de Ballesteros.

Winter looked at it, puzzled and frowning, and sent for old Muddeh Khan, the head bearer. Muddeh Khan looked unhappy and avoided her eye. The Huzoors, he explained apologetically, had been in a merry mood and had damaged the portrait somewhat in sport. He would have removed it, save that the wall also . . .

Winter dismissed him, and when he had gone she crossed to the portrait and pulled away the square of olive-green velvet, and knew why the smell in the room had reminded her of Hazrat Bagh. Conway and his guests had used the vast painting as a target, and the dark beauty of the magnificent canvas was spattered with bullet holes which had smashed through it and broken and pitted the wall at its back. The haughty, hollow-cheeked Spanish face with its faint suggestion of scornful amusement was a mess of ruined canvas, and there was nothing left of the portrait that was worth repairing.

Looking at it, Winter was dragged down without warning into helpless rage. That he could do this to her father's house!—to Pavos Reales! That he should bring his coarse, drunken friends and his cheap, loud women to this beautiful, silent house and vulgarize it as he had done last night!

She turned and walked out of the house and down to the river terrace, hatless in the hot sunlight, shivering with shock and anger and disgust as she had shivered on the morning that had followed the nightmare of her wedding.

I cannot bear it! thought Winter, staring out across the wide reaches of the river with eyes that only saw the senseless ruin of that magnificent canvas. I cannot bear it. . . . And yet what was she to do?

I will go to the hills, she thought. That will at least please Alex. Or—or will it? No, not please him. He does not want me to go because I am I, but because I am merely one of all the women he would like to be rid of so that we cannot get in the way of military decisions if there is a crisis. What was it Alex—or Nicholson—had said? "Women . . . in some crises are such a very minor consideration that they cease to be a consideration at all."

Quite suddenly her anger and despair fell away from her. If a crisis was brewing in India her own problems were indeed trivial, and they must be put aside. Conway intended to return to Lunjore at the end of the month, and she would go with him and arrange to leave for Simla or Naini Tal toward the middle of May. Then by the time the next cold weather came this threatened crisis would either have broken or blown over, and Conway would have resigned his post and be leaving India. She must do nothing until then. Except the hardest thing of all—wait.

It was midafternoon and the hottest and quietest time of the day, for few went abroad while the sun sucked the moisture from the earth and the marrow from men's bones. The river and the stone-flagged terrace lay empty in the sun glare, and the far bank was deserted. A mile or so upstream the city shimmered in the heat haze, and there was no cloud in the sky and nothing moved except the soundless river and a solitary boat that drifted down with the stream.

It was a flat-bottomed country boat with a matting roof curved above it to keep out the sun, poled by an ancient rheumy-eyed man in the scanty garb of a fisherman, and it drifted closer and closer to the stone wall of the river terrace until its prow grated on the water steps. It was a small enough sound but astonishingly loud in the hot, silent stillness of the afternoon, and Winter moved to the balustrade and looked down.

A woman's partially veiled face peered out from beneath the matting screen and looked cautiously up and down the empty reaches of the river, eyes narrowed against the sun glare, and then glancing upward, saw Winter. The eyes widened suddenly and a dark clawlike hand beckoned. There was something so furtive and yet so urgent in that gesture that Winter turned involuntarily to look behind her. But the terrace and the park beyond it was deserted, and not even a butterfly moved in the blinding sunlight.

She went quickly to the water steps, holding her wide skirts clear of the hot flagstones, but at the top of them she hesitated for a moment. There was no one within sight or call, and she did not know who was in the boat. The hand beckoned imperiously again and Winter descended the steps slowly and stooped to peer under the shadows of the curved matting. The face that had looked up at her dropped its chuddar for a brief moment. It was Hamida.

Winter gathered up her skirts and holding them about her she scrambled into the darkness of the tentlike enclosure. There was a clink of silver bracelets and a scent of attar of roses, and a soft, slender hand that was not Hamida's stretched out of the gloom and caught her bare arm.

"Ameera! Is it thou?"

"It is I, *querida*—" Ameera spoke in halting Spanish. "Luck is indeed with me, for I did not think to find you here. Hamida was to fetch you from the house. I came at this time because I knew that there would be few abroad at such an hour. I cannot stay long."

She spoke with a soft, breathless haste that made Winter say sharply: "What is it? What has happened?"

"I cannot come to see you again. It is not safe, either for you or for me. And if it were known that I have come now—"

The sentence broke off into a shiver, and all at once the hot dimness of the little matting shelter, the bright stillness of the land and the wide, slow-flowing river were filled with fear, and even the sly chuckle of the water under the wooden boat seemed a sound full of menace.

Winter took Ameera's hand between her own small, cool palms and held it tightly. "Tell me what has happened."

Ameera sank her voice to a whisper: "You must go, *querida*. Quickly! Very quickly. There is danger here for all of your blood. No, not in Lucknow only, or in Oudh, but in all India. I have heard—things. Things I dare not tell you. But it is true what I say. Therefore I come to tell you that you must not go to the hills, but to the sea, and take ship and return at once to your own country."

"This is my country."

"It is not—it is not!" said Ameera passionately. "I am of this land, but you are not! But for love of you, because we two played together as children and because your father was brother to my mother, I betray my countrymen to beg you to go!"

Winter said slowly: "Dear, you must tell me more. I cannot go just for this."

"I can tell you nothing—nothing! Already I have said too much. If my husband knew that I had told you aught, he would kill me—even me, who am the mother of his sons and whom he loves. Yes, loves!"

Winter's eyes, accustomed now to the gloom after the sun glare of the terrace, could see that Ameera's laughing face was drawn and haggard with fear and anxiety, and that there was a reflection of that fear on Hamida's face also. But she had to know more. She had to know when.

She said carefully, trying to keep the urgency from her voice: "I will try to go, but it will not be easy to leave soon. We do not return to Lunjore until the end of this month, and I had thought to go to the hills by mid-May."

Ameera said: "Not to the hills. To England. Even the hills may not be safe."

"It will take three weeks to reach Calcutta," said Winter slowly.

"That I know. Did I not say that you must leave at once?"

Winter's fingers released the slim hand she held, and she said as though frightened: "But is it safe to travel? If there is danger, would it not be safer to stay where there are regiments?"

"No harm will come to you before the last day of May, but after that there will be no safety anywhere, least of all where there are regiments! You will go? Promise me you will go?"

Winter drew a long breath and found that the palms of her hands were wet. A wetness that had nothing to do with the airless heat of the small boat. She had got what she wanted. She leant forward and kissed Ameera swiftly: "I will try, *querida*. But if my—my husband," she hesitated on the word, "will not go, then I cannot."

"Then go to the hills. It may serve—I do not know. And now I must go. Already I have stayed overlong. Good-by, *querida*—" She lapsed into Urdu: "Good-by, Little Pearl. Do not forget me! I will make a prayer to my God, and to Bibi Miriam also, who was a woman and may hear me, for thy sake and thy safety."

The tears were running down her cheeks and she clung to Winter for a moment and then tore herself free and thrust her away. "Go now—go quickly! It is late. Hamida, tell the *manji* to make haste!"

Winter stood on the water steps in the hard sunlight and raised her hand in farewell as the old man thrust off with his pole.

The little ripples lapped and hissed softly against the hot stone steps, and she watched the small boat through a mist of tears until the sun dazzle on the water blotted it out. Something moved on the terrace above her and she whirled about, her heart in her throat. But it was only a peacock rustling his splendid tail along the flagstones. Her sudden movement and the swish of her hooped skirts startled the bird, and lifting his tail clear of the ground he scuttled for the shelter of the bamboos with undignified haste. But the momentary panic he had caused her served to remind Winter that Ameera had risked her life to bring that warning. It was a horrible thought, and it sent a small, icy prickle of fear down Winter's spine, so that she shivered in the afternoon heat and turned back again to the river, peering under the palm of her hand. But the boat had gone and the river ran quiet and undisturbed from bank to bank, and nothing moved upon it save a corpse that drifted down on the stream, turning lazily with the current.

Standing on the deserted terrace Winter looked out across the wide river and the wide land beyond, as her mother Sabrina had done on an evening almost eighteen years ago: and was seized as Sabrina had been by a sudden horror of India—of the savage, alien land that lay all about her, stretching away for hundreds of miles and yet hemming her in; of the dark, secretive, sideways-looking eyes; the tortuous, unreadable minds behind the bland, expressionless faces; the incredible cruelties that were practiced in the mazes of that city and of which the servants whispered. I must be careful, thought Winter. I must be very careful. For Ameera's sake.

She did nothing for three long days, forcing herself to inactivity and her face to smiles, for fear that her actions or her expression should be watched by someone who might have had knowledge of Ameera's visit. She wrote no letters and paid no visits. She received and entertained her husband's guests and gave no outward sign that might be interpreted as alarm or disquiet, feeling like a traitor to her own race because she did not run at once to Sir Henry with that vital information.

On the fourth day her chance came when she and her husband attended an evening party at the Residency. Shamianahs had been erected on the Residency lawns and the trees hung with colored lanterns, while the band of one of the regiments stationed in the cantonments provided music for the delectation of several hundred guests who included almost all the British residents and a large proportion of the nobility and gentry of Oudh.

Perhaps the most spectacular guest, and certainly one who aroused the most interest, was Dundoo Pant, the Nana of Bithore, who attended the party accompanied by an impressively large retinue. The Nana was a man who cherished a grievance against the British, the government having refused to recognize him as the legal heir or to allow him the pension granted to the Peishwa, Baje Rao, who having no son had adopted him under Hindu law. But he did not appear to have allowed his grievances to sour him, and was most friendly and affable toward the British guests, with several of whom he seemed to be on excellent terms. He was a fat man, strangely dark skinned for a Mahratta, and very splendidly dressed, and he wore a pair of large diamond earrings which flashed and glittered in the light of the colored paper lanterns. Alex, had he been present, would not have recognized the earrings—the ones he had seen had been rubies—but he would have had no difficulty at all in recognizing the wearer.

The Chief Commissioner had been surrounded by a ring of guests wherever he moved, and it was clearly impossible to have any private conversation with him. But Winter had managed to speak with George Lawrence. She had asked him to show her the rose garden and had put her hand on his arm and walked away with him, talking with unusual animation.

"It is Sir Henry I wish to speak to, but the people follow him about so and I do not wish to go apart with him. So you must tell him." She looked up into her companion's face and said: "Please will you smile, as though I were telling you something of no matter?"

George Lawrence smiled an obedient and somewhat puzzled smile and managed to retain it, though with some difficulty, through the next few minutes. But if he found her tale a trifle confusing, he at least realized that young Mrs. Barton was in deadly earnest; though he was inclined to treat her story with some reserve. There had been so many rumors of late, and this was just one more—and apparently one brought by an overexcited Indian woman who by some curious twist of fate was first cousin to this girl who walked beside him. He promised nevertheless to relay it to Sir Henry.

"He must tell no one who it came from," begged Winter earnestly. "But it is true—tell him that I am sure that it is true! Ameera risked her life to tell me, and I am risking hers by telling you. Tell him that!"

She looked up into his face and smiled as she spoke, but her eyes were wide and bright and full of a desperate urgency.

"I will tell him," promised George Lawrence. "But you must not allow yourself to become overanxious, Mrs. Barton. We hear many of these rumors. I feel sure that this cloud will blow away as others have done. It will pass."

It will pass. . . . It has passed. . . . In cantonments and offices, in residencies and British bungalows, in government houses and council chambers and in the home of the Governor-General himself, wherever the British met to talk, the words were spoken again and again. The brief flare-up at Berhampore in February and the uglier and more recent outbreak in Barrackpore had died down without leading to any further demonstrations, and men who had been smelling the wind uneasily relaxed again, and concurred with the popular conviction that the peak of the general unrest had passed, and that any serious danger—if there had ever been any, which the majority were inclined to discount—was over.

Winter heard from Lottie who was now in Delhi, Edward having been transferred from Meerut on special duty. They were not living in the cantonments but in a house lent them by a friend, inside the city itself and not far from the Kashmir Gate.

"I fear that Mamma is a little disappointed that we would not reside with her," wrote Lottie, *"but I see so little of Edward that I like to have him to myself when he is off duty. Sophie is away on a visit to friends of Mamma and Papa's in Cawnpore, and will be returning on the fifteenth of the next month. It is really not so very hot as yet, and I begin to think that reports as to the heat of the plains have been greatly exaggerated, although I am told that this is quite an exceptionally cool year, and many old hands say they have known nothing like it before. I wish you would come and stay with me. It would be so delightful to see you again. You must come next cold weather, and only think! I shall have a little Edward to show you then! I cannot bring myself to believe it. Mamma sends her love. . . ."*

Lottie's news disturbed Winter, for she had thought that Lottie at least was safe. There were well over a thousand British soldiers in Meerut, forming the strongest European garrison in the North-West Provinces, and surely any woman would be safe there? But Delhi—!

She wrote to Lottie, urging her for the sake of the coming child to go to the hills and to take Sophie with her, and begging that Mrs. Abuthnot accompany her daughters—they would all spend the hot months together in a bungalow among the pines and be cool and have pleasant times. But Lottie would not leave her Edward or Mrs. Abuthnot her George. Winter wrote again, and more urgently, but they were not to be persuaded. *Even if I told them all that Ameera had said, they would still not come,* thought Winter. *Because they would not believe it! Or they would hope that it was not true, and soon they would make themselves believe that it could not be. There is nothing I can do.*

On the last night of their stay in Lucknow Conway had given a farewell party. It had been a riotous affair and had lasted well into the small hours of the morning, and he had to be carried to the carriage in which they were to make the journey to Lunjore. He had expressly forbidden Winter to ride, saying that he had no desire to have her down with heat stroke on the journey; nothing could be more inconvenient! But the sight of her husband's brandy-sodden and inanimate bulk being disposed in the carriage proved too much for her, and she had Furiante saddled.

She looked back over her shoulder at the Casa de los Pavos Reales as she rode away: at the orange trees and the lemon groves and the pomegranates, and the tree-shaded levels of the park that had changed so little with the long years, and thought, Perhaps I shall never see it again. But she left it without regret, for the gracious, peaceful house held no happiness for her and no memories. It was the Gulab Mahal that held those, but the Gulab Mahal was closed to her. It was still a fata morgana—a glimmering mirage. The moon out of reach.

24

It was evening, and the last day of April, when the Commissioner and his wife drove once more through the massive gateway of the Lunjore Residency. And two hours later they were dining with the same raffish company that had celebrated the Commissioner's wedding.

They were all there—with the exception of Mr. Josh Cottar who had departed to Calcutta on a business trip. Lou Cottar, Chrissie and Edgar Wilkinson, Colonel Moulson, Major Mottisham and half a dozen others. "Wrote ahead and invited 'em," said Conway. "Didn't think that we'd take that extra day, but what's the odds? Nothin' like havin' a celebration to welcome us home, eh?"

"I assure you the place has been like a morgue—or a Quaker Meeting —while you have been away," said Lou Cottar. "I have had such a fit of the bore that I have yawned two more lines into my face, and heaven knows that is has enough already! You do at least provide the only tolerably amusing parties in Lunjore, Con."

"It wasn't only my parties you found amusing once," said the Commissioner, reaching out to pat her arm. "Eh, Lou?"

"Ah, but that was at least five years ago. Or was it more? You were a heavy, handsome brute in those days, and I believe I actually lost almost two nights' sleep over you once!"

"Shall I see if I can make you lose two more?"

"You couldn't do it. You're gross, Con. And you drink a deal too much. If it wasn't for your parties I'd be tempted to drop you! But you're a habit with me, and I'm too idle to break it."

The Commissioner glowered at her. "You've got the most poisonous tongue of any woman I know, Lou. By God, I don't know why I put up with you!"

"Because I'm a habit with you, and you've never been able to break yourself of bad habits," said Mrs. Cottar.

Nothing has changed, thought Winter. It is just the same. It is as though I had never been away to Lucknow. . . .

But that was not true. She herself had changed. The noisy, raffish party and the sight of her husband with his arm about Chrissie Wilkinson's waist no longer had any power to hurt or disgust her. If Ameera was right, all these people here might die within a few months—perhaps in less. The last day of May, Ameera had said—"and after that there will be no safety anywhere." And it was the first of May tomorrow. May Day!

The following morning, when she had breakfasted, she wrote to Alex.

It was a short letter and the first she had ever written to him. She asked a servant to deliver it to him, but the man said that Randall Sahib was in camp among the outlying villages. "Then someone must take it to him," said Winter. "Send Yusaf to me." The man looked slantingly at her under lowered lids and went away to summon the syce, but the look had frightened Winter.

Quite suddenly, in that brief moment, the full meaning of what a major insurrection in this country would entail came home to her. She had never really visualized it in its entirety before. But now, standing in the big, cool drawing room of her husband's house, she thought for the first time of exactly what such a rising would mean. Of the handful of white people who held this vast country, and the dark, teeming millions who surrounded them and who lived cheek by jowl with them, watching their every movement and listening to their every word—and waiting. There was little privacy to be had in a land where a dozen servants were always within call, and where a punkah coolie, a chuprassy, or a *dazi* sitting cross legged before a pile of sewing was as natural a part of every veranda as the matting on the floor.

She tore up the letter that she had written to Alex and having burnt the pieces, wrote another. She handed it to Yusaf, telling him in a tone that was sufficiently clear to carry to the punkah coolie, a chuprassy and a loitering mali who was cutting off the dead heads of the canna lilies in a flower bed below the veranda, that a friend of the Captain Sahib's whom she had met in Lucknow wished to come over for some shikar (shooting), and as the sahib was in camp he must be informed in case he wished to return.

Yusaf had ridden with the letter, and Alex had read it late that evening by the light of a flaring oil lamp. There had been only two lines, but he had read them and reread them and then folded the paper carefully and put it into the inner pocket of his coat.

"Tell the mem-sahib that I return tomorrow or the next day."

Yusaf saluted and slipped away into the darkness, and Alex returned to his tent and blew out the light that was attracting too many creeping and flying things to their doom.

Niaz had put up the camp bed in the open, and lying on it later that night Alex stared up through the mosquito net at the blaze of stars, and saw a comet cross the heavens from east to west, not with the rush of a falling star, but slowly, dragging a long train of glowing light that appeared red rather than white or golden, and taking a full ten minutes to traverse the spangled ceiling of the sky. From a dozen yards to his left he heard Niaz move, and looking in his direction he saw the silhouette of his lifted head and knew that he had seen it too.

They will say that too is a sign—or an omen, thought Alex, and I am not sure that one can blame them for it.

A red star, smearing a trail of blood from the east to the west. Were there such things as signs and wonders in the sky? A star had once brought Wise Men out of the East to search for that Sword that had come into the world so many centuries ago and had not yet been sheathed. That the heavens foretold the future was perhaps the oldest superstition in the world, and men had watched the skies for thousands of years, believing that their fate could be read there.

In the hot weather many men slept out in the open, in roadways and on rooftops and at the doors of their huts. How many would have seen the red comet? And how many—or how few?—would not regard it as a sign from heaven? An evil sign: not because of its color, for red is worn in the East for rejoicing, but because the times and men's thoughts were evil.

A hundred yards away a pariah dog thrust its gaunt nose at the sky and howled long and very mournfully, and the howl was taken up and repeated again and again in a barking, wailing chorus by all the dogs of the near-by village as though they bayed the moon. Beyond the tank and the mango tope where Alex' camp was pitched, a light pricked the darkness, and another and another, and presently a conch brayed in the temple and a tom-tom beat. They have seen it, thought Alex. This is how legends are born.

He did not start for Lunjore until early next afternoon, and he and Niaz rode hard through the heat of the day and into the dusty sunset and the brief green dusk. They had drawn rein as the sun sank below the horizon, so that they could eat and drink, for the Mohammedan fast of Ramazan had begun with the new moon, and while it lasted Niaz and all other followers of the Prophet might not eat or drink between sunrise and sunset.

They had stopped at the edge of a tank, and as they dismounted a lone pigeon with a hawk on its tail flew low above their heads, twisting and turning in its flight, and flumped heavily into a large peepul tree on the far side of the tank. A flock of crows rose up from the peepul, cawing hoarsely, and the hawk flew off, and presently the pigeon, undisturbed by the narrowness of its escape, fluttered down onto a half-submerged slab of stone at the edge of the green, scum-covered water to drink. It rose again almost instantly with a noisy, startled flap of wings as though something had frightened it, and they saw it circle upward and then turn and make for the west where the glow of the setting sun was turning the dust veils to gold.

Alex looked across the tank with narrowed eyes, trying to see what it was that had startled the bird, and became aware that there was a man seated among the roots of the peepul tree. A naked, ash-smeared sadhu who sat so still that he might almost have been part of the tree. The squirrels played about him, running casually to and fro, and a dozen birds who were making preparations to roost quarreled and twittered within reach of his hand, as completely undisturbed by his presence as the crows and the parrots who perched in the boughs over his head. He had made no movement—Alex was sure of that, for had he done so he would have alarmed the other wild creatures about him—yet the pigeon had been frightened. It was a trivial incident, but it occupied Alex' mind to the exclusion of much else for the remainder of the ride.

It was dark by the time they reached the bungalow, and Alex took a hot bath to remove the dust and sweat of the long ride, and having changed into the white mess jacket that was almost a uniform of the hot weather, he walked across in the hot starlight to the Residency.

He found Winter sitting on a sofa in the center of the drawing room with the slow-moving punkah stirring the air above her. She had a book in her hands, but it was obvious that she had heard his voice in the hall. There was a suggestion of rigidity about her slight figure, and she was smiling. It was a pleasant smile; the smile an actress might have employed to indicate pleasurable surprise. But she was not as a rule, reflected Alex walking leisurely toward her, much given to smiling, and it occurred to him to wonder if that smile was for his benefit, or for Rassul's who had shown him in? Some instinct for danger made him return it, and as he took the hand that she held out to him he knew that he had been right, for her fingers were cold and not quite steady, and they tightened warningly upon his for a moment before they were withdrawn.

Winter said: "Do sit down, Captain Randall. I am afraid my husband is busy just now. A card party, you know. How much English do these people understand? I did not expect to see you until tomorrow." She laughed as though she had made some joke.

Alex' eyes narrowed suddenly but he replied without the least hesitation: "There was nothing much to keep me, and camping is hot work in this weather. A good deal more than most people would think."

He saw Winter's quick breath of relief, and smiled. Had she really been afraid that he would misunderstand her and demand explanations? She threw an anxious glance at the two doors that opened onto the veranda. *Chiks* hung before both to keep the room from filling with bats and night-flying insects, but there were, he knew, at least three servants on the veranda. He shook his head very slightly.

Winter said: "Yes, I thought it might be so. Mr.—Brown wished to know if there was any good shooting to be had in Lunjore at this time of the year. He has a few weeks' leave soon and was considering coming here. I told him that I could not possibly say, but that you would write."

Alex talked trivialities for a quarter of an hour by the drawing room clock. Whatever it was that Winter wished to tell him, he had no intention of hearing it now. He finished his drink and rose. "Do you ride tomorrow?"

"Yes. A little before five. It is too hot now, once the sun is up."

Alex said: "You should ride by the river. It is cooler there. Good night, Mrs. Barton."

There were no signs in the skies that night and the pariah dogs were silent, but the city was not. The city was awake and restless, and tom-toms throbbed and conches blared as they had in the little village beyond the tank and the mango tope.

"It is Ramazan," said Niaz, but he said it uneasily, looking over his shoulder.

"It is dewanee—the madness," said Alex. "We ride an hour before sunrise. Bring a gun."

"Which? Do we shoot partridge or *kala hirren?*"

"Pigeon," said Alex briefly.

"Ah!"

Alex turned swiftly at the tone. "Didst thou see, then?"

"Nay. It was too far. But that bairagi did not wish us to see the bird, and therefore he told it to go. Wherefore I wondered—"

"I too," said Alex. He had seen such things done before, and it did not strike him as in the least impossible that the man could order a bird's departure without speech or movement. He had heard it said that even little silent Zeb-un-Nissa, Akbar Khan's granddaughter, could do the same.

It was cool in the early light of the May morning. Cooler than Alex ever remembered it to have been at this time of the year. May and June were normally burning months in the plains, but this May was not like others, and he could only regret it. An early hot weather and soaring temperatures would have sent many women hurrying to the hills with their children, but the unusual mildness of the weather had caused them to linger, putting off the day of separation.

Winter had ridden out by the wooden bridge that spanned the nullah behind the house, instead of by the main gateway. She saw the two horsemen far out on the plain ahead of her as she emerged from the thick belt of scrub and jungle that covered the far bank of the nullah and was an arm of the denser jungle that stretched away to the eastward and closed in upon the river bank three miles farther down, where the river joined the main stream that formed the boundary between Lunjore and Oudh. She threaded Furiante between the rough tussocks of grass where the narrow jungle track ran out onto the plain, and gave him his head, riding to cut them off before they reached the river bank, and she was laughing as she reined in beside a lone clump of three tall palm trees where Alex had pulled up to wait for her.

Alex greeted her, unsmiling. He wheeled his horse beside her and they moved off together parallel to the river bank, Niaz and Yusaf falling back out of earshot. "What is it that you wished to tell me?"

"It is something Ameera told me," said Winter, and she told him of that hot, still afternoon on the river terrace of Pavos Reales, and of the thing that Ameera had told her in halting Spanish so that even Hamida should not know what it was that she had said.

Alex did not say any of the soothing and reassuring things that George Lawrence had said. He said nothing at all for a long time, riding beside her in silence and looking out over the brightening river through narrowed eyes.

So he had been right! A day and a date. The last day of May—and it was already the third. Three days gone. Twenty-seven left. Twenty-seven days in which to turn aside the wind that was rising steadily and blowing hot and fitfully through every cantonment in India. How did one stop a wind that had been whistled up by the blindness and obstinacy and ego-tism of men who imagined that it was a simple matter, and one worthy of all praise, to pry the East loose from its centuries-old laws and customs and force it into a Western mold?

I can do nothing about the regiments, thought Alex, but some of the Tulakdars will stand behind me—or at least stay quiet. And so, I think, will the villagers. The city is the trouble. There are always budmashes (scoundrels) by the score in the kennels of any city, and the scum of the bazaars and the back alleys will rise at a word simply for the chance of murder and loot. . . . Will the police stand if the Army breaks? I must see Maynard again. . . .

A mile and a half down the river, and out of sight of the city, they turned inland through grass and low scrub and drifts of sand, and pres-ently a small, white-bearded man as thin as an arrow rose up apparently out of the ground, and Alex stopped and dismounted.

"The Huzoor is in good time," said Amir Nath. "Will he fly the *jurra* himself?" He lifted the hooded goshawk that held to his wrist, and the bird turned its head with a faint jingle of bells and flexed and unflexed its taloned feet, stretching a little and ruffling its feathers.

Alex shook his head. "No. I have not handled one for too long, and I would not have him miss."

A small boy rose up from the tall grass and grinned shyly at Winter. He carried a peregrine falcon on his wrist and was Nunni, Amir Nath's great-grandson. Winter sat down on a tussock of grass beside him and they carried on an animated conversation while the sky paled above them and the partridges awoke and a flight of parrots swished overhead, making for the river.

Five hundred yards above them Yusaf, sitting his horse at the bend of the river, stood up in his stirrups and raised his arm, and Niaz, three hun-dred yards below him, whistled.

Alex had brought a gun, but the pigeon was well out of range. It came flying steadily, making for the borders of Oudh.

It is too high, thought Alex. The hawk will never see it. But Amir Nath had removed the hood and now, with a high, shrill cry he hurled the bird up and into the air. There was a rush and a whirr of wings and the goshawk mounted with the speed of a feathered arrow, and hung motionless for a moment, sixty feet above them. Then it had sighted the pigeon and was away.

Niaz, who had ridden up, stooped from the saddle, and Nunni, thrusting the tercel at his great-grandfather, clutched at his hand and scrambled up before him with the agility of a squirrel, and they were away in pursuit.

The pigeon flapped and jinked in the air, turning and twisting, making for the shelter of the dense miles of jungle that blanketed the borders of Lunjore and Oudh. But she did not reach them. The goshawk towered above her, seized her and clung to her and dropped to the ground.

Three hours later Alex was confronting the Commissioner with a small strip of native-made paper on which was written a few lines in *shikust*. "And that, I think, sir," he concluded, "is how news seems to get about this country so quickly. There's probably a chain system of 'em."

"What the devil does it say?" demanded the Commissioner peevishly.

"'It is too soon. Be patient and await the auspicious day.'"

"Well—well? What of it? Can't see any harm in that?"

"I take it to refer to some premature outbreak in Oudh," said Alex with exemplary patience. "If we hear within the next day or so that any such incident has occurred, I think we can take it as conclusive. I know that it does not prove much by itself, but added to all the rest it seems to me to have points of interest. Not the least of them being that we now know that there are leading agents and agitators in the city. It also bears out the theory that what is planned is a simultaneous rising on a given date."

"Nonsense!" retorted the Commissioner. "Probably refers to a wedding!"

"As you like, sir," said Alex in his most expressionless voice; and departed to see Major Maynard, who commanded the police.

Major Maynard alone confessed to uneasiness; but not on account of his police, whom he believed to be stanch. "It's old Packer," he said. "Unless something can be done to stop him preaching the Word to his men we shall have trouble. Can nothing be done to gag the old fool?"

"I've done my best," said Alex tiredly, "but he told me that he was 'rendering unto Caesar the things that are Caesar's and to God the things that are God's.' He has a good deal of support in Lunjore."

"Among the sepoys?"

"Good God, no! Among the ladies. They look upon him as a saintly man and a shining example to the less devout—such as Moulson!"

"Moulson's too much of a martinet," said Major Maynard gloomily. "Seems to be no happy medium. There's old Gardener pottering around with his watering can, cherishin' his fellows as though they were tender plants, and Packer looking upon his as erring sheep to be gathered into the fold, while Moulson goes to the opposite extreme and slings his sepoys into irons if they so much as blink on parade! He'll go too far one day, but there's no denying that his lot are the best disciplined of the bunch. I'd say there was a lot less chance of them cracking than of Packer's strayed lambs!"

"And your own?" inquired Alex.

"Oh, they're all right," said Major Maynard easily. "But I'll bear in mind what you say and keep a sharp eye on 'em. Personally, I'm inclined to think that the worst is past."

"I envy you your optimism," said Alex dryly, and rode back slowly to his bungalow through the blinding sunlight.

25

THE telegraph did not as yet operate in Lunjore, and so it was not until two days later that the news trickled over the border from Oudh that on Sunday, May the third, the 7th Regiment of Oudh Irregulars had refused to accept their cartridges, and had mutinied. Sir Henry Lawrence had apparently acted with great promptness and succeeded in disarming the regiment—a good many of whom had absconded—and fifty of the ringleaders had been seized.

"It is too soon," said Alex, rereading that laconic dispatch. "Be patient and await the auspicious day." He crumpled up the tiny scrap of paper and stood looking out at the jacaranda trees in the garden, thinking: We have only one chance, and that is that their ringleaders will not be able to hold 'em until a given day. They're too worked up. Something will set them off. Some ass will put his foot in it and provoke a premature explosion that will sound the alarm. It's our only chance. But if it does go off on time, and in every cantonment in the country, they can write our obituaries now!

The weather continued unusually mild, and all over India women who had intended to leave for the hills delayed and put off the day of departure while the nights remained cool, and the Commissioner of Lunjore informed his wife that he could not arrange for her to leave for the hills before the twenty-second of the month. Mrs. Gardener-Smith and Delia, Mrs. Hossack and her four children, and Captain and Mrs. Batterslea and their young family were all leaving on that date, and therefore it would be more convenient if she were to travel in their company, as Captain Batterslea's presence would save him the trouble of arranging an escort for her. "Plenty of time before it gets too hot," said the Commissioner. "No hurry."

Plenty of time . . .

In the cantonment of Meerut, forty miles to the northeast of Delhi,

Colonel Carmichael Smyth, the commanding officer of the 3rd Light Cavalry, had ordered that fifteen picked men from each troop were to parade on the following morning to learn to use the new cartridges. "I'm not standing any damn' silly nonsense from *my* sepoys!" said Colonel Smyth. The ninety men were duly paraded—and eighty-five of them had refused to handle the caste-breaking cartridges. They were immediately tried by court-martial and sentenced to ten years imprisonment. A parade of all troops was ordered by the aged divisional commander Major General Hewitt to watch the sentence put into execution, and for hour after hour, in the broiling sun on the Meerut parade ground, the regiments stood in stony-faced silence and watched the eighty-five picked men of a picked regiment stripped of their uniforms and fettered one by one with the iron fetters that they would drag with them through ten dreary years of captivity. And when at long last the ordeal was over, the terrible, clanking file of manacled men were marched away in the bright, merciless sunlight, calling and crying to their comrades: "Is this justice? Because we will not lose our caste so that none of our own will speak with us or eat with us, must we suffer this fate? Is there no justice? Help us, brothers! Help us!"

"Art thou of the 3rd Risala?" shrilled a harpy in the Street of the Harlots in Meerut City to a group of prospective clients as night fell. "Then thou canst not enter here! Out! Out! We do not lie with cowards! Where are thy comrades who eat dirt and walk in chains? *They* were men! But thou—! Chicken hearts—children! Cowards all! *Pah!*" She spat in derision and a chorus of jeering, painted faces applauded from a dozen latticed windows and balconies, screaming like peacocks: "Out! Out! We lie with no cowards! If ye indeed be men, and not the boneless babes we take you for, release your brothers from bondage!"

Their taunts and their jeers pursued the men of the 3rd Cavalry through the hot, crowded, snarling bazaars of Meerut City, driving them from rage to a murderous frenzy. . . .

The night was hot and very still. So still that every small sound of all the small sounds that go to make up silence separated itself from its fellows and emphasized that stillness. The cheep of a muskrat; the dry scrape of a scorpion crawling up the wall; the flitter of a bat's wings in the dark veranda; the drone of the mosquitoes and, from very far away, the echo of a jackal pack who howled on the plains beyond the river.

There are no tom-toms in the city tonight, thought Winter, listening by her open window. And no conches. This is the first night for almost ten nights that I have not heard them. Perhaps it is the heat. It has not been really hot until now.

Somewhere in the dark recesses of the house a clock struck one. Three more hours before she could dress and go out to ride by the river. Would it be cooler by the river? It was so hot here, and so airless.

I will go up to the roof, she thought, turning restlessly away from the window. It will be cooler up there. She groped for her slippers in the darkness and put them on, and slipping her arms into the wide sleeves of the muslin wrap that lay at the foot of her bed, left the room and walked softly down the veranda and up the steep flight of stone steps to the first level of the flat-topped roof.

A shadow moved on the stonework and she looked up, startled, to see a small white figure standing above her by the narrow parapet that surrounded the upper roof. It was Zeb-un-Nissa.

Winter called up to her in a whisper, but the child did not answer or make any movement to show that she had heard. She was staring out across the lawns and gardens and the distant bulk of the Residency gateway toward the southwest, and her face and body looked curiously rigid, as though she were straining to catch some faraway and almost inaudible sound.

I believe she's sleepwalking! thought Winter, suddenly anxious. She waited for a moment or two, looking up at the child's tense face, and then went up the steps very softly so as not to frighten her. Zeb-un-Nissa did not move. Her eyes were wide and fixed, and standing beside her Winter could see that her small face was drawn with fear. She laid a gentle hand on the child's thin arm and spoke softly: "Nissa—"

Zeb-un-Nissa did not start or turn, but she moved her head a little and looked at Winter as though she were perfectly aware of her, her eyes full of horror. "Hark!" she said in a hoarse whisper. "Dost thou not hear them?" She began to shiver, and Winter put an arm about the frail little shoulders and drew the child against her: "What is it, *piyaree* (darling)? What is there to hear?"

The child pulled herself free and turned again to the parapet, clutching at the stone with small clawlike hands.

"It is the mem-*log*—the mem-sahibs! They are screaming! Canst thou not hear them scream? There be children also! Listen—*listen!* They are killing the mem-*log*. Thou canst hear the sword cuts. There! That was a child!—Hark to its mother shriek! *Ai! Ai!*" She wailed aloud and put her hands over her ears, cowering down below the parapet and weeping. "I cannot bear to hear them scream! They are killing the mem-*log*—they are killing the mem-*log!*"

Winter dropped to her knees and gathered the small, wailing figure into her arms. "Nissa—Nissa! There is no one screaming. It is only a dream, *piyaree*. Only a bad dream. There is no killing."

She had heard no sound behind her, but a shadow fell across them, black in the moonlight, and she turned swiftly, her heart in her mouth, to see Akbar Khan, the gatekeeper, salaaming deferentially behind her. His face was dark against the moon and the night sky, but Winter could see the gleam of his teeth and the glitter of his eyes, and though her first momentary panic had died at sight of him, an odd flicker of fear went through her, making her pull the child closer.

"Her mother missed the unworthy one from her bed," said Akbar Khan softly. "She has been sick with a fever these few days past and she must have left her bed while her mother slept. I am sorry that the child should have troubled the lady-sahib."

"She has not troubled me," said Winter. "Let her be. She can sleep in my room for what is left of the night."

"Nay, nay!" said Akbar Khan, shocked. "It would not be seemly! And her mother is anxious, and sent me in search of her."

Winter felt the frail body in her arms stiffen and writhe and become rigid, and then quite slowly it relaxed. Nissa sighed and her head nestled down against the shoulder that supported it, and looking down at the small face and feeling the shallow, even breathing, Winter realized that she had fallen asleep.

Akbar Khan reached down and took the child from her. "It was a fit," he said placidly. "She has always been a sickly child, and I fear that the time of her release is near. Her mother will grieve; but what is written is written." He cradled the thin body of his grandchild comfortably in his arms and went away, his bare feet making no sound on the warm stone.

Winter watched him go and she shivered in the hot night air. Akbar Khan had always been courteous and placid, and his greeting to her whenever she passed through the gateway was dignified and respectful, containing no trace of the veiled insolence that she had sometimes detected in Conway's other servants. But tonight there had been something in his manner that frightened her. Or was she being foolishly imaginative? But he had told a lie when he had said that Nissa had been sick for some days. That at least was not true, for she had seen Nissa daily at dawn.

What did the child think that she had heard? It was a dream of course. She had been dreaming. And yet she had not behaved as Winter imagined that a sleepwalker would do. She had appeared to be aware of Winter, and awake; caught up in horror—but awake.

The servants said that Akbar Khan's granddaughter had second sight, and they were afraid of her. And there had been that day when she had said—or seemed to say—that Alex would come to no harm; and he had come to no harm. But she could not have known that he was in any danger. It had been a coincidence.

"She was dreaming!" said Winter aloud and firmly. But she shivered again, and drawing her thin, beruffled wrap tighter about her, she left the roof and returned to the hot, dark, silent rooms and her hot, tumbled bed.

Alex heard her running along the veranda of his bungalow the following morning, and knew who it was even before the startled chuprassy lifted the *chik* and she was standing before him, tense and white faced, her hands clutching at the edge of his desk.

"Alex, do something! They've killed her! I know they've killed her! Conway won't do anything. He says it's all nonsense. It's her grandfather —it's Akbar Khan. He did it. I know he did it!"

Alex came round the desk and caught her by the shoulders and propelled her forcibly out of the office and into the living room. He pushed her down into a chair, splashed a generous quantity of brandy into a glass and held it to her mouth while she drank it. Winter gasped and choked, but it took some of the shivering rigidity from her.

"Now tell me."

"It's Nissa!" said Winter, and described the happening on the roof. "I went to see her this morning and—and they said she was dead. They didn't want me to see her, but I made them. I—I have never seen anyone dead before—only Great-grandfather. I think they smothered her—" Her voice broke suddenly on a shudder of horror.

Alex said quietly: "You can't know that."

He walked back with her in the full glare of the blazing morning and saw her go into the house, and an hour later he sent over a brief message asking if she would ride with him that evening.

Winter heard the wailing in the servants' quarters for half that hot afternoon, and later a small wooden box was carried out by a side door in the wall to the Mohammedan burial ground outside the city; but she did not see it go.

"There is nothing we can do," said Alex. "The child appears to have been subject to epileptic fits, and Dr. O'Dwyer, whom I asked to look at the body, says that it is quite possible that she died as a result of one of them—with general debility and the heat as contributory causes. He was not prepared to take any further action on it. He said—and rightly—that there was enough tension in the place already without giving rise to any more alarm and excitement. I'm sorry, but that is all there is to it."

"Then you won't do anything?"

"There is nothing I can do, beyond what I have already done. The child was buried at four o'clock." He turned his head and looked at the set white face beside him and said after a moment: "I'm sorry, Winter."

But Winter's account of what the child had said last night disturbed him. It was not that he believed Zeb-un-Nissa to have had second sight, but it seemed to him quite likely that she was repeating something—or dreaming of something—that she had heard discussed. If so, she might well have been assisted to die. The words that the child had said repeated themselves again and again in his brain as they had repeated themselves in Winter's last night—"They are killing the mem-*log!*—they are killing the mem-*log!* . . ."

Perhaps it was just as well that Zeb-un-Nissa was dead, and that there had been no one to call out during that long, burning day that they could hear the mem-*log* screaming.

Delhi was far away, hidden behind the dust and the dancing heat and the parched, blazing plains. And Mrs. Abuthnot had not screamed as she died in the hot sunlight within the Kashmir Gate where so short a time before the officers from the cantonments by the Ridge had held that gay moonlight picnic. But little Miss Jennings had screamed and shrieked as the clawing, bloodstained hands snatched at her and the reddened sabers cut and slashed. And all through that long, hot day the shrieks of women and the terrified screaming of children, the crackle of flames and the howl of the mob, rose up from Duryagunj—that once quiet quarter of Delhi where the European and Eurasian clerks and pensioners and Indian Christians had lived and were now dying in terror and agony in the blinding, merciless sunlight.

All through that long, hot day frantic officers in Meerut, where the terror had broken out and from where the mutineers, after a night of murder, had ridden for Delhi, ground their teeth and waited, or pleaded for permission to ride after them—there were more British troops in Meerut than in almost any other garrison in India, and not all the native regiments had revolted—only let them follow after the mutineers and save Delhi before it was too late! But General Hewitt was old and fat and infirm, and the magnitude of the crisis had left him too bewildered to take any decisive action, while Brigadier Wilson, left to take the initiative, hesitated and was lost. "We must think of the women and children," said Brigadier Wilson uneasily. "We cannot risk a repetition of last night's massacres. We must protect the remaining women and children."

All through the long, hot day the Delhi Garrison waited and hoped, and watched the Meerut Road for the help that they could not believe would fail them. And every moment that the help delayed, the mutineers of the 3rd Cavalry, and those who had joined them, grew bolder, and more and more of the city rabble gathered before the palace where the tatterdemalion court of the aged King of Delhi grew hourly more confident.

"It is true—it is true!" urged Zeenut Mahal, the scheming favorite of old Bahardur Shah. "They say that they have killed every Feringi in Meerut; men, women and children also! It must be true, for see—there is no dust cloud on the Meerut Road! If any remained alive, think you they would not ride with all speed for Delhi to take vengeance? They are dead! They must all be dead! Let us kill all the Feringis in Delhi also, and then thou wilt be King indeed!"

"It is true—it must be true!" said the scum of the city, sharpening swords and knives for the slaughter. "They have killed every Feringi in Meerut. Let us do the like here!"

Lottie had seen her father cut down by his own men, an expression of utter disbelief upon his rubicund, cherubic face, as though he could not and would not believe, even in the moment of his death, that this thing was possible. She had made no sound, because she herself did not believe what she had seen. Standing with her mother, and a dozen other women and their children who had taken refuge at the Main Guard within the Kashmir Gate, she had seen him ride up to the gate with his men. She had heard his fussy, fatherly voice—this pleasant, kindly little man of whom she knew so little—raised in expostulation when his men had checked before the gate. And a minute later she had seen him dragged from his horse and three bayonets plunged into his body.

Lottie, looking down dazedly from the rose-red walls where she had picnicked and walked in the peaceful autumn days of the vanished year, had thought how red and bright the blood looked on the hot white dust.

"It cannot be happening," said Lottie. "It cannot be true. . . ."

"I don't see 'as 'ow we can 'old out much longer, sir," said Conductor Buckley to Lieutenant Willoughby who commanded the Delhi Magazine. "The perishers 'ave brought scalin' ladders—" His words were barely audible above the howling of the mob and the incessant rattle and crash of gunfire.

They had been holding the magazine since morning, and now the sun was moving down the sky again. Was it only four o'clock? Nine of them, against a howling, yelling mob of thousands. Nine of them to man ten guns.

"Scully says the train's laid, sir," yelled Conductor Buckley. "Any sign from the Meerut Road yet, sir?"

Young Lieutenant Willoughby ran to the river bastion and strained his eyes for a last look down the hot, empty road where the heat haze danced and shimmered under the brazen sky. "No. They are not coming. Perhaps they are all dead. We cannot wait any longer."

He looked up once at the blue of the sky, his eyes calm and youthful in the sweating, dust-grimed, powder-blackened mask that was his face, and then glanced at the swarming thousands who clambered in, monkey wise, over the walls, hemming the defenders into the last narrow square of ground.

"We shall take a good many of them with us," said Lieutenant Willoughby. "All right, Buckley. Give him the signal to fire it. . . ."

An appalling crash of sound silenced the savage roar of the mob, and a vast cloud, rose-red and beautiful in the level sunlight, lifted up above the domes and minarets, over the groves and gardens of the city of the Moguls, reaching up higher and higher into the still air and spreading out like a blossoming flower on a tall white stem. And as though the sound of the explosion had been a signal, the sullen, hesitating sepoys within the Main Guard turned upon those who had taken refuge there, and Lottie, who had run down from the wall at the sight of Edward, saw her mother fall without a sound, and saw a saber slash down through her husband's head, laying it open almost to the shoulder.

She had screamed then, and fought to go to him, but someone had caught her arms and dragged her, struggling and shrieking, to the battlements, and then hands were gripping her wrists and she was being lowered down from the wall, swaying and turning against the hot stone, and screaming for Edward. The makeshift lifeline of hastily knotted belts broke, and she fell and struck the hard ground and rolled into the ditch, the breath knocked out of her body; and then she was caught again and dragged on and up the steep escarpment, running and stumbling over the rough ground to plunge headlong into the tangled thickets of the Kudsia Bagh. . . .

The crash of the explosion shivered through the hot stillness, and rocked the flagstaff tower on the Ridge where the terrified families from the cantonments had been crowded together in helpless confusion all that long day, waiting for news and straining their eyes through the heat haze toward the city and the empty Meerut Road.

"We can't wait here any longer," said a haggard-faced officer pacing the Ridge. "What in hell's name are they doing in Meerut? They *cannot* all be dead! For God's sake, why don't we do something to help those poor devils in the city? There's still the river arsenal to draw on. We could have made some sort of a show, instead of just leaving them to be slaughtered!"

"Don't be a fool, Mellish! We've got to think of the women and children. We can't try any forlorn hopes while we have their safety to consider."

"Then why the devil didn't we send them away this morning? No one seems to have done a damn' thing in Meerut, and no one is doing anything here—except young Willoughby who has evidently had the guts to blow up the magazine! Look—what's that! There's a cart coming up the road! Is it news at last?"

A bullock cart creaked and jolted slowly up the road in a cloud of dust to halt by the flagstaff tower, where the sinking sun illuminated its contents with brutal clarity—the slashed, stiffening, bloodstained bodies of half a dozen British officers, thrown in as carelessly as though they had been so many bales of straw. A challenge flung at the Ridge by the triumphant city. A challenge that would not be taken up for many days.

"It will be dark in half an hour," said the Brigadier, his eyes still straining toward the empty Meerut Road. "The women had better go, and they will need protection. You had all better go while the road to Karnal is still open. I shall stay here."

The glare of burning bungalows in the cantonments made a second sunset in the sky as carriages and dogcarts and men on foot and on horseback streamed away into the gathering darkness to begin that long torment of flight through a hostile land, during which so many were to die.

The Brigadier's shoulders sagged tiredly, and he turned at last and rode away from the Ridge, leaving the deserted cantonments to the night and the looters. The day was over, and high above the darkening city the last of the daylight and the first rays of the moon lit a fading cloud that still hung above the shattered magazine and marked the only decisive stand that had been made in all that terrible day.

Alex drew rein before the Residency gate and spoke for the first time in almost an hour. "I understand that you leave for the hills on the twenty-second. I shall see you before then. Good night."

He turned his horse and cantered away in the direction of his bungalow, and Winter went on under the arch of the gateway past the stately, sa-laaming figure of Akbar Khan.

Something within her shrank as she passed him. They hate us, she thought, thinking of herself for the first time, and unconsciously, as an alien in this land. It is the Mussulmans who hate us most. And she re-membered the stories that Aziza Begum had told her of the fiercest of all Faiths, and the war cries of the armies of the Prophet. *"Deen! Deen! Futteh Muhhammed!"* ("For the Faith! for the Faith! Victory to Mo-hammed!") There was little mercy in the creed of those who fought un-der the banner of the crescent moon, and even if Akbar Khan had not murdered little Zeb-un-Nissa, Winter was suddenly sure that behind his blandly respectful manner he was coldhearted enough to kill anyone who stood in his way.

Conway was in the drawing room, sprawled on the sofa with a glass of brandy in one hand. He was wearing a thin, native-style shirt over white cotton trousers, and both were dark with sweat. It was not late, but he was already unmistakably drunk. There was a silver-mounted hookah on the floor, and the cushions of the sofa were indented as though someone had recently been sitting beside him. Winter had told him once that if the woman Fatima entered the house—she excepted his private rooms—she herself would leave it; and she wondered now what had made Fatima bold enough to return. Should she make a stand now and carry out her threat? But the apathy that had descended upon her an hour ago pressed down on her with an almost tangible weight. She had not slept at all during the previous night and now she was very tired. Too tired to care about Con-way and his fat, musk-scented mistress. It did not matter any more. Noth-ing mattered any more. Perhaps it was true that their lives were plotted out for them and none could avoid their fate. "What is written, is writ-ten." How often had Zobeida said that! Perhaps this also was written.

Winter slept soundly that night despite the heat and the creaking of the punkah. As soundly as Zeb-un-Nissa who lay in the Mohammedan ceme-tery and did not hear the yelling of the jackal packs who slunk among the graves. As exhaustedly as Lottie who lay asleep—her thin slippers and frilly skirts torn and ripped by thorns and stained with dust and blood—in a curtained ekka, whose kindly owner had found her and her two com-panions crouching in a ditch by the roadside, and had befriended them.

"I go to Lunjore, and with all speed," said the driver of the ekka. "Delhi will be no place for a man of peace for many moons, and I have a brother in Lunjore with whom I will abide until this madness is past."

26

ALEX had hoped to sleep late but he was awakened at sunrise by Imam Din. "Huzoor," said Imam Din softly, "there is a red kite caught in the thorn tree by the city road."

"Damn!" said Alex wearily. "Damn and blast! Oh, all right. *Acha*, Imam Din, *main jaunga*."

He shook himself awake and twenty minutes later he was riding through the croplands in the direction of Chunwar. The mile-long road that led across the open plain to the city boasted a solitary thorn tree that grew near its edge some two hundred yards from the cantonment end, and this morning there was a cheap paper kite, such as children fly, caught up in its scanty, spiked foliage. A vivid scarlet thing, visible from some considerable distance.

Alex did not pass the thorn tree and barely glanced at it. He took a narrow side path that skirted a field of mustard, and presently checked the Eagle by a culvert where the elephant grass grew high and a wild fig tree threw a patch of shadow, and dismounted as though to tighten a girth.

There was a rustle in the grasses, and a voice whose owner remained invisible spoke in a whisper that was barely audible above the creaking of a distant well wheel and the indignant chittering of a striped squirrel.

"There is a word in the bazaar that the pultons have risen in Meerut and have slain all the *Angrezi-log* and ridden on Delhi, which has fallen also. It is said that they have proclaimed Bahardur Shah as Mogul and put all Feringis to the sword."

"When?" asked Alex, wrestling with a strap.

"Yesterday only. The city hums like a hive."

"Will they rise?"

"Who knows? There be many budmashes in the bazaars, but the Mulvi's men call upon them to hold back and to wait for the Word. It were better that none of thy people were seen in the city today. If even a stone were thrown, there is no knowing what might follow. Thou knowest the temper of crowds. If they see blood they run mad like jackals."

Alex said softly: "Go back and bring me word tonight. I will ride by the tomb of Amin-u-din at sunset."

"I will try. But I am afraid—afraid. If it were known, they would tear me in pieces!" Alex could hear the man's teeth chatter, and he laid a handful of silver coins in the dust by the rim of the culvert and said: "There will be fifty more tonight."

He returned to the cantonments by way of the rifle range, riding for

the most part at a leisurely walk that necessitated a considerable effort of
will, and pausing to exchange greetings with carters, cultivators and casual
pedestrians by the way. It was well past eight o'clock by the time he
reached the Residency, and although the day was already gruelingly hot
the closed and shuttered rooms of the big house were surprisingly cool.

He found the Commissioner still in bed, naked save for a width
of thin cotton cloth wrapped about his waist in the manner of a Burmese
lungi. The room reeked of musk and stale spirits, and the green-
tinted *chiks* over the closed windows toned the light to a twilight dimness.

"Well?" demanded Mr. Barton sourly. "More mares' nests?"

"I hope it may turn out to be no more than that," said Alex curtly.
"There is a story being circulated in the city of a rising in Meerut and
in Delhi. It may be entirely untrue, or there may have been some
trouble there that has been grossly exaggerated by rumor. But the story is
that the regiments in both places have mutinied and killed all the Europeans, and that Bahardur Shah has been acclaimed as King."

"What rubbish!" said the Commissioner angrily. He sat upright, and
the movement appeared to be painful, for he groaned and put a hand
to his head. He glowered at Captain Randall and said: "Why, Meerut's
crammed with British troops! Crammed with 'em!—at least two thousand.
Strongest garrison in India! Poppycock! It's only another bazaar rumor."

"Perhaps, sir," said Alex shortly. "The point is not so much whether it
is true, as that the city believes it to be true. I should like, with your
permission, to put the city out of bounds to all Europeans until the
excitement has had time to die down. With rumors such as these flying round the bazaars, a white face in the city might lead to stone throwing, and with a mob that is only a short step from murder. May I take
it that you agree to putting the city out of bounds, sir?"

"Oh, yes, I suppose so," said the Commissioner ungraciously. "Do what
you like about it and leave me in peace!"

Alex did not linger. He went to the Commissioner's office and wrote
briefly and to the point, using the Commissioner's official paper. When
he had finished he returned to the darkened bedroom with pen and ink-
well to demand the Commissioner's signature. He saw the chuprassies
leave with the sealed documents and returned to the hall to ask if he might
see Mrs. Barton.

"The mem-sahib left but half an hour ago," Imam Bux informed him.
"She has gone to the city."

Alex whipped round on the speaker with a suddenness that startled him
considerably. "*Where?*"

"To the shop of Ditta Mull, the silk merchant, near the Sudder Bazaar."

"Who is with her?"

"Huzoor, the mem-sahib went on horseback. I do not know which syce
—I will make inquiry, if the Huzoor—"

But Alex had gone.

It was after nine and the tree shadows were shortening on the white dust. Already the heat danced on the open plain so that the mile-distant city appeared to shimmer and waver in the blinding sunlight as though it were made of molten glass. There was a white foam of lather streaking the Eagle's neck and flanks, and Alex' coat was wet with sweat, but his hands and his stomach were cold with fear and rage—a rage that was entirely directed at himself.

If I get myself involved in a riot, I may have to shoot, thought Alex, and if I do that— They won't harm her! They know her too well. I ought to let her take her chances. If they kill me that fool Barton will lose his head, and I have not given the order about the bridge, and—I can't *risk* everything just because of one woman! . . . Nicholson was right—the safe-guarding of women and children in some crises is such a very minor consideration that it ceases to be a consideration at all—I must not go. . . . But he went.

He reined to a canter as he neared the city gate, and fought down his fear, for a mob was a purely animal thing and like an animal could sense fear. He rode in under the gate at a walk, sitting loosely in the saddle, and called a greeting to the police havildar who saluted him as he passed.

He could feel the pulse and panic of the city swirling about him from the very dust and beating down upon him in the blinding heat. There was an ominous silence as he passed and a menacing mutter that rose at his back, and the faces that watched him were avid or insolent or uneasy. Those men he knew and spoke to as the Eagle shouldered his way through the crowded bazaar avoided his gaze and shifted unhappily, observing their neighbors with furtive anxiety. Normally, when he rode through the city, men cleared a path for him, but today he found that he must force the Eagle between men who made no attempt to move out of his way, and who jostled and obstructed him with deliberate insolence. His progress became slower and slower; and then a stone hurtled out of the crowd. It missed him and struck a woman, who screamed shrilly.

An indescribable sound rose from the crowd, a sound like the soft, growling snarl of a gigantic cat, and Alex rose in his stirrups, and facing the quarter from whence the stone had been thrown, raised his voice and called a jest across the heads of the crowd. It was a coarse jest relative to the proper treatment of prostitutes, and the crowd, taken by surprise, laughed. The tension snapped and a man called out: "Has the sahib heard the news from Delhi?"

"*Beshak!* I hear many lies with every morn, Karter Singh. But I wait for the evening, and when the heat of the day is past the truth becomes known."

"Is it then the truth?" cried another voice.

"The heat has surely turned thy brain, Sohan Lal!" said Alex with a laugh. "Abide a little and let it cool!"

The laugh had its effect upon the crowd. Hostility waned and doubt took its place. Perhaps the rumors that had spread like wildfire through the bazaars since dawn were false, for the sahib, it was plain, had also heard news—yet he laughed. Would he laugh if the news were bad? The crowd drew back and let him pass, their faces sullen and unsure, and twenty yards ahead Alex caught sight of the Mulvi of one of the city mosques making his way along the street. He urged the Eagle to a quicker pace, and drawing level with the man, leaned out and touched him on the shoulder. The Mulvi turned sharply.

"As Salaam aleikum, Mulvi Sahib," said Alex pleasantly. "Canst thou spare the time to lead me to the shop of Ditta Mull in the street of the silk merchants? I cannot call to mind the way."

He saw the anger flash in the man's eyes, and the cunning replace it as the Mulvi looked up at him and then back at the watching crowd—and knew that he had guessed aright. This was one of Ahmed Ullah of Faizabad's men, and Gopal Nath, hidden in the culvert by the fig tree, had whispered that the Mulvi of Faizabad's men were preaching patience. The man who stood at Alex' stirrup knew quite well that he was familiar with every street and alley and shop in the city, and was demanding protection, and he would have given much to refuse it. But it was as much in his interests as in Alex' own to prevent a premature outbreak in Lunjore, and so he smiled sourly and murmured the conventional reply to the greeting.

"Wa aleikum Salaam. If the sahib will come with me I will show him."

Furiante's impatiently tossing head and the frightened face of the syce who was endeavoring to control both horses were visible above the heads of a noisy, jostling crowd who swayed dangerously to and fro before Ditta Mull's shop. The panic on the face of the syce did nothing to reassure Alex, and once again he felt fear clutch at his throat, and forced it back. The Mulvi, walking beside him, took the Eagle's bridle and thrust his way through the crowd, who fell back and cleared a passage to the bottom of the five rickety wooden steps that led up to the shop front.

Winter was not visible, for Ditta Mull had hurriedly dropped the heavy chiks before the open entrance of his shop. He peered out anxiously on hearing Alex' voice and grasped feverishly at his sleeve: "Take her away, Huzoor!" begged Ditta Mull. "By the back way! I do not know what madness has taken hold on the city this morning. Already there have been stones flung at my shop. It is not our own people. They know her well. But there are others—budmashes from Suthragunj and Shahjehanpur and Barelli who have been stirring up trouble in the city with wild tales. The mem-sahib wished to leave, fearing the people might harm my shop on her account, but I would not let her. It is well that thou hast come. I will tell the mem-sahib."

He hurried away through a dark doorway in the back of the shop, wringing his small, fat hands and making little moaning noises, and returned a minute or two later with Winter. She was perfectly calm, and quite uninterested, thought Alex furiously—irrationally swinging from the extremes of fear to the limits of exasperation—in the dangers of the situation. She frowned a little at the sight of him, but refused to leave without a large quantity of rose-colored sari silk that she had previously selected. She watched Ditta Mull wrap it up in a length of muslin, his hands shaking like leaves in a wind, and having accepted and paid for it, she said with a touch of impatience: "Do not show them that face, *Lala-jee*. If they see that thou art afraid, then they too may behave foolishly."

She handed the package to Alex, who received it in grim silence, and went out under the lifted *chik* into the fierce glare of the sunlight. The crowd had ceased to shout and sway and had become silent. As Winter stepped out, a mutter rose from them and swelled ominously, but she appeared unconscious of it and Alex saw her look up to smile at someone in a second-story window at the far side of the narrow street, and sketch the Hindu gesture of salutation with one hand.

The crowd, instantly diverted, turned as one to see who it was whom the mem-sahib had greeted, and saw a small, fat child hanging out over the edge of a fretted window ledge and beckoning. Winter shook her head at it and called out: "Have a care, Bappa, or thou wilt surely fall! I cannot come today, but I will come soon."

"Tomorrow?" shrilled the child.

"Not tomorrow. Perhaps next week."

The brief conversation changed the mood of the crowd, but Alex could feel the dangerous pendulum swing of their emotions with every nerve in his body, and knew how little it would take to sway them toward senseless savagery. Was Winter unaware of it? She seemed to be. He heard her murmur a polite and conventional greeting to the Mulvi, and then she was in the saddle and moving off down the packed street, controlling the nervous impatience of Furiante with apparent ease.

The next fifteen minutes seemed endless to Alex, riding behind her and frequently separated from her by the shifting, jostling crowds. He heard her speak to a dozen people as they edged their way through the streets, her voice light and gay.

The Mulvi left them abruptly at the turn into the wide stretch of the Sudder Bazaar that ended at the Rohilkhand Gate, and vanished down a side street. Three hundred yards to go . . . two hundred . . . one hundred . . . fifty. Slowly, keep to a walk. . . . A man was holding forth excitedly to a dense knot of people as thick as a swarm of bees, and scraps of sentences separated themselves from the sullen murmur of the crowd. ". . . with two heads! My cousin's wife's brother saw it . . . it is a sign! What else but a sign? Their days are accomplished. . . ." Muttered curses and a man spitting loudly and contemptuously as they passed. A low-caste woman shouting at the frightened, furious syce: "*Hai, ghora wallah*, do they feed thee on bone dust now that thou hast taken service with the sahib-*log*?"

And then they were through the gate and out on the open, empty, glaring road that led across the plain to the cantonments, and Furiante had broken into a canter and then into a gallop. Winter had attempted to slow him after the first hundred yards or so, but Alex had brought his whip down on the horse's quarters and they had flashed at full gallop under the shadows of the trees that lined the cantonment road. He reined in at last before the gate of his own bungalow and waited for the syce to come up with them. He had not spoken once since he entered Ditta Mull's shop, and he did not speak now. He put up a hand and wiped the sweat out of his eyes, and knew that his hand was shaking.

Winter said abruptly: "You're very angry, aren't you? But I did not know that there was trouble in the city. You should not have come for me. I do not think that they would have done me any harm. They were more likely to harm you." She looked at him doubtfully and added: "It was—kind of you to come. Thank you."

"You have nothing to thank me for," Alex said shortly. "I probably endangered your life, and that of everyone else in the cantonments, by going there."

The syce cantered up, dusty and sullen but still clutching the package of rose-colored silk, and Alex observed him tight lipped, and then turned back to Winter. He said: "The city is out of bounds until further notice, and I should be obliged if you would curtail your rides in future, and keep only to the cantonments and the maidan."

"But—"

"That is an order," said Alex, and turned into his own gateway.

He had ridden out at sundown that evening to the ruined tomb of Amin-u-din on the far bank of the river, but Gopal Nath had not been there. There had been no one there but the bats and the lizards and a flock of green parrots, for Gopal Nath was lying face downward among the high grass at the edge of the grazing grounds with his throat cut from ear to ear. And the work that the jackals and the hyenas began that night was completed the next day by the kites and the vultures and the remorseless heat, so that twenty-four hours later no one could be quite sure who those reddened, scattered bones had once belonged to.

There had been a party at the Residency that night. The last of the Tuesday parties, although no one there knew that it was going to be the last.

A dispatch rider from Suthragunj on a lathered horse had arrived in Lunjore at noon the next day. The Commissioner, handed a sealed letter on a salver by Imam Bux during luncheon, had stuffed it into his pocket, unread, and forgotten about it until the following morning, and it had been nearly midday when he read it at last. His pale eyes bulged with shock and the paper had dropped from his nerveless hand and slid to the floor where the draft from the punkah sent it fluttering lazily across the drawing-room carpet like a bird with a broken wing.

It had been Winter who had picked it up and Winter who had sent for Alex.

Less than an hour later a hurriedly convened conference of a dozen appalled men met round the Commissioner's dining-room table to discuss the emergency arising out of the incredible, the impossible news that it had contained, and to decide what measures, if any, might belatedly be taken to safeguard Lunjore from the mutiny and massacre that had over-taken Meerut and Delhi.

Alex had urged the supreme measure of disarming the regiments and the suggestion had been treated as an outrage.

"Your suggestion, Captain Randall," said Colonel Moulson, "is not only beneath contempt, but one which it is not your place to advance."

Alex gave a faint shrug of his shoulders. "I am sorry, sir. Then may I suggest that we send the women and children to Naini Tal immediately? Today if possible. There may still be time. The mutinies at Meerut and Delhi were premature. I am sure of it. As I have already told you, I have reason to believe that a date for a general outbreak has been set for the end of this month. That belief is not only supported by information, but confirmed by the behavior of the city. There may still be time to send the women to safety."

"We cannot do it," said Colonel Gardener-Smith heavily. "At this stage it is surely a matter of vital importance not to show any sign of panic. You must see that."

"I agree. I entirely agree," said Colonel Packer. "To show alarm may precipitate the very crisis we seek to avoid. We must place our trust in the Lord. His rod and His staff shall not fail us."

"Which means," said Alex with shut teeth, "that no precautionary measures whatever can be taken, for fear that any change in the present routine may be translated as panic."

"You exaggerate, Captain Randall," said Colonel Gardener-Smith coldly. "Reasonable precautions will of course be taken."

"Will you name one, sir?" demanded Alex tersely.

There was a sudden silence about the table.

Alex came to his feet and leant on the table, his hands gripping the edge. "May I *beg* you to reconsider? I am well aware that it will give rise to alarm if we send the women and children away. But the maximum efficiency cannot be obtained while the garrison is hampered by a horde of women whose personal safety will be placed above military expediency. How can any man make a coolheaded decision, which he knows may in-volve grave risk, while he is thinking that to take that risk may mean the murder and mutilation of his wife and child?"

He looked about the table at the circle of grim, drawn faces and saw hesitation and doubt, and for a moment he was hopeful. Then Colonel Moulson spoke.

"My dear Captain Randall, you allow your fears to run away with you. I would like to point out that we have three Infantry Regiments here as well as half a regiment of Military Police. So you must really not expect us to make a public exhibition of ourselves by ordering a panic-stricken exodus of all the women and children just because you yourself feel nerv-ous!"

Alex said softly: "I can only say, sir, that in the event of my timorous fears proving justified, I hope that you will obtain some comfort from the realization that you will have sacrificed the lives of these women, and jeopardized the safety of the Company's possessions, in order to demonstrate a confidence in the fidelity of your sepoys which you do not wholly possess."

Colonel Moulson's face was suddenly scarlet with rage and he half rose from his chair. "You are impertinent, Captain Randall! Must I again remind you that you are a junior officer—and can be disciplined?"

"Because I speak the truth, sir?" Alex' precarious hold on his temper had departed and his voice was raw edged with a rage that matched Colonel Moulson's. "You all have your doubts! Every one of you! But not one of you will admit it. You will not even institute a few inquiries, because to do so would be tantamount to an admission that disloyalty among your men might be possible. All very laudable, but, in the present crisis, you will give me leave to say that it is hardly practical!"

"In the present crisis," said Colonel Moulson furiously, "it is the panic-mongers that we have to fear! If we could rid ourselves of them we should be a deal better off! There is no lack of confidence here, I assure you, but as you yourself feel so insecure, I can only suggest that you should apply for sick leave and go yourself immediately to Naini Tal!"

Alex' right hand that lay flat upon the table clenched slowly into a fist—and as slowly relaxed again. It was no use. They were courageous enough, but they did not even now realize the magnitude of this thing that was overtaking them. They had refused to take any precautions while the emergency was far away, and now that it was upon them they would take none—for fear of showing fear.

Alex sat down without further words, and did not speak again while the conference dragged to its inconclusive close. But when it was over he dispatched a telegram to the Governor-General, in the name of the Commissioner of Lunjore, requesting plenary military powers. The nearest telegraph post had until recently been seventy-five miles away in Suthragunj, but it was not twenty by the Hazrat Bagh Road, and Alex reflected grimly that Kishan Prasad's road was proving its usefulness in a way that had not been intended by those who had made it.

That night the first of the fires started in Lunjore, and the surgeon of the 105th N.I., Colonel Packer's regiment, had his bungalow burnt to the ground. It had been a thatched bungalow, and an arrow wrapped in blazing, oil-soaked rags had been fired into the roof shortly before midnight.

Lottie and her companions, though suffering tortures from the heat in the closely curtained ekka, were still safe in the charge of its kindly driver. In this they were luckier than the majority of the fugitives from Delhi, for scattered over the sun-scorched countryside that surrounded the captured city of the Moguls, men, women and children hid and starved and died. They crouched all day in ditches and canebrakes, gasping in the relentless heat, stripping themselves of uniforms and crinolines, wading rivers, crawling through the dying grass, skulking in the jungle; scratching shallow graves with their bare hands in the hot, iron-hard earth to cover the corpses of children, and leaving the bodies of adults to the vultures and the jackals. Robbed, stripped, insulted; hunted through the croplands and murdered for sport. Lured by promises of protection into villages whose inhabitants gathered to watch them die, and laughed as the naked bloodstained bodies were flung on the village dung heaps.

A few—a very few—fell into the hands of kindly people who gave them food and shelter and risked their own lives, and the lives of all their families, in order to save a hunted helpless fellow creature. But on the morning of the sixteenth of May, in an open courtyard of the palace of the King of Delhi, where there stood a little cistern shaded by a peepul tree, some fifty dazed and terrified people, of whom all but six were either women or children, were herded together like sheep. The last of the Europeans and Christians left alive in Delhi, dragged up from the heat and stench and darkness of the dungeon in which they had spent five days, to be butchered in the harsh sunlight by men whom the sight and scent of blood had turned into beasts. Men who cut and slashed and howled in frenzy until the last scream and the last moan was silenced, and who drew back then, shuddering, from the shambles and the stench of fresh-spilled blood and brains and entrails that steamed up from the pile of the newly dead.

Now at last there were no more Feringis in Delhi! Now at last the reluctant, trembling old King and every man, woman and child in the city was committed irretrievably to the path that had been chosen. There could be no drawing back now, for the massacre of the women and children whose mutilated bodies strewed the courtyard, and whose blood soaked into the silent stones and curled and dried in the searing heat, had sealed them to their path. This was irrevocable. The die had been cast.

All that day, while the shadows of the peepul tree and the cistern crawled across the paving stones and the quiet dead, a shifting, peering crowd pressed ten deep about the courtyard, gaping and whispering. And toward evening half a dozen mehtars, men of low caste who act as sweepers and disposers of filth, heaped the stiffened, mangled bodies onto carts which dragged them to the bank of the placid Jumna, there to fling them one by one into the river—food for the crocodiles and the mud turtles, the jackals and the scavenger birds: and a sign and a warning to a hundred villages as the bodies drifted down with the slow stream to be stranded on sand bars and burning ghats and fish traps, or caught in the eddies that washed the walls of fortified towns.

27

LOTTIE had arrived in Lunjore at last. Lottie and Mr. Dacosta and Mrs. Holly—that same Mrs. Holly who had embarked on the steamship *Sirius* and had nursed Mrs. Abuthnot and her daughters through a bout of seasickness.

Stout, cheerful, sensible Mrs. Holly was considerably less stout and no longer cheerful. Her clothes hung in folds and her round, pleasant face sagged in deep, harsh lines; for she had seen her husband's head struck from his body with a single swing of a sharpened tulwar in the blazing charnel house of Duryagunj, and only the sudden collapse of a burning roof beam had saved her from a similar fate. Somehow—she could not remember how—she and Mr. Dacosta had escaped from the carnage and reached the Main Guard at the Kashmir Gate, where they had witnessed the final tragedy and escaped over the battlements. But although her stoutness and her cheerfulness had gone, her placid good sense remained. She had taken Lottie and Mr. Dacosta under her wing, and it was she who had cajoled the driver of the ekka into taking them up, and so brought them at last to Lunjore.

Mr. Dacosta was an olive-skinned, middle-aged Eurasian, a clerk in a government department. He had been wounded by a sword cut and badly burned, but he had struggled on valiantly and had not complained.

Lottie had been delighted to see Winter, and she had forgotten Delhi. She wondered sometimes, a little hazily, why it was that she should suddenly have decided to come to Lunjore. Edward must have insisted. It was odd that she could not remember. Perhaps it was something to do with having a baby that made thinking an effort? It was easier not to think—so much easier. Thinking made her head ache, and with that ache fear would well up inside her like ice-cold water bubbling up out of an unseen spring, and her heart would begin to hammer and her breath come short. She must not think. It made her feel ill, and that was bad for the child. Edward's child—

"Edward wants a girl, you know," she confided to Winter, "but I want the first one to be a boy and just like Edward. He is to be christened Edward—I have quite made up my mind."

"Alex," said Winter desperately, "do you think she will ever remember?"

"One day," said Alex. "She's better off as she is at the moment. When is that baby due?" He frowned at the sight of the sudden color that burned in Winter's cheeks and said impatiently: "You don't really suppose that hitching a hoop higher and carrying round a shawl disguises a thing like that, do you?"

Winter said with as much composure as she could muster: "I think she expects it in about two months' time. But Mrs. Holly says one can never be sure with a first child, and that it may not be born until—"

She stopped abruptly and put her hands up to her hot cheeks. It was one thing to answer a direct question, but one did not—one *could* not—discuss such things with a man!

A corner of Alex' mouth curved in the shadow of a grin and he said: "Don't be missish, Mrs. Barton! It's a perfectly natural function."

Alex had talked to Mr. Dacosta—Mrs. Holly avoided questions—and had heard the first true account of that last day of British rule in Delhi.

"We looked all day for thee troops from Meerut," whispered Mr. Dacosta, hoarse with weakness and fever, "but they did not come. If only twenty British troops had appeared before thee gates that morning, those men would have run away. It is all lost—all lost. It is not good to have seen what I have seen and still live. It is not right!"

Two days later he had died.

Almost every night now there were mysterious fires in the cantonments, and though extra guards patrolled the area they never made any arrests. The Police Lines burnt down one night, and then the dak *Khana*, and the following night the bungalow of Lieutenant Dewar, whose wife and young family were only saved with difficulty, for they had been sleeping on the roof on account of the heat, and the fire, which broke out in the living room, had taken firm hold before they were aroused.

It was difficult to allay panic among the families of the officers, who lived in bungalows near the lines surrounded by large gardens where trees and shrubs provided cover for lurking incendiarists. But the three commanding officers still refused even to consider disarming their men, although now, when it was too late, they would have sent the women away—and dared not do so, for each day new reports of disaffection and murder came in. Lunjore was still quiet, with the tensed, twitching quietness of a cat at a mousehole; but it was not so with the districts that surrounded it. "They are safer here," said Colonel Gardener-Smith, whom the past ten days appeared to have aged by as many years. And even those who had previously made arrangements to send their families to the hills canceled them.

The Commissioner did not appear to notice that his wife had put off her departure. He noticed little in those days, and that little through an alcoholic haze. He was afraid, and his fear drove him to his familiar refuge, the bottle. Even Fatima had forsaken him. She had packed her clothes and her jewels and everything else she could manage to lay her hands on, and had slipped away one night with her three fat half-caste children, her relations and her servants and Nilam, the blue macaw, and had not come back. Her defection had frightened the Commissioner far more than the nightly fires, the news from Delhi, the inaction of the Meerut Brigade or the endless tales of murder and massacre that trickled in daily from the outside world.

"Rats leavin' the sinkin' ship!" whispered the Commissioner hoarsely, staring into space with eyes that did not see the sly, inscrutable face of Imam Bux who had broken the news. "That's what it is. They know. The rats know! We're sinking. She knew it, and she's gone—the lying, cheating black bitch!"

He had flung his glass furiously at the impassive butler and that afternoon he had advocated immediate flight. They must all of them go, and by night, in boats down the river. The British Raj was finished. Unless they were all to die, those who were not already dead must fly the country —reach the coast, using the rivers and avoiding the roads, and abandon India. They could not hold it. It was impossible to hold it! If they stayed they would all be murdered.

"Better that than to turn tail," snorted Colonel Moulson, observing him with disapproval. "If we can keep our heads we shall weather the storm. Calcutta can't be idle, and strong reinforcements are certain to be on their way."

"How do we know that there are any Europeans left alive in Calcutta?" whispered the Commissioner.

He had retreated to the brandy bottle, and had taken no interest in the information—relayed to him three hours later—that the sepoys of Colonel Packer's regiment had refused to accept their consignment of commissariat flour, saying that it was known to be adulterated with bone dust for the purpose of destroying their caste. The flour had been duly taken away and thrown into the distant river.

The sepoys, having won their point, had become noticeably insolent and out of hand, and many, from all three regiments, had that evening openly looted the ripe fruit from the gardens of the cantonment bungalows. Their officers had soon succeeded in putting a stop to it, but it was plain that discipline was deteriorating rapidly.

That same night Major Wilkinson, who had dined at the Residency and returned drunk to his bungalow, fired at and wounded one of a patrol who challenged him. There was an inquiry held on the following day and Major Wilkinson was acquitted of any intent to wound—on a plea of being unconscious from intoxication at the time.

"Bloody fools!" said Alex exasperated. "They should have cashiered him—sent him off to be court-martialed at Suthragunj—anything but this! Are they mad? If it had been the other way round, they'd have given a sepoy ten years' penal servitude or hung him! If this doesn't start something, I'm a bigger fool than Packer!"

There was a ball to celebrate the Queen's birthday on the first day of the new week. Victoria's birthday had fallen on a Sunday that year, so the ball had been held on the day following it. It had been, too, the end of the fast of Ramazan, and there was a new, slim sickle moon in the sky. It hung in the green of the evening, a curved thread of silver, like the crescent of Islam embroidered on the green banners of the Faithful—like an omen in the sky.

"La Ill-ah ha! Il ill-ah ho!" cried the muezzins from the minarets of the mosques in the city. "There is no God but God!"

The band of the 2nd Regiment of Lunjore Irregulars stood smartly to attention, their dark faces creased with concentration, and watched the conductor's baton fall. *"God save our Gracious Queen, long live our Noble Queen. . . ."* The familiar tune, the national anthem of an alien race, blared out through the open windows across the dark parade ground and the sepoy lines.

She was thirty-eight—that dumpy, imperious, self-confident housewife who had ascended the throne as a slim, self-confident girl in the year that Sabrina Grantham had married Marcos de Ballesteros; the year that Ameera, wife of Walayat Shah, had been born to Juanita in the little pink stucco palace in Lucknow City.

"Send her victorious, happy and glorious. . . ."

Sabrina's daughter danced at the Queen's Birthday Ball in a wide-skirted ballgown of water-green tarlatan looped up with garlands of camellias. She smiled as she danced—the same smile that was on the face of every woman who danced in that flag- and flower-decorated room; the smile of women who watch their men and strain their ears to listen, and who will not show that they are afraid.

Alex too had attended that ball and there was nothing in his face to show that he had spent the greater part of the afternoon arguing, urging, pleading fruitlessly and for the last time with three courageous, obdurate men for the disarming of the sepoys.

But they were not to be persuaded. They did, however, decide on taking one precautionary measure, for the sake of the ladies, whose nerves were beginning to suffer from the strain of constantly being on the alert. It was the custom among the European families in Lunjore to drive out in the early mornings to get what little fresh air they could before the sun rose and the heat forced them into the dimness of shuttered rooms. Word was conveyed to the families that on the morning following the ball the women and children were to drive instead to the Residency, taking with them such clothing and necessities as they would need for a stay of a few days. The Residency was sufficiently large to shelter them all without too much discomfort, and a party of Military Police were to be posted in the grounds as extra protection. Four guns, under the charge of native gunners of Colonel Moulson's regiment, were to be placed in between the Residency and the lines, and another two between the Residency and the city.

"The Residency is admirably situated for defense," said Colonel Gardener-Smith. "With that nullah and the jungle behind it, and a wall round the rest of it, nothing could be better."

"I agree," said Alex, "providing one were defending it against a rabble from the city. But if the sepoys should mutiny, it will turn into a trap."

"My sepoys will not mutiny!" said Colonel Gardener-Smith obstinately. "I will stake my life on that."

Alex said nothing more. He was tired of vain repetitions. He had gone across to the Residency and spoken to Winter. "What have you done with that pistol I gave you?"

"I have it."

"Good. Keep it loaded and keep it within reach. I've brought you some more ammunition for it. And see that there is always a horse kept saddled, and—" He did not complete the sentence but looked past Winter's shoulder at the blank wall for a long minute, his brows drawn together in a frown, and then shrugged. What was the good of saying anything else? He had done what he could. *"Remember the auspicious day"*. . . .

Two more days to go, thought Alex that night, leaning against the wall and watching a quadrille danced at the Queen's Birthday Ball.

But there were no more days. Only hours.

The Hirren Minar

28

It was Major Beckwith, second-in-command to Colonel Gardener-Smith, who informed his commanding officer half an hour before sunrise on the morning after the ball that the regiment had not dispersed after parade and could no longer be trusted. He wept as he said it, for Major Beckwith, like his colonel, had believed with a wholehearted belief in the fidelity of his men.

"I will go back and speak to them," said Colonel Gardener-Smith.

"It's no good, sir. They will listen to no one."

"They will listen to me," said Colonel Gardener-Smith stubbornly. But they had not listened.

"We will not harm thee, or permit thee to be harmed," said the ring-leaders, "for thou art a good man. But we take no more orders from Feringis who have plotted to destroy our caste and enslave us. Go quickly while there is yet time, for we know what we know, and the men of the 105th are not as us, and if they can, they may slay thee."

They had thrust him from the lines, shouting down his words, and had rushed to the bells of arms, and seizing their rifles had announced their intention of marching immediately for Delhi to offer their services to the Mogul. They had opened fire on their officers, two of whom had been badly wounded, and there had been nothing for it but to leave before worse befell, and the Colonel had left.

His bungalow was empty, for his wife and daughter were already at the Residency, and it seemed intolerably dark and quiet. As quiet as the tomb. As quiet as old age. I am an old man, thought Colonel Gardener-Smith. An old man and a fool. I have given my life to a lie. They will disband the 93rd and remove its name from the Army list. *My* 93rd! It will go down in the records—*Disbanded for Mutiny*.

He left the bungalow and went to the deserted mess, walking bareheaded in the blaze of the newly risen sun, and took down the colors and burned them in the grate, pouring lamp oil on them and watching until there was nothing left but a heap of evil-smelling black ash. And then he shot himself.

"The bloody idiot!" said Alex furiously, hearing of it half an hour later —he had ridden out to speak to the Kotwal of a village beyond the city and had returned late. "Just when we need every man who can fire a gun! Goddamn these sentimentalists! Art thou ready, Yusaf? It may be that thou wilt have to wait two days. No matter, there is food and water enough for a long wait. If they come, wait until the first of them are abreast of the rocks by the two palm trees. Go now and go swiftly. *B'ism Illah—*"

Colonel Packer's regiment had broken out in mutiny less than half an hour after the 93rd, and had seized the treasury and possessed themselves of the money and all available arms.

Colonel Moulson had been breakfasting at the Residency, together with several officers who were engaged in assuring the ladies assembled there that there was no cause for alarm. The Residency was noisy with women's voices, the laughter or yells of children, and the rustle of poplin, muslin and *barège* dresses and ruffled pantalets. Almost every woman there had danced until a late hour at the ball, and many had had no sleep before starting out for the Residency, but all were gay and in good heart, for the presence of the police guard, the sight of the guns with their attendant crews of native gunners, the high white wall of the Residency and, above all, the company of their fellows, had worked wonders on their failing spirits. There was a lighthearted and picnic-like atmosphere in the crowded rooms that even the nonappearance of their host, and the news that he was indisposed, did nothing to dispel.

Delia, unlike the majority of the women present, had elected to wear her widest crinoline and a dress that was more suitable for an afternoon party than an early breakfast. Colonel Moulson found her enchanting, and was in process of telling her so when the sound of galloping hoofs interrupted him. . . .

"I might have known it!" fumed Colonel Moulson. "Always said that fool Gardener was too soft with his men! I'll show 'em! Marching to Delhi with the treasury, are they? Where the hell's my horse! If we double three companies across the maidan we'll cut 'em off and cut 'em to bits!"

He galloped off into the glare of the morning, his adjutant and a senior captain riding behind him, and his regiment received him in silence. They listened to his bellowed commands, and no man moved—their shadows lying motionless on the hot ground. Then a man laughed, loud and scornfully, and another took aim and fired.

Ten minutes later the adjutant, his arm pouring a bright scarlet flood, slid from his wounded horse onto Alex' sunny veranda and gasped out the news.

"They shot him down—and Mottisham too—and Halliwell and Reeves and Charlie and little Jenks. They're all dead. Packer's fellows have broken too. They've killed him—saw his body. Cut to bits. And old Gardener-Smith has—"

"I know," said Alex, knotting a strip torn from a curtain with furious haste about Captain Wardle's shattered arm and shoulder. He turned his head and called out to Niaz who had ridden full tilt round the corner of the bungalow from the direction of the stables.

"The Lunjore Pulton also! Ride for the river. Get the charges from the Hirren Minar. I will meet thee there. Go quickly!"

Niaz lifted a hand in salute and turned his rearing, frantic horse as Alex helped the adjutant back into the saddle. "If Moulson's men have broken that means the gunners will go," said Alex. "Get over to the Residency and tell 'em to get the women and children away over the nullah and into the jungle at once—at *once*, do you hear? Think you can make it? Good. Alam Din, run with the sahib—be swift!"

He leapt down the veranda steps and caught at the bridle of his horse. "Where—where are you going?" gasped the adjutant, wheeling his own wounded animal.

"Magazine."

Niaz, already halfway to the gate, caught the word and reined in hard.

"What is it?" called Alex, spurring down the drive.

"I go with thee!" said Niaz between his teeth, and rode out level with him.

"Do as I tell you!" said Alex savagely and in English. He cut at Niaz's horse with his whip and drew ahead, the Eagle easily outdistancing the heavier horse, and yelled back over his shoulder and in Urdu: "It is an order! This is in thy hands. Do not fail me, brother!"

The magazine was a small, square, unpretentious building of whitewashed stone that stood in the center of the cantonment area and was surrounded by a high wall and several shade trees. The guard that month had been furnished by Colonel Gardener-Smith's regiment, but now there was a yelling mob of sepoys milling around it, and Alex heard the crackle of musketry and reined back in the shadow of a clump of bamboos. Someone was holding the magazine then! He caught a brief glimpse of a pink boyish face, hatless—the red hair bright against the whitewashed stone above the inner parapet—and recognized young Eyton, one of the two new-joined "griffins," barely a month out from Home. The other lay face downward thirty yards from the gate and on the edge of the yelling crowd, his brains splashed in an oddly symmetrical, star-shaped pattern on the hot dust.

Another face appeared beside young Eyton—a dark, bearded face that showed a gleam of white teeth; a rifle cracked and another man in the crowd fell. There were some, then, who had remained true to their salt. But the fight was an unequal one, for already fifty men or more had swarmed over the outer wall, and the gate was creaking under a heavy log of wood wielded by a dozen men as a battering-ram.

Alex knew that he should go. There was nothing he could do. But he did not move. He saw the boy appear briefly again on the parapet and peer down at the yelling besiegers, duck to avoid the shots and hold up his hand as though he gave a signal—and even as he watched, Alex knew what that signal meant, and he turned his horse and set him at a low wall fifty yards away, cleared it and was racing across a stretch of open ground. As he reached the far side of it he heard the roar of the explosion and felt the shock of the blast like a blow between his shoulders. "Well *done!*" said Alex, unaware that he was shouting aloud. He spurred across another piece of open ground, leapt a compound wall and found himself among the flowers of Captain Batterslea's garden.

Mrs. Batterslea had been one of the five women who had considered the move to the Residency quite unnecessary and had elected to remain in her own bungalow. "The children are far better off here. Why, my servants adore them! I am quite sure they would die for them!"

Mrs. Batterslea's extravagant statement had proved to be no more than the truth. Her ayah lay huddled among the plumbago bushes below the veranda, in death as in life striving to protect the small, silent figure in its white frock and blue sash that her stiffening body and outstretched arms still covered. In the servants' quarters behind the bungalow portly Farid, the butler, the thin-legged purbeah *mali*, Captain Batterslea's Brahmin orderly, and Bulaki, the low-caste sweeper, had died side by side, fighting to protect the three small boys who had been reached at last only over the bodies of four men of an alien race and divergent faiths who had fought their own kind in defense of a foreigner's children.

The bungalow was burning and the heat of the flames joined the furnace heat of the sun and shriveled the few plants that still brightened the flower beds. The flower beds had been Mrs. Batterslea's special pride, and in them she had striven, not always with success, to grow the flowers that reminded her of Home—larkspur and mignonette, pansies, gillyflowers and roses. Of these only the roses now remained, wilting in the relentless heat: the roses and Mrs. Batterslea herself, who lay wide eyed and openmouthed among the withered flowers, staring up at the brassy sky. The frilly pink and white wrap she had worn had been torn away, and where her breasts had been there was now only blood. And she had been raped before she died. That means the bazaar scum and the city have broken out already, thought Alex automatically, knowing that no sepoy would have done such a thing, for to do so would have defiled him.

The sight of her mutilated body checked Alex and turned him back from the road he had meant to take. From the moment that he had heard the first news of the outbreak he had thought of only one thing and seen only one thing: the thin, tired, dauntless face of Henry Lawrence who had said: "If it comes, I shall look to you to hold the western road for me." And when he had learned that the 93rd had expressed their intention of marching for Delhi he had been conscious only of relief. Let them go to Delhi! Let them go anywhere as long as it was not eastward into Oudh.

But now, looking down at Mrs. Batterslea's dead, staring face and breastless, outraged body, he saw another face—Winter's. Saw it as clearly and as distinctly as though it were she and not Alice Batterslea who was lying at his feet among the trampled rosebushes. And he turned back and rode for the Residency, hating himself; cursing aloud in a breathless, blasphemous whisper, but driven by an emotion and a fear that he could not control.

The heavy, iron-studded doors of the Residency gate had been closed that morning and the police guard ordered to keep them barred, but the door of the narrow wicket in the main gate, through which only one at a time could enter, stood ajar. There was a crowd before the gate, a swaying, yelling crowd who were being harangued by a wild-eyed figure in a white turban—Akbar Khan, the gatekeeper.

"Kill them!" screamed Akbar Khan. "Slay all, and let not one escape! For the Faith! For the Faith! *Maro! Maro!* (Kill!)"

They heard the sound of the furious galloping hoofbeats and scattered like a whirl of dead leaves as Alex rode into them. He fired only once and saw Akbar Khan topple forward with an expression of ludicrous surprise on his face, and then he had flung himself from the saddle, the Eagle's rearing body protecting him momentarily from the crowd, and in that fractional moment he was through the narrow wicket. A bullet fired by someone within the gate smacked into the woodwork within an inch of him and he stumbled over the body of a man who lay across the threshold, and turning, threw himself against the narrow door and dropped the heavy bar into place.

He turned from it, pistol in hand, and saw the faces of the police guard, sullen and unsure as they fidgeted uneasily with their muskets, and knew that there was no security there.

"Sorry, Randall," said a gasping voice from the shadows of the gate. "Nearly got you. Thought it was another of those swine."

Major Maynard, commanding the Military Police, was sitting on the ground with his back to the wall and one hand pressed to his side in a vain attempt to stem the red tide that welled out between his fingers. He held a smoking revolver in the other.

"Y're just in time," said Major Maynard. "Tell 'em up at the house—run for it. 'Fraid these bastards of mine won't stand."

Alex faced the watching men and said harshly: "Take up the sahib and carry him to the house. Quickly!"

"No!" gasped Maynard. "No—wouldn't be any use. I've got—fifteen minutes perhaps—and as long as—I'm here—they'll do nothing. When I'm gone—they'll open the gate and run fer it. Get up to the house—tell 'em t' get out. I'll hold 'em for—a few minutes—"

Alex did not wait. He had told Wardle twenty minutes ago to get the women away, and they must have gone already, but he had to be sure. He turned and ran for the distant house, across the iron-hard lawn and over the flower beds, and reaching the veranda leapt up the steps, with the noise of the mob beyond the Residency gate rising into a roar behind him.

But no one had gone. They were all there still. Perhaps a dozen men and more than twice as many women and children. A flower garden of women in preposterous, pale-colored, wide-hooped skirts, tight-fitted bodices and thin, inadequate flat-heeled slippers. Women whose faces, sallow from the heat and inactivity of the hot weather, were now greenish-white with fear.

"Good God!" said Alex furiously, "what the hell d'you think you're doing? Go on—get these women away! Wardle, I thought I told you—"

"Safer here," gasped Captain Wardle. "The gunners are loyal and the police'll hold—"

"The gunners have broken and the police will run within five minutes—and half the riffraff of the city is out there!" snapped Alex. "Go on—out by the back and over the bridge. Get into the jungle! It's your only chance. *Run!*"

He saw Winter's face across the width of the room. She had one arm about Lottie and her eyes were wide and enormous but quite steady. There was a sudden and louder burst of yelling and a crash that told its own tale, and Alex ran to the window, took one look and was across the room and had flung open the door that led out of the drawing room and to the back of the house. "*Run!*"

They ran—picking up screaming children, clasping babies, sobbing and panting, tripping over their wide skirts. Winter said: "Take Lottie, Mrs. Holly," and pushed them out through the door. She stood back, urging the women to speed, and then Alex had caught her wrist and was running with her, dragging her. He pulled her down the steps of the back veranda and thrusting her ahead of him said breathlessly: "Over the bridge—quick as you can!" and then he had left her.

After the dimness of the shuttered house the sunlight was unbelievably hot and bright. The heat and the glare met her like the glaze from a blast furnace and added to the complete unreality of the moment. Far across the gardens, through the intervening trees and shadows, she could see a crowd of little figures pouring through the gate.

"Run, damn you!" shouted Alex from the turn of the house. She saw him jerk up his arm and fire, and picking up her wide skirts she ran after Lottie and Mrs. Holly and a dozen others who had made for the bridge over the nullah.

But they had not all run for the bridge. Many of them had checked and turned back, daunted by the glare and the empty spaces and the yelling of the mob; and deeming the shuttered house a safer refuge they had run to hide instead in closets and cupboards and under the frilled valances of beds, locking themselves into darkened rooms and cowering behind the furniture. Others, confused by terror and the blinding sunlight, had lost their sense of direction and were running helplessly to and fro like panic-stricken animals, dodging behind trees and shrubs.

Winter saw Lottie and Mrs. Holly reach the bridge and cross it and run on toward the tangled thickets thirty yards beyond it. Her wide skirts swayed and swooped and the ground under her thin, flat-heeled slippers felt unbelievably hot. She had almost reached the bridge when a shriek behind her made her check and turn, and it was Delia, running toward her from the direction of the house.

Delia's muslin ruffles flared about her like the petals of a huge peony in the wind, and the ribbon had fallen from her hair so that her long chestnut curls streamed out behind her. Her face was a mask of terror and her mouth a screaming square. Men were running behind her, covering the ground with great bounds—two men wearing dirty turbans and scanty garments that were spattered with blood, one of whom had armed himself with a grass-cutter's sickle. His teeth looked astonishingly white in his dark face and he was gaining on Delia easily.

This is not happening, said something in Winter's brain. Her hand went to the deep pocket in her skirt and she pulled out the revolver and leveled it, but she could not fire, for Delia was directly between her and the pursuing man. And even as she hesitated, he caught her. A dark, sinewy hand clutched at Delia's curls, caught them and dragged her back. The sickle swept, and Delia's severed head, its mouth still open and its blue eyes wide in terror, remained in the man's hand, dangling by its curls, while her body fell sideways in a foam of gay muslin flounces.

Winter fired and the man tripped and fell, and Delia's head, released from his outflung hand, struck the bridge, rolled and came to a stop almost at Winter's feet. The second man had stumbled over the body of the first and had fallen also, but he pulled himself to his knees. He carried a butcher's knife in his hand and there were fresh bloodstains upon it. As he scrambled to his feet she fired again and missed, and then the revolver jammed. The man ran forward, howling threats and obscenities, and Winter flung the useless weapon in his face. She heard a shot and saw him stagger and fall, and then from somewhere Alex had appeared running toward her. He leapt the sprawled body of the man, stooped swiftly to snatch up the fallen revolver, and said breathlessly: "Run—"

"No!" gasped Winter, catching at the rail, "we can't! Look—"

There were screaming women and children in the Residency garden, running across the lawns, blind with terror; dodging like hunted hares while rifles cracked and dark-faced, bloodstained, blood-crazed men pursued them, yelling and laughing.

Alex thrust the revolver into his belt, and gripping her arms he tore her free and dragged her by main force across the bridge and down the path that stretched for thirty yards or so over open ground before entering the narrow arm of jungle that lay between the back of the Residency and the plain. He did not keep to the path but plunged off it right handed, dragging her with him and thrusting his way between the high grass and the thin scrub, the bamboo brakes and the dhak trees, and when he stopped it was only because Winter's crinoline was hopelessly impeding their progress. From behind them they could still hear clearly a bedlam of shots and shouts and screams, but they did not appear to be pursued. There were too many victims in the grounds of the Residency, and a too alluring prospect of loot, for anyone to bother with chasing the few fugitives who had vanished into the jungle.

Winter was sobbing and struggling. "Let me go! You can't leave them! You can't! You've got a gun. There are children there—listen to them—*listen!* You coward—you coward!" She struck at him wildly, trying to break his hold.

Alex slapped her across the face with the flat of his palm. It was a hard blow and it jerked her back against a tree trunk and effectually checked the torrent of words and her rising hysteria. "I may yet be of more use alive than dead," said Alex brutally. "Get those hoops off— quickly!" He released her wrist and stood waiting, breathing quickly and listening, his revolver in his hand.

The pain of the blow had made her head ring and Alex' curt voice did not permit of argument. She pulled up the voluminous poplin skirts and the frilled petticoat and unfastened the hooped crinoline with feverish haste, wincing and gasping at the sound of those distant appalling screams that seemed to tear thin scarlet gashes through the hot sunlit morning. She saw Alex' face flinch and stiffen but he made no move to return. He reloaded her revolver with steady hands and gave it back to her. "Come on!"

It was easier to move without the hooped skirt, though her dress had to be lifted up to prevent it trailing on the ground. But her shoes were not made for rough walking and she knew that they would not stand up to it for long. Something rustled in the shadows, and two women who had been crouching among a tangle of grass and creepers stood up, white faced and breathing in short gasps. Lottie and Lou Cottar. And behind them, in a panting huddle on the ground, sat Mrs. Holly.

"*Winter!*" said Lottie in a sob. She ran to Winter and clutched her, her eyes wide and glittering. "What happened? Why did they make me run? Why? *Why?*" Her voice rose to a scream and Winter, remembering the murderous rabble so short a distance behind them, spoke frantically: "Hush, Lottie! You must be quiet!"

"Why?" sobbed Lottie. "*Why!*"

Alex reached out and caught her, pressing her head against his breast and holding it there with one hand. His eyes were anxious and alert but his voice was neither. He spoke to Lottie in an entirely matter-of-fact tone that somehow carried complete conviction: "We have to go to Meerut. You want to see Edward, don't you? The carriage has broken down, you know, so I am afraid we must walk. We were only running to get out of the sun. This is a short cut—and you must not make too much noise because—because I have a bad headache."

The hysterical tension ebbed from Lottie's body and she lifted her head and smiled her sweet, dazed smile. "I didn't know. I'm sorry. Why, of course I want to see Edward! Mrs. Holly did not tell me that we were going to Meerut, and I thought—let us hurry!"

Alex released her and said quietly: "Are there any more of you?"

Mrs. Cottar shook her head and answered him in a whisper: "Only the three of us. I think there are others hiding in the nullah, and some of them ran on down the path." Her face was chalk-white except where a thorn had scratched it deeply, and her hair had tumbled down her back. Her smart morning dress—she too had discarded her hooped underskirt—was ripped and torn, and she was trembling violently. But her eyes and her voice were steady.

"They'll have to take their chance," said Alex curtly. "We can't wait." He glanced at Lottie and said: "She'll have to take those hoops off. And you'd better do something about your shoes, or we shan't get far. Tie 'em with strips off your skirts—we can spare a few minutes." He knelt swiftly to help Mrs. Cottar who was already ripping the frills from her petticoat with quick, unsteady fingers. "You've got a gun, I see. Can you use it?"

"Yes," said Mrs. Cottar briefly, and sat down to tie the strips of cloth round her shoes, binding them strongly about the ankle. Alex performed a similar office for Lottie, while Winter, having tied her own slippers with the ruffle torn from her petticoat, coaxed Lottie out of her crinoline and turned to Mrs. Holly who had not moved.

"Hurry, Mrs. Holly—you must take off your hoops. Let me help you—"

"It's no use, dearie," said Mrs. Holly hoarsely. "I can't go no farther."

"Of course you can," began Winter, but Lou Cottar, who had heard the words, whipped round. She said in a harsh whisper: "It must have been that man in the servants' quarters. He fired at us as we went past. I thought he'd missed her—"

Alex pushed Winter to one side and knelt to put an arm about Mrs. Holly, lifting her a little. His hand touched a warm wetness that there was no mistaking and he saw the gray look on the plump, homely face, and recognized it.

There was a sudden renewed clamor of shots and shouting from the direction of the Residency and the screaming of someone in intolerable pain. Lottie flinched and began to breathe quickly again, and Mrs. Holly said urgently: "Go on, sir! It ain't safe to wait. You can't do nothing for me. I know that. Go on quick."

Winter flung her arms about Mrs. Holly, holding her tightly; feeling, as Alex had felt, the warm tide that soaked out upon the grass. She looked up at Alex and said jerkily: "You and Lou can take care of Lottie. I'm going to stay here."

"That you're not," said Mrs. Holly with sudden energy. "You'll do what you're told, Miss Winter! An' there's Miss Lottie. She'd be that scared without you. 'Er Ma was good to you. You owe 'er something. Get along now, dearie—hurry now."

Winter looked up at Alex with wide, imploring eyes and he shook his head in answer to the question they asked. Her cheeks were suddenly wet with tears and she bent and kissed Mrs. Holly, released her and stood up.

Mrs. Holly looked at Alex and her lips moved. He bent swiftly. "Take me shoes," whispered Mrs. Holly. "She'll need 'em. Stout they are. Not like those flimsy—I can't reach—" Alex turned without a word and removed the stout, sensible shoes and thrust them into his pocket. He jerked the revolver from its holster, looked at it for a fractional moment and then laid it beside her on the grass.

"No, sir," whispered Mrs. Holly. "I might use it if they come, an'—an' I don't 'old with it. The Commandments is plain. The Lord didn't say kill 'em if they kills you. 'E jus' said—*don't!* An' then you see—I might be tempted ter use it on meself, sir, an' that wouldn't be right neither. Take it—"

Alex picked it up again. He lifted one of the rough, work-worn hands, kissed it swiftly and rose to his feet. He knew that she had no chance; he knew that she might take hours to die; but he had other things to think of and he had to reach the river. He would have shot her himself and taken her death on his conscience, but he did not dare, for he did not know who might hear that shot and follow it up.

He swung round on the three white-lipped women who watched him and said savagely: "Don't stand there! For God's sake get on—quickly." He thrust them ahead of him into the hot, rustling grass and the shadows of the *runi* trees, and did not look back.

Two and a half hours later they had covered less than four miles. The intolerable heat, the absence of trodden paths and the necessity of forcing their way through high grass and scrub, raging thirst and the unsuitable shoes and garments of the women had combined to slow them down to a mere matter of keeping moving.

Lottie had struggled on manfully, supported at first by Winter or Lou Cottar, while Alex went ahead, but it had soon become obvious that she could not keep up with them, and eventually Alex had carried her. Lottie, even seven months pregnant, weighed astonishingly little, but the lightest weight becomes intolerable after a time, and Alex' muscles ached and the blood drummed in his ears and he had been forced to stop and lay her down at shorter and shorter intervals.

It was Winter who said suddenly, watching his grim, exhausted face as he rested for a moment, sitting with closed eyes and his back to a tree trunk: "Where are we going?"

Alex opened his eyes and looked at her and his face was suddenly bleak. But for her and Lottie and Lou Cottar he could have turned back and tried to get a horse from the stables and make a detour by the plain, and he might still have reached the bridge in time. But for them he could still reach it in an hour. The bridge was ten miles by road, but barely half that through the jungle, and he had gone this way on foot often enough before, though the jungle was thick and there were no paths. But for Winter—Winter and Alice Batterslea—he would not be here at all. . . .

"The safety of women in some crises is such a very minor consideration that it ceases to be a consideration at all. . . ."

IIe said in a parched whisper: "There's a ruin—use it for shikar—a mile above the bridge. Put the stuff there—weeks ago." He closed his eyes again.

"What stuff? What stuff, Alex?" Winter knelt beside him shaking him.

"Gunpowder," said Alex without opening his eyes. "Blow up the bridge."

Across his body Winter's eyes met Lou Cottar's. She had never liked Lou Cottar, but now something in the older woman that matched something in herself made a sudden bond between them. They looked at each other for a long moment and it was as if each of them had asked the other a question, and answered it.

Winter looked back at Alex. "How much farther is it?"

"Hmm? Oh—a mile. Get there soon." He moved his shoulders uneasily and dragged himself to his feet.

Winter said with a break in her voice: "Alex, you fool! You should have left us—"

Alex said: "You don't know these jungles. You'd have gone round and round in circles until—" He shrugged his shoulders uneasily and winced with the pain of the movement.

"Well, we are all right now. We'll bring Lottie. Go on as quick as you can, but—but mark the way. If it's only a mile we can follow you."

Alex looked at Lottie, who lay asleep with her head in Lou Cottar's lap, and then at Lou Cottar and Winter. They were exhausted from heat and thirst and the slow miles they had walked. Their faces and hands were scratched by thorn scrub and sharp-edged grasses; their feet were blistered—Lou was already wearing Mrs. Holly's shoes—and their clothing was torn and soaked with sweat. But their eyes were calm and they looked back at him steadily. Two pairs of eyes, so very different—so entirely alike.

He said: "Don't rest too long or you'll find you can't move. Keep moving, even if it's slowly. I'll mark the way. Hide if you hear anyone, and don't fire unless as a last resort. The sound of a shot carries." He turned away and the high grass and the thorn scrub, the choking bamboo, the *runi* trees and lantana and the hot, checkered shadows closed behind him, and he was gone.

They listened to the sounds of movement fade and die, and all at once the jungle was intolerably still. A soft, monotonous ticking crept into the silence, and Winter looked down and saw that it was Alex' watch which must have fallen from his pocket. She reached out and picked it up and the broken chain clinked as she lifted it. Alex must have forgotten to wind it, for the hands pointed at ten minutes past ten.

Ten minutes past ten. Only ten minutes past ten! It had not been eight o'clock when Alex had burst into the crowded Residency and told them to run—and to keep running. Surely that had been a year ago—a lifetime—an eon ago? How many people had died in the hour that preceded that? In the quarter of an hour that had followed it? How many people

were dying now? How many were hiding in the jungles like themselves,
and how long would they—and those others—be able to stay alive? Ten
minutes past ten . . .

Lou Cottar spoke in a whisper. "He was right. We'd better keep moving.
We can follow him fairly easily if we go now, but the grass stands up
again so quickly."

Lottie rolled her head in Mrs. Cottar's lap and whispered: "Water—
please."

The two women looked at each other and looked away quickly, their
own throats parched.

"We shouldn't have thrown our hoops away," said Lou Cottar, getting
stiffly to her feet. "We could have made a hammock out of them. Oh, well
—too late now. It will have to be my dress. It may hold." She slipped
out of it as she spoke, and they folded it and tied it with strips torn from
Winter's petticoat and made a rough-and-ready hammock in which they
laid Lottie. It was a precarious enough conveyance and put an intolerable
strain on them, but they managed it somehow, with the air of a makeshift harness that took the weight on their shoulders.

It was an agonizingly slow performance, but they kept moving. The sun
scorched them and blistered Lou's arms and face—Winter's, more inured
to the sun of late, suffered less. The dense shade held no coolness, and
Lottie turned and twisted and begged for water and it became more and
more difficult to persuade her to lie still. Once a tiger bounded across
their path, but they heard no other movements in the jungle, and almost
an hour later they saw something loom up out of the tangle of scrub and
sal trees and bamboo that was not a shadow but a solid wall of creeper-
covered stone, and knew that they had reached the end of that day's
journey.

The ruin that Alex and Niaz had stumbled across three years ago, while
tracking a wounded leopard through the jungle, had perhaps once been
the hunting lodge of some forgotten king, or all that remained of a long-
vanished city. Niaz had named it the Hirren Minar—the Deer Tower—for
they had found the antlers of a buck in the grass by the threshold, and
they had kept its discovery to themselves. Only Imam Din and Kashmera,
Alex' shikari, were aware of its existence, for despite the fact that it lay
barely a mile from the bridge of boats, the jungle here was dense and
scored with deep nullahs choked with scrub and high grass, besides being
known to be the haunt of tigers. They had frequently used it as a base
when on shooting leave, and over the last three years there had lurked
at the back of Alex' mind the germ of the thought that someday a hiding
place such as this might prove more than useful.

All that remained was part of a two-storied building topped by a low,
ruined dome. Thickets of bamboo grew closely about it, and lantana and
the rank jungle grass smothered the fallen blocks of stone and pressed
up between the paving. It was hot and very dark inside, and smelt strongly
of the wild boar and his family who had recently been inhabiting it. There

was also a distinct scent of leopard. The stairway that had led up to the top story had fallen centuries ago, and only a gaping hole remained in one corner of the black, bat-haunted ceiling of the single cell-like lower room.

The trodden grass showed where Alex and at least one other had passed in, but the ruin was as silent as the silent jungle, the hot sunlight and the checkered shadows.

"There is no one here," whispered Lou, and the dark stone walls about her whispered back, ". . . *no one here.*"

"But there is a ladder," said Winter. "Look!"

Hanging from the jagged hole in the roof was a serviceable rope ladder, and they tugged at it tentatively. It appeared to be quite fast. Winter set her foot on it, and Lou Cottar caught her arm: "Be careful—there may be someone up there!"

They stood still and listened, holding their breath, but they could hear no sound. "Water—" moaned Lottie. "*Water,*" whispered the echo. Winter gave a little jerk of her shoulders and started upward, and a minute later she had vanished through the broken aperture. Presently her head reappeared. "It's all right. Can you get Lottie up? There's water here—there's—there's everything!" Her voice broke.

Two rough-and-ready beds, a roll of matting, some tin boxes, an oil lamp and an earthenware chatty would not have been considered "everything"—or even "anything"—a few hours ago. But the world had dissolved under their feet during those hours, and the sight of these few and homely objects helped in some way to solidify it again.

The water in the chatty was warm and stale and there was not a great deal of it. There was a tin mug, recently used, standing beside it, and they watched while Lottie drank, and then drank thirstily but sparingly themselves, and wetted their handkerchiefs in it to cool Lottie's hot body.

"There, there, darling," said Winter, forcing her voice to placid reassurance. "You'll be all right now. We're safe now—we're safe."

But for how long?

29

NIAZ had left the cantonments half an hour and more before Alex, and on horseback. He had meant to ride to within half a mile of the bridge and strike off at a tangent into the thick jungle, making for the Hirren Minar by a route which he and Alex had used before. He should by rights have reached it several hours before Alex, but he did not do so.

By the irony of fate it was a bullet fired by one of the five British women who had preferred to remain in their own bungalows rather than take refuge at the Residency, that had brought down his horse. Laura Campion, standing over the body of her dying husband on the veranda of her bungalow, had fired his musket at a mob of sepoys who had pursued the wounded man from the lines. The bullet went wide, and Niaz's horse, neck stretched at a gallop, had crossed the line of fire.

Niaz struck the dry grass verge of the roadway, rolled into a ditch and lay still.

He recovered consciousness within a few minutes, and not long afterward, shaken and badly bruised but otherwise unhurt, he was crawling down the ditch toward a culvert where the drive leading into Captain Garrowby's bungalow branched off the road. As he did so he heard the explosion of the magazine, and did not know if it also signaled Alex' death; but he did not turn back.

There was a tangle of oleanders growing by the gate of Captain Garrowby's bungalow, and Niaz, waiting his opportunity, left the culvert and took refuge among them. He must have a horse, and there would be horses in the stables behind the bungalow.

There was a smell of smoke in the hot air and a crackling sound, and emerging from the shelter of the oleanders he saw that the bungalow was on fire. He ran across the garden, keeping to the shelter of the shrubs and trees, and saw a mob of sepoys between the back of the bungalow and the stables, cutting off his approach. Niaz did not linger. He scrambled over the compound wall and fifteen minutes later he was a quarter of a mile away, wriggling along a drain behind Mr. Joshua Cottar's stables. But Josh Cottar had taken four of his horses with him when he had left for Calcutta, and Mrs. Cottar had driven to the Residency in a carriage and pair, accompanied by a syce riding the remaining horse. The stable doors stood open and the stables were empty. It had not proved at all easy to steal a horse that morning, but an hour later Niaz had dragged a portly *bunnia* from the back of a starved-looking pony, and was riding as hard as he could persuade the animal to gallop in the direction of the bridge of boats.

He abandoned the pony when he took to the jungle, finding it easier to make his way on foot, and had arrived at the ruined hide-out barely fifteen minutes before Alex. He was in the upper room collecting sundry packages with feverish haste when Alex arrived, and they had looked at each other for a long moment before Alex turned away, and dipping a tin mug into the water that stood in the covered earthenware chatty, drank deeply. There was brandy there too, and he drank some of that, and fetching the Westly Richards rifle from its hiding place in the ruined dome above, he loaded it. Niaz fetched a shotgun from the same place, and Alex looked up and shook his head. "Nay, leave it, I have this." He touched the revolver. "How much time have we?"

Niaz shrugged his shoulders. "An hour—two hours—a day. Who knows?

I do not think they will come too soon. They are mad from killing and they are breaking into the bungalows to rob and burn."

"When there are no more left to kill they will be afraid and come away quickly," said Alex, filling his pockets with spare ammunition and reaching for powder flask and shot. "I came away across the nullah with three mem-sahibs whom I left half a *koss* from here. They follow, but slowly. I have marked the way. Let us go."

They descended the swaying ladder, and shouldering their burdens went out into the hot shadows of the forest. The river ran past less than two hundred yards from the Hirren Minar, and the road and the bridge of boats lay away to the right, a scant mile from the hidden ruin. No paths led there, but Alex and Niaz knew this part of the jungle well and they had their own tracks through the apparently trackless thickets.

They moved with more and more caution as they neared the road, and presently the jungle thinned out a little and they heard the gurgle of the river running between the boats and the creak and strain of the bridge.

"Wait here," whispered Niaz. "I will go forward and see if the road be clear." He laid down the things he carried and wriggled away like a lizard through the thick scrub.

Alex sat with his back to a tree trunk and tried not to think of a dozen things that he had seen that morning. Things that made his stomach heave and cramp with rage, and a red haze swim in his brain so that some primitive, unreasoning, tribal instinct had made him for one dreadful instant want to get his hands round Niaz's throat at the Hirren Minar, because of the things that men of Niaz's race had done that day. He had seen too, for a fractional moment, a like antagonism in Niaz's face, and known that the drag of race and blood had pulled at him also.

But we are not only our people—we are ourselves, thought Alex, *ourselves!* No, we are not—we are chained together by environment and custom and blood. . . . "*I arm their hands and furnish the pretense.* . . ." He found that he was unable to think clearly and wished that he need never think again.

The undergrowth rustled and gave up Niaz, who said cheerfully and without troubling to lower his voice: "I have locked the tollkeeper and the police guard in the tollhouse and have taken away their muskets. Remains now those on the far side."

Alex said: "Had they heard aught?"

"Nay. Two slept, and that they would not have done had the news been told." Niaz lifted his discarded burden and said: "Why do we not cut the boats loose? That would suffice."

"For a time only. The boats would strand and they would use them again. And I would close this road."

They came out cautiously into the thinner belt of jungle by the bridge-head where the grass was trampled down and the ashes of old fires showed where travelers had stopped for the night. The small stone-built tollhouse was silent, and there was no sound to be heard except the gurgling of water between the close-lashed boats.

Alex glanced at the tollhouse under frowning brows and Niaz said sweetly: "They will not cry out. I have bound them."

"And the others in the huts behind?"

"They sleep. And all the muskets were in the tollhouse. They will not move for some hours yet. Why should they? There was no outcry."

They walked down the slope of the road onto the bridge, into the full blaze of the blinding noonday and the sun-dazzled water; the creaking planks hot under their feet. The heat shimmered off the wood in quivering waves that smelt of tar, and the glittering river that slid beneath them did not cool it. There were row upon row of mud turtles basking in the glare at the edge of the sand bars on the far side of the river, but except for the turtles there seemed to be nothing else alive within a dozen miles, and the hollow sound of their footsteps on the planks of the bridge was loud in the hot silence.

A drowsy tollkeeper heard it and came reluctantly to the door of the mud hut that served as a tollhouse on the Oudh bank of the river. Seeing a sahib he salaamed and hurriedly straightened his turban. Alex returned the salute and inquired as to the prospects of shikar in the jungles by the bridge? He had, he said, glancing down at the stain on the sleeve of his coat, shot a leopard that morning not a mile up the road. While he talked Niaz moved between them and the hut.

Five minutes later the two men in the hut who constituted the bridge guard, together with the horrified tollkeeper, were sitting gagged and bound in the inner room, and Niaz was making fast the door. He carried the two antiquated muskets out and flung them into the water as he and Alex ran back along the causeway and onto the bridge.

They worked swiftly and methodically in the broiling sun, laying the charges, tamping and connecting fuses, never certain that the intense heat of the hot wood and the burning metal would not detonate the explosive of itself. The sweat poured off them and the dazzling glare off the river scorched their faces and hurt their eyeballs.

"Listen!" said Niaz suddenly. "There are horses on the road!"

Alex leapt to his feet and stood for a moment listening intently, and heard the faint faraway sound of hoofs. He snatched up the rifle and thrust it at Niaz. "Four more and we have done. Hold them off for a little."

Niaz turned and raced for the bridgehead and Alex bent to the charges again, working with feverish speed. The sound of horses' hoofs was clearer now, and presently he heard the crack of a rifleshot, but he did not lift his head or look round. He must have more time—only a little more time. The noise of the river was astonishingly loud under his feet, and the heat of the iron bands that reinforced the planking burnt his hands as though it were red-hot. Once again he seemed to hear Sir Henry's voice speaking from the shadows of the veranda in the Lucknow Residency: "*I need time . . . time most of all!*"

"Only five minutes!" prayed Alex. "It isn't much to ask—only five minutes!"

He heard a fusillade of shots and a bullet sang past his head like a hornet, but still he did not look up.

Niaz reached the tollhouse, and leaping the step of the shallow veranda he unbarred the door and ran to the small window that looked down the long Lunjore Road, ignoring the groans of the three bound and gagged men who watched him from the floor with starting eyes.

There were perhaps twelve or fifteen riders, sepoys from Lunjore, advancing at a leisurely trot for the bridge; either men bringing the news of the rising to Oudh, or an advance party sent to secure the bridge for the main body of the mutineers who would cross later that day.

Niaz waited until they were within range and then fired, aiming deliberately for the leading horse in order to create the maximum confusion. He saw the horse rear and fall, and the dust rose in a choking cloud as the men drew rein and came to a sudden stop. He reloaded swiftly and fired into the dusty smother; heard a yell and the screams of a wounded horse and saw the riders scatter to either side of the road. They would not come on for a moment or two, and he fetched the muskets belonging to the police guard that he had piled against the wall out of their reach. With several muskets and Alex' rifle he should be able to save time on loading.

He reloaded the rifle again and watched with interest, reserving his fire, while the skirmishers at the road's edge conferred together. Presently one of them cupped his hands about his mouth and, evidently under the impression that it was the bridge guard and the tollkeeper who were firing upon them, bellowed that they were friends and urged the guard to join them—the Feringis being dead and all Lunjore in the hands of its rightful owners.

The man moved incautiously out into the road and Niaz shot him and watched his riderless horse bolt down the road and gallop wildly past the tollhouse. There was a crash and a splash as the frenzied animal went wide of the bridge and plunged headlong into deep water, and Niaz heard shrill feminine screams from the three small huts twenty yards behind the tollhouse where the tollkeeper's family lived. A fusillade of shots spattered up the dust and chipped flakes of stone from the walls, and he saw the remaining horsemen hurriedly dismount and disappear into the jungle.

Now they will come up under cover on either side of the road, thought Niaz, and remembered with dread that Alex, working alone on the empty bridge, would provide an admirable target. He fired again at random into the jungle just ahead of where the men had entered it, discharging each of the muskets in turn and reloading again with feverish haste.

A woman ran out across the sun-scorched ground opposite the window, and a musket ball fired from the jungle on the far side of the road whipped past her and smacked against the corner of the tollhouse, sending a shower of chips flying. She screamed and ran back again and Niaz grinned and fired in the direction from which the shot had come. Three more riderless horses galloped past with trailing reins, and he heard their hoofs thunder on the bridge and hoped that they had not ridden Alex into the water.

There was a back door to the tollhouse and a woman beat upon it and screeched to her husband to come out and take refuge in the jungle, for they were being attacked by dacoits. The remainder of the police guard had presumably either run away or joined the sepoys. There were men now in the jungle opposite, and a bullet entered the open door and ricocheted round the small room. Niaz turned from the narrow iron-barred window in the end wall, and running to the door he fired into the thick scrub on the opposite side of the road. As he did so something struck his chest and he fell sideways, the rifle jerking from his hand to slide along the floor and come to rest against the far wall.

After a moment he came dizzily to his knees and crawled toward the rifle, but he could not reach it. He groped instead for his revolver, and dragging it painfully from its holster he raised himself a little and fired at a face that peered through the high grass at the road's edge, and saw a man lurch forward and fall on his face in the dust. And then he heard the sound of running feet, a crash of shots, and Alex had leapt the single stone step of the veranda, stumbled over him, and turning, had fired his revolver at a man on horseback who rode shouting for the bridge.

The shouting voice stopped as though cut off with a knife and there was the sound of a fall, a clatter of hoofs and a brief moment of silence. And then the crashing blast of an explosion—and another and another that joined together in a single shuddering roar of sound, until the glaring day was dark with flying splinters of wood and choked with the reek of black powder. Then the silence slammed down like an iron shutter and the river gurgled no longer, but ran quiet and unimpeded from bank to bank.

Alex spoke breathlessly into that silence: "Quickly, before they recover —out by the back!" He had barred the door behind him and was across the room, pulling at the heavy bolts that closed the back door. He drew it open a crack and said: "There is no one there—quick!"

"I cannot," said Niaz.

Alex whipped round, seeing for the first time that Niaz had not been merely kneeling to fire, but was wounded, and he crossed the floor in a single bound. He knelt swiftly and thrust an arm under him, lifting him: "Hold about my neck and I can carry thee."

"No," said Niaz urgently. "This is the end for me. Go—and go swiftly, while there is yet time—*mera kham hogya* (my work is finished)."

Alex looked down at the graying face against his arm and the bright, swiftly spreading stain that soaked the dusty tunic, and pulling back the reddened cloth he saw that there was nothing that he or anyone could do. A desperation and a wrenching rage beyond anything he had felt that day tore at him with the savagery of a taloned paw.

Niaz said: "Thou hast seen how it is with me—go now. I can still—fire

a gun—it will hold them—for a little. Get to the jungle—there be the mem-
sahibs to be—thought of—"

Lou Cottar—Lottie—Winter . . . If it had not been for them he, Alex,
would have reached the river an hour or more ago. This would never
have happened. How long would they live if he died? He had left Mrs.
Holly to die alone—and slowly. He had had to—because of those three
women. And because of the bridge. But the bridge had gone. He had
stopped at least one road into Oudh, and perhaps by doing so had bought,
at the price of his friend's life, a little more time. Only a very little more,
for there were so many other roads.

Once again, and for a brief moment, he saw Winter's face quite clearly
against the rough stone walls of the shadowed room; as clearly as he had
seen it in Alice Batterslea's garden; as clearly as though she had been
standing there looking at him with those grave dark eyes that had seen so
little of happiness. But it did not mean anything to him any more. She
would have to take her chances. He would not leave Niaz to die alone as he
had left Mrs. Holly.

Alex drew his arm away very gently, laying Niaz back, and getting to his
feet he closed and bolted the back door and dropped the shutters across
the two windows, fitting the iron bars that held them into the sockets. He
took up the guns one by one and loaded them methodically. There was
a jar of water in the room and he brought it to Niaz, lifting him carefully
against his shoulder.

A bullet struck the heavy wood of the door and another cracked against
the stone. Alex looked down at Niaz and smiled, and Niaz grinned back at
him—the old carefree grin with which he had greeted every chance and
mischance of life through the twelve eventful years that they had known
each other, and said in a clear strong voice: "It is better this way. It is not
good to have a divided heart, and there is that in me, which, were it not
for thee, would have me follow such men as the Mulvi of Faizabad. We
have had a good life, Sikunder Dulkhan—a good life—and though thou art
an unbeliever, and therefore hell doomed, thou hast been as my brother.
Lift me up, brother—it will be a good fight—"

His voice failed, and presently he began to mutter names and odd
scraps of sentences, and Alex realized that in imagination he was back at
Moodkee, watching the opening of the Khalsa Cannonade, and fretting
for the order to charge. Then suddenly he laughed and raised himself in
Alex' arms, pressing up as though he rose in his stirrups, and shouted aloud
as he had shouted on the day of that charge, *"Shahbash bhaiyan! Dauro!
Dauro! Da—"* A rush of blood choked him, pouring from his mouth and
dyeing Alex' coat and hands, and he fell back and was still.

A musket ball struck a leaf of the wooden shutter over the window
and filled the room with flying splinters. There were shouting voices
and another fusillade of shots from outside the tollhouse, and the bound
men on the floor writhed and groaned in terror as a second bullet smashed
through the shutter and struck the wall above their heads; but Alex did

not move. He stayed quite still, holding Niaz's body in his arms; his mind entirely blank. The noise outside the tollhouse seemed to come from very far away and to have nothing whatever to do with him, and he was only aroused at last by a bullet fired at much closer range that smashed through the panel of the door and passed within an inch of his shoulder.

He laid Niaz down very carefully and stood up. His gaze fell on the water jar and he picked it up and drank thirstily, and poured what remained of it over his head and neck. He did not know how many men there were outside. A dozen? Twenty? They would get him in the end, but he should be able to account for some of them before the ammunition ran out. He took stock of it and discovered that unless the police guard kept their ammunition elsewhere they had only been issued a few rounds each. But there was still the supply he had brought for the rifle.

He picked up Niaz's revolver and loaded the single chamber that had been fired. A rifle, five muskets, two revolvers. A pocketful of ammunition. He might hold them off for an hour—perhaps a little longer.

There were two string charpoys in the stifling room and he stooped, and lifting Niaz he laid him on one of them. He took up the rifle and loaded it, and crossing to the window he lifted the bar of the shutter and pulled it aside. There were three sepoys not a dozen yards away, and putting down the rifle, he jerked the revolver from its holster and fired, killing one and wounding a second.

It was nearing five o'clock when Alex fired the last round and dropped the useless weapon to the floor.

The heat of the closed stone building was appalling and his head and every muscle of his body ached abominably. The sun was sinking down toward the treetops and the walls of the room were hot to the touch. The three bound men who lay against the wall had ceased to move or whimper, and he wondered incuriously if they were dead from fear or thirst or one of the ricocheting bullets. He closed the shutter again, and sitting down on the charpoy beside Niaz, he leaned his head against the wall and waited, watching the patch of sunlight from the broken shutter creep slowly across the floor and up the wall, and thinking odd, disjointed thoughts. For the moment there was silence outside, but he knew that it would not be long before it dawned upon those outside that he must have come to the end of his ammunition. He had met every move with a shot so far and made it too dangerous to approach across the open, but after a time they would find that they could move without one, and draw their own conclusions.

He heard horses' hoofs galloping down the Lunjore Road toward the river, and heard them check some distance above the tollhouse. Reinforcements? He wondered how soon the mutinous regiments would arrive. They should be here by now—unless, which seemed likely, someone had ridden back to tell them that the bridge had been destroyed and that there was no further point in their coming that way.

He wondered how Yusaf had fared, and if the blowing up of the Hazrat

Bagh Road had been as successful as that of the bridge? It should have been—they had worked it out with considerable care. He hoped that Yusaf would not be too impatient, but wait until the guns and the wagons were well on the mined stretch of road. That should not only effectively block the road, but dispose of a considerable quantity of ammunition at the same time. Would they come that day, or would they wait until the thirty-first? A harlot's taunt had sprung the mine of the mutiny before its time; but now that it had been sprung, that premature explosion, like the charges he had laid on the bridge, was setting off a succession of other explosions, and not all the pleas of the leaders could prevent the inflammable material they had prepared from catching fire from the flying sparks.

The hot room stank of sweat and urine, black powder, betel nut and blood, and the gloom was noisy with the buzz of flies. Alex pulled down the end of Niaz's puggree so that it covered his face, and folded the quiet hands across his chest. They were stiff already. It must be getting late. He rose and turned the charpoy so that the dead man's head was toward Mecca. There was no more water, so he could not wash as the ritual prescribed, but he rubbed his hands partially clean on his soiled handkerchief, and spoke the words of the Du'a over the quiet body, there being no one else who would ever speak them for Niaz.

"*May the Lord God, abundant in mercy, keep thee with the true speech; may he lead thee to the perfect path; may he grant thee knowledge of him and his prophets. May the mercy of God be fixed upon thee for ever. Amen. . . . Oh, great and glorious God, we beseech thee with humility, make the earth comfortable to this thy servant's side, and raise his soul to thee, and with thee may he find mercy and forgiveness.*"

Alex sat down again, and presently, from very far away, borne on the hot silence and scarcely more than a vibration of sound, he heard the faint, faint boom of an explosion. It was followed a second later by another, and then a third. Yusaf! thought Alex contentedly. The Hazrat Bagh Road had gone, and with it a large proportion of the contents of the Suthragunj Arsenal, for the charges that he and Niaz and Yusaf had laid had not been sufficient to account for that sound at so long a range. That had been ammunition wagons blowing up. He leant back against the wall and closed his eyes.

A voice from outside the tollhouse shouted for those within to come out and give themselves up. Alex made no reply, and emboldened by the silence, footsteps clattered at last on the shallow stone veranda and rifle butts battered on the door and the window shutters. They were followed after an interval by other sounds—dragging sounds, footsteps and voices all about the small building—and quite suddenly Alex realized what it was that they were doing. They were piling wood and dry grass against the doors and windows and about the house. They were going to make a pyre of it. A funeral pyre for himself and Niaz.

One of the men on the floor stirred and moaned, and the sound cleared

some numbness from his brain. He and Niaz were not the only occupants
of the tollhouse. There were three other men there, and he could not
let them be burnt alive. "Wait a minute," said Alex, speaking aloud.
"Wait a minute—"

He dragged himself to his feet and walked unsteadily to the door, and
as he did so he heard a man outside say triumphantly: "Did I not say
so? It *is* a sahib! There are sahib-*log* in there!" and realized that he had
spoken in English.

A voice immediately outside the door said loudly: "Who is it? Who
is within?" and Alex' hand dropped from the bolt, for he knew that voice.
He leant against the door because it was an effort to stand, and said:
"It is I, Rao Sahib. Call off your butchers, for there are three in here
who are bound hand and foot and who had no part in this. You cannot
burn them alive. I will come out."

He heard Kishan Prasad catch his breath. "Who else is with thee?"

"None but Niaz Mahomed Khan, who is dead."

There was a shouting and a rush of feet, and he heard Kishan Prasad
say furiously: "Stand back! Stand back, I say!" and a moment later the
sound of a grumbling and reluctant retreat.

"Open then," said Kishan Prasad.

Alex picked up the empty revolver from the floor and thrust it into
the holster with a gesture that was purely mechanical, and straightening
his shoulders with an effort, he drew back the bolts and opened the door.

Kishan Prasad stared at him for a long moment and then he stepped
over the threshold and threw a quick look about the small room. He
looked at Alex again and then turned away and stood blocking the narrow
door, facing men whom Alex could not see.

"There is but one sahib here," he said. "The other man is dead and
the three men they have bound are alive. This sahib I know, and because
he once gave me my life at risk of his own, I say that he shall go free.
Stand away."

There was a rush of shouting men, but Kishan Prasad did not move
from the narrow doorway and his voice rose clearly above the tumult:
"Stand back!" said Kishan Prasad. "I am a Brahmin; and if you would
kill this man, you will first have to kill me."

The babble died down abruptly and the men drew back, for they were
Hindus, and to kill a Brahmin would be sacrilege unspeakable, dooming
them to the nethermost of hells.

"Go," said Kishan Prasad, speaking over his shoulder to Alex. "Move
out behind me and run for the jungle. I can do no more. The debt is
paid."

Alex said tiredly and without emotion: "Rao Sahib, if I had one bullet
left, I would shoot thee now for the things that have been done this
day because of men like thee."

"That may yet come," said Kishan Prasad. "Go now."

He moved out of the doorway, keeping between Alex and the group of snarling men at the far end of the veranda, and Alex backed away behind him, one hand against the wall, and reaching the end of the veranda he stepped down and to one side behind the shelter of the house, and turning ran for the jungle behind the tollhouse and the huts.

He heard the uproar break out behind him, and a single shot whistled past his head. And then he was into the high grass and had turned parallel to the road and was running and stumbling through the thickets, keeping as close to the road as he dared, in the belief that the pursuit would imagine him to be making straight for the thicker jungle instead of turning back up the Lunjore Road. They would watch to see that he did not cross the road, and would not search the far side of it, so he must cross as soon as he could do so without being seen.

He wriggled into a thick patch of thorn bamboo and lay still, listening for sounds of pursuit. There were no more shots, and though he could still hear shouting it seemed to go farther and farther away, proving that his guess had been correct, and that they had expected him to run in a straight line and were beating the jungle behind the tollhouse. Alex crawled with infinite caution to within sight of the road and lay there for a long time, wondering if he dared cross it. He had reached a point roughly five hundred yards above the tollhouse, but the road here ran straight as a spear for a mile or more, and there would be men watching from the tollhouse. He must not draw them to the far side of the road.

The sun touched the rim of the jungle and slid slowly below it, and the shadows lay long and blue, and a peacock called from the thickets behind him. A horseman galloped toward him from the direction of the river, raising a long cloud of dust. And suddenly it was simple.

The rider drew level with him and passed him, and Alex leapt to his feet and ran for the opposite side of the road, screened by the choking cloud of dust.

30

In Lunjore City the conches brayed and horns blared in the temples, tom-toms beat and rockets flared, while men rioted through the streets shouting that all Hind was free forever from the Company Sahibs' rule— that all the Feringis were dead, and that the great days had returned.

A mile outside the city the cantonments lay silent and deserted. Here and there a bungalow still burned and creeping figures still slunk between the silent houses, searching for any loot that might have been overlooked during the day-long orgy of murder and robbery. But as the evening shadows lengthened, the dead who lay about the cantonments filled even the

scum of the city with uneasiness and superstitious fear, and they fired a
few more bungalows, leaving the night breeze to carry the sparks and
fan the flames, and ran away shuddering.

The sepoys who were to have marched into Oudh for the retaking of
that province had turned westward toward Delhi when the news had been
brought that the bridge had gone, and the lines were deserted. In the
silent Residency the dead lay scattered through the quiet gardens and
the darkening rooms, and a quarter of a mile away, in the jungle beyond
the nullah, Mrs. Holly died at last.

The jackals and the hyenas, the crows, the kites and the naked-necked
vultures would feast to the full for many days to come, for there were
other dead on the plain that stretched toward Hazrat Bagh.

The garrison of Suthragunj had risen at the news of the mutiny at
Lunjore and had killed their officers and seized the treasury and the
arsenal, and had left, as Kishan Prasad and his friends had planned,
by the kutcha road to join with their fellow mutineers and march in
strength upon Oudh. They had taken the guns and wagonloads of powder
and ammunition, and Yusaf had waited until those guns and wagons were
between a given mark. The charges set each other off for a quarter of a
mile, and the wagonloads of ammunition exploded with a crash and a
detonation that was heard ten miles away and more. And when the smoke
and the flame cleared there was no road, and what remained to be seen
was not pleasant to look upon.

Yusaf waited until there was no more movement from the shattered
road. Then he drank deeply from his water bottle, ate his fill of cold food
and wriggled out backward from between the rocks.

He did not return to Lunjore, but moved off westward, making like a
homing pigeon for the North-West Frontier. From what he knew of Nikel
Seyn and Jan Larr'in and Daly Sahib, the Guides at least would be fully
employed, and he had many friends among the Guides. Who knew—they
might already be marching to attack Delhi? and if so, he would join them
on that march.

Winter and Lou Cottar had heard the faint, faraway crack of rifle fire
at the bridgehead, and the distant roar of the explosion. All that afternoon
the firing had continued, and they had guessed what it meant and watched
and listened—and waited.

For want of anything else to do they had set about turning the stone
chamber into some semblance of a home. It had at least kept them occupied. The room was large and square and windowless on three sides.
The fourth side consisted of three pillared arches, two of which still re-
tained broken fragments of stone tracery, and which led out onto a flat
roof surrounded by a low, ruined parapet.

There were several *chiks* in one corner of the room, and though the
white ants had damaged them they were in reasonably good repair, and
Lou Cottar had hung them between the pillars, remarking that they

would keep out the worst of the flies and mosquitoes. They had also curtained off a section of the room with sacking for Alex' use, convinced as they did so that he would not return, but denying the fear by that action.

Bamboo and dried grass had made primitive but efficient brooms, and they had swept and dusted, cleaned and tidied, in a desperate attempt to keep their hands occupied and their minds from thinking of the many things that did not bear thinking of. For to think of them was to sink into clutching quicksands of panic and horror. It was better to occupy themselves with make-believe domesticity, and they were grateful to Lottie because she needed attention and care, and because to keep from frightening her they themselves must not show fear.

Lou Cottar, standing at the edge of the open roof by the crumbling parapet, had reported that she could see a glimpse of river and would fetch water. She had taken the chatty—Winter had lowered it after her on a rope—and set out to find her way through the dense jungle to the river bank that lay so near and yet took so long to reach. She had not returned for over an hour and Winter had received her with breathless relief. "I'm sorry," Lou apologized, "but it's so thick out there that I lost my way coming back, even though it is so near. We must mark the way when we go again. We'll have to pull the water up. I can't carry it up that ladder."

The water was cool and refreshing, and they filled a small rusted tin with it and arranged a spray of wild gourd and jungle berries in it for Lottie. "I bathed," said Lou Cottar, knotting up her wet hair. "It was wonderful. The bank is very steep and there are no shallows on this side, but there is a place where the river has cut in between a tree and made a little beach, and I held on to the roots. You had better go too, before it gets dark. It gets dark so soon once the sun is down, and—" She stopped as though she had forgotten what it was that she had meant to say.

The sun was almost at the level of the treetops, and they had heard no shots for some time. They looked at each other and looked away again, saying nothing because they were both thinking the same thing—that Alex must be dead.

We are on our own now, thought Lou Cottar. We shall have to get out of this by ourselves—if there is a way out. It's a pity about Lottie English— It's going to be difficult with her on our hands. I wonder if Josh will hear what happened? I wonder if— No! I won't think about it. I won't think of it!

He is dead, thought Winter. If he were not, he would have come back by now. The bridge went hours ago—hours. And I called him a coward because I thought he should have stayed and been killed at the Residency instead of doing something sensible and dying at the bridge instead. I wish I were dead too; it would be so much easier to be dead. But there is Lottie—and Mrs. Cottar. And—and perhaps there are others somewhere. Or are they all dead?

Conway must be dead too. He at least had been in no condition to make his escape. It was odd to think that he had been her husband, and now he was dead—and that she could feel nothing at all. Alex had told her once that you felt nothing but the blow when a bullet hit you, and that the pain only came when air reached the wound. The air had not breathed upon her brain or her heart yet, for she could feel no pain. Only numbness.

The faint, faraway crack of a lone shot broke the brooding stillness, and the two women turned their heads as one to listen. But there were no more shots. It was, somehow, a very final sound. Like a period at the end of a chapter.

"I'll take some of Lottie's clothes and wash them in the river," said Winter abruptly, "and my own. They'll dry in an hour."

She removed her own torn, dusty, sweat-soaked clothes and wrapped herself in a length of faded blue cotton cloth that they had found rolled up in a bundle and stuffed in among a collection of odds and ends in one of the tin boxes. It made a skimpy though adequate sari, and she wound it about her in the fashion of the Indian women.

"You know," said Lou Cottar thoughtfully, "you could almost pass as an Indian, if you'd get a little more sunburnt. It's your hair and eyes. It may be a help yet."

"I should have to learn to walk without shoes," said Winter.

"We may both have to," said Lou Cottar grimly, and turned away to collect a few of Lottie's underclothes for Winter to rinse in the river.

They made a bundle of the clothes and Winter took the loaded revolver and went down the rope ladder. The jungle that had been so silent all day was waking to life as the shadows lengthened, and there were rustlings among the dry, golden grass, and birds sang and twittered and called from the thickets. A peacock fluttered up to a low bough of a tree, his gorgeous tail glinting in the low rays of the sun, and a chinkara fawn looked at Winter with soft, startled eyes over a tussock of grass before bounding away in the direction of the river. Making her way through the tangle of dry grass and leaves and creepers her ears were filled with the sound of her own progress, but she could hear the bird song above it. With a vivid remembrance of the tiger which they had seen that morning, she kept the revolver in her hand, but she had little fear that she would need to use the weapon. The shots and the blowing up of the bridge would have scared any large animal for miles, and after the heat and sweat of that terrible day the lure of cool water was not to be resisted.

The river ran gold in the evening light by the time she reached it, and the far bank was already in shadow. The water slid past like silk, so smooth and still that it seemed impossible that there could be strong and treacherous currents beneath that placid surface. It chuckled softly between the exposed roots of a great tree that the wash of the stream had undermined, and lapped against a small shelving beach below the steep bank. Winter clambered cautiously down the bank, and removing her makeshift sari, tucked it and the bundle of soiled clothing into a crutch among the tree roots, and let herself down into the water.

It was cool and delicious beyond belief, and she lay along the shelf of the bank and let the river run over her, drawing the heat and the ache from her tired body. Her hair spread out and rippled like waterweed in the pull of the stream, and the gurgle of the current slipping through the tree roots made a soothing, monotonous murmur in the silence.

She did not know how long she lay there, mindless and still, with closed eyes, but presently the slow thought drifted through her brain that it would be easy—easy and pleasant—to slide into the main stream and let the current carry her out and down into the cool darkness of the deep water. There was nothing to live for and she was very tired.

She turned her head in the shallows and opened her eyes. The sky and the river were no longer gold, but rose-pink, and the leaves and flowers of the tree that leant over her made a stiff, formal pattern against the wash of color.

Something moved in the pattern—a green parrot with a scarlet beak and long green and blue tail feathers. And all at once the Gulab Mahal was there before her. The enchanted garden of her childhood: the formal patterns of leaves and flowers and brightly colored birds that moved against a sunset sky, and that had remained fixed in her memory as a bright promise through all the gray, intervening years.

There was something to stay alive for after all. Somehow, someday, she would reach the Rose Palace. She had promised herself that for too long to relinquish it now.

A new energy seemed to flow through her with the thought, and she came to her feet and wrung out her wet hair, and reaching for the bundle of clothing among the roots, she washed out the torn, soiled garments in the river and climbed the bank again, wrapping the makeshift sari about her once more and leaving her wet hair hanging loose.

A peacock cried in the jungle, and the call echoed across the wide river and was repeated by another on the far bank. *Pea-or . . . Pea-or . . . Pea-or!* The cry seemed to underline the loneliness of the silent river and the dense miles of jungle, and to wail for all those who lay dead and who had been alive when that sun rose that was setting now. A savage and unbearable pain stabbed through the numbness about Winter's heart. The air is getting to it, she thought, and she picked up her wet bundle and the revolver and turned from the river to make her way back to the Hirren Minar, stumbling through the tangled grass and the thickets as though she had been blind and must feel her way.

She had stayed far longer by the river than she had meant to do, and now the sun had gone and the swift twilight was closing in. She had marked her way carefully, but she had lost those marks and was unsure of her direction. Fear replaced the pain in her breast, and she stood still, trying to remember the landmarks that she had taken note of when she had left the ruined building, and presently she began to move again, but with more care. But she had gone less than a dozen yards when she stopped again at the edge of a small clearing.

Something was moving in the jungle ahead of her, as though some large animal were walking slowly toward her through the dry, rustling undergrowth; and remembering the tiger she froze into stillness, her hand gripping the revolver. The noise came nearer and nearer, and now she could see the grass and bushes on the far side of the clearing sway to the movement of something or someone who was moving directly toward her. *Someone*—was the hunt so close?

Winter crouched down where she stood, seeing again in an ugly flash of memory the dark, contorted face of the man who had pursued and murdered the screaming Delia. Her finger tightened upon the trigger of the revolver as the high grass at the far side of the clearing rustled and parted. And it was Alex who stood there.

For a moment she did not believe it. She had given him up for dead, and the sight of him—filthy, bloodstained, dazed but alive—was a greater shock by far than the sight of his dead body would have been. The revolver slipped from her hand and she stood up with a choking cry and took a swift step forward, the bundle of clothing falling unheeded to the ground.

Alex checked, swaying, and his hand moved automatically to the butt of his useless revolver. Through the haze before his eyes he saw a slim Indian girl confronting him in the dusk, the blue of her thin cotton sari and the blue-black of her long, unbound hair melting into the shadows of the darkening jungle behind her. Then the haze cleared—and it was Winter.

They stood staring at each other for a minute that seemed like an hour, and then Alex stumbled forward, and as she ran to him he dropped on his knees and she caught him, holding him to her, and felt his arms go about her in a desperate grip.

She held his head against her, rocking him as though he had been a child. His hair smelt of dust and sweat and the reek of black powder, and she pressed her fingers through it, whispering endearments that he did not hear, and listening to the terrible, grinding sobs that seemed to wrench his body to pieces. She could feel the heat of those tears soaking through the thin cloth and wetting her body, and she held him tighter, straining him against her, until they stopped at last. The racking shudders ceased, and presently he lifted his head and looked up into her face.

His eyes in the fading twilight held an odd, blind anger, and his arms lifted and pulled her down onto the grass. She felt his hands on the thin cotton of the sari, wrenching it away, and he hid his grimed and smoke-blackened face between her small firm breasts. Her skin was cool from the river, and smooth and sweet, and he kissed it with an open mouth, moving his harsh cheek and his aching head against it, holding her closer. Then his hands moved again, and for a fleeting moment the fear and the horror of her wedding night returned to Winter. But this was not Conway, drunken and bestial. This was Alex—Alex. . . .

There was neither love nor tenderness in Alex' hands or his kisses. They were deeply and desperately physical, and she knew that for the moment her cool body meant no more to him than an anodyne to pain—a temporary forgetfulness and release from intolerable strain. But it was enough that she could give him that.

Conway was dead—they were all dead. All those people who had lived and laughed in the cantonments at Lunjore and at Delhi. Mrs. Abuthnot —Colonel Abuthnot—Zeb-un-Nissa—perhaps Ameera too. The whole world was breaking into pieces and dissolving into blood and tears and terror. But here in the quiet forest there were only herself and Alex—Alex' arms and his mouth and his need of her. Alex who was alive . . .

At long last his hold slackened and he lay still. The sky darkened above her, turning from green to a violet blue that was strewn with stars. The starlight and the thin moon made odd shapes out of the trees and the thickets and the tussocks of grass, and sometimes something rustled in the jungle or an owl hooted in the darkness. Once, very far away, a barking deer called a warning that a tiger was passing, and once a nilgai, the wild blue bull of the jungles, crashed through the dense undergrowth not a dozen yards away. But Alex slept the sleep of utter mental and physical exhaustion, and Winter held him in her arms and watched the stars and was not afraid of the night noises or of anything else.

His head was heavy on her breast and the weight of the arm that lay across her and pressed her down on the warm dry grass seemed to increase with every breath she drew, while her own arm beneath him had passed from numbness to prickling pain. But she did not move except to hold him closer, her cheek against his hair, and presently a breeze arose, a hot breath of wind that the river had cooled until it blew pleasantly through the jungle with a sleepy, soothing, rustling sound, dispersing the mosquitoes and night-flying insects and lulling her at last into a sleep as deep as Alex' own.

The sky was paling to the first light of dawn when Winter awoke and felt Alex move and draw away from her.

After a moment or two she opened her eyes slowly and sleepily, aware, despite the rough grasses below her and the numbness of her arm, of a feeling of miraculous restfulness and physical well-being. Alex had risen and was standing beside her, his profile dark against the graying sky, and although it was as yet barely light enough to distinguish more than the outline of his face, she knew that he was frowning.

He was not looking at her, and she lay and watched him with an aching, possessive love as the light grew and deepened and his features and the forest about him ceased to be flat silhouettes and became three-dimensional, emerging from the surrounding grayness and taking on form and shape. As the sky brightened she saw that the sleeves and breast of his torn coat were black with dried blood, and the sight brought her suddenly to her feet, clutching at his arm.

"Alex! You're wounded! You're covered with blood!"

"It isn't mine," said Alex in a flat and entirely expressionless voice. "It's Niaz's. He's dead."

He looked down at the stained, discolored coat and began to remove it, stripping it off slowly and with difficulty as though his muscles were stiff, and letting it fall to the ground. The blood had soaked through to his shirt, and seeing it, he frowned with a faint distaste. He said, without turning his head: "I'm sorry about last night."

His voice did not express sorrow, or anything else—unless it was perhaps the same faint distaste that had shown in his face when he had looked down at his stained shirt—and Winter's heart contracted with the familiar little ache of pain that she had felt so often when she looked at Alex. Are you, my darling? she thought. Are you really? Don't be sorry, my dear love! Anything but that!

She wanted desperately to put her arms about him and to tell him that she loved him, and that nothing in all the terrible things that had happened or would happen mattered more than that. But she knew that she must not do it. He did not want to hear it, and he would not understand it.

She disentangled the length of blue cotton from among the grasses and rewound it about her slender body, and the movement brought life back to her numbed arm and wrenched a sobbing gasp of pain from her. Alex heard the small sound and misinterpreted it, and she saw him flinch, but he did not turn.

He said: "I'm going down the river. I shan't be very long. Stay here."

He disappeared into the jungle, and Winter stood listening until she could not hear him any longer. She stooped then, and picked up his discarded coat. He would need it, and she could soak the stains out. She shook the dried fragments of grass from it, and as she did so something fell out of one of the pockets. A small folded square of paper. She picked it up and smoothed it out mechanically. It was her own note—the one she had written to him when she had returned from Lucknow, and which Yusaf had taken to him in camp. He had kept it. She stood looking at it for a long time and then she folded it again very carefully and replaced it.

Alex returned at long last. He had evidently bathed in the river, for the dirt and grime and powder stains were no longer on his face, and his hands and arms were free of dried blood. His hair was black and smooth from the water and he had washed out his shirt and trousers and put them on again. The saturated material clung to him wetly, molding his slim, hard body, but it was already beginning to dry in the dry heat. He took the revolver and the bundle of clothing from Winter and said: "What have you done with Lou Cottar and Lottie? What were you doing out here last night?"

"They're all right—at least—at least I think so," said Winter, turning to follow him. "I went to bathe in the river and I lost my way coming back."

Alex appeared to know his way through these jungles, for he walked ahead of her unhesitatingly, and suddenly the dark entrance of the Hirren Minar was before them.

There was no sound from the ruined building, and he groped in the gloom and found that the rope ladder had been withdrawn. He said softly: "Lou—are you all right?" and there was a swift movement above his head as though someone had been standing there with held breath, listening, and a voice said: "Alex!" The rope ladder dropped and two minutes later they were both in the upper room. Mrs. Cottar said: "What happened to you? I thought—" She leant against the wall and burst into tears.

Alex pushed aside the *chik* that she had hung across the open archway, and went out onto the flat roof outside. The sky was bright now, and the day was already breathlessly hot. The tall bamboos that concealed the Hirren Minar, towering to the level of the ruined dome, walled in all but a small part of the roof, leaving a narrow gap through which he could look out across the jungle and catch a glimpse of the river. He sat down on the crumbling parapet and stared at that small square of brightness.

There were things that he had to think about. Things that must be thought about soon. But all at once he knew that he could not do it now. He could not think about anything at all. He had not eaten for over twenty-four hours, and for months past he had considered problems that were now of no further importance. He would give himself a day in which to get what rest he could. At least he was clean again, and that in itself seemed enough of an achievement for one day. He had not expected to be clean again. He had expected to die grimed and filthy and with his face stiffened and caked with dust and blood and sweat.

The problem of the three women in the room behind him would have to wait. They could not stay there indefinitely, but they could at least stay there for a day or two, perhaps longer. He noticed incuriously that the ruined roof which was normally a foot deep in dead leaves and the debris of dying bamboos had been swept clean. A man would not have bothered. The thought of the three women pressed like a heavy weight on his shoulders, and his mind rejected it, turning tiredly away.

Winter came out onto the roof behind him, and a ray of the rising sun, piercing through the heavy screen of bamboos, caught her in a brilliant shaft of light. Alex turned and surveyed her with a faint surprise as though she were someone he had never seen before. She was still wearing the blue cotton sari and the scanty length of cloth molded the slender beauty of her body with a classic perfection. Her skin glowed gold in the golden sunlight and her black hair had blue lights in it, and he thought with an entire lack of emotion that she was the most beautiful thing he had ever seen—and a stranger.

The wary, withdrawn creature whom he had met at Ware; the seasick child in the cabin of the *Sirius*; the Condesa de los Aguilares; Mrs. Conway

Barton—they had all gone. The wariness and the withdrawal had gone too, and the great dark eyes were no longer unsure but quiet and untroubled. There was a serenity and a glow about her. Something that was almost happiness.

How can she look like that? thought Alex with a faint twinge of irritation. As if she were entirely content and there were no longer any problems that mattered. Had women no imagination? Had nothing of all that she had seen made her realize that her life from now on—all their lives—was only a matter of living for an hour or a day more, by luck and cunning and the grace of God?

Winter said: "Breakfast is ready."

The incongruity of the commonplace, matter-of-fact statement at that time and in that setting suddenly struck him, and he laughed for the first time in many days.

31

ALEX lay flat on his stomach in a thicket at the edge of a glade in the jungle. He held one end of a thin cord in his hand and he was watching the leisurely approach of a peacock and his retinue of wives. The cord operated a primitive trap some twelve feet ahead of him which had, during the past fortnight, accounted for several jungle fowl, two green pigeons, a peahen and an unwary porcupine. The porcupine, as a culinary problem, had proved insoluble, and after struggling with it for an hour or more Winter had handed the charred and unsavory remains to Alex for immediate burial.

The Hirren Minar was well stocked with salt and parched grain and a miscellaneous variety of the more durable stores, but they needed fresh food, and Alex did not dare fire a gun for he knew that the sound of a shot would carry far in the long, hot silent days. They had fishhooks and lines, however, which had proved more than useful, and he had found that it was possible to trap birds.

Cooking was a difficulty, for they were afraid of showing smoke. In that still air it would have risen straight and betrayingly above the treetops, and they did not know who might see it. There were probably other fugitives in the jungles, and the hunt might well be out against those who had taken refuge there. So they cooked only after dark or before dawn, and in the lower room of the ruin, blocking the door with a homemade curtain of grass and bamboo to avoid showing a gleam of light. It was a hot and choking performance, but Winter and Lou Cottar managed it without complaint.

They had been in the Hirren Minar for over two weeks now, and already it seemed as though they had lived there for months—for years even. They had settled into a routine of living, occupying themselves with petty domestic details; living a curious dreamlike life in the hot, silent, shadow-barred jungle. They might have been castaways on a desert island surrounded by a thousand miles of empty sea, but the three women appeared to be contented enough. They never spoke of Lunjore, or of anything that had happened there. At least not before Alex.

Lottie's gentle, trancelike daze had survived that second escape from massacre, and though she talked continuously of Edward, her clouded brain accepted the simplest lie, and the presence of Winter and Alex convinced her that all was well. When Edward's maneuvers were over they would be able to live in their own bungalow in Meerut again. She must be patient and not complain.

Lou Cottar, too, schooled herself to patience. At first it had been enough—and more than enough—to be alive and safe when so many were dead or living in dread and discomfort and danger. But as the days went by she began to take the security for granted, and ached to escape from the jungle and at least attempt to reach civilization. The British could not all be dead. That was nonsense! If only they could escape they would surely find that life elsewhere was going on much as before.

Lou had lived only for amusement, and for men, and she yearned for the society of her own kind again. For lights, noise, music, laughter—all the things that made life an entertaining affair. She had never taken any interest in her own sex and had little use for them, and to live cooped up in the company of two young women with whom she had nothing in common was tedious and irritating. But Lou possessed common sense and courage, and she knew that because of Lottie English they must take no chances. She had, surprisingly enough, begun to feel an odd fondness for the little creature. Lottie frequently irritated her, but she knew that she could not abandon her.

If Alex had paid her some attention Lou might have felt more reconciled to the situation. She had always considered that Alex possessed more than his fair share of sexual attraction, and she had been interested in him both as a male and as a personality. But Alex did not see her. He did not see any of them, except as a responsibility and a collective mill-stone about his neck. Hampered by them he was tied to the Hirren Minar until such time as he could get them to safety, and he did not know when that would be.

Outside the jungle that sheltered them and yet hemmed them in there must be so much to be done. So much that needed doing. Delhi to be retaken. Somewhere beyond the borders of Lunjore William would be doing the work of ten men: and John Nicholson, of whom it had been said that singlehanded he could cow an entire mutinous Army corps into obedience. Henry Lawrence in Lucknow, John Lawrence in Peshawar, and a hundred others. None of them would be standing still, and they would need every pair of hands and every brain and heart they could muster to save the country from falling into ruinous and disorganized anarchy. Yet he, Alex Randall, sat here idle, tied hand and foot by the necessity of protecting the lives of three women.

He had slept most of that first day at the Hirren Minar, and awakened to a ravenous hunger that had been only partially appeased by a mess of dried corn and a somewhat muddy-tasting fish that Lou Cottar—who had found the lines and fishhooks—had caught in the course of the afternoon.

He had been unreasonably angry on discovering that Winter had cooked it over a fire that she had made in a corner of the stone chamber below, and had informed her tersely that she had shown a lamentable lack of intelligence, and that in future no fire would be lit by day. Winter had smiled warmly at him, rather in the manner of an adult humoring a cross and convalescent child, and had apologized with a lightness that had further infuriated Alex, for he took it to be an indication of the fact she had no conception of the precariousness of their present position. He would have to take charge of them. Left to themselves they would be lost—

He had left them to themselves the next night and all the following day, and had made no mention on his return as to where he had been. For he had been back to the Residency.

He had found it deserted except for the kites and the crows and the scavenging pariah dogs. A sickly sweet stench of corruption had hung over it in a cloud almost as tangible as the clouds of bloated flies that buzzed over the dead, but there was nothing to be learned there. Not even the names of those who had died, for apart from the Commissioner and some half a dozen others, very few were still recognizable.

Alex had nerved himself to search among them for some evidence as to who they had once been, but he had been forced to abandon it. His own bungalow was empty, and like the rest it had been systematically looted. There had been an attempt to set it on fire, but the flames had not taken hold. The office, however, was reasonably intact, for the mob had not been interested in files and papers and had not troubled to destroy them, and Alex, having collected certain records of importance, had hidden the documents in the roof of the deserted stables. He had made a small bundle of various objects which he considered worth removing, and filled a torn haversack with fruit and corn from the trampled garden. There had been few people in the cantonment area, and he had kept out of sight himself, crouching behind walls or in the shelter of tamarisk scrub or other available cover, at any sound or sign of movement.

On the following night he had gone to the village where his shikari, Kashmera, lived; walking through the crops by the light of a narrow moon. It had been a grave risk, for he was well known in the village. But it was a risk that had to be taken, for he could do nothing without news. The old shikari had come to the door of his hut and had known who it was even in the faint starlight, and he had followed Alex out into the night, and they had crouched among the shadows of a cornfield for half an hour, whispering together.

Three days later it had been Amir Nath and his hawks who had met Alex at sunset at the third milestone outside the cantonments. Sometimes it would be Kashmera, sometimes Amir Nath, and once it was a friend of Alex' from the city, Lalla Takur Dass, a bazaar letter-writer who lived in an alleyway near Ditta Mull's silk shop. And so he had heard the news of the city and the villages and the surrounding districts.

It was not yet safe to move, they told him. There were still too many sepoys in Lunjore, and it was they who were keeping the district in a ferment. Several of the local Tulakdars were taking an active part in the revolt, and the lower elements of the city could always be relied upon to create trouble. But others among the Tulakdars had remained quiet and were watching to see which way the cat would jump, as were many men in Lunjore.

"But if thy people do not take Delhi soon," said Amir Nath, "they too will join with the others. There is no news of that yet, but there is talk that all the sahib-*log* are not slain, as was at first believed, and that an Army marches from Ambala to retake Delhi. If that be true, and Delhi be taken, then many who now waver will stay quiet. Remain thou quiet also, and in hiding, until the worst is past. To move now were to run all heads into a noose, for there is no safety east or west, north or south. Oudh also has risen and it is said that Lawrence Sahib and all the *Angrezi-log* in Lucknow will soon be slain, and that the *Jangi-lat-sahib* (Commander-in-Chief) is dead at Ambala."

There was nothing to be done but to keep the women in hiding, and Alex chafed at the inaction and occupied himself with snaring birds.

Winter alone of the four fugitives had no need to pray for patience. She was, for perhaps the first time in her life, entirely content. The jungle and the river and the ancient, hidden ruin held a strange enchantment for her. They did not belong to the everyday world. They were something lost and forgotten and right outside reality. She shut her mind to the memory of all that had happened to her in Lunjore—to the heartbreak and bitter disillusionment that had awaited her there; to the long months of degradation and misery; to the horrors of that last day and to the thought of the worse things that might even now be happening in the world beyond the forest. She would not think of the past or the future. Only of the present. And the present was Alex.

It did not worry her that Alex hardly looked at her and rarely spoke to her, or that when he did it was generally with an unmistakable undercurrent of exasperation. She felt as though she had loved him all her life and knew everything about him; and ever since the night following their flight from Lunjore she had felt so completely a part of him that she could sometimes follow the processes of his thoughts as though they had been her own. Harsh experience had taught her to expect little of life, and now it contented her that Alex was alive and within reach of her, and that she could watch him and listen to his voice, and feel his presence even when she could not see him.

The only unpleasant times were when he would go out to get news from the villages. She had never asked him where he went or whom he saw, and she was always frightened, with a sick, shuddering fear, that he would not return.

Lottie and Lou Cottar, in spite of the appalling heat, still wore the dresses they had worn when they left Lunjore. Alex had brought back needles and thread from one of his night excursions, and they had mended them neatly. He had also, somewhat unexpectedly, brought Winter a wine-colored cotton sari with a deep blue border, and a narrow cotton bodice such as the village women wore. Lottie and Lou Cottar could not be persuaded to wear such things. They had discarded their petticoats, stays and pantalets, but they clung to what they considered a civilized garment, as though it gave them some assurance that this was only a temporary interlude that would soon give place to normality.

"You're letting yourself go native, Winter!" snapped Lou Cottar one hot evening. She looked resentfully at the girl, and in the same moment thought how well the draped folds of the cheap sari became her, and how much more effective the silky, blue-black hair was when it swung in thick plaits almost to the knee, than when it was rolled up into the conventional heavy chignon. She said irritably: "You are the only one of us who doesn't look out of place in this Godforsaken hole—and who doesn't seem to mind being here!"

"I don't," said Winter dreamily.

Lou Cottar stared at her with an indignation that changed to sudden comprehension. She said abruptly: "You're in love with him, aren't you?"

Not so very long ago Winter would have considered such a question an unwarrantable impertinence and in the worst possible taste, while to answer it honestly would have been unthinkable. But this was not the civilized world. This was Eden. She smiled at Lou and said: "Yes."

"Is he in love with you?"

Winter thought of the letter that Alex carried in the inner pocket of his coat. But he might not even know that he still had it. She shook her head, and Lou said tartly: "Then he's a fool!"

"I think he has too much on his mind to bother about anything like that," said Winter reflectively. "Just now he can only think of me as a nuisance."

"Not only you," said Lou with a twisted smile. "All of us. And I can't say that I blame him. If it wasn't for us he could go. And if it wasn't for Lottie—"

She glanced toward the bed where Lottie lay asleep. Her thin features sharpened with anxiety, and she said with suppressed violence: "That damned baby! It's hanging over us all like—like the monsoon! Something that you know is coming and that can't be stopped. How much longer has she got?"

"About six weeks, I think," said Winter doubtfully. "Perhaps seven."

"Six weeks! Oh, God—and here we are doing nothing. *Nothing!* What in heaven's name are we going to do if she has it here? Do you know anything about babies?"

"No," admitted Winter.

"Neither do I. Not a damned thing! I've never had any of my own and I've never been interested in women who did. They look frightful and become dead bores. We've *got* to get her to some civilized place where there is a doctor! Why doesn't Alex do something?"

Alex, lying under a canopy of leaves in the hot, dry jungle grass and watching the shadow of a sal tree draw out across the clearing, was making the same calculations and coming to the same conclusion.

It was a conclusion that he had come to days ago, but he could still see no safe way of translating the thought into action, for it was inviting death to travel anywhere. There were bands of budmashes, looters and mutineers all over Rohilkhand and Oudh and throughout the North-West Province, and to remove from Lunjore would be to leave the frying pan for the fire. The thing was impossible as yet.

Six weeks . . . perhaps seven. But anything might have happened by then! Troops must be being hurried out from Home or stopped on their way to China. Reinforcements *must* be coming. And once the tide had turned it would be possible to demand help from those who at present were too busy watching the swing of the pendulum and unwilling to commit themselves one way or the other. For the moment Lottie was safer where she was.

That damned baby! thought Alex with an exasperation and anxiety that equaled Lou's. Why on earth do women have to—

And then without warning a thought that had never occurred to him before struck him with the sudden violence of an unexpected blow over the heart. It wiped the problem of Lottie from his mind and substituted a far more frightening one, and he stared blindly across the clearing, seeing only a slim figure in a faded blue cotton sari.

No, thought Alex desperately—no! It couldn't happen. It was only once— He had not thought of Winter for days, except as one of three women who were, unavoidably and infuriatingly, his responsibility. And at the back of his mind there had lain an unjust and illogical anger because she had been the means of turning him aside from the course he had set for himself, and by so doing had been indirectly responsible for the death of Niaz.

He did not want to think of her now, and with an abrupt movement he buried his head in his arms as though by doing so he could blot her out of his mind and from his conscience.

That night he took a graver risk than he had yet taken, and went into

the city, riding a thin village pony that he had procured with the assistance
of the apprehensive Kashmera.

"It is not safe!" urged Kashmera. "The Huzoor is too well known in
Lunjore!"

"There are few who will recognize me now," said Alex, and it was perhaps true. His face was thinner, and there were no longer any curves in
it; only hollows and angles—and lines.

There was elation in the city, for the reports and rumors that had been
received were all of successful risings and of European and British garrisons murdered or besieged, and it lacked only ten days to the twenty-
third of June—the centenary of the Battle of Plassey which an ex-clerk
of the East India Company, Robert Clive, had fought with three thousand men against an army of sixty-eight thousand, and in winning it had
won half India. The rule of the "Company Sahib," said the prophecy,
would last for a hundred years from the date of that battle, and now
that day was near. . . .

The talk of the bazaars only served to convince Alex that he could not
move the women yet. He had bought food and tied it in a corner of
cloth, and ridden back in the bright moonlight with angry despair in his
heart.

"Is there no news, Alex?" demanded Lou Cottar the next morning, following him out into the jungle and facing him among the hot shadows
of the sal trees. "You must have heard something! Even if it is bad we
would much rather know than be kept in the dark."

"All the news is bad," said Alex shortly. "We can't leave yet."

Lou said: "But we must go soon! Can't you see that if we don't, Lottie
may—"

"Do you think I haven't thought of that?" interrupted Alex brusquely.
"Don't be a fool, Lou! She may have a bad time of it if she stays here,
but she'll certainly die—and so will the rest of us!—if we are mad enough
to attempt a cross-country trip just now. The jungle at least will do us no
harm."

But he had spoken too soon, for the jungle that had seemed to befriend
them suddenly showed its claws.

They had gone down to the river that evening, all four of them, as they
did every evening because it was cooler there and there were always
clothes and cooking pots to be washed and fishing lines to tend. Winter
had not seen the cobra until it lashed at her, hissing, as she bent to dis-
entangle the edge of her sari that had caught on a thorn. Her foot touched
the cold coils, and the fangs bit into her left arm just above the elbow.

Alex had been less than a yard away from her and he had swung round
as she cried out, and had seen the snake slither across her path, and the
two small punctures on the smooth, tanned skin. The next second he had
leapt at her and caught her; his fingers tight above the wound, forcing the
blood down, and his mouth against it, sucking at it with all his strength.

Lou had come running and had beaten the grass with a stick, and then

snatched up a petticoat that was to be washed and ripped at it frantically, tearing at it with her teeth. It tore at last and she wound a strip of
it above Alex' straining hands and pulled it tight in a tourniquet.

Alex lifted his head and said hoarsely: "Permanganate—on the ledge
at the left back—quickly," and Lou turned and ran, stumbling and tripping among the grass and thorn and creeper, while Lottie wrung her hands
and wept.

Alex jerked the knife he carried from its sheath, and caught Winter
to him, holding her hard against him so that she could not move, his
hand a vice about her wrist. He said: "It'll hurt. Don't move," and cut
the wound across deeply, twice.

He felt her teeth clench on the thin stuff of his shirt and her body
twist to the pain, but she did not cry out and he dropped the knife into
the grass. The blood poured down her arm and his in a red tide and he
lifted her and carried her swiftly back to the Hirren Minar.

Lou Cottar met them a dozen yards from the entrance with the little
tin of permanganate crystals clutched in her hand, and they had filled
the wound with them, and had got Winter up the rope ladder. Alex had
let the arm bleed and she had looked at it with a frown of pain and said
in a dazed whisper: "It will make such a mess on the floor."

He had bound it up eventually and given her as much opium as he
dared, and later, when he had realized that she would not die, he had
gone out and been exceedingly sick behind the impenetrable thicket of
bamboos.

Winter had run a high fever that first night and Alex had held her
clutching hands while she twisted and turned and muttered unintelligi-
bly, and Lou Cottar bathed her burning body with cool water. "Is she
going to die?" Lou had asked once, and abruptly. There had been a break
in her voice, and her face had been barely more than a pale blur in the
darkness beyond the line of moonlight that lay between the broken
archways.

"No. She'll be all right in a few hours," said Alex with more confidence
than he felt. "Give me that cloth and go and lie down, Lou. If you crack
up too, I swear I'll go out and shoot myself!"

Lou had laughed on a sudden breath of relief and had obeyed him,
and Alex had taken the small fever-wracked body into his arms and held
it close, his cheek pressed to the burning forehead. The moonlit night had
been breathlessly hot and Alex' own body was wet with sweat, but his
hold seemed to soothe her, and after a while he felt her slacken and lie
still in his arms, and knew that she was asleep at last and that the fever
had broken.

My love! thought Alex, moving his mouth against the hot smooth skin
and the damp waves of silky hair that were as dark as the darkness about
him. My little love . . .

All at once the gnawing restlessness that had lived with him hourly
during the last weeks fell away from him, and he no longer cared what

became of anyone else—or of India—as long as Winter was safe. He could wait patiently now. She was no longer a burden and a responsibility, but part of his heart, as she had always been. What did it matter if they had to wait here in hiding for months—or years?

Only after this, thought Alex, I must not kiss you again or touch you again, because if I do I shall only take you again—I couldn't stop myself—and it may be months, or a year, before we can get away. . . .

He thought of Lottie and shivered.

32

WINTER had suffered remarkably little ill effect from the incident. The wound that Alex' knife had made had healed cleanly and given the minimum of trouble, and though the fever and loss of blood and the pain in her arm had kept her on her back and feeling absurdly weak for several days, she had soon been about again.

She saw very little of Alex after that, and suspected that he was deliberately avoiding her, but she knew that some tension in him had relaxed and that he was no longer impatient or irritable. She was aware too that he had developed a habit of watching her under his lashes. He would lie on the river bank in the evening while she and Lottie and Lou washed the clothes and cooking pots, and she would look up and find his eyes on her, and feel, as always, that familiar contraction of the heart.

Alex had taken to wearing nothing but a loincloth these days, so that his body was burnt as brown as his face and he could have passed anywhere for a Pathan. He had been out less for news than for food of late, and but for the relentless, exhausting heat the days passed peacefully enough.

Alex, like Winter, found the heat unpleasant but bearable. But to Lou, and more especially to Lottie, it was an interminable torture. They watched the skies daily for signs of the monsoon, and longed for rain, but though the clouds would sometimes gather, and they would hear thunder rumble along the horizon and see the heat lightning flicker, no rain fell to temper the intolerable heat, and they lived for the early mornings and the late evenings when they could lie and soak in the coolness of the river.

Alex became afraid of the river, and he drove in stakes about the narrow curve of the little beach where they bathed, in case their continued use of it might attract the attention of a mugger, and that one day one of them might be dragged down by yellow-toothed jaws into deep water. But there was too much food in the river these days for the muggers to bother with live prey. The bodies of the British came down on the current, bloated and bobbing to the undertow, and once one had stranded by the little beach: a woman whose long hair had caught in the tree roots so that her mangled corpse swung gently to and fro in the ripple as though she were swimming—or struggling.

Alex had sawn through her hair with his knife and pushed her off into the current, and the others, arriving five minutes later, had wondered why he was looking so unusually grim. That night he had gone to the city again, and when he had returned at dawn his eyes were hot with restlessness once more, for it seemed that the tide was turning at last. The British were known to be encamped upon the Ridge before Delhi; the Guides had marched from Mardan and were now with the Delhi force, and Hodson Sahib, the "*Burra Lerai-wallah*" ("Great in Battle") was also there, in command of a regiment of horse that he had raised.

There was a noticeable breath of uneasiness in the bazaar. It was disconcerting to find that the sahib-*log* were not all dead. And it was said, whispered one man to an awed group in the Sudder Bazaar, that Nikel Seyn (Nicholson) himself was riding for Delhi! Nikel Seyn—the sound of whose horse's hoofs could be heard, so men said, from Attock to the Khyber and whom many declared to be a god, and no man. The speaker had shivered and thrown a quick backward look over his shoulder as he spoke.

"It won't be long now," said Alex, his eyes blazing in the gray dawn light. "We shall have to stick it out here a little longer, but the monsoon must break soon, and then it will be cooler. And when Delhi is taken we'll be able to get away. A good many of the waverers will come over to us then, and we shall be able to get help on the road."

Another ten days. Perhaps a fortnight—or a month. But what did it matter now that the end was in sight? They could afford to wait a week or two more.

"We've been very lucky," said Lou, wiping the pouring perspiration from her face with the back of her hand, "luckier than so many others. Perhaps the luck will hold."

But it did not hold.

That same evening Lottie had strayed away to pick jungle berries, not twenty yards from the river bank, and she had heard someone moving through the bushes and had turned, expecting Lou who had been fetching water.

But it was not Lou. It was a bearded, turbanless native in torn and soiled clothing, who carried a heavy bundle upon one shoulder and bore on wrist and ankle the marks that are made by iron fetters.

She did not know that this was one of the criminals who had been released by the mob from the city jail, nor that he had subsequently murdered a Hindu merchant and his family, and escaped with the loot to the jungle. But Lottie was under no illusions as to his intentions.

He had stared at her unbelievingly, and then his lips had stretched into an evil grin. A mem-sahib!—a Feringi! His eyes glittered and he dropped the bundle he carried and drew a stained sword from its sheath. He moved toward her quite slowly, crouching a little, the dry jungle grass rustling and crackling about him, and Lottie's mouth opened in a soundless scream. She made no attempt to turn and run, but stood frozen and still like a trapped rabbit, and she did not hear Lou coming up from the river.

Lou never moved from the Hirren Minar without a revolver, and she dropped the chatty, and as the man looked round, checked by the sudden sound, she pulled the weapon from the sling she had made for it and fired. The man jerked upright and his eyes and his mouth opened in a look of incredulous astonishment, and then he swayed, coughed, crumpled at the knees and fell sideways with blood pouring from his mouth.

"No!" screamed Lottie. "No! No! *No!*"

Alex had been reinforcing a bamboo ladder that he had made to replace the rope one that Lottie found difficulty in climbing, and hearing the shot and the screams, he dropped it and ran. He had taken one look at the man on the ground and at Lou who was holding the screaming Lottie, and said: "Where's Winter?" And then Winter had run through the bushes, white faced and panting, and he had gripped Lou's shoulders and shaken her and said: "Were there any others?"

"No. I don't know," said Lou jerkily.

Alex said: "Get on, get back—all of you. He may not have been alone."

But Lottie would not go. She had struggled and screamed, and Alex had turned and taken her from Lou and carried her back to the Hirren Minar, holding her with her face pressed hard against his shoulder to muffle the screams. He had put her on her feet for one moment at the foot of the ladder, and she had turned and fled, and when he caught her she had fought him, writhing and twisting and clawing at him, her thin, distorted body suddenly possessed of surprising strength, so that it had been all he could do to get her back into the upper room.

Alex said: "Pull up the ladder, Winter; and close the entrance. Lou, give me the opium—and the brandy. It's all right, Lottie dear, you're safe now."

But Lottie screamed and shrieked and fought as she had screamed and fought at the Kashmir Gate at Delhi when she had seen a grinning, bearded man leap at Edward with a sword, and had seen her husband fall, spurting blood from that terrible wound, and had been dragged away to be lowered over the battlements and fall into the dry ditch below. "Let me go! Let me go! They're killing him! Edward—*Edward!*" screamed Lottie. And then quite suddenly she had gone slack in Alex' arms and they saw with unutterable relief that she had fainted.

Alex laid her down on the narrow camp bed, and letting down the rope ladder, he ordered Winter to pull it up after him, and went out into the twilight jungle.

He turned the dead man over, and recognizing him, realized that he was probably on the run, and he stood still, listening, for a long time, but could hear no sounds that suggested anyone moving through the jungle. Presently he made a cautious circuit of the immediate area but found no one, and returning to the corpse he dragged it to the river bank and pushed it off into deep water.

The bundle the man had dropped proved to be full of valuables. Silver coin, a large quantity of Indian jewelry and an assortment of objects that could only have come from the looted bungalow of some European, and one object that told its own story: a woman's hand that had been hacked off for the sake of the rings it bore and which had presumably proved difficult to remove. Alex disposed of this gruesome and decomposed relic and carried the bundle back to the Hirren Minar. The money might come in very useful.

There was an appalling smell of burnt feathers in the upper room of the Hirren Minar, and Alex climbed the ladder to find Lottie still unconscious and Lou and Winter, their faces no more than white blurs in the dusk, making desperate efforts to revive her.

"Leave her alone," advised Alex. "If she has remembered Delhi she is better off like that. We'd better light the lamp."

They used the oil lamp as little as possible, partly to conserve their scanty stock of oil, but mostly because it necessitated covering the open archways with solid screens that Alex had made from bamboo canes, roots and dry grass, so that the light would not show. In the daytime when the hot wind blew they poured water on those screens and it helped to cool the room, but after sunset when the wind dropped the screens made it unbearably hot, and there was no breath of wind blowing tonight.

Winter went below to prepare the evening meal, and Lou lit the small oil lamp while Alex mixed brandy, opium and water. "It may keep her quiet for a bit when she comes round," he said, and pushed the brandy bottle at Lou. "You'd better have some of that yourself. You look as though you need it." They had been as sparing with the brandy as they had been with the oil, but Lou drank, and felt grateful for the fiery liquid.

Lottie had not recovered consciousness for another hour, and when at last she had moaned and stirred they had been able to make her drink the opium brew without much difficulty. She had sat up, propped against Lou Cottar's shoulder, and had stared up at Lou's face and at Alex and Winter, and her eyes had lost the dazed sweetness that they had worn for so long.

She said at last: "Edward is dead, isn't he? They killed him. I—I remember now. And they shot Mamma—and—Papa. Where is Sophie?"

"Sophie is safe, darling," said Winter. "She is in Cawnpore."

"They killed Edward," whispered Lottie. "They—they cut him with their swords, and there was a man with a knife who—"

Winter said: "Don't think of it, darling—don't."

"I should have stayed with him, but they wouldn't let me. I should have stayed with him—" She turned her head against Lou Cottar's shoulder and wept, and Alex got up and went out.

He had slept in the jungle that night, in the grass before the entrance of the Hirren Minar, but he had lain awake for a long time, listening to the night noises and straining his ears for any sound that might be made by men. He could hear, intermittently, a murmur of voices from the upper chamber of the ruined building behind him, but it came at longer and longer intervals and at last there was silence.

There were clouds in the sky that night, but they held no promise of rain; only of hot winds and dust, and it seemed as though they intensified the heat, pressing it down onto the gasping earth so that it could not escape, as though they were a lid on a gigantic caldron. They were gone when Alex awoke with the first light of dawn, and the sky was clear again. Clear with the hazy clearness that promised a day of grinding heat.

Alex went down to the river and lay in the water on the narrow ledge below the bank. It was only when the sun flared in the treetops that he realized that none of the three women had come down to the river that morning. They were usually there well before sunrise, and he would leave the small beach to them and return to the Hirren Minar. But today they had not come.

He left the water reluctantly and felt it dry on his back almost before he had reached the top of the bank. Between the tree shadows the sun was like a raw flame on his shoulders as he walked back to the Hirren Minar, and he had reached the entrance when he heard that agonized moaning, and stopped.

He stood quite still for perhaps five minutes, knowing with despair and anger and pity what it meant. Then he turned away and sat down in a patch of shadow on a fallen block of stone that fronted the low stone ledge before the Hirren Minar. This at least was not his affair. There were two women with her.

The problem of this unborn child had been hanging over them all ever since the day of their escape from the Residency. The appalling inevitability of birth marching steadily toward them, unavoidable, inescapable. Lottie would have to bear this child even though her husband, mother, father and half her friends were dead, and India awash with blood and anarchy. Except by dying, she could not escape it. Listening to the moans he wondered why the Almighty had thought fit to inflict on womankind such a lengthy and agonizing method of populating the earth? And why, in the name of Allah the Merciful and Compassionate! had this got to happen now?

Probably just as well to get it over, thought Alex. After all it was a perfectly natural process. Happened half a million times a day and was a simpler matter than one would suppose. He had assisted at the arrival of Chytuc and helped a bitch who was in difficulties to produce her litter, and once he had sat up all night reading by the light of an oil lamp a manual on midwifery, and receiving terse instructions from a doctor who had crippled himself in a fall from his horse when riding fifty miles to attend the wife of a surveyor in a lonely forest camp, who was about to give birth to a seven-months child. It had proved a slow but comparatively simple affair. But the woman had been wide-hipped and healthy, and not in any way comparable to the childish smallness and fragility of Lottie.

What are those women doing to her? thought Alex impatiently. He could hear Winter's voice and Lou's, and Lottie's agonizing moans going on and on. The moans rose to a scream that was more fear than pain, and suddenly he could bear it no longer. He leapt the stone ledge and was up the ladder and in the comparative coolness of the upper room.

Lottie was lying on the camp bed, fully dressed and clutching at the sides of it, her eyes wide with terror. Winter knelt beside her and Lou Cottar leant over her with a tin mug in her hand. They turned their heads toward him and on both their white faces was the same terror of the unknown that was on Lottie's, and Alex, seeing it, realized in that moment that not one of them had the least idea of the mechanics of birth.

The suffocating prudery of the age saw to it that the majority of young women were kept in complete ignorance of such matters, and neither Winter nor Lottie had even seen a cat having kittens. All three of them had only the haziest idea of what happened when a child was born, for the whole affair was shrouded in the deepest mystery and only referred to in whispers. It was, moreover, considered by many that the less a young mother knew about childbirth the less likely she would be to panic about it in advance, while once the birth had begun—well, there was nothing for it then but to endure it.

Alex could see all these things written clearly in the desperate, terrified faces of the three women, and a sudden fury of exasperation took him by the throat. He thrust Winter and Lou aside and said savagely: "What in hell's name do you think you're doing? Come on—get her out of those clothes!" And saw again the same expression reflected on three faces. Even in this extremity they could feel it to be unspeakably shocking to remove Lottie's dress in his presence, and his exasperation mounted. He bent over Lottie and took her hands, feeling them turn and clutch frantically at his, and said: "Listen to me, Lottie. You've got to think of your baby now and not of anything else. Forget that I'm a man—or anyone you know. Just try and do what I say. Will you do that?"

Lottie nodded, clinging to his hands, and he released them with difficulty and said shortly to Lou: "Pull that fan and keep the flies off her. Have we got enough water in the place?"

"I—I think so," said Lou. Her face was quite white and her assurance had suddenly forsaken her. Lou had not flinched in the face of danger, but Lottie's pain and fear were something that she could do nothing to relieve, and it left her feeling sickened and helpless.

"Well, make sure! And if we haven't, get it." He turned to Winter who had removed Lottie's clothing and said: "Get down there and heat some water. And here—" He reached for a clasp knife from the stone ledge and handed it to her. "Boil that in some water—let it boil for five or ten minutes and then take it off and leave it in there."

She turned without a word and descended the ladder and Lou said: "The smoke—"

"We shall have to chance it."

He heard Lottie's moans rise to a scream again and went to her swiftly, taking her hands again, and Winter heard him talking as she fetched wood and dry grass and lit the fire that they had never yet lit by day. He was telling Lottie about the child. What it was doing, and what her own body was doing to help it in its struggle for release, and what she must do to help them both. It sounded, suddenly, entirely natural and reasonable, and no longer some dark and mysterious and unexplainable process fraught with terror and uncertainty.

"You can't avoid a certain amount of pain, dear," said Alex, "but there isn't anything to be frightened of and it will be here soon."

" '*He*,' " said Lottie. "Not 'it.' "

The long morning wore away, and the appalling heat filled every corner and crevice of the Hirren Minar as though it were a tangible thing. That day, when they had needed it so badly, the hot wind failed and the air was as still as brass. Lou and Winter took turns pulling the bamboo punkah and sponging Lottie, while Alex sat by her; holding her hands and pulling against her as she clung to them, dragging at them and screaming. The sweat ran down their faces and blinded their eyes, and Winter and Lou flinched and gasped at every scream, but Alex' voice remained steady and reassuring and Lottie's eyes clung desperately to his—as desperately as her hands. But before the morning was out Alex knew with a sick despair that he was fighting a losing battle.

Lottie's meager strength ebbed with the day, and Alex gave her brandy and cursed both man and nature for allowing any woman born with that narrowness of hip to conceive. He could not see how it was possible for the child to be born at all—let alone be born alive. And yet it was so nearly born. But the afternoon had gone, and Lottie's strength with it. She could do no more. He would have to do the rest himself. He looked at Lou and saw that her hands were shaking, and he turned his head and spoke over his shoulder to Winter: "Hold her for me."

Lottie's daughter was born just as the sun touched the level of the treetops, and long before the gold had left the sky, Lottie was dead. She had survived the birth, and she might have lived if she had fought to do so; but she had neither the strength nor the desire to hold onto life.

She had spoken only once. Lou had washed the tiny, whimpering creature and laid it against Lottie's thin shoulder, and Lottie's sunken eyes had opened slowly and painfully and she had looked at it. A last ray from the sinking sun had pierced through the bamboo screen and touched its small head, and Lottie's bloodless lips had curled in the shadow of a smile.

"Red hair," she whispered. "Like Edward's. Take care of him, Lou." And then she had died.

Lou had wept, but Winter had not cried for Lottie. That tiny red-headed morsel of humanity, if it lived, might have comforted Lottie, but it would never have made up to her for the loss of her Edward, or wiped out that picture of him dying cruelly before her eyes. She washed Lottie's light little body and dressed her again, and went out to the river before it became too dark to see, leaving Lou with the child.

Alex was sitting on a fallen block of stone among the jungle grass near the entrance to the Hirren Minar. He had his head in his hands, and in the dusk he had been almost invisible against the background of the bamboos that towered up behind him.

Winter stood watching him for a moment or two, and then she had gone to him and put her arms about him and laid her cheek against his hair. He turned his head against her shoulder with a tired sigh and his arms went around her quite gently. He stirred at last, moving his head so that his lips lay against the curve of her throat, and his arms had tightened about her, drawing her close. And then a peacock had screamed from beyond the bamboo brake—a harsh, grating cry that seemed to echo the gasping screams that had rung in their ears all that hot agonizing afternoon—and Winter felt Alex' body jerk almost as though he had been abruptly awakened from sleep. He pushed her away from him suddenly and violently, his hands coming up to grip her arms and wrench them away, and he stood up swiftly and said in a voice that was as hard and as rough as a steel file: "No, I'm damned if I will! Not after today. I won't let that happen to you. Go on—get back in there—" He bit the sentence off, swung round and disappeared into the dusk.

He had returned an hour later and fetched the heavy-bladed knife that was used for cutting through thick jungle, and gone out again. It had taken him the best part of the night to dig a grave that would be deep enough to protect Lottie's little body from marauding animals, but he had managed it at last.

They had buried her in the clear pearly light of the early morning, an hour before the sun rose, and Alex had said as much as he could remember of the service for the burial of the dead over her grave. He remembered a good deal of it, for India was a country where that service was used with regrettable frequency. Afterward he had gone off to bathe in the river at a spot higher up the bank, leaving the narrow beach by the tree to Winter and Lou, and had not returned until an hour after the sun had risen.

The upper room of the Hirren Minar was clean and swept and tidy, and yesterday and all the nerve-racking torture of those long, hot, agoniz-

ing hours seemed a year away. Winter had handed him food which she
had kept hot for him in a covered cooking pot among the embers of a
fire, and he had eaten it and watched Lou, who was feeding the baby
with water in which she had boiled a little rice. She dipped a clean rag
in the liquid and gave it to the tiny creature to suck, and there was a look
on her face that Alex had not thought it possible for Lou Cottar to wear.
A soft, absorbed wonder. He observed it with interest and a certain as-
tonished amusement—Mrs. Josh Cottar, of all people!

Lou said thoughtfully and with entire seriousness: "You'll have to get
me some milk. I wonder if we could keep a goat?"

Alex finished his meal and came over to look at the skinny, wrinkled
little object with the fluff of reddish-gold down on its head that had cost
Lottie her life, and looking at it he had a sudden warm feeling of achievement. He had not been able to save Lottie, but he had at least saved
this minute scrap of new life from dying before it had lived, and all at
once that seemed a thing as well worth doing as the saving of a Province. He touched the tiny waving hand, and felt it close about his finger
with the instinctive and unexpected tenacity of a sea anemone.

Alex laughed and said: "You shall have your goat, Lou, if I have to
steal it! What are you going to call her?"

"Amanda," said Lou promptly.

"Good Lord! Why? Did Lottie—"

"No," said Lou. "Lottie was sure it was going to be a boy. She never
knew it wasn't. It's just that I think Amanda is a nice name for her. It
means 'worthy of love.' "

Alex stroked the downy head with a forefinger and Lou looked up at
him and smiled. "Still three women on your hands, Alex."

"Four," said Alex with a grin. "You've forgotten the goat. And I can
clearly see that a goat is going to be more trouble than the rest of you
put together."

It was a prophecy that was to prove lamentably correct.

Alex had slept most of that day and had gone out at sunset. He had
returned at dawn dragging an exceedingly vocal goat procured for him
with suspicious ease by Kashmera, whom Alex suspected of having stolen
it. The goat had been loathe to accompany him, and he had been compelled to carry it for the best part of the way.

Lou and Winter had attempted to milk it, collectively and severally,
and had been reduced first to desperation and then to helpless mirth in
the process. Alex had refused to help. He said that he considered that
he had discharged his part in the affair by procuring the animal, and that
he was damned if he was going to turn *gopi*. They must learn to deal
with it themselves.

They had done so, and the baby throve. It was astonishingly tenacious
of life, and survived the untutored treatment to which it was subjected, as
it had survived the horrors and hazards of that pregnancy and premature
birth. The goat gave far more trouble. It evidenced a desire to stray and

could be trusted to eat its way through any and every rope. Alex constructed a strong door of thick bamboo poles to replace the flimsier curtain of grass over the entrance to the Hirren Minar, and they kept the goat in the lower chamber at night.

It had awakened them the second night by bleating plaintively and monotonously, and when at last it had ceased they had heard a rasping, scratching sound, and Alex, who had been sleeping on the open roof, had looked down over the ruined parapet and seen by the clear starlight and a waning moon the beautiful black-barred body of a tigress who crouched before the bamboo door, clawing at it with a taloned paw. The tigress had heard the movement above her and had looked up, her eyes glinting like green moons, and she had stared at him for a full minute before leaping away into the thickets.

Alex had strengthened the door, lashing a double layer of bamboo poles the thickness of his arm across and across it, and the next night the tigress had been back again. He heard the scrape of her claws, and lifting a lump of earth that he had taken the precaution to bring up with him, dropped it on her from above. There was a sharp and untiger-like yelp and she had bounded away into the jungle.

"Why didn't you drop something heavier?" demanded Lou, who had been an interested spectator.

"Because I have no desire to have a wounded tiger in this bit of the jungle," said Alex. "They are unpleasant things to have around."

"But it will only be back tomorrow night."

"Probably. But it won't get through that door. There's that baby of yours starting now! If it isn't one thing it's another! Who wouldn't be a bachelor?"

Lou had laughed and hurried back to feed the wailing child, and the next night they had been awakened at moonrise by a leopard snarling and tearing at the bamboo door. But apart from these disturbances the long, burning, breathless days passed peacefully enough.

The jungle dried and shriveled and turned brown about them, and the river shrank, but still the monsoon delayed. They never spoke of Lottie, as they never spoke of all those whom they had known in Lunjore, or of anything that had happened there. Their life went on as before, except that now there was the baby to look after in place of Lottie, and Lou had lost her restlessness.

Lou had never liked children; she had never wanted any of her own, or been in the least disappointed when none had been born to her. She had looked upon it as a blessing. But somewhere, unsuspected by anyone, least of all herself, there must have lurked an unquenchable spark of the maternal instinct, and now, unexpectedly, it had sprung alight. Perhaps Lottie, dying, had been able to sense its presence and its potential strength, for it was not to Alex or to Winter that she had spoken. She had said: "Look after him, Lou," and Lou had taken the child and looked at it with a sudden awe-struck and exultant sense of possession.

That sense of possession had grown stronger every day, and now she did not mind how long they stayed in the Hirren Minar. She was afraid of moving from it. They were safe here, and they must not take any risks. She could even bear the intolerable heat better because the child seemed to take no harm from it, but she waited and panted and prayed for the rains. If only the rains would break!

"Alex, how much longer will it be?"

"God knows!" said Alex. "Any day now."

The news from the outside world, if it could be believed, was not encouraging. Sir Henry Lawrence had fought a disastrous action at Chinut and had been heavily defeated, and now he and the British in Lucknow were closely besieged in the Residency. General Wheeler and the Cawnpore Garrison were reported to be at their last gasp in the torn and shattered and pitifully inadequate entrenchments that they had scratched up out of the earth, and where they had held out under the glaring heat and the rain of shot and shell since the sixth of June. Mutiny had broken out in Allahabad and the sepoys had murdered their officers and massacred all Christians. The only news that seemed to hold out hope was that the British still clung to the Ridge before Delhi, although their force was as yet more besieged than besieging.

"Wait yet awhile," urged Kashmera, as he had urged so often before. "Thou art safe in the jungle."

But the jungle had finished with them, and it would not let them wait.

33

ALEX had been setting a snare at the entrance to a small clearing some fifty yards from the Hirren Minar when he smelt smoke.

He had not been feeling at all well that day. His head ached, and he thought angrily that Lou or Winter had disobeyed orders and lit an early fire. Then he had realized that the hot wind that was rustling the dry grass and dead leaves was blowing toward the Hirren Minar, and not away from it. There was someone else in the jungle, and upwind of him. He left the snare and returned swiftly, pulling the grass back over the path that he had taken, and ordered the two women, who were about to leave for their evening bath, to get back into the upper room.

"Pull up the ladder and keep a revolver handy," said Alex peremptorily. "And drag the slab over that hole. I'm going to have a look around. Don't move until I come back."

. He had disappeared and they had waited a long time, making no noise and listening to the interminable croon of the hot wind and the monoto-

nous rustle and clank of the dry bamboos. Presently Winter had lifted
her head and sniffed as Alex had done.

"Smoke! So that's why—Lou, suppose it's some of the others! It might
be. We can't have been the only ones to get away."

"More likely charcoal burners," said Lou in a whisper. "And if it were
men hunting for us they wouldn't warn us by lighting fires."

Alex had returned half an hour later and called to them that they
could come down. He looked strained and uneasy. The smoke had come
strongly on the wind, but the wind was dying now with the dying day,
and soon it would be dark enough for him to verify his fears.

Lou, carrying the baby, had made straight for the river, but Winter
had stopped and looked at Alex with anxious eyes: "What is it?"

Alex' gaze was on the sky to the southwest. There had been clouds
in the sky all day. Dirty copper-colored clouds which he had hoped
might mean rain at last. But was there something more than clouds there?
He said: "I think the jungle is on fire somewhere over there. It may burn
out, but— Oh, well, we shall know soon."

The wind died and the smell of smoke died with it, but later, as the
sky darkened, a pink wavering glow that was not the sunset grew steadily
brighter, until it drowned out the last of the daylight and spanned the
horizon from north to south.

Alex watched it from the roof of the Hirren Minar. It may miss us,
he thought. Or it may burn out before it reaches us. But he had little
hope of it doing either. So little hope that he made a bundle of those few
things that seemed to him urgently necessary, and carried them down to
the river bank.

Presently the wind rose again, and now it brought with it not only the
smell of smoke, but drifting ash. Soon there would be sparks, and the
forest was tinder-dry from the scorching June days. He returned to find
the two women standing on the open roof watching the sky, their faces
clearly illumined by the distant glow. They turned together to face him,
and once again, as on that day in the jungle when they had fled from
Lunjore, their eyes were wide and strained, but without panic, and he
knew that the anxiety in Lou's was not for herself, but only for the child
she held.

Looking at them, Alex was conscious of a confused mixture of emotions
that included gratitude, relief, tenderness and a passionate admiration. He
found that his voice was a little difficult to control and said with unnecessary curtness: "Can either of you swim?"

"Yes," said Winter, who had spent a few weeks every summer at
Scarborough—Lady Julia considering the sea air good for growing girls.

"A little," said Lou Cottar. "But—but Amanda—"

Alex said: "We'll have to make some sort of raft. Just in case. Get me
all the ropes you can, Lou, and give that child some food. Light the lamp,
Winter—and get a fire lighted below. We'll have to see what we're doing."

He disappeared down the ladder and they heard him hacking down the heavy bamboo door that he had built to protect the goat.

They worked with feverish haste, tearing down the split-cane *chiks* and using them to face that triple platform of bamboo, and carrying down the box that Lou had been using as a cradle. The door made an admirable raft, and Alex found himself feeling grateful to the goat for the first time since they had acquired it. The perspiration poured off them as they worked, for the heat of the fire added itself to the remorseless heat of the June night, and the wind blew that heat across them so that soon it hurt to breathe. The air was full of smoke now and they could hear the crackle of the flames, while the light of the fire that Winter had lit in the stone room was no longer necessary, for the world about the Hirren Minar was as bright as though it were bathed in a red sunset.

Alex said: "Bring anything that isn't too heavy and that you think is worth bringing. I can manage this; it doesn't weigh so much. We may have half an hour or so yet, but it isn't safe to bet on it. Be as quick as you can."

He departed with the raft, and they went back up the ladder for the last time, and collecting all the food they could carry, took a last look about the queer stone chamber in which they had lived in such discomfort and found such strange happiness and content, and Winter smiled at it with sudden tears in her eyes, as though she were saying good-by to a dear friend. Then she helped Lou down the ladder with the baby, and they were out in the jungle and Lou was hurrying toward the river while Winter followed her, dragging the goat.

The fire was no longer a distant crackling chorus now, but a steady roar, and the sky was a brilliant rose-pink pall of smoke shot through with sparks. A bird was singing gaily among the branches of a thornbush as though it imagined that the dawn had broken, and the undergrowth was alive with movement. Peacocks, jungle fowl, porcupine, a fox, three jackals and a chital hind ran past them, making for the river, and there was a crashing among the bushes as a bull nilgai thrust its way into a clearing, saw them, and backed away snorting.

If the wind had died the fire would not have reached them for several hours, but the wind drove the sparks ahead of the wall of flame, and where they fell they started new fires, so that the roaring blaze leapt forward with seven-league boots and ate up the miles with terrifying swiftness.

Alex was waiting for them on the little shelving strip of bank where they had bathed so often. The makeshift raft floated high and light in the water, and he was lashing the tin box to the center of it. He took the baby from Lou and laid it in the box among an assortment of bundles, and stretched a strip of wet cloth above it as an added precaution against smoke and sparks. It was less easy to get the goat on board and safely tethered, but they managed it.

"You can't swim in that, Winter," said Lou, hurriedly divesting herself of her dress. "I'm sorry, Alex, but this is no time for modesty."

Alex grinned at her, and waded out as far as the steeply shelving bank allowed, while Winter, following Lou's example, removed her sari and rewound it, wrapping it around her in a straight strip so that it covered her from armpit to thigh.

Lou said anxiously, looking back at the jungle: "Don't let's go until we have to. It may miss us after all. It's still quite far away." Crouched in the cool water under the shelter of the high bank the heat was not so intolerable, and the river looked appallingly wide—the far bank as though it were miles away—and Lou remembered the muggers who haunted every Indian river, and shuddered.

Alex said: "Not a chance, I'm afraid. Look over there. They know."

Lou Cottar turned her head and looked. A herd of nilgai were plunging down the steep bank not twenty yards below them, and taking to the water to swim out steadily into the red-dyed river; the current taking them down in a long, slanting line toward the far shore. A moment later there was a crash above them as a wild boar, his tusks and his little pig eyes gleaming in the leaping light, slithered down the bank and without paying the smallest attention to them, launched himself into deep water. And then suddenly there were animals all about them, so that the steep banks seemed alive with terrified forest creatures, and for a moment or two they forgot their own danger in the wonder of that sight.

A tawny, spotted shape leapt down the bank and crouched on the narrow ledge almost within reach of their hands, snarling with terror; its tail lashing wildly. But the leopard's green eyes passed them by, for his fear and his hate were not for them, but for the fire behind him, and presently he too took to the water. From somewhere further up the bank they heard the unmistakable snarling roar of a tiger, and a troop of frantic monkeys leapt and howled in the tree above their heads. One of the monkeys, a mother clutching a skinny big-eyed baby, sprang down upon the raft and huddled against the bleating goat, chattering and grimacing.

"Come on," said Alex. "If we wait any longer we shall have a cargoload of stowaways." He found that he had to shout to make himself heard above the roar and crash, and that he felt oddly stupid and lightheaded. He would have liked to sit down in the water and stay where he was, but he pulled himself together with an effort and said: "Listen, Lou, I've rigged up a sort of towrope and I'll go ahead with it. If you're not much of a swimmer, keep hold of the raft and keep upstream of it. Winter—" He turned to look at her and fought down the choking fear that threatened him; the fear of the current, of the man-eating muggers of the river—"Winter, you push from behind. Give me as much help as you can, and—and don't for God's sake let go."

He had made a rough-and-ready harness of rope, and with it across his shoulders he struck out from the bank and felt the current catch him and draw him and the raft downstream, as a shower of sparks fell hissing into the river.

He did not glance back but swam on steadily, striving with everything in him to keep from being drawn too far down the stream, for the road and the shattered remains of the bridge lay only a mile away, and there would be men there—the mud-and-wattle tollhouse on the Oudh bank where he and Niaz had tied up the occupants on the day they blew up the bridge, and the huddle of huts behind it.

The oil-smooth surface of the water was filmed with ash and charred leaves and full of frantic, swimming animals, many of whom clawed at the raft and held onto it, dragging sodden, shivering little bodies onto the sheltering bamboos; squirrels, rats, mice and a bedraggled mongoose. There were pigs and deer—sambhur, chital, kaka, blackbuck, nilgais, jackals, panthers, tigers, a scaly four-foot iguana and a solitary elephant with a broken tusk in the river that night, swimming as desperately as the three humans for the safety of the far bank.

It seemed to Alex as though they would never reach the shallows. As though the river were endless. His head ached and his muscles seemed to have no strength in them, and there was a cramping pain in his stomach. The rope bit into his shoulders and caught across his throat and choked him, and he could feel the drag of the dead weight pulling to the pull of the current, for Lou could do little more than cling to it and keep afloat. And then quite suddenly there were sandbanks ahead of him, as though they had lifted from the river, and the current no longer pulled at him, and he had reached the shallows.

All about him wet furry shapes were dragging themselves onto the warm white sand, licking their fur and shaking themselves and crawling or scuttling away toward the distant line of trees, and Alex freed himself from the rope harness and dragged the makeshift raft forward until it grounded in the shallows.

He turned then at last, and saw that they were all there. The shivering goat, the baby lying placidly in its box, the monkey still clutching its round-eyed offspring, Lou Cottar on her knees, staring blindly ahead of her and breathing in deep gasps, and Winter lying full length in the shallows with her long hair cloaking her slim body in blackness and her chin on the edge of the raft. He walked over to her unsteadily and reached down a hand to pull her to her feet.

"I can't," said Winter, and laughed up at him. "I've got no clothes on."

"I like you without your clothes on," said Alex, and pulled her up into his arms and kissed her, holding her cool wet body close to him and tasting the water that ran into his mouth from their wet faces and their dripping hair. He held her for perhaps a minute, oblivious of Lou Cottar, and then released her gently, and putting her away from him bent to untie the goat.

The monkey, abruptly taking fright, leapt from the raft and fled across the sand: and suddenly they were all laughing. Laughing helplessly from strain and overwhelming relief, and because they were still together and still alive. They stopped at last, and turned to look at the wall of flame that was the bank that they had left.

They had left it only just in time, for hissing, burning branches were falling into the water and there was nothing but flame to the turn of the river that hid the bridgehead. The Hirren Minar must be somewhere in the center of that furnace, and tomorrow there would be nothing but miles of black, smoldering desolation where yesterday there had been dense jungle.

A hot spark fell on Alex' bare arm and he winced and swung round suddenly to look at the line of trees behind them and beyond the long stretch of the sand. Lou Cottar, following his look, said with a catch in her voice: "It can't reach as far as this!"

The flames could not leap that wide expanse of river, but the wind was carrying stray sparks across it, and the jungle everywhere was tinder dry. But they dared not remain exposed to the brilliant light at the edge of the shallows. They would have to make for the trees.

Alex bent without a word, and untying the box from which Lou had removed the baby, filled it with the various things that they had brought with them, while Winter retrieved the wet folds of her sari from about her ankles, and dragging the goat, followed them across the wide level of the sands to the shelter of the grass and the casurina scrub that fringed it.

The long swim across the river had cooled them, but now they were hot again. Unbelievably hot. The air scorched their lungs with each breath that they drew, and the river and the wide sandbanks and the line of the jungle were lit with a bright pulsating glare as though it were a stage in the full blaze of footlights and gas lamps. Every blade and leaf and twig of the jungle behind them stood out from its fellows, high-lighted and black-shadowed, and here and there a floating spark would alight and wink and go out, or catch at a brittle powder-dry spear of grass and show a brief spurt of flame.

A tuft of pampas grass twenty yards from them caught alight and flared up, and Lou caught her breath in a harsh gasp, and snatching at the end of Winter's wet sari, dragged the end of it free and drew it across the child's face. She said desperately: "It's almost dry already! We shall have to get back to the water. Alex—"

Winter saw Alex' face stiffen queerly and knew that he was visualizing taking to the river again and going down with the current—for how far? And for how long? They might have to go for miles, hemmed in between two walls of fire, with only that makeshift bamboo raft to hold to. Then suddenly and unexpectedly he gave a dry sob of relief, and holding out his hand, palm upward, said: *"Rain!"* It was the monsoon at last.

Unbelievingly, incredulously, they turned their faces up to the furnace of the sky, the hot drifting ash and the falling sparks, and felt something warm and wet splashing upon their parched skins.

"Wait here," said Alex. "I'm going to get the raft." He leapt down the bank and they saw him race across the sands as the first heavy, blessed drops began to fall. He upended it and shouldered it and presently he was back again, panting and breathless. "Get in among the trees; under the thickest stuff you can find," he said jerkily. They forced their way into the thicker jungle, with the raindrops splashing onto their shoulders and the glare from the burning trees on the far bank lighting their way, and using the raft as a roof, wedged it at an angle to carry off the rain and make a rough shelter among the trees, stowing the bundles and the baby under it as the first slow drops turned to the full, drumming downpour of the monsoon.

They stood out in it, letting it pour over them as it roared out of the sky like some tidal wave such as the one that had overwhelmed lost Atlantis, drowning out the roar of the burning jungle. It was not rain as Winter had known rain. It was a solid wall of water falling on them and smothering out thought; and cool—and cool.

The glare diminished and died at last, and they were in wet darkness in the drumming, drenching rain. The thick jungle and the platform of bamboo and matting were an inadequate shelter against that torrential downpour, but they did not care. It had cooled that appalling heat and they could breathe again.

It was still raining when the dawn broke grayly over the drenched miles of blackened, smoking wasteland, the pock-marked face of the river and the sodden jungle around them where the canes and the tall grass sagged under the weight of water.

Winter heard Alex stir, and opened her eyes to see him walk out into the pouring grayness. She sat up pushing the wet hair back from her face and shoulders, and saw that Lou was still asleep, wearing nothing but the cotton chemise in which she had swum the river, and with her arm about the box in which the baby slept. They had propped up the lid with sticks last night so as to provide extra shelter for the baby and the various belongings that were wedged at one end of the box, and the baby, though presumably damp in the manner of babies, appeared to be otherwise dry.

Winter rose to her knees and wringing out her wet hair, plaited it and looked ruefully at her damp sari. But there was nowhere in the jungle that was dry, for the warm rain drummed on the leaves, pouring off them in fountains and cascades and runnels, and the steady voice of the water drowned out all other sound. There would be no need to bathe in the river today, thought Winter, and then realized with a sense of shock that it was not going to be so easy to reach the river from this bank, for to gain the brink would mean exposing themselves at the edge of a wide belt of open sand a long way from the safe shelter of the trees.

Struck by this thought she turned to rummage cautiously among the few articles they had brought with them from the Hirren Minar, and found a cooking pot which she set to catch the water that was sluicing off the roof of their temporary shelter. The noise and the movement failed to wake Lou who slept on while Winter instituted a search in the near-by jungle for any fuel dry enough to burn. Only yesterday the whole forest could have been lit with a single match, but this morning it was no easy matter to find a handful of grass and dead leaves with which to make a fire.

Presently the baby raised a feeble wail and the sound woke Lou, who sat up, rubbing her eyes and after a time came out and joined Winter. She looked up at the gray, weeping skies and round at the sodden jungle and said briskly: "We shall have to build a hut."

Winter looked at her and smiled, remembering Lou's previous restless desire to escape from the jungle, and contrasting it with her present and instant desire to construct a more permanent shelter so that she could remain safely in hiding during the coming months. Lou returned the smile. They could still smile in spite of all that had happened to them, and they were still smiling when Alex returned, pushing through the drenching undergrowth. But at the sight of his face their own faces were suddenly sober.

"What is it?"

"That bloody goat!" said Alex forcefully.

Lou gave a choked cry and ran to the side of the shelter where they had tethered the goat, but there was nothing there but a chewed piece of rope, and the goat had gone for good.

"I can only hope that some wet and hungry tiger has made good use of it," said Alex sourly. "It will be a richly deserved end. Don't be silly, Lou! Give it some rice, or boil some flour and water. No one is going to notice smoke today."

"Will you stop calling her 'it!' " snapped Lou in sudden and irrational fury.

Alex grinned. "You're getting damned maternal, Lou. One day you'll persuade yourself that it—sorry, she—is your own child."

"She is," said Lou, and went to join Winter who was building a fire in a hollow tree that she had discovered some twenty yards from their shelter.

Alex looked after her with a half-smile that turned into a grimace of pain. He went into the shelter and found the small tin of opium pills and swallowed down a few of them with brandy. I cannot go sick now, thought Alex dizzily. Not now—

But no amount of brandy and opium could keep the fever at bay, and half an hour later Winter, bringing him hot food on a plate of leaves, found him lying under a tree a few yards from the shelter, his body jack-knifed with pain and his breathing harshly audible above the steady patter of the rain. His brown, sunburned skin had an oddly gray tinge to it and seemed to be stretched too tightly over his cheekbones, and there were dark patches under his closed eyes. Winter put the food down very carefully, surprised to find that her hands were steady when her heart was beating with such terrified swiftness, and laid a hand lightly on his forehead.

The harsh heat of it appalled her, and Alex opened his eyes and looked at her between narrowed lids. He seemed to have some difficulty in focusing her. His forehead creased in a scowl of pain and he said in a blurred, difficult voice: "Be all right—only dysentery. Tell Lou—keep that baby away—dangerous—"

There had followed a nightmare interval of days and nights—none of them could ever have said how many, it had seemed like a month and was probably no more than three days—in which Alex' body had been torn and burned and wasted with dysentery and raging fever, and it seemed to Winter that he could not live. She had not known the meaning of dysentery, for though it was a plague common to all India, any explanation of it, or of what a severe attack entailed, was not considered a suitable subject for the delicate susceptibilities of ladies. She had stayed with him day and night, doing everything that it was possible to do for him, endlessly and tirelessly; holding his head on her lap, forcing the brandy and opium that were the only medicines they possessed down his parched throat, feeding him with rice water, listening to him rave when the fever mounted and feeling every cramping pain as though it were a pain in her own body.

She slept only when exhaustion overtook her, and then with her hand on him so that she woke when he moved. She had never in all her short life seen an illness like this, or imagined it, and at times it seemed worse to her than the birth of Lottie's baby had been. But Alex held onto life, and it was, in the end, Lou who betrayed them.

Lou had looked at Alex and said: "I don't think it's only dysentery. I think he's got some sort of fever on top of it. Unless—unless it's cholera."

She had kept away for fear of carrying the infection to the baby. But the pouring rain, and the sudden breaks when the rain would stop and the sodden jungle steamed under the molton heat of the sun, had not suited the baby as the dry heat of the Hirren Minar had done. The baby wailed endlessly and heartbreakingly, and vomited up the rice water and the thin gruel that Lou made with flour and coarse country sugar. And the supplies of even those commodities were running low.

"She will die without milk!" said Lou, wild-eyed and desperate. "She must have proper food—she must!" She had walked up and down, clutching the wailing infant to her breast and said passionately: "Why can't I feed her myself? Why aren't we made so that we could if we wanted to? She needs it, and I can't give her anything—*anything!*"

Winter did not hear her. She watched Alex' haggard, burnt-out face and dry, cracked lips, and her mind and her heart were as desperate as Lou's. She did not even notice when Lou went away, and it was only when she found that there was no fire lit—for Lou had been dealing with all the cooking—and no food prepared, that she realized that Lou and the baby had gone. And even then she imagined that they could not be far away.

The rain had stopped and the jungle that had been so brown and brittle only a few days ago was now a hot, humid greenhouse in which new grass and leaves and creepers and every variety of growing thing had sprung up overnight in lush abandon. The damp heat was less bearable than the dry heat had been, and Alex seemed to struggle for every breath he drew.

The sound of his labored breathing tore at Winter's heart, and for the first time in the long weeks since she had run from the Lunjore Residency she turned her face away and wept: wept hopelessly and helplessly and silently; the hot tears running into the grass roots as swiftly as the raindrops that had poured down onto them the day before.

She did not know how long she lay there, face downward on the steaming ground, and she did not hear Alex move, but his hand touched her and she lifted her head and saw that his eyes were open. There was a faint frown in them but they were entirely lucid and no longer clouded and unfocused or blind with pain. He spoke with a palpable effort and in a voice that was barely a whisper: "Why are you crying?"

Winter brushed away the tears with the back of her hand and said unsteadily: "I'm not—not now."

She had left him and stumbled away to light the fire and boil water. And it had been the first time in days that she had not left him expecting to find that he was dead when she returned. She had made a brew of flour and rice water and sugar, and stirred brandy into it and taken it back to him; and his eyes were still lucid.

He drank the concoction because he was too weak to refuse it, and lay still afterward looking ahead of him under half-lowered lids. Presently he said: "How long?"

"I—I don't know," said Winter. "Days. Don't talk."

"I shall be all right now," said Alex in the same difficult whisper, and he had closed his eyes and gone to sleep with his head in her lap.

Winter had slept too, her head thrown back against the tree trunk behind her; and when she heard voices and someone had shaken her she thought it was Lou.

But it was not Lou. It was a party of men armed with lathees and in charge of a man who wore a rusty sword and carried an old-fashioned musket.

"These are not sahib-*log!*" said one of the men scornfully. "They are but the *naukar-log* of the mem."

But one of them had peered closer and said: "Nay, they have *Angrezi* blood in them at least. We will take them. Up, thou!" The speaker stirred Alex with his foot and Winter said furiously and in the vernacular: "Let be! Canst thou not see that he is sick?"

The tone and the quality of the Urdu she used gave the men pause, and they looked at her doubtfully. It occurred to them suddenly that this might after all be an Indian lady of good family. Her fingers tightened imperatively on Alex' shoulder, and he had obeyed the unspoken warning and remained silent. He could not have risen if he had tried. The man with the musket said uncertainly: "Of what city art thou?"

"Of Lucknow," said Winter without hesitation. "Of the household of

Ameera Begum, wife of Walayat Shah, who is my cousin and lives in the Gulab Mahal by the mosque of Sayid Hussain. This man is of Persia, and my—my husband."

The men observed her, owl eyed, and consulted in whispers, and Winter heard the leader say: "What matter? The order is for all to be sent to Pari. Send these also."

They had rifled the contents of the shelter in which Lou and the baby had lived, removing the revolvers and the shotgun and anything else they could find, and ten minutes later they had moved off through the jungle, taking Winter and Alex with them.

Alex, helped to his feet, had not been able to stand without support, let alone walk, and they had used the roof of the shelter to carry him on. It had taken them surprisingly little time to reach the road, and Winter realized that they must have been swept down by the current further than she had supposed on the night that they crossed the river. There had been a bullock cart waiting, on the road, and a curious crowd of villagers— and Lou Cottar.

Lou had stared at Winter and Alex in horror and said hoarsely: "I didn't mean—I didn't know this would happen! I thought I might find a village where I could get milk. And—and they did help me. They were kind. I didn't realize they would go back to see if there was anyone else. I only came by the sand because it was easier, and—and they followed the marks. I thought—"

Her voice choked and stopped and Winter said: "It's all right, Lou." And then they were thrust into the cart and jolted away down the long, uneven road toward Pari.

34

It had been dark by the time the captives reached the little walled town near the jheel; the town that Alex and Niaz had skirted on that autumn night when they had ridden from Khanwai and crossed the bridge of boats hidden under the sacks and the sugar cane in the bullock carts.

The cart that now carried Alex, Winter, Lou and Amanda, creaked to a halt beside a gateway in a mud wall, and they were taken out and hustled across a dark courtyard and into a long, low-ceilinged room lit by a single guttering cresset. The two men who had carried Alex laid him on the floor and the door banged behind them. An iron bar clanged into place and someone at the far end of the room stood up in the shadows beyond the circle of light and said hoarsely and incredulously: "Winter!"

Winter was on her knees beside Alex, and she looked up, startled; blinking a little in the dim light that seemed dazzling after the darkness outside. A face moved into the range of the lamp and stared down at her wide-eyed: a strange, haggard face, dirty and unshaven and with a bloodstained bandage tied about its head. She looked up at it for a long moment, puzzled and uncertain, before she recognized it. And then at first she did not believe it, for it was, incredibly, Carlyon who stood there. Carlyon whom she had last seen on the veranda of the little dak bungalow beyond the ford on the road to Lunjore, and whom she had thought to be —if she had thought of him at all—several thousand miles away in England.

There were other voices behind him, and other faces. Eight other faces; tired, dirty—and British.

Carlyon said hoarsely: "Winter! What are you doing here? They said you'd all been killed!" His voice was as raw-edged and ragged as his clothes, and other faces that Winter knew separated themselves from the shadows: Captain Garrowby—Dr. O'Dwyer—Mrs. Hossack—

Mrs. Hossack clutched at Lou Cottar and wept, and Captain Garrowby said: "Mrs. Barton!—Mrs. Cottar! We thought you must all be dead! We thought that we were the only ones who had got away. Who is that with you?" He lifted the lamp and said: "Good God!—it's Randall!"

"Only just," said Alex in a whisper. "Hello, Garrowby. How did you— get out?"

There were charpoys in the room, six of them, placed end to end along the walls, and Captain Garrowby and Dr. O'Dwyer had lifted Alex onto one of them, and he had lain there and listened to the story of another escape.

The Garrowbys and Dr. and Mrs. O'Dwyer and Mrs. Hossack and her four children had not been to the Residency and so had escaped the massacre. Mrs. Hossack had intended to go but had been delayed, for Dr. O'Dwyer had been at her bungalow to see her eldest child, a seven-year-old girl, who had been suffering from hot weather fever. Captain Hossack, of Colonel Packer's regiment, had been shot down on the parade ground by his men, and his orderly had ridden to warn Mrs. Hossack to escape. The doctor, whose bungalow was next door, had run to fetch his wife and they had all entered the Hossacks' waiting carriage, intending to take refuge at the Residency. But the Garrowbys had stopped them. Captain Garrowby of the 93rd had been warned by his men, and he had ridden for his bungalow and bundled his wife into the trap and had turned the corner into the Residency road to see an obviously hostile crowd collecting before the gates. He had turned the trap, deciding to make for the river, and had met the Hossacks' carriage. They had all made for the bridge and had crossed it at least two hours before Alex and Niaz reached it.

They had said no word at the bridge of the panic in Lunjore, for fear of being stopped, but at Pari they had been attacked by a mob which had included mutinous sepoys from the disbanded 7th Regiment, and had turned and driven back furiously the way they had come. Abandoning the carriage and trap they had taken to the jungle and hidden there.

One of the Hossack children had been killed and Captain Garrowby and Mrs. O'Dwyer had been wounded in the firing, and Mrs. O'Dwyer had died two days later. They had wandered in the jungles, living on roots and berries, and first one and then another of the two elder Hossack children had died, and later Mrs. Garrowby too had died of heat stroke and exhaustion. Captain Garrowby and the doctor, with Mrs. Hossack and her remaining child—a baby of six months—had been driven to ask help at a village on the outskirts of Pari, and the villagers had taken them in and treated them kindly. But three days earlier they had been put into a covered cart and brought to this house—they did not know why, or how long they would remain there. They had been given food, and had not been ill-used, but the atmosphere and the attitude of their jailers were not reassuring. The four other captives had arrived on the following day: Lord Carlyon, the Rev. Chester Dobbie, Mr. Climpson, and Miss Keir— the sole survivors of a party of fifteen Europeans who had hoped to escape from Oudh and had been attacked and massacred at a village five miles away. They too had been fugitives for many days before being captured and brought here.

Winter had paid no attention to the recital of escape and misery, for her eyes had looked past Carlyon to Dr. O'Dwyer, and she had gone straight to him and pulled him across the room to Alex, and after that she had only watched his face and listened to what he said. "He'll do," said Dr. O'Dwyer reassuringly. And then a native woman had brought coarse food and a bowl of fresh milk, and Lou had fed the baby and told the story of the last weeks, and the voices and the faces and the heat of the low-ceilinged room had mixed and melted together and Winter had fallen asleep and had not stirred or wakened until the sun was high in the sky.

There was an enclosed courtyard on the far side of the room where the prisoners had spent the night, and the door leading out into it had been unlocked at sunrise.

The same native woman had brought food again for the captives, but she had refused to answer questions and had gone out to the far side of the courtyard to join a crowd of gapers who peered curiously at the Feringis, discussing them and speculating about them and chewing pan.

"What do you suppose they mean to do with us?" said Lou uneasily, rocking the baby.

"Keep us as hostages, I think," said the Rev. Dobbie, who thought no such thing but trusted that God would pardon him that comforting lie.

"Hostages for what?" inquired Lou.

Mr. Climpson, a middle-aged magistrate who had escaped from his burning bungalow with the assistance of a loyal servant, said: "The local Tulakdar has been wavering for some time. He cannot decide which side is going to win, and he seems to have given orders that any Europeans found in these parts were to be taken prisoner but not harmed. I think he means well enough, but he is getting nervous. The whole of Oudh is now in revolt, and since the Chinut affair the British position looks bad. I think that is why he has had any of us known to be in the district brought here."

"Yes, yes," said the Rev. Dobbie, nodding reassuringly at the women. "I am sure that is right. He feels that we shall be safer here. That bar on the door may keep us in, but it also serves to keep others out."

Carlyon, leaning against the jamb of the open door, surveyed him under drooping lids and wondered if the little man really believed that? Carlyon had heard the story of Jhansi and the public slaughter of the Europeans who had accepted the Rani's terms of surrender. That hapless garrison had been roped in three lines—children, women and men—and bound and helpless they had been butchered in that order, so that the women had been forced to see their children die before their eyes, and the men to see both die in turn before their own end came.

He had heard too—for the news had been told to Mr. Climpson by the headman of the village where they had lain hidden before being brought to Pari—of the massacre of the Cawnpore Garrison who had accepted the offer of surrender and safe conduct by Dundoo Pant, the Nana Sahib. The exhausted survivors had been allowed to embark in boats that were to take them to Allahabad, but once the last man was on board the rush roofs of the boats had been set alight by the boatmen, who leapt out into the water as the watchers on the bank opened fire on the blazing, drifting targets. And so the last of the Cawnpore Garrison had died, with the exception of some two hundred women and children who had struggled ashore and been taken captive.

In the light of these stories Carlyon was inclined to take a very different view of their situation from the ones advanced by either Mr. Climpson or the Rev. Dobbie. It seemed to him far more likely that they were being kept alive in order to provide a Roman holiday for the mob when a suitable occasion should arise: the type of public spectacle that the hapless garrisons of Jhansi and Cawnpore had provided.

I should have gone home, thought Carlyon. I must have been mad. . . . He had meant to go. He had returned to Delhi, raging because Winter had escaped him, and had heard later, through friends of the Abuthnots, of her marriage. But he had not gone home. He still wanted her more than he had ever wanted anything in his life, and he could not bring himself to admit defeat and return to England.

Leaning against the door he watched her now as she lay asleep. The three other women, in their soiled bedraggled Western clothes, looked haggard and ugly with anxiety and exhaustion. But this relaxed, sleeping creature managed still to be beautiful, though it was a different beauty from that which had attracted his instant attention in the ballroom at Ware.

This was a woman, and no longer a girl. A woman thin-faced from strain, and sleeping the sleep of utter exhaustion; but still as lovely a thing to look at as any man—even one as weary and desperate and as frightened as himself—could wish to see. In that hot, horrible room, surrounded by her fellow captives in their stained and ragged clothes, she looked as colorful as a poppy growing on a rubbish dump, and merely to look at her in some way served to lessen his fear and his despairing fury, and serve as an assurance that the world still contained other things besides hate and terror and violence.

Carlyon became aware that he himself was being watched, and looking beyond Winter he encountered Captain Randall's gray, speculative gaze, and was conscious of a sudden flare of hostility and antagonism. That familiar antagonism that this man had aroused in him from the moment that he had first seen him in the drawing room of the Abuthnots' bungalow in Delhi.

They had both escaped from violent deaths by the narrowest of margins; they had lived as hunted animals, and they were herded together now as captives. They had seen sights that would haunt their sleep as long as they lived—and they did not know if they might live as long as another day, or another hour. But for a moment they could forget it all and stare at each other with antipathy and cold anger; the greater issues giving place to an instinct as elementary and as animal as that which drives rival stags to fight in the spring.

Yet another bedraggled captive had come to swell the ranks of the prisoners that day. An elderly Eurasian clerk who had been found hiding in a village some five miles to the south.

"It is not the country people who are cruel," said Mr. Lapeuta in his soft singsong voice. "They are like us, you know—veree ordinary people. It is thee townspeople and thee sepoys who are hot against us. I think that thee Tulakdar of these parts will not kill us, but I think that he wishes to be rid of us, for he is fearful of thee mulvis, who preach against us, and he would like to wash his hands of us all. If there is better news, then doubtless he will keep us here, so that he can show how he has sheltered us, and gain much reward. But if thee news is bad, then I think he will send us away."

The accuracy of Mr. Lapeuta's forecast was proved within three days. News from Lucknow trickled into Pari: news that took the heart out of the captives, put heart into the rabble and frightened the Tulakdar into ridding himself, Pilate wise, of the responsibility of the fugitive Europeans whom he was holding captive.

Sir Henry Lawrence was dead. He had been killed in the beleaguered Residency at Lucknow, and all over India men heard the news with a catch of the breath. Now that he had gone it would surely be only a matter of days before the Residency was captured and its defenders massacred as the garrison of Cawnpore had been.

The Tulakdar wavered no longer, and hastened to rid himself of the haggard band of British before they were murdered by the mob under circumstances that might involve him in trouble in the event—which now appeared less likely—of the Hellborn ultimately defeating the insurgents and regaining power.

He sent in more and better food, permitted the services of a barber, allowed the women facilities for the washing and mending of clothes, and having impressed his excellent intentions upon them, had them hurried by night into a covered cart such as purdah women travel in, so that they might not be seen and dragged out by the way, and sent them off under guard, the men in one cart and the women and the two children in the other.

The four days and nights that followed were a horror that equaled anything that Winter and Lou had yet endured. The cart made slow progress, for the heavy rains had turned the roads into quagmires, and the torrential downpour soaked through the inadequate covering and drenched the huddled occupants. And when it ceased the sun turned the hooded cart into a steam bath in which the perspiration poured off them, soaking them afresh and less pleasantly, and the temperature rose until it became difficult to breathe.

There had been no sign or sound of the second cart. They did not know what had become of their fellow captives, or if they would ever see them again; and they heard no news in those days and so did not know that on one of them the last survivors of the Cawnpore Garrison had died, and with them, Sophic Abuthnot.

Little Sophie Abuthnot, as small and fair and fragile as Lottie had been, had survived both that ghastly siege in General Wheeler's pitifully inadequate entrenchments, and the horrors of the massacre in the boats at the Sati Chauri Ghat, only to meet a more terrible fate. For the guns of the British advance could be heard at Cawnpore, and Nana Dundoo Pant had heard in them the bitter knell of his hopes. All the evil fury and hate of which he was capable, and which Alex had seen in his face and heard in his voice in the vault beneath the ruins at Khanwai, had been let loose on the only victims that remained in his hands—the two hundred exhausted, hopeless, helpless women and children who were herded like animals in one small building, the *bibigurh*. He had listened to Havelock's guns and had given the order for their murder.

It had taken all day to kill them, for they had shrieked and dodged and twisted and striven to protect their children. But it had been done at last, and by nightfall the floor of the *bibigurh* was deep in blood and littered with the bodies of the dead and dying, and when the new day dawned the butchers had dragged out the corpses and flung them into a well outside the house. Sophie had not been dead when they had thrown her down, but she had died under the weight of the dead. And half India shuddered in horror and drew back from the edge of the pit they had digged, for that massacre turned many men who would have fought the British to the bitter end to lay down their arms and return to their homes.

"There can be no blessing on such a deed," said Ameera's husband Walayat Shah, who had hated the British and had himself taken part in attack after attack upon Sir Henry Lawrence's beleaguered garrison in the Lucknow Residency. But on the day that he had heard the news of the murder of the women and children in the *bibigurh* at Cawnpore he had broken his sword in two and thrown away his musket, and had come back to the Gulab Mahal and had not left it again. "We cannot prevail," said Walayat Shah. "The Jehad is dead. Those who slew the women and the babes have slain it also. To slay in battle or in hot blood, that is well. And to kill men, if they be unbelievers, is to achieve Paradise. But to slaughter captive women who have suffered the harshness of war and sorrow, and been robbed thereby of all strength and will, is a deed to blacken the sun. I will fight no more against the Feringis, for God can no longer be on our side."

The four women in the covered cart had been given little food and insufficient water, and Lou Cottar's face aged with every crawling hour. Mrs. Hossack, cradling her small son, had wept and moaned with a hopeless and despairing monotony, and Miss Keir had suffered from bouts of sickness that added to the stench of the broiling, steaming cart. They had given the best of the food and almost all of the water to the two children, and Lou had made a paste of boiled rice and water and fed it to the baby with her finger tip.

The scarcity of food had been bearable, but the lack of water in that terrible heat had been a torment that had only been partially relieved on the fourth day when Janet Keir began to shriek and rave and tear frantically at the side of the cart, and Winter had flown at the escort with a flood of words that she was not even aware that she knew. Daunted by this blazing-eyed virago who could curse them so efficiently in their own tongue, the men had produced at the next stopping place not only water but milk, though little enough of either.

The sun sank in a blaze of blood-red light that pierced through the chinks of the cart and its covering, but the darkness brought no relief. Winter's mouth was dry and her tongue swollen and her throat parched with thirst. Her head and her body ached with one vast throbbing ache that seemed to beat like a gong in her brain. How many days had they been in the cart? How many times had the sun gone down? She could not remember. Mrs. Hossack moaned no more, and the child who had wailed weakly all day was silent. Miss Keir too had ceased to writhe and mutter and beg for water, and lay still at last. Were they dead? Or were they only asleep like Lou?—or was Lou dead too?

She became dimly aware that the cart was passing through crowded streets. Lights and voices and noise pressed about it and somewhere guns were firing; guns and a ceaseless, distant crackle of musketry. There was a smell of cooked food and a pungent aromatic scent of ghee and dung fires and *masala*; of roasting *chunna*, hot dust and decaying matter; of sandal-wood and sewage and burning oil—the scent of an Indian bazaar.

The noises fell away and at last the cart stopped with a creaking jolt, and there were more voices. Rough voices, angry voices, shrill voices, whispering voices; and then the stout cloth that was bound over the end of the cart was unfastened, and the four dazed, semiconscious women were dragged out to stumble and fall to the ground, their legs giving way under them.

There was a man with a drawn sword in his hand, shouting, and another man with a musket, and Winter thought numbly: They are going to kill us, but it seemed a matter of supreme indifference. And then someone ran to her and lifted her, and the voices and the lights and the shouting men spun together in a circle and turned into darkness.

The Gulab Mahal

35

WINTER awoke to find herself lying on a low bed in a strange room. It was still dark, but the graying sky beyond the window gave enough light to show the outline of the room.

A gray fog of utter hopelessness filled her mind, and she closed her eyes and lay still, feeling that grayness engulf her. Alex had gone—everything had gone. There was nothing to live for any more—not even Lottie.

The light brightened slowly, turning from the first pallid whisper of dawn to the clear glow that precedes the sunrise, and the silence gave place to familiar sounds; faint and few at first, but gathering in number and volume. A rustle and a twitter of birds; the chatter of a squirrel and the creak of a well wheel; a conch blowing in a distant temple and a muezzin crying the call to prayer from the minaret of a mosque.

The brightening light beat against her closed eyelids, and the gray fog in her brain lifted and shredded away like mist drifting off the river in the early morning, and slowly and almost imperceptibly the pain in her heart lessened and peace took its place.

The glow beyond her closed eyes brightened and she opened them on the same vision that she had seen once before when she had lain in the river by the Hirren Minar and had wished for death. The rose-pink sky and the formal patterns of leaves and flowers and birds. The vision that had once before drawn her back from despair and the dream that had glowed before her mind's eye for so many cold years. But this time it was real. This was the Gulab Mahal. . . .

She lay quite still, not stirring, barely breathing; thinking confusedly that she was asleep—or dead. It could not be true! When at last she moved it was to stretch out a hand and touch the green parrot on the wall beside her.

Firishta—it was Firishta! The old, long-forgotten name from her childhood returned to her. So he was not a real bird after all. She had thought that they were real—the flowers and trees and birds who lived and moved against a rose-pink sky. They were not alive and they had never been alive.

They were carved and molded in painted and polished plaster. Why had she not remembered that? But it was still Firishta. And it was, incredibly, wonderfully, the Gulab Mahal.

She was safe at last. She had come home.

From somewhere in the distance there came the sound of gunfire, but she did not hear it. She rose and walked slowly about the room in a waking dream, running her hands over the dear familiar flower patterns, caressing the painted birds and beasts. She did not know that this was the room in which she had been born and in which Sabrina had died. She knew only that every foot of it was familiar and beloved. She saw the crescent-shaped shadow steal across the floor, and remembered it too, and did not fear it, as Sabrina had done, for it was linked with love.

She did not know how she had come there, or know that it was the Tulakdar of Pari's determination to play safe that had been responsible. The Tulakdar had remembered what his men had told him of the woman who was no *Angrezi* and who claimed kinship with the wife of Walayat Shah of Lucknow. He would send them to the care of Walayat Shah, and thus his hands would be clean. Walayat Shah might spare the woman if she were indeed blood kin to his wife, and although he would undoubtedly hand over the remainder of the party to those who would make a public spectacle of their death, the woman at least would be able to testify that he, the Tulakdar, had only acted for the best.

The heavy curtain over the doorway rustled and lifted, and Winter turned at the sound and saw that it was Ameera. They clung to each other and wept and did not speak for a long time, and then Ameera had held her off at arm's length and looked at her.

"It is true then!" said Ameera. "I thought it a dream. So thou hast come home; but in no auspicious hour. Dost thou know that I have spent the night upon my knees before my husband, begging for thy life and for the lives of those with thee? He would have turned all from the door, but Hamida was in the courtyard and she saw thee and ran to me. At first I did not believe; and then I knew that it could be no chance that brought thee here. This surely was written. For hadst thou come two days ago, or even one, I could not have saved thee. My husband was hot against thy people, and he hates them still and would rid himself of all whom the Tulakdar of Pari sent hither. But because of the word that was brought from Cawnpore, he will hold his hand."

So it was Sophie who had saved them—Sophie and all those women who had died in such fear and agony in the *bibigurh*.

For all the captives from Pari had arrived at the Gulab Mahal, though they had been brought for safety's sake by different roads, and all had been given shelter. Walayat Shah, remembering Cawnpore, had looked upon it quite simply as a penance laid upon him by God that he should risk his own life, and that of his sons and the whole household, in order to protect the lives of a weary handful of hated Feringis. He knew that if it should become known in the city that he was housing these people, their lives, and probably his own, would not be worth a moment's purchase. But he had taken them in. They were lodged in a secluded wing of the Rose Palace adjoining the zenana quarters. The rooms were hot and cramped, but the one on the ground floor, allotted to Lou, Mrs. Hossack, Miss Keir and the two babies, gave onto a large private garden that was separated from the rest of the gardens by a high wall, and was full of orange and loquat trees and a tangle of roses and jasmine. Six of the men shared a room immediately above it, and above that again, reached by a steep, narrow stair, was an isolated square of roof screened from the view of the zenana roofs by a wall and a pavilion that enclosed one end of it, where they had put Alex.

The pavilion was little more than a shallow porch opening onto the roof, with a boxlike enclosure behind it for sanitary purposes, and it had been allotted to Alex who, as a sick man, it had been thought best to segregate from the others instead of allowing him to share their cramped quarters: Walayat Shah having no desire to find all his unwelcome guests falling sick.

Winter had been given Sabrina's room as by right, and she had begged that Lou might share it, instead of being penned in a far smaller apartment on the ground floor with Mrs. Hossack and Janet Keir. Three of the most trusted servants of the household had been put in charge of the Feringis, who had been given native dress to wear in place of their own ragged garments, and were not permitted to go even into the secluded garden except between sunset and dawn. They were kept completely segregated from the other inhabitants of the Gulab Mahal, and they had little fault to find with this, for they lived in daily and hourly fear of discovery and death.

The continuous rattle of musketry, punctuated by the boom of guns, came clearly to their ears all day and for a large part of every night, and was a continual reminder to them not only that they were not the only British in Lucknow, but of the peril in which they stood. They could hear the crash of exploding mines as the mutineers tunneled toward the defenses of the Residence and the stubborn beleaguered garrison ran out countermines and blew up their galleries; and whenever there was a lull in the firing, the fugitives in the Gulab Mahal shuddered and waited and prayed for it to begin again, fearing that silence might mean that the Residency had fallen at last.

The garrison in the Residency had numbered barely a thousand combatant British and seven hundred loyal Indian troops when the crisis had arisen. They were hampered by the presence of well over a thousand women, children and noncombatants; by lack of adequate food, by sickness and appalling problems of sanitation and the disposal of the dead. The position they held had never been intended for purposes of defense. The hurriedly constructed and inadequate fortifications were flimsy in the extreme, and the forces surrounding it numbered twelve thousand fighting men, many of them British-trained sepoys, backed by the rabble

of the city. It could not have withstood a single concerted assault that
had been pressed home, but the mutineers possessed no leader of real
ability. The attacks were never delivered in sufficient strength, and so the
siege dragged on.

Alex made one unexpected friend in the Gulab Mahal: Dasim Ali, uncle
of Juanita's husband Wali Dad and great-uncle to Ameera, who was
first cousin to Winter de Ballesteros. Dasim Ali was now an elderly gentleman whose beard was dyed scarlet with henna, and his shrewish wife
Mumtaz was the senior lady of the pink palace. Mumtaz was as bitter
against all Feringis as Walayat Shah, and disliked her husband's great-
niece Ameera as much for her foreign blood as for her beauty. But Dasim
Ali was a placid and pleasant person who harbored no bitterness toward
anyone—except on occasions toward God, who had granted him no sons.

He paid frequent visits to Alex' rooftop, and would bring him the news
of the city and the progress of the siege, together with such scraps of
news as trickled in from beyond the borders of Oudh.

Winter too made friends in the Gulab Mahal, and she was the only
one who went freely to the women's quarters. Dressed in Ameera's clothes
and wearing Ameera's jewels, with her blue-black hair in a heavy plait and
her slim feet bare or in a pair of Ameera's flat, curl-toed slippers, she
would have passed anywhere as an Indian woman of good family, or from
the hills, where women's skins are fairer than they are in the hot plains.

Even Dasim Ali's sour and shrewish wife ended by grudgingly accepting her presence, and had once even condescended to instruct her in the
art of making a certain sticky sweetmeat of which the children of the
Gulab Mahal were particularly fond.

Once again, after so many years, sitting on the zenana roof in the dusk,
Winter heard the old, familiar stories of her childhood told to those children, as Aziza Begum had once told them to her. And as she listened
she heard too the ugly sound of gunfire from the beleaguered Residency,
and was disturbed by conflicting emotions.

"What will happen when all this has ended?" she inquired one evening
of Alex. She had brought him a herbal draught prepared by Ameera, and
had stayed talking to him in the twilight. There were rockets going up
from the city, for it was the festival of Bakr Id, and from somewhere in
the zenana quarters a woman was singing to the accompaniment of a sitar:
a song of Akbar's day. "It is such an old country," said Winter softly.

"No, it isn't," said Alex. "It's new. It's as new as—as Russia if you
like."

Winter turned to smile at him in the dusk. "Now you are just arguing
for the sake of argument!"

"No, I'm not. Anything that has such tremendous possibilities and
horizons is new. We are old. You can predict more or less what will happen
to us. But you cannot predict what will happen to her. She has lain fallow
for centuries—they still use the same methods of plowing and irrigation
that they used when we were wearing skins and living in caves! They've

gone to seed. But seed if it's plowed into the ground produces something new. Think of what they could do! We've started them off again—plowed them in if you like. They'll hate us for it, but they wouldn't have done anything for another hundred years or so if left to themselves. We've tried to go too quickly and force our way of life on them, but in a hundred years from now—or two hundred, or three—their history may show that Plassey wasn't an end or a defeat, but a beginning. Even this that is happening now was probably needed."

"And when we go?"

"When we go Hinduism will probably come into its own again, and if they aren't careful the country will drift back into an Eastern version of the Balkans. But I shall have been dead a long time before then. And so will you!"

There were only three British women now in the Gulab Mahal. Four, if one counted Lottie's daughter. Miss Keir had never recovered from that nightmare journey in the covered cart. She had lingered on for a few days and died one hot night within a week of their arrival at the Gulab Mahal, and Lou Cottar had moved into Mrs. Hossack's room in her place.

Lou had said that it was because Mrs. Hossack was afraid of being alone, but Winter suspected that it was because Mrs. Hossack, as the mother of four, was a mine of information on the subject of infants, and could be relied upon to give helpful advice in a crisis.

"Lou of all people!" said Alex. "I should have said that she was as unmaternal as a goldfish; yet here she is, reduced to a state of crooning imbecility in a mere matter of weeks. I am beginning to think that I made a great mistake in assisting that infant to get born. It will be a lesson to me to mind my own business in future."

He turned on his elbow to look at Winter, and said disagreeably: "I don't see you making much fuss over the creature. Are you devoid of any maternal instincts, Mrs. Barton?"

"No," said Winter, giving the matter thought. "But you see, it isn't my baby."

"It isn't Lou's," said Alex.

"Yes, it is. Lottie gave it to her."

"And I wonder," said Alex unpleasantly, "what Edward English's parents are going to say to that?"

It was a thought that frequently worried Lou. Supposing that Edward's parents demanded the child?

They can't have her! thought Lou. She's mine! They couldn't take her. . . .

"Has she been christened?" asked Mrs. Hossack one day.

"*Christened?*" Lou looked up from bathing Amanda in a small metal basin. "No, of course not. How could she be?"

"There's Mr. Dobbie," said Mrs. Hossack. "He could do it. She should be christened."

The thought of having the child christened had taken possession of

Lou. Edward English's parents might have their own ideas as to names, and the child was going to be christened Amanda, and also Cottar: the surname of "English" would be hers by law. Fired with this idea Lou had approached Mr. Dobbie who had instantly agreed to perform the ceremony.

Amanda Cottar English was christened "in the presence of this congregation" on Alex' roof in the late evening; Alex, Winter and Mrs. Hossack standing as godparents. The ceremony brought a considerable portion of relief to Lou. It seemed to make Amanda more her own, and the claims of the misty and faraway Englishes—she was not aware that Edward had been orphaned for several years—faded and became less alarming.

But its repercussions were unexpected.

The fact that there was a clergyman available who was qualified to perform Holy Offices had dawned suddenly upon Lord Carlyon, and he had managed to get Winter to himself in the garden two evenings later.

Moonlight had filled the garden with pale shadows before the last of the twilight had faded, and Carlyon had stood among the orange trees and once again asked Winter to marry him. Not at some future date when they could escape from this house and from Lucknow—if they should ever escape—but now, at once. Tonight or tomorrow. Dobbie could marry them—

"You need someone to look after you, to protect you. I would take care of you. I love you! What does it matter whether you love me now or not? You would one day. I could make you."

He had caught her hand, and she drew back quickly: "I am sorry. I cannot. Thank you for—for wanting to, but—" The moonlight showed him a sudden abstracted look in the wide, black-lashed eyes, and he was seized with an angry and wounding conviction that she was not thinking of him at all, but of something or someone else.

He reached out and caught her hand again, gripping it by the wrist in a hard grasp that she could not break, and said hoarsely: "Is there anyone else? Is that why you won't marry me? Is it Randall? I've seen the way you look at him sometimes! You were in the jungle with him for weeks, weren't you?"

His rage boiled up until it seemed that it must choke him. "It is Randall, isn't it? What is he to you? Are you his mistress? Do you spend your nights with him on that roof? Is that why you persuaded your black relatives to let him sleep up there instead of with us?"

He saw the shadowy reflection of a succession of emotions cross Winter's face: disgust, anger, contempt, and finally—and surprisingly—pity. It was the pity that hurt most and which drove him to the final stupidity.

He released her wrist and caught her swiftly into his arms as he had done once before in Delhi, and kissed her with hungry violence. Kissed her mouth and eyes and throat again and again as though he could not stop.

She had not struggled or cried out. She had stood entirely still, endur-

ing his bruising kisses as though she had been a lay figure without life
or emotions; and her very immobility had brought him to his senses as
nothing else could have done. He released her at last and stood back
from her, breathing in hard gasps. She had not spoken, and after a moment she had turned and walked unhurriedly away between the orange
trees of the walled garden, her pale-colored Indian dress showing like a
moth among the shadows and the Indian jewelry she wore making a soft
chinking sound that died away into the dusk.

Drawing the muslin veil over her head and across her face as Ameera
and the other women did on the rare occasions on which they moved outside the women's quarters, she passed along a narrow enclosed veranda
and up the final flight of stairs that led to the roof where Alex lay.

Alex' bed had been dragged out into the open, presumably by Dr.
O'Dwyer. He was lying on it with his back to her, wearing only the scanty
loincloth that alone made the heat of the day bearable, and his body
looked painfully thin and very brown against the pale-colored *resai* that
did duty as a mattress. He heard the chink of Winter's jewelry, but he
did not turn, and she came to stand beside him, looking down at him
and wondering if he were asleep. After a moment or two, as she did not
speak, he said ungraciously: "Well, what is it?"

Her hands gripped together tightly and she took a deep breath and
forced herself to speak calmly:

"Alex, will you marry me?"

Alex did not move for an appreciable time, and then he turned slowly
and looked up at her. It seemed to him that there was a tight band made
of some hot metal round his forehead, and he could not think at all
clearly.

"What did you say?"

"I asked you if you would marry me," said Winter steadily.

"Why?"

She sat down on the edge of the low bed and as she did so the muslin
veil slipped off her shoulders, and the clear moonlight showed red marks
on her throat. The hand she raised to catch at the veil was bruised too
about the wrist with the plain prints of the brutal grip that had held it.

Alex reached out and caught her hand, holding it with thin, hot fingers,
and looked at those marks; and Winter, noticing them for the first time,
jerked it quickly away.

Alex said thickly: "Carlyon?"

"Yes. No—I mean—it doesn't matter."

He sat up and found that it tightened the band about his head by
several notches. It should surely be impossible to feel so ill and so angry
at one and the same time? Separately perhaps, but not together. He said:
"Yes, I'll marry you. And what's more, I'll do it now. Go and tell Dobbie
I want to see him. And wait a minute—give me some of that opium—"

Winter never knew what he had said to Mr. Dobbie, but whatever it
was it appeared to have persuaded Mr. Dobbie to accede to the unexpected

request for an immediate marriage. Lou knew, for Lou had come in search of Winter and had heard a murmur of voices from the roof. She had almost reached the top of the stairs when she had heard Alex say: "Very well then. I'll have her without. And you can take that on your conscience! It won't be on mine."

Lou had turned round and come down again, looking thoughtful.

36

WINTER had been married at night and by moonlight, as Sabrina had been. And like Sabrina, with no preparation at all and in a wedding dress that did not even belong to her.

She would have worn Ameera's scarlet and gold wedding dress with its wonderful fringed and tasseled head veil, but out of deference to the doubtful and anxious Mr. Dobbie she had worn instead a dress of heavy white silk, yellowed by the years and scented with the neem leaves and tobacco in which it had been kept, that had belonged to Ameera's mother Juanita de Ballesteros.

Alex had worn Mussulman dress, borrowed for the occasion from Dasim Ali, and had only managed to keep on his feet with the assistance of opium and one of the pillars that divided his room from the roof. He had stood with his back to it, and had looked so entirely un-English in the moonlight that poor, worried Mr. Dobbie had suffered yet another qualm.

But to Winter there had been nothing strange about this wedding. It was the fulfillment of the promise that the Gulab Mahal had always stood for—that old Aziza Begum had given to her and Zobeida reaffirmed so often—that once she returned to it, all would be well.

The scent of orange blossom rose from the walled gardens of the Rose Palace and reached the flat rooftop where Winter stood in Juanita's white dress and felt Alex' parched, fever-hot fingers push a heavy ring of beaten gold and silver that had once been Anne Marie's, onto the finger that had once worn Kishan Prasad's glowing emerald. And as once, long ago and on just such a night, Sabrina too had done, she was suddenly aware of an uplifting sense of timelessness—as if all Time were one, and she would live forever in the future in Alex' children and hers, as she lived in the past with Marcos and Sabrina; with Johnny and Louisa. . . .

But her wedding had not ended peacefully as Sabrina's had done.

They had all been gathered there on the roof: Lou Cottar and Mrs. Hossack, Captain Garrowby, Dr. O'Dwyer, Mr. Climpson, Mr. Lapeuta and Lord Carlyon. Even Ameera and Hamida had been there; standing in the darkness behind the lowered *chiks* that screened the interior of the pavilion from the roof, in deference to the fact Ameera was in purdah and could not be seen by strange men.

The guests had come forward to offer congratulations and good wishes at the end of the brief ceremony, and Carlyon had confronted Winter and said in a deliberate drawl: "Am I permitted the privilege of kissing the bride?"

Alex said: "Not in future," and hit him.

It had been luck more than strength or science, and rage more than luck, that had caused the blow to send Carlyon sprawling, for although Alex had recovered a good deal of his strength, the fever had once again drained an appreciable amount of it from him during the past twenty-four hours.

Carlyon had come to his feet, white with fury, and had returned the blow with a good deal more science and considerably more strength before the remainder of the wedding guests had rushed in to separate them. Alex had been unable to defend himself, for the well-meaning Mr. Dobbie had leapt at him, catching his arm, and Winter had turned and clung to the other. Carlyon's clenched fist had taken him under the jaw and he had fallen between them as though he had been poleaxed, hitting the back of his head on an angle of the pillar as he fell, and had not recovered consciousness for some considerable time.

"Men!" said Lou furiously. "As if we were not in enough trouble already! Now they'll try and kill each other as soon as they get the chance! You'd think there was enough fighting going on without—oh, God! *Men!*"

Winter had spent her second wedding night, as she had spent her first, in tears and terror. But this time it was on her bridegroom's behalf and not on her own.

Alex' own recollections of the night were hazy. His head hurt abominably, his jaw ached, his body burned with fever and his parched mouth was full of blood from a cut that his teeth had made in his tongue. Someone periodically gave him water to drink and persuaded him to spit out the blood instead of swallowing it, and somebody else—or the same person—put a pleasantly cool and aromatic-smelling compress on his forehead and changed it at intervals.

The fever had lessened toward morning, and he had fallen asleep at last and had not wakened until the sun was hot on the roof. And then it was Lou who was standing by one of the pillars of the pavilion, peering through the slats of the *chik* and listening to the crackle of rifle fire and the boom of guns that had been silent during the past night but had begun again with the dawn.

She had turned when she heard Alex move, and he said: "What are you doing here at this time of the morning, Lou? Got a sudden fit of the bore with that baby at last?"

"No," said Lou. "I promised your wife that if she'd go to sleep I'd see that you were all right."

"My—?" said Alex, and stopped. "Good God! Of course. Then I didn't dream the whole thing. I seem to remember hitting that bastard Carlyon —I'm sorry, Lou; I apologize."

"He hit you a good deal harder," said Lou with a grin.

"Did he? Hmm. He must have done! I don't seem to remember that. What happened to—my wife?"

"I rather think she spent the night bathing your fevered brow," said Lou. "She doesn't seem to have much luck with her bridegrooms. Conway was filthy drunk."

A sudden black scowl replaced the frown of pain on Alex' forehead, and he said: "Shut up, Lou. If you want to play at being Miss Nightingale you can give me some water. If you want talk you can go away."

Lou brought him food and water and prepared to depart, but with her hand on the *chik* she stopped and turned back.

"Alex—"

"What is it now?" demanded Alex ungraciously.

"Lord Carlyon . . ." Lou hesitated and bit her lip. "You know as well as I do that someone may give us away any day, and then—and then it will be all over with us. We've got to stay together, and that man has got a bad temper and not much control over it."

"I don't seem to have had much control over mine lately," said Alex wryly.

"I know. But that's different. You wouldn't do anything that might jeopardize all of us just because you were in a rage. But he would. You don't know what a lot of nonsense he's been talking. About escaping from here. Lord Carlyon doesn't understand more than half a dozen words of Urdu. If he once got out of this place he'd be caught before he'd gone a hundred yards, and that might give us all away. So you see—"

Lou jerked restlessly at the edge of the *chik* and turned away to peer through it again, her back to Alex. He did not speak, and presently she said: "Alex, *please!* Don't quarrel with him! Don't goad him into doing anything that may jeopardize all of us. Promise me you'll leave him alone?"

Alex said: "Provided he leaves my wife alone."

"Of course he will; now. But you can't expect him not to speak to her, and if you're going to hit him every time he does—"

"My dear Lou," interrupted Alex wearily, "at this moment I could not successfully hit a fly. No, of course I will not start another brawl! Get on back to your baby, there's a good girl. My head is splitting and I can see six of you. And just at present one is more than enough."

Lou had gone and Alex had lain on his back all through the grueling heat of the day, and had thought as coherently as the pain in his head would permit.

Lou did not realize that there were only two things that had kept him from leaving the Gulab Mahal as soon as he was capable of walking, and that they were neither of them what she supposed. The first was the fact that a sick man was a liability and not an asset. The second was Carlyon: Carlyon and Winter. Winter was safe enough—or as safe as she would be anywhere at this time—with the occupants of the Gulab Mahal. But she was not safe from Carlyon.

He realized the sense of Lou's request, for they were none of them safe with Carlyon.

Carlyon had urged that they should attack the servants who cared for their needs, overpower the adult males in the house, seize any weapons they could find in the house, and provided with arms, money and food, escape to Cawnpore where Havelock and his army were known to be encamped. It was no distance—less than forty miles.

He had produced other schemes, equally rash and impracticable, but he would not escape alone and leave Winter. And now Winter, to escape him, had married Alex Randall.

She must have been very frightened of Carlyon to have taken such a drastic step, thought Alex, staring up at the flaking plaster of the ceiling while the heat danced upon the open roof outside. What had he done to her? Tried to rape her? Alex felt rage rise in him again at the thought and turned over and buried his face in his arms.

He himself would have to continue to keep Winter at arm's length. The fact that she was now his wife made no difference to that situation. It merely made it more difficult. They might be here, or on the run again, for months—perhaps a year—or more than a year. And he thought again of Lottie. He could not run the risk of watching Winter die as Lottie had died, and for the first time he was grateful for the ill health that would provide him with an excuse to keep her at a distance.

The gunfire had continued for the greater part of the day with a fury that told of a large-scale attack upon the Residency, and an hour before noon the thunderous explosion of a mine shook the Gulab Mahal. Alex could hear the boom of the guns and the crash of the shells with shuddering clarity, and the shimmering heat of the rooftop seemed to vibrate to the sound and strike his body with the same savage regularity.

And so the day that marked the second serious assault on the Residency passed. And the flimsy defenses still held.

There had been a third assault on the eighteenth of August, and Alex had worked out the date and scratched it with a nail on the wall of the pavilion. They had waited, all of them, with a tension that seemed to make it difficult to breathe, for the sound of musketry fire to start again after the silence that had followed the din of the assault. And when they had heard it they had felt their nerves and muscles go slack with relief, and had breathed as though escaping from near suffocation.

But the next day there had been another sound. The sound of gunfire from the southeast.

"By God—they're here!" cried Alex running to the parapet of the roof in the drumming, drenching downpour of the monsoon rains, and straining to listen while the water poured off him in a warm torrent.

It could only mean one thing. Havelock was marching on Lucknow. And presently, as the downpour ceased and a hot wind began to blow, the sound of those guns came clearly through the humid, clean-washed air.

They had heard them at intervals all that day and for much of the following one, and it occurred to Walayat Shah for the first time that perhaps God had been at his side when he had agreed to shelter those bedraggled fugitives for the sake of the dead of Cawnpore, for perhaps, because of it, he and his household would one day be saved from destruction.

But they had heard Havelock's guns no more: nor any news of what had happened to his Army. August dragged out its slow length, and it was September. And still the dwindling, dying, fever-racked garrison in the Lucknow Residency held out, and still the torn rags of the Union Jack fluttered defiantly from the flagstaff that had been shot down and replaced so often, and at the cost of so many lives, on the topmost roof of the shattered Residency.

It seemed to the fugitives in the Gulab Mahal that they had lived in their hot, cramped quarters in the little pink stucco palace in Lucknow for a lifetime.

Day succeeded day with an appalling, crawling monotony, and nerves grew ragged and tempers flared.

The lack of news from the outside world was the worst affliction they suffered. The heat was endurable because of the frequent downpours that roared off the roofs and gutters and drenched the gardens, cooling the hot stone and turning the dust to liquid mud where frogs croaked and winged ants hatched out in drove after fluttering, crawling drove.

The food was scanty, for there was little money to spare for the feeding of a band of hell-doomed infidels, but it was enough, and the sanitary arrangements, though primitive, were adequate. They were, compared with thousands of their fellow countrymen, living in comfort and safety. But not to know what was happening to the garrison in the Residency, to Havelock's forces, to the regiments on the Ridge before Delhi, to the rest of India and the Empire of John Company, made the long days longer and frayed their nerves to the breaking point.

They had discussed, endlessly, the possibility of escaping from Lucknow and trying to make contact with the relieving army, and one night three of them, Captain Garrowby, Dr. O'Dwyer and Mr. Climpson, had climbed out of the enclosed garden, scaled the outer wall by standing on each other's shoulders, and vanished into the maw of the city.

But they had not gone far. They had kept together instead of taking the wiser course of separating, and they had lost their way in the maze of streets so that dawn had found them still in the city. They had been stopped and questioned, and that afternoon they had been shot and their bodies hung up by the heels for an encouragement to the mob.

Dasim Ali had brought Alex the news on the following evening. The

men, he said, had been tortured first to make them tell where they had
been hiding, for it was suspected from the state of their garments and
their shoes that they must have been sheltering in the city itself and had
not, as they claimed, entered it only that night.

They had died without divulging their hiding place, but Walayat Shah
and Dasim Ali's wife Mumtaz and others of the Gulab Mahal had been
frightened and angry, and had taken immediate precautions to see that
none of the remaining Feringis jeopardized them by escaping. The doors
were locked now at night and the gardens patrolled, and what little liberty
the fugitives had previously possessed was drastically curtailed.

Winter was far from happy in those days. She might never have been
married to Alex, and she was often tempted to wonder if that brief ceremony on the moonlit roof had ever taken place, or if she had only dreamt
it. She still slept and spent the greater part of each day in her own gaily
painted room, and Alex still lived in the little pavilion on the roof. She
saw as little of him, or less, in these days as she had when they had first
come to the Gulab Mahal. His manner to her was much as it had always
been, and he did not appear to think that the fact that she was now his
wife necessitated any change in the monotonous routine of their days.

Alex had recovered much of his former health, and the maddeningly
recurrent bouts of fever left him at last. But Winter could not forget
that he had been ill with fever on the night that she had asked him to
marry her, or that he had been drugged with both fever and opium when
he had actually done so. If he had been in full possession of his faculties,
would he have consented to marry her? She began to wonder why he had
ever agreed to do so, and if he had really not known what he was doing,
and had subsequently regretted it? She had had her own reasons for asking Alex to marry her instead of waiting in the hope that he might one
day ask her himself, but she did not divulge them. Ameera and Hamida
knew; and if Lou guessed she did not ask any questions.

With the coming of autumn the heat ceased to be a grinding torment,
and the garden was pleasantly cool before the sun rose. But Winter was
seen there less frequently in the early mornings, and there came a time
when for three days running she failed to join the others on Alex' rooftop. He had asked Lou for the reason, and Lou had replied shortly that
she was not feeling very well but that it was nothing to worry about. Winter herself, taxed with it on her reappearance, had said lightly that the
heat and an overripe papaya that she had eaten had been responsible,
and Alex had accepted the explanation, and might have continued to do
so for some considerable time if it had not been for an unexpected storm
that had blown up out of a clear sky some four nights later.

He had been sleeping out on the open roof and the first intimation he
had received of the storm was when he was awakened by what appeared
to be a tub of cold water emptied over him. This was not the warm rain
of the hot weather, but the colder rain of autumn. And a wind was behind
the rain, driving it against him and chilling him to the bone. He was

drenched almost before he was awake, and the roof appeared to be awash with water.

This is where I catch pneumonia, thought Alex exasperated, wrestling in the pitchy darkness to release the sodden *chiks*. He became aware of someone else on the roof, and of Winter's voice calling his name through the lashing of the wind and the rain and the infuriating flapping of the *chiks*.

"Alex—Alex—where are you?"

"I'm here," shouted Alex. "What do you think you're doing? Get on back! Where are you?"

He groped for her in the blackness and caught a wet arm, and as he did so the brief, fiendish blast of the wind that had driven the storm before it died out as quickly as it had arisen, and there was only the rain falling steadily onto the roof with a soft splashing sound as though it were falling into a lake.

Alex said furiously: "Winter, are you mad? You'll be drenched! Get on back to your room!"

He heard her laugh a little shakily and she said: "I'm drenched already. And I won't go down unless you come with me. You can't stay up here for the rest of the night. You'll only get ill again, and we've had enough trouble with you already."

"You sound," said Alex, "regrettably like a nurse I used to have when I was about six. All right, I'll come. Be careful of those stairs. If we fall down them in the dark we shall break our necks."

The room that had once been Sabrina's seemed hot after the coldness of the wet, windy roof, and there was an oil lamp burning. The flame wavered in the draft and the painted plaster trees and birds and flowers seemed to move with the moving light as though they were alive, and the curve of the rose-colored ceiling was full of soft shadows so that it was difficult to tell how high it was.

Alex took the cloth that Winter handed him and rubbed himself dry with it, removing his wet loincloth and appropriating a length of turquoise blue muslin—evidently a head veil—to replace it. He sat down on the carved and painted bed and looked about the room, charmed by the gay, childish grace of the formalized patterns and the clear colors which, though rubbed and worn in many places, were still jewel-bright. And then he looked at his wife.

Her hair had been unbound for the night and she was wringing the water out of it and twisting it up out of the way in a heavy shining knot at the back of her head. Her arms were lifted, and her thin cotton sari was drenched with rain and clung wetly to her body, outlining and revealing every rounded curve of a figure that was no longer the reed-slim one he had known.

Winter finished knotting up her hair and said: "There's another *resai* over there. Will you mind sleeping on the floor?"

He did not answer her and she turned to look at him and saw that he knew. There was a white line about his mouth and his eyes were wide and very bright, and she stood quite still, looking back at him gravely, her gaze steady and a little apprehensive.

After a long minute Alex spoke as though speaking were difficult. He said: "Is it mine?"

"Yes."

He held out a hand to her and she came to him as slowly as if she were walking in her sleep. Alex reached up and drew her down into his arms and said in a voice that she had not known he possessed: "Why didn't you tell me?"

He laughed suddenly, a laugh that broke on a dry sob. "And to think," said Alex, "that I have been keeping my hands off you for weeks—for months—because I was afraid of this!"

His hands stripped away the sodden sari and his fingers pressed through the heavy wet waves of hair. And then his mouth closed down on hers, blotting out thought.

37

THEY were allowed three days of unclouded happiness. Three days and nights of complete and unalloyed rapture and contentment, made the more sweet by being snatched out of the ugly mire of blood and fear and frenzy that fouled half India.

They had come into possession of a kingdom, and Sabrina's room was an enchanted garden a thousand miles removed from the harsh realities of the warring world outside. They had so much to talk of and to tell; so much to ask and to remember and to forget, and so much to give that needed no words for its expression.

They went up to the rooftop only after the others had gone, and lying in the crook of Alex' arm, counting the stars that shimmered and blinked and blazed in the tented velvet of the sky, Winter no longer heard the firing from the Residency or the night noises of the city, but only Alex' quiet breathing and the steady beat of his heart under her cheek.

She was entirely and completely happy with a happiness that many touch once but do not hold. At Ware she had longed for the Gulab Mahal as a child cries for the moon, and on so many nights and through so many years she had wished on a star. Now she did not need to wish for anything more, for all that she could ever have wished for had been given to her—together with every star in the sky. She knew now that whatever happened, and however much pain or horror or parting the future might hold, she had touched every one of those stars and held the moon in her hand, and that if she died tomorrow she would die content.

They had seen little of anyone else during the three days that followed the night of the storm. Only Ameera and Hamida and Lou. Alex had not seen Ameera before, except as a veiled figure on the night of his wedding.

"But thou art the husband of my cousin now, so for a time I will forget that I am of India, and a Mussulman, and be of my mother's people, who keep no purdah," said Ameera smiling at him.

Alex had looked from one face to the other and seen the similarity of the de Ballesteros blood, and had laughed and said: "Thou art not of India only, Begum Sahiba. The West is there also."

Ameera shook her head so that her earrings jingled. "Nay, that is not so. There may come a time when it is possible for one person to be of both, but that time is not yet, and I do not think that my children's children will see it. Their children, perhaps. I shall be dead then, and shall not know. But those who are, as I am, of the East and of the West, must cleave only to one if they wish to avoid unhappiness. To stand with a foot in each is to be neither. I have chosen the East."

Lou had come in search of Winter on that same day and had found Alex there. She had looked relieved and said: "So you've told him, have you? I wondered how much longer you were going to be about it. Is it—" She bit the sentence off abruptly and blushed hotly for perhaps the first time in her adult life.

"No," said Alex shortly. "It's mine."

Lou drew a deep breath of relief. She said: "I thought it might be, because you didn't come back that night; but I was afraid it was Con's and that was why she wouldn't tell you."

Winter said: "How long have you known, Lou?"

Lou laughed. "Probably almost as long as you have. It wasn't difficult, living as we do."

Alex said: "I didn't know."

"Oh, *you!*" said Lou, and left them.

They had not seen any of the others, and did not know that their absence had driven Carlyon to the ragged fringes of desperation and rage. Everything that had happened to him since his arrival in this appalling, barbaric abomination of a country was Winter's fault! Winter's and Randall's. The rage of disappointment and the wound to his vanity and egotism. The sleepless nights and the gnawing, unsatisfied hunger for a woman who had escaped him. The four walls of a hot, bare room and the all too brief daily sight of Winter—as lovely and disturbing and desirable as ever, and always out of reach. Of Randall, always watching.

And then after three days Alex and Winter had come down to the garden again, and together, and even in the soft uncertain dusk Carlyon had been able to read Winter's face. They could all read it, and the others had looked at her and smiled, because she was young and lovely and so in love.

But as Carlyon watched her, the jealousy and resentment of the last three days—and of all the days that had gone before—boiled up in him like a seething bubble of lava breaking through the thin crust of a volcano, and the fumes of it rose to his brain so that he saw her through a red mist of rage as the sole author and architect of all his misfortune.

She had been standing less than a yard away from him, her face clear in the pale moonlight, and he had leapt at her and caught her by the throat, shouting a torrent of accusations and obscenities, shaking her to and fro as his hands choked the breath from her in a strangling, frenzied grip.

Alex had reached them first and had hit him between the eyes with all his strength, and he had released Winter and staggered back, and then come at Alex, screaming senseless, futile words.

They had overpowered him at last and dragged him, still struggling and shouting, back to the room he shared with Lapeuta and Dobbie, and Alex had carried Winter up to the painted room and held her in his arms while Ameera and Hamida put cold compresses on her bruised and swollen throat.

Later a message had been brought him by Rahim, and he had left her to the care of the women and gone up to the moonlit roof to find Mr. Lapeuta and Dasim Ali waiting for him.

"It is not safe that that man remain longer in the Gulab Mahal," said Dasim Ali. "Who knows but that his shouts may have been heard by those outside the walls? He cried aloud, and in *Angrezi,* and while he remains he is a danger to us all. He must go."

Alex' face whitened and the lines cut deeper about his mouth. Half an hour ago he would have killed Carlyon if he could. But to send him out of the Gulab Mahal meant sending him to his death as surely—and less mercifully—as though they had put a loaded gun to his head and pulled the trigger.

"We cannot do it," said Alex. "It were better to kill him here. It would be quicker. They tortured the others. He would be caught in an hour—less!"

"If he went alone, yes," said Mr. Lapeuta. "But perhaps not if we go with him—Rev. Dobbie and myself. We have discussed it and we think it is possible. I, as you see, can pass veree easily as an Indian. Also I know Lucknow, and so does Rev. Dobbie. Lord Carlyon need not talk. We will tie a bandage over his eyes with much blood on it, and say that he had been injured in thee fighting, for his eyes are of a color that is not usual in this country. We can lead him. We may be caught, as thee others were, but I think we have more chance than they, for Rev. Dobbie has dark eyes and speaks the language with great fluency. It is worth thee trying, sir. To leave him here endangers all in this house. And he can endure no longer. This has come harder on such a man than on us, sir. He is, I think, a brave man, but not a patient one."

" 'The raft of the benevolent gets across,' " murmured Dasim Ali, looking thoughtfully at Mr. Lapeuta. "It may even be that thou wilt all reach safety." And so they had gone.

Their skins had been darkened with dye and they had been given food and a little money and what clothes they would need, and had been smuggled out by a small side door in the wall.

Alex had not seen them go, for he did not wish to see Carlyon again. He had gone back to Winter and held her and kissed her with a passionate intensity as though he were saying good-by to her. And she had known then that he would go too.

It had rained again that night, but in the morning the skies were clear and the clean washed air brought the sound of guns. Havelock's guns.

All that day the sound of those guns shivered through the hot sunlight, coming nearer and nearer until it seemed as though they could be only a few miles from the city, and as twilight fell the four who were left of the British in the Gulab Mahal gathered on the rooftop to watch and listen, knowing that men they knew would be fighting and dying out there—pressing on with everything that was in them to the relief of the battered, indomitable Residency.

The wind shifted that night, and in the morning the cannonade was less easy to hear. But on the following day the guns were no longer a mile or so outside the city, but firing from within the city limits as the Highlanders and the Sikhs and the British and Native Cavalry and Infantry under Havelock's command fought their way through the streets.

The gates of the Gulab Mahal were barred and barricaded and every shutter closed and bolted, and none stirred outside while the city shook to the savage din of battle. And as the sun sank, the wind blowing from the direction of the Residency brought with it a new sound, faint but unmistakable. A roar of cheering.

"*They've got there!*" said Alex with a catch in his voice and a lunatic desire to cheer himself hoarse. "Listen to that! They've got there!"

They had got there at last. But the garrison of the Residency, though sure now of survival, had not been relieved after all. They had only been reinforced. The regiments who had fought their way through the streets had been too badly mauled, their losses too great, for them to be able to do more than join the exhausted defenders in the Residency, and to stand siege there themselves.

The tumult in the city died down and the stench of death rose from the street like a tangible cloud to foul the air. And once again the familiar rattle of musketry fire, punctuated more frequently now by the boom of guns, sounded from the direction of the Residency.

Alex waited for several days, gleaning what news he could from Dasim Ali and Ameera. But from what they told him there seemed to be little chance of the situation developing into more than another stalemate, if

not a retreat. For the garrison was hampered by an inordinate proportion
of women and children, and these could not be jeopardized. Now that
Havelock and Outram with the relieving force were also penned up in
the Residency, it seemed likely that they would have to remain where
they were until they in turn were relieved, for to fight their way out with
the women and children would be no easy task. And should they succeed
in doing so, they would have to retreat, not only from Lucknow but from
Oudh, and it might be many months before another and stronger force
could be marched to attack and take the city.

Alex had talked for a long time with old Dasim Ali on the last evening
of September, and then he had gone down to the painted room and to
Winter.

The light of the oil lamp played upon the rose-colored walls and the
painted plaster birds and flowers as it had on the first night that he had
seen that room, and once again it seemed to him that the trees swayed
and the birds moved, and that the shadows made a mist under the curved
ceiling so that he could not tell how high it was.

Winter was combing out the long waves of her hair, and he sat on the
low Indian bed, as he had sat that first night, and watched her; and did
not speak.

After a moment she laid down the comb and turned toward him. The
light of the lamp behind her fell upon his face but left her own in shadow,
and the soft wavering flame threw an aureole around her, glinting on the
long ripples of her black hair and outlining her small head.

She looked at him in silence, as she had done once before in that room,
seeing in his face what it was that he had come to say. And once again
he held out a hand to her, and she came to him and put her arms about
him, standing between his knees with his head against her heart as she
had stood in the dusk outside the Hirren Minar on the day that Lottie had
died. Now, as then, he held her quite gently, leaning against her, and
presently he said: "I can take you with me. There are troops at Alam
Bagh just outside the city. It will not be too difficult or too dangerous to
get you there, for you can pass as an Indian. And once you were there
you would be safe. After that it would only mean reaching Cawnpore,
and then by river to Allahabad and Calcutta. If Havelock is here it means
the road must be open."

Winter said: "Would you come with me?" and knew the answer before
she asked it.

Alex moved his head against her as though he were in pain. He said in
a harsh, difficult voice: "I must go back to Lunjore." He felt her flinch,
and said as though she had spoken: "I must, dear! I should never have
left. There was so much that I could have done there—or tried to do. It—
it is my work; my responsibility. It's my *own* district! There is no one to
keep order there now, but once they see someone in authority again it
will quiet them and bring back order and sanity. Give them the assurance
that there is still a stable government and a law that does not depend

on the will or the whim of any individual who happens to be temporarily in power. That is what they need: peace and quiet and that assurance. If I go back now I can . . . Dear heart, I must go back! Give me leave to go. . . ."

Winter said: "And if I will not? Would you still go?"

"I—I must. But I would go happier if I went with your leave."

She said in a whisper, because she could not trust her voice not to break: "Go with it, my love," and felt something that had been strained and taut relax in his mind more than his body. "When are you going?"

"Tonight. In an hour."

She did not make any sound, but he felt the effort to control it shudder through her body, and knew what that effort had cost her. He said: "Can you be ready by then?"

She did not answer him at once, but her hand relaxed its pressure against his head and began to stroke his hair again, quite gently, and presently she said: "I am not going."

He looked up then, quickly, and saw her face wet and sweet and calm above him.

"Dear, I could not go. They would send me away to Calcutta. I should be at the other end of India. I shall be nearer to you here and far, far safer than you will be. Ameera will take care of me, and I shall be among friends. I was born in this room, and I have thought about it and loved it all my life. Perhaps your child will be born in it too. I will wait here for you."

Alex said: "Dear love, I can't let you stay. One day we shall attack the city, and take it. You don't know what that would mean, but I do. I have seen a city sacked. If you were here—"

Winter's hand moved to his mouth, covering it so that he could not speak, and above it his eyes looked into hers steadily and for a long time. And then his lashes dropped and he kissed the warm palm that closed his mouth, and did not argue with her any more.

He had gone before midnight, slipping out by the narrow side door by which Carlyon and Lapeuta and Dobbie had left, and there had been only his wife and Dasim Ali to see him go.

Winter had stood pressed against the little iron-studded door and listened to the sound of his quick, light footsteps dying out on the dusty road outside, and presently the night had swallowed up the sound, and old Dasim Ali had touched her on the arm and she had turned away.

She had cried again on the bed in the painted room when he had gone, and Ameera had comforted her. But in the morning it was the room that had comforted her most. She had woken to find it bright with the dawn, and as the sun rose and the familiar shadow crept across the floor and touched the bed on which she lay, peace and reassurance flowed back and filled her heart and her mind and her body. Nothing could hurt her while she was here. Alex would come back. She had only to wait. . . .

The year wore slowly on, and it was not until mid-November that once again the roar of guns and the din of battle rattled the rickety fabric of the Gulab Mahal as another British force fought its way toward a second relief of the Lucknow Residency, and once again the ugly tide of war surged through the narrow streets of the city.

Havelock died in that month, and on the day after his death word had been whispered in the dusk at the barred gate of the Gulab Mahal that the *Jangi-lat-Sahib* Sir Colin Campbell was going to retreat from Lucknow and fall back once more upon Cawnpore, and that the evacuation would take place that very night, and in great secrecy. The women and children were to leave in carts and doolies at midnight while the city slept, and make for the Alam Bagh, which was strongly held by the British.

Ameera had brought the news to Winter. "My husband and Dasim Ali," said Ameera, "say that if it be thy wish, it can be arranged that thou and the two women with the children go also. There are doolies here, and men to carry them, and they will join with the other mem-*log* at a place that is known to them, and take thee to safety. But it must be decided swiftly, for already it is dark."

Winter had smiled lovingly at her. "I will tell the others. It may be that they will choose to go. But I will stay here—unless thou and thy husband wish me to go. And if that be so, then thou wilt have to send me away by force!"

"That we never shall do," said Ameera embracing her. "Is this not the house in which thou wast born? Go and tell thy friends to make ready if they would go."

They had gone.

Lou had, somewhat unexpectedly, kissed Winter. They had smiled at each other with affection and respect, their hands holding tightly for a moment, and had kissed again, saying nothing because there was so much to say—and yet so little that need be said. And then Lou had gone. Lou, Amanda, Mrs. Hossack, Jimmy.

The gate creaked shut behind them, the bars and bolts grated hurriedly back into place, and the shuffling footsteps of the doolie bearers faded and were swallowed up by the night as Alex' quick, light ones had been. With the morning the bearers had returned, saying that the memsahibs and their children had reached the Alam Bagh in safety and had been sent forward with all the other mem-*log* to Cawnpore. So Lou and Mrs. Hossack at least were safe, and Winter hoped that Lou would not find that escape had robbed her of Amanda. Lou deserved Amanda.

The year drew to its close, but the mutiny still raged. Men still fought and died, and in Lucknow the mutineers dug defenses and built barricades in preparation for the attack that they knew could not be long delayed. But within the faded, pink-washed walls of the Gulab Mahal the days passed peacefully, and Winter sank into the life of the Rose Palace and became part of it as she had been part of it in the long-ago days when Juanita and Aziza Begum had been alive, and Winter herself had been a small black-haired child playing with the painted plaster birds in the room that had been Sabrina's.

Twice a day, morning and evening, she would go alone to the rooftop where Alex had lived, and look out across the treetops and the lovely battered city toward Lunjore.

"He is not dead," she told Ameera. "If he were I should feel it; here, in my heart."

And then in January she had heard news of him at last. Old Dasim Ali, who had friends everywhere, had heard by a roundabout route that there was a sahib again in Lunjore who had brought back order to the district. The rumor gave no name, but Winter did not need one. She knew that it must be Alex, and that he had been right to go.

All through January the insurgents had kept up their attacks on the Alam Bagh, and toward the end of February a last and desperate assault was launched against the garrison.

Winter heard the opening of the cannonade in the early morning, and it shook the walls of the Pink Palace and sent the startled crows and pigeons cawing and whirling above the roofs of the city. But the roar of the guns meant no more to her than the cawing of the crows, for her pains had started before dawn, and the guns were only a dim and disregarded background to the ordeal of birth.

It was not an easy birth, and there had been times when Ameera and Mumtaz Begum and Hamida looked at each other in fear and anxiety. But Winter remembered a long, hot, agonizing day in the Hirren Minar, and Alex' voice talking to Lottie—explaining, encouraging, soothing; and it was as if he spoke to her now as he had spoken then to Lottie—explaining, encouraging, soothing; telling her not to be afraid. And she had not been afraid.

The sun had set and the moon had risen. Ameera had lit the oil lamp, and her shadow and Hamida's and other shadows of women moved and leapt upon the walls, and the ceiling was lost in a rosy mist as it had been on the night when Alex had come down from the roof, and on the night that he had left her. And then suddenly she had thought that he was in the room, and had screamed to him by name—a scream that rang out through the open windows and across the silent garden and awoke the echo that lived within the high encircling walls—"Alex! . . . Alex! . . . Alex!" And to the sound of that echo, Alex' son was born.

It was March when the long-expected attack upon Lucknow began, and day after endless day the guns had roared in the city while the streets became battlegrounds and graveyards and charnel houses, and the dead had littered every yard of the contested ground.

Colin Campbell's army—Highlanders, Sikhs, Punjabis, British and Indian regiments of Cavalry and Infantry, Peel's Naval Brigade and Jung Bahadur's Gurkhas from Nepal—had stormed the defenses and flung themselves on the guns, fighting yard by yard through the red, reeking streets, through the storm of grape and canister and round shot and the choking smoke of burning houses.

Curiously enough—or perhaps justly—it was Carlyon who was largely responsible for saving the Gulab Mahal from the sack and slaughter and destruction that overtook almost every house in that shattered city. Mr. Lapeuta, the Rev. Dobbie and Lord Carlyon had all reached safety. And later, when Sir Colin Campbell's Army moved to the final attack upon Lucknow, Carlyon had used his considerable influence to urge that the Gulab Mahal should be granted as much protection as was possible in such circumstances. Even in the frenzy of the fighting that promise had not been forgotten. With the terrible tumult of battle ebbing and surging through the streets, rifle butts had knocked on the barred door of the Gulab Mahal and men's voices had shouted above the clamor, demanding entrance.

Winter had gone down to them alone, wearing Juanita's white dress, and not knowing who it might be. But she had heard the English voices and had opened the gate, tugging at the heavy bars and locks with her small hands—for the gateman had run away in terror—and had opened it at last to see the smoke-blackened, blood-streaked faces that filled the once quiet street.

A man on horseback laughed down at her and dismounted to take her hand. "Do you remember me, Mrs. Alex? I met you at Delhi—William Hodson."

"Yes," said Winter, looking up into the white, battle-grimed, laughing face of the man whom Alex had said would always be twenty paces ahead, and thinking that no one who had ever met him would be likely to forget him. "I remember."

"I cannot stay," said Hodson. "I came only to tell you that as far as possible this house will be protected. If you see Alex before I do, tell him that the astrologer in Amritsar was right! He will know what that means. But if we get these wretches on the run I may see him before you do."

He sprang back into the saddle, saluted her, and wheeling his horse he galloped away with his men behind him; his face as eager and his eyes as hot and bright and glittering as though he rode to meet a friend or a lover, instead of the death that awaited him that day.

The door had been barred again and an order signed by Sir Colin Campbell himself nailed to it; and while the fighting lasted a guard had stood at the gate and protected the Gulab Mahal from the looting and the frenzy of battle-crazed, blood-drunk troops, until the worst of that delirium was past and Lucknow was taken.

April brought with it once again a warning of the molten heat to come, and the small bare rooms of the Gulab Mahal seemed airless once more, and stifling. Food was scarce and milk was scarcer: but news was scarcest of all, and what there was of it was never reassuring.

The mutiny was being stamped out and the savage reprisals that Alex had feared and predicted were accompanying that process—in the old and evil belief that only blood and savagery can repay and wipe out the stain of blood and savagery. But although it would be many months yet before peace was fully restored, it was already plain that the prophecy of the Hundred Years was to be fulfilled. India had become too great a thing to be the private possession of a trading company, and would have to be taken over by the Crown.

"We have not won back Hind," said Walayat Shah, "but it was the Company's Raj that we had hoped to pull down, and *Shook'r Khooda*, we have succeeded in that; for now the Company's Raj will go, and their long reign of robbery and confiscation will be ended."

Soon it would be May again, and the hot, burning days that a year ago had seen the fuel catch fire would see it still burning fiercely, though with a dying flame, in Jhansi and Rohilkhand and Gwalior and Oudh. But there was still no news from Lunjore.

"Surely if her husband were alive he would send word?" said the women of the Gulab Mahal. "It must be that he is dead."

The thought was often clear on their faces and in their kind, troubled eyes, and one day it had been too clear to be borne, and Winter had answered it as though it had been spoken aloud:

"No. It is not true! He is not dead. He will come for me someday. I have only to wait. . . ."

And she had snatched up her son and carried him up to Alex' rooftop, and had strained her eyes in the direction of Lunjore as though her love could reach beyond the horizon and pierce the dust clouds and the distance and the heat haze that hid it from her sight.

The sun dipped down toward the horizon and bathed the shattered city in beauty, hiding its blackened, gaping scars; and she remembered what Hodson had said to her—Hodson whose star, as the astrologer in Amritsar had prophesied so many years ago, "would rise and burn bright among much blood," and who had died in the battle for the city. "*I may see him before you do.*" Had he too spoken prophetically? Had he indeed met Alex?

Quite suddenly she could bear it no longer, and she turned and ran desperately, as she had run before, to the refuge of the painted room, sobbing and shuddering.

The reflected glow of the sunset filled it with a warm rosy light, touching the trees and the birds and the flowers into the same enchanted life that lamplight could give them, and the leaves and the petals welcomed her and the birds and the beasts nodded to her and Firishta watched her with a bright, friendly, reassuring eye.

She pushed the bed to one side and sank down on the matting with the child in her arms, and leant her head against the cool carved plaster, pressing her cheek against the comforting curve of Firishta's round green head. Her eyes closed and gradually the helpless trembling of her body lessened as little by little the fear ebbed away from her.

The baby went to sleep in her lap and the glow faded from the room, taking the gay brightness from it and leaving it as cool and as softly colorful as an opal.

"Someday," she said, whispering the words against Firishta's green head. "One day—"

There were footsteps and a murmur of voices in the passage beyond the doorway, and then someone lifted the heavy curtain that hung before it, and she opened her eyes and looked up. And it was Alex.